# The Flame and the Dragon

## A Legends of the Five Crowns Novel

### MISTY EVANS & MICHELLE MILES

Book Cover by GetCovers

First edition 2026

ISBN: 9781964028309 (eBook)
ISBN: 9781964028361 (paperback)

Edeia

Aurelia
Kingdom of Light

Drakenholt
Kingdom of Beasts

Evermere
Kingdom of Heroes

Thornveil
Kingdom of Shadows

Seabright
Kingdom of the Seas

Solerian Sea

Frozen Wastes

Wintermark
Wilds

Moonfall
Bay

Solara

Jaxton

Wraithlands

Fen Mountain

Klamere

Longmere

Fableholow

Evermere River

Windhelm

Tereen

Jonwick

Silver
Cove

Tidewatch-
by-the-Bay

Thurmarsh

Silvermist
Bay

Larkfell

Seabright
Haven

Grey Harbor

Drifthaven

Brightwater
Port

Starfall
Fjord

Evermist Woods

# PROLOGUE
## RENWICK

THE THRONE ROOM OF Klamere burns bright with golden light that flickers along with laughter. A string quartet plays from the dais beneath giant twin dragons carved in shadow-glass, their instruments sawing through memory like a blade through silk. I've rebuilt this dream a dozen times in story form, never quite getting it right—never quite brave enough to face what really happened.

But tonight, I let it play out—all of it.

Across the polished marble floor, nobles twirl in gowns that shimmer. Goblets catch the chandelier light, sparkling with stardust, the illusion perfect in its deception. It was a celebration, after all. The new dragon library was finished, the finest, most revered collection of knowledge and stories in the realm. The air smelled of roasted meat and honeyed wine, and my father wore a smile that reminded me of a wolf with a crown.

And me? I was the young prince in velvet who thought prophecy couldn't touch us.

The air glimmers, bubbles. Dessalyn appears near the edge of the ballroom, barefoot in the dream, her moss-green cloak fluttering as if caught in a phantom wind. Her eyes—sharp, guarded—match the cloak's hue. She looks around, her back going straight as a blade when she spots me. It's not the first time we've met in dreams, and it's one of the only ways I can communicate with her. She's the only one who still has some memory of Drakenholt, my kingdom. Of me.

I cross through the ghosts on the dance floor, moving slowly, carefully, so as not to frighten her. I fail. She takes a step back, fear and wariness in those pretty eyes, but lifts her chin in defiance. "Where are we?" she asks.

"Home," I answer, though the word tastes like ash in my mouth.

The music stops, the dancers freezing in mid-step, my father's goblet suspended in a toast. Her eyes go sharp as flint when they land on the throne. "The palace in Klamere?"

I nod. "The night your mother spoke the prophecy of Drakenholt."

She stiffens. Her fists curl at her sides. "I've seen this," she says. "In a mirror."

A mirror? Has she forgotten she witnessed it in person? "You were here." I point to a table in the far corner of the giant hall. She gasps as she sees herself, her younger sister Calliope, and her parents. Thand Lorewyn was the architect of the library, and the

Lorekeeper family had been here for weeks. "The mirror only made you remember."

Dessalyn covers her mouth with a hand, her eyes tearing up as they rest on her mother. I let the dream play out, and the scene jolts to life. Laughter resumes. The music swells. A pair of dancers twirls past us without seeing either of us, their smiles unnaturally wide.

*If only I could stop time right here and not allow the rest to play out.* But I must.

Dessalyn's mother, Serenelle Lorewyn, a Fae woman of indescribable beauty, rises from the table to present herself to my father. Dressed in sunflower gold, her hair braided with glimmering ribbons, she walks with regal grace. The crowd parts, barely disguising their curiosity, their whispers like wind through reeds.

My father lifts his chin, intrigued. He cuts off the band with a flourish of his wrist before waving her forward.

I tense, remembering the moment as if my bones recorded it. He expected flattery, perhaps a gift. Instead, he received a prophecy.

*"A thief will come,"* she says, her soft-spoken voice clear enough throughout the crowded hall, *"not for your riches, but your remembrances. He will wipe your story from the realm."*

A shocked silence falls. Everyone holds their breath. Even the chandeliers flicker and dim, waiting for the king's reaction.

My father laughs, a low, patronizing chuckle. I remember joining in from my perch at the royal table, swirling wine in a goblet too fine for my years. I am seventeen and drunk on importance. "Our story will live forever," I say.

*If only I'd known...*

Dessalyn, barely fourteen but wise for her age, rushes to her mother's side, glaring at me like she could set me aflame with her scowl. Elbows too sharp for court, chin too high to bow. She starts to speak, but Serenelle hushes her, saying the words I see in Dessalyn's eyes. "You arrogant, stupid boy." Serenelle's voice is almost sad. "You fancy yourself a king, but you will never sit on the throne."

I had earned her wrath. Now, I hope to earn her daughter's help.

"You didn't believe her," Dessalyn says from her dream place.

The sound of her low voice tightens my insides. She owes me nothing. I owe her much.

I don't look at her. No matter how much I hate the younger version of me, I can't change the facts of that night. "No. I didn't," I say.

She steps closer, her bare feet silent on marble that doesn't exist anymore. Her hand reaches out as if she could touch her mother's dress. "Why show me this?"

"Because it matters. Because you've forgotten."

Her eyes don't leave her mother, who stands now with her hands clasped in front of her like she's holding her own anger in check. "I remembered this night for years. Then..."

I risk a glance at her. The music shifts. The dream stutters.

She inhales a sharp breath. "I don't want to see her like this."

I don't want to see my kingdom the way it is now, everyone gone. "She deserves to be remembered."

"She *deserved* to be believed."

If I could, I would rewrite the story and change the past. While my dragon magic once made me a scribe to rival any in our realm, even that can't undo what's been done.

She rounds on me, only now fully remembering what happened. "You and your father ignored her warning. You buried it as if that would stop it from coming true."

I can't argue. I don't try. "It didn't work."

Her eyes glimmer with unshed tears. "She died believing no one had listened."

Died? The word spears me right in the gut. I step forward, voice faltering. "Serenelle is...dead?"

Dessalyn sucks in another breath. She looks nothing like the girl in the dream. This version is not only older; she's haunted. Strong. Filled with grief, just like me. She doesn't need to confirm it's true.

I reach for her, but she recoils. I drop my hand. "I'm sorry. No one told me."

Her eyes flash with anger. "Why would they? You cared nothing for us. Your father banished us from the kingdom after Mother delivered that prophecy, sending us home as outcasts." She takes a step back as if being too close to me is offensive. "She was never the same after that night. She faded into...nothing."

The dream begins to fracture. The chandeliers above us crack. The walls tremble.

"Wait—" I reach for her. "Don't go."

But her emotions cause her form to flicker and unravel, smoke caught in the wind.

"Dessalyn—"

Her eyes turn hollow. She speaks, the words too faint for my ears, before she vanishes.

Smoke coils where she stood. A single gold ribbon flutters to the marble and disintegrates before it can land. The ballroom collapses. Flames lick the curtains. The musicians crumble to dust. My family fades into nothingness.

I'm left standing in the ruins of the dream memory, alone with the echo of what I could've done differently. Above me, the throne sits empty. Cracked. The golden crest of our house is fractured down the middle.

I kneel in the ruins, alone again, as I always am.

Only now, I know something I didn't before.

Serenelle *died*. A pure-blooded Fae's life expectancy is thousands of years. *She faded into nothing*. I clutch my chest and shake my head. She didn't pass from time or illness. Not from some natural end.

She was severed.

My father's banishment was more than it seemed. The Severance Decree, a curse spoken in the old language and sealed with his blood, caused Serenelle to fade.

I never realized the Decree had been used. Not then. Not until now. It explains so much.

Dessalyn's mother, the great Fae Lorekeeper with ties to every kingdom, was *severed* from Drakenholt. From our magic and our laws. My father's decree made that kind of exile a death sentence for someone like her.

Lorekeepers don't just live inside stories. They *breathe* them. Strip away a thread woven tight inside one, and what's left unravels.

The heat of my dragon magic flares under my hand with the realization, but just as quickly burns out. Creating these dreams leaves me drained, vulnerable to the Story Thief. "You were right, Serenelle," I say to the air. "I was the stupid boy who thought himself a king."

But what I don't say, not even here, in the safety of a memory-dream, is what I now suspect—my father didn't simply try to erase Serenelle's prophecy.

He erased *her*.

# Chapter One
## Dessalyn | Waking Curse

*A quest never begins when you expect it to—it waits until your guard is down and your heart is unready.*

I WAKE WITH FIRE searing in my chest, heat coiling beneath my ribs. My fingers twitch against the blankets, still reaching for the gold ribbon that slipped from my mother's hair in the ballroom before dissolving into nothing. For a moment, I'm still there, in Drakenholt's throne room, with Renwick's gaze fixed on me in the midst of the smoke and gilded ruin. Then the dream splinters into smoke, and I'm alone in my narrow bed, the dark of night pressing close like it means to keep me.

I shove upright, the quilt slipping into my lap. My breath is uneven, each inhale edged with the phantom burn of fire. The air in the room feels close, heavy with the scent of rosemary from the bunches drying above the window, and faintly of ink and parchment from the desk crammed against the wall.

I grope for the oil lamp on my bedside table and strike the flint. The flame flares, casting a golden haze over the sloped ceiling patched with story parchment. The parchment is warped now, the ink faded to ghost-gray, but still holding on.

Like me.

Barefoot, I pad across the faded blue rug. My boots—two pairs lined in a neat row on the edge of it—watch me like silent sentries. I unhook the window latch and push it open.

Cool night air spills in, brushing my damp temples. Below, the garden sleeps, the rows of herbs silvered under the partial moon. Beyond, the barn's dark shape hunches against the hill, no sound from the animals inside—no restless stamping of hooves, no cluck of disturbed hens. Only the hum of the night and the thrum of my own unsettled heart.

I press my palms to the sill, gripping the cool wood, and replay the dream in my head—the ballroom, my mother, Renwick's voice threading between us like smoke. His insistence that I'm the only one who remembers him, the only one who can save his kingdom.

The fact should make me want to help him. It doesn't.

Underneath it all is the same old anger—the memory of Drakenholt's prince who stood silent while his father humiliated my family and cast us out. Who laughed when my mother delivered her prophecy. Who thought himself above me in every way.

And yet, there's an undeniable pull. Always the pull I feel to him.

I have my mother's gift. The dreams have never lied to me, no matter how much I've wished they would. My visions, either. And the soul-deep certainty that my quest is somehow bound to Ren's—that's the cruelest part of all.

I let my hand drift to the pendant at my throat, the one Mom gave me the day before she disappeared. The familiar azurite stone warms under my fingertips, though it can't warm the cold twist inside me.

A breeze caresses my cheek, strands of my hair tickling my neck. My braid has unraveled completely, my hair a wild snarl from my restless sleep. I rake my fingers through it, more to occupy my hands than to fix it, and glance over at my cramped desk.

My quest journal lies there, closed, its leather cover catching the lamplight. My pulse quickens.

Besides the dreams, it's the only way Renwick and I can speak. The Story Thief—a nameless, faceless shadow I can't seem to find—has stolen his kingdom and his voice. Any attempt to speak directly to me of Drakenholt's fall leaves Ren in crippling pain. Any attempt to rewrite its stories makes them vanish all over again.

Except when he writes them for me.

He is a storyteller like me, only not of Fae heritage. Rather, he is of dragon lineage. As his world has been erased, he's tried to rewrite it, only to fail over and over again because of the Story Thief's curse. He's the only one left behind, and the rest of the realm—except me—has forgotten them all.

Why hasn't the Story Thief erased him yet? I've questioned this a dozen times. The only answer I've found is me. As long as I still remember him, even if it's only a few images, his voice, it's enough. I'm connected to him, and it is this connection that keeps him from completely disappearing.

I doubt there's anything Ren could compose right now that would make me feel better. Yet, the pull to check my journal is too strong. There's no undoing what the dream has reminded me of or what my quest to restore Drakenholt demands—there is only going forward from this moment.

If he's written an apology, will I accept it? If he's recorded more of Drakenholt's fall, will I have the courage to save the legend?

If he hasn't written anything, leaving the next page in my journal empty...

I don't know what I'll do.

Fiddling with the edges, I take a deep breath. This is *my* quest. The thing I've longed for my whole life. There's no backing out now.

I run my hand over the cover, steel my nerves, and open it.

The page is blank.

My heart falls. I stare at the empty page as the lamplight flickers, shadows pooling in the corners of my room. Then I feel it—low and steady, a pulse that's not mine.

*Vellicor.*

The sensation is faint at first, the thrum of a distant drumbeat, but grows stronger with each breath. The Lore Language stirs in my chest, its syllables ghosting in my lungs and tingling my fingertips, urging me toward the scriptorium.

Vellicor doesn't summon without reason.

I close the journal, the leather warm from my hands, and slip it under my arm. My robe hangs from a peg by the washroom door; I wrap it tight around me, tugging the sash until the knot bites. My bare feet make no sound as I take the lamp and ease into the hall.

Calliope's door is shut. Moonlight through the nearby window pools at its threshold. I pass by slowly, holding my breath as if the floorboards might betray me.

A shadow moves at the far end of the corridor. My heart jumps—until the shadow meows.

"Marsh," I whisper.

Calliope's cat stares at me from the spot in front of the invisible scriptorium door, pupils wide as coins. His bushy tail lashes once, twice, then he slips into the shadows, a hunter on the prowl.

The heartbeat draws me farther down the hall, where my fingers trace along the plaster until they meet an invisible seam. The air is cooler here, edged with a whisper only I can hear.

I stretch out my hand. The scriptorium only reveals itself to Lorekeepers. The concealed brass knob blooms into existence, warm beneath my palm as if it's been waiting. The latch clicks, and I slip inside.

The scriptorium exhales around me.

Ink and parchment, sharp and comforting, wrap me in their familiar scent—but beneath them lingers the ghost of jasmine. My throat tightens. No matter how many moons pass, my mother's perfume clings to this space as if she's only just stepped out, leaving the air tasting faintly of summer nights and secrets.

Candle stubs are scattered over our Lorekeeper desks like tiny monuments to a thousand unfinished pages. Their wax has congealed into trays we never remember to replace. My favorite bottle of violet ink hums on the nearest, eager to record the next story Vellicor gives me.

Will it be mine?

Beside the ink bottle rests Mom's heirloom quill, the silver feather catching the lamplight. It sleeps now, its magic dormant, but I know it would flare gold in the presence of corruption. It never tolerates lies.

Setting down the lamp, I assess the shelves lining the walls, filled with hundreds of volumes bound in leather and paper. Shadows thrown by the flickering light creep over legends, fairytales, myths, maps, and more. The thrill of so many stories always stirs my blood, and their whispers invite me to get lost in them.

But it's Vellicor that demands my attention tonight.

The sentient book lies in its cradle of carved blackthorn, as old as our bloodline. Its cover shifts like a living hide, symbols crawling faintly across the surface before fading into stillness.

Bulin watches me from his perch above the sentient book, unblinking. The owl's feathers are shadow and starlight, his gaze stoic. A Fae creature, he never eats, never sleeps, only guards.

I step closer, my journal still tucked under my arm, and the book's pulse strengthens. The Lore Language shivers in my bones. Vellicor's cover stirs as if it's breathing, and then, slowly, the single eye with its predator's slitted pupil opens.

"Hello, friend." *Pulse.* I murmur the words to unlock him: "Once upon a story..."

With a shudder, the cover opens. The first page flips past. Then another and another. They eventually still themselves, the pulse slowing to a steady rhythm under my fingertips. A single line of script unfolds across the open parchment in shimmering gold, the Lore Language ink curling into letters I can read.

*"Seek the border where two stories meet—one lost, one about to be stolen."*

My heart lurches. One lost—Drakenholt. One about to be stolen?

A map unfurls across the page, in the same shimmering gold that makes me think of sunrise on water. Landmarks rise and fade, borders shifting as though the realm is breathing. Evermere's familiar outline takes shape, our town of Fablehollow marked with a quill and storybook. My breath catches when my finger traces northward—past the river lands, past the high forests—to a narrow, shaded strip Vellicor names: Jairton.

The word pulses. I trace it with my finger.

It appears to be a border town—the kind of place where travelers slip between kingdoms unnoticed. But here, it's drawn like a seam in fabric, fraying at the edges, and on the other side...there's only fog.

Where Drakenholt should be.

A thrill runs through me, sharp enough to chase away some of the anger curdling in my belly. If Vellicor is pointing me there, it means the next piece of my quest is waiting—something important enough for the book itself to stir from its slumber.

I place my quest journal on my desk and start pulling down reference tomes from the shelves. Their spines creak in protest, coughing up dust. Jairton appears in a handful of them—always mentioned in passing, never as the subject. A trading hub and temporary garrison for border skirmishes, nothing more. But the older the book, the more the details blur.

One crumbling gazetteer shows a caravan route that vanishes halfway across the border. Another lists a series of taverns that no longer exist, their names scratched away as if the parchment itself refuses to remember.

The Story Thief's shadow is here. I can feel it.

And somewhere beyond that fog, so is Ren.

The lamp flame dances low, throwing pools of gold across the desk as I flip to another atlas, hunting for a sharper outline of Jairton. My pulse is too loud in my ears. Vellicor rarely speaks so plainly—if plainly is even the right word—and the urgency in that single line won't let me sit still.

I'm leaning over the map, tracing the fogged edge of Drakenholt's absence, when a faint creak snaps my head up.

Footsteps.

I snap the atlas shut, slide it under the desk, and pull the quest journal onto my lap just as Calliope's sleepy voice floats from the hall.

"Dessa? What in the stars are you doing up—"

She stops in the doorway, her robe belted haphazardly, red-gold curls spilling loose over her shoulders. Her eyes are puffy from sleep, but there's a glint of suspicion in them that could pierce steel, even in the dim light. "You're in the scriptorium. Again."

I force a smile. "Couldn't sleep. Thought I'd sort the—" I wave vaguely toward the shelves "—Fablehollow trade records."

Her gaze sweeps the desk, catching on the stack of open books, the map edges peeking from beneath them. "At midnight?"

"It's...calming." I shrug, the lie heavy on my tongue and on my shoulders. "Like counting sheep, but with more dust and fewer hooves."

She pads closer, eyeing me the way she does when she knows I'm keeping a secret—which, in her mind, is always. Marsh slips past her ankles, tail flicking high, and hops up onto the desk with the imperious grace of someone who owns every surface in the room.

He noses at the quest journal on my lap, and I have to tighten my grip to keep it shut. The little traitor purrs, like he's announcing I'm hiding something.

Calliope narrows her eyes. "You've been dreaming again." It's not a question.

My pulse quickens. "We all dream."

"Not like you do. Every time you have a Fae dream, you look like this." She gestures at me—hair wild, eyes too bright, nightdress rumpled from tossing. "And you're always down here afterward, pawing through books and parchments like the next page is going to leap out and crown you quest-queen."

I snort, searching to keep her from knowing she's hit the mark. "Quest queen. I'm not—" I start, then stop.

Calliope folds her arms, waiting.

Denial is useless with her. I glance at Marsh, who blinks at me like he knows exactly which border I've just been told to cross. I stroke a hand down his back, the purr vibrating through my palm like it might steady my thoughts. But Calliope is still staring me down, and the longer I keep my mouth shut, the more I feel the pressure building inside.

So I let the words slip. "Vellicor gave me a message."

Her arms drop, and she leans toward the sentient book. "What kind of message?"

I slide the journal aside and go to the cradle, fingers brushing its scaled, breathing leather cover. The clue is still there, golden ink sunk deep into the parchment: *Jairton*.

Calliope's frown deepens as she traces the map with her eyes. "That's on the Evermere border."

"Exactly." My pulse skitters at the thought. "It must be the next thread in the Drakenholt story. Maybe even a way past the fog."

Her answer is instant, sharp. "Dessa, Father will never let you go. Not after Longmere."

I flinch at the memory of that night—the reek of blood, the Storyspawn wolves attacking us, their eyes glinting like oil in moonlight. The way they'd circled, cutting us off, faster and more vicious than anything I'd ever seen.

And the moment Renwick had slipped like armor between them and us and told us to run.

I hadn't recognized him then, the Thief having already nearly erased all of my memories, along with everyone else's. But if Ren hadn't been there...

We would have died—me, Calliope, and Falena, the young girl traveling with us.

What happened after I did run was even more shocking. As we fled, I looked back, sure that our savior would be torn to pieces by the unnatural wolves, but he...

Transformed.

Into a dragon.

I shut down the thought. "I have to go, Calli. Read that line about *one lost, one about to be stolen.* Evermere borders Draken-holt. Our kingdom could be next to be erased. Jairton could have answers."

She shakes her head, curls bouncing. "Or more wolves."

The scriptorium presses in on me, as if even the ink and parchment know I've stepped too close to dangerous ground. Calliope's right—Father will never let me go—but I can't let that be the end of this. The next step of my quest is within reach. I must accept it.

I open my mouth to argue, but a rustle from my journal cuts me off. It's faint at first—paper shifting against paper—then sharper, like something dragging across the parchment. A quill?

Heart hammering, I open it to the last written page. Ink stains the empty space beneath it, spilling into words before my eyes, each stroke jagged and uneven.

*Don't come to Jairton.*

My hand flies to my mouth.

Beneath the warning, a single drop of something dark soaks into the parchment. Not ink.

Blood.

# Chapter Two
## Dessalyn | Blood on the Page

*All warnings are stories in disguise—some too late, some too true.*

THE PAGE DRINKS HIS blood.

The words spread, adding to his warning. *It's not safe. The Story Thief's evil is here.*

I can't breathe. My eyes stay locked on the words, afraid they'll vanish. Is there more to come? The crimson gleam glistens under the lamplight, but nothing else appears.

The heat from earlier—the dream fire lodged under my ribs—ignites again, sharper now. Raw. His words crawl beneath my skin, into the hollow place that hasn't known peace since I remembered Drakenholt.

Renwick Ravelle, dragon prince and ghost of a forgotten kingdom, has bled to send me this. Every word trembles with his pain, the letters uneven, clawed in desperation. How did he know Vellicor was directing me there? How did he know I would come? Is it our connection?

Well, he's followed up the dream with a message, just not the one I anticipated.

I brush trembling fingers over the parchment, careful not to smudge the ink or blood. My pendant warms, the way it always does when the Lore stirs. And beneath my fingertips, the page hums.

Vellicor is listening.

The sentient book stirs in its cradle. Calliope leaves my side to rush to it, but shakes her head. The words on the page in my journal shiver.

Another line begins to write itself below Renwick's warning—not in his hand this time, but in the curling script of the Lore Language.

> *To find what's lost beyond the flame,*
> *seek the border etched in blame.*
> *When memory frays and dragons fall,*
> *the silent call will break them all.*

A riddle. A summons.

Or a curse?

"Look." I show it to Calliope.

She pales. "That's...Mom's handwriting."

Goose flesh rises on my arms, but it seals the truth in my gut. This *is* part of my quest. Jairton lies on the edge of Evermere and the forgotten land of Drakenholt. Ren's trail leads there. The Story Thief's, too.

I continue to stare at the writing, my pendant pulsing as if it senses Mom near. "The prince is in danger." My voice shakes. "I have to go to him—before it's too late. Before it's too late for all of us."

Because if I wait—if I hesitate again—he might be gone.

I jump up, closing my journal and heading for the door.

Calliope grabs my wrist. "You can't just go running off again. Not after Longmere."

Her voice cuts through the spell of the moment, yanking me out of the dream's haze. I blink at her, the journal a heavy weight in my hands, and see the fear rising in her eyes—sharp and familiar.

"I have to." Even now, a ticking clock beats in my heart along with my pulse. "Mom even wants me to."

She steps between me and the door, a shield blocking my path. "No," she says, firmer now. "You could have died in Longmere. Falena and I, too. Storyspawn wolves, remember? If Renwick hadn't—" Her voice breaks. "It's a long journey to Jairton, and you don't know what you'll find once you get there. You need a plan."

My pulse pumps hot with anger. "I remember. All of it. Every breath, every vision. And I remember that you chose to come with me." It's not a plea for her help, because I can do this on my own, but we're always there for each other. Going to Jairton alone is my quest, and yet, I can't imagine being separated from her for days, weeks, maybe months.

She crosses her arms. "And I still would—but not like this. Not in the middle of the night, chasing a blood-soaked riddle and some prince's warning. I don't care if Mom sent the riddle or Vellicor orders you to leave right now. You're the smartest person in this family, so act like it. We have to talk to Father, form a plan, make sure this isn't some clever trick by the Story Thief."

She's right, but I laugh, short and bitter. "Oh, yes. Let's ask the great Thand Lorewyn for permission. After he forbade me from ever leaving again after what happened in Longmere."

Calliope's jaw tightens. "You know I don't agree with him, and I know this is your quest, but you think I would let you make a stupid decision based on emotion and too little information?"

"I think you're trying to stop me."

"I'm trying to protect you!" Her nostrils flare before she softens her voice. "Please, Dessa. Sleep. Just a few hours. We'll speak to Father in the morning. If this truly is your quest path, he can't stop you. You know that."

The tension stretches between us, a string pulled taut and on the verge of snapping.

Marsh jumps down from my desk and circles my ankles. Vellicor's pages twitch behind us. The journal falls open in my hand, and I glance once more at the riddle, the curling words that might be my mother's, and the glimmer of Ren's blood now drying to rust.

Could this be a trick?

Calliope places a hand on my shoulder. "You always say no one should quest alone."

My breath stutters. *She's right.* And yet—

I nod once. "Fine. I'll wait until morning after I speak to Father." But as I turn away, I already know I won't be sleeping.

Calliope and Marsh walk with me to my room. The house is too quiet when I slip inside, too still. I'm going to go crazy in here.

I leave the lamp burning low on my desk and drop onto the edge of the bed, quest journal in hand. The heat from it has dissipated, but the impression of Renwick's blood on the parchment burns behind my eyes.

I don't change out of my nightdress. Don't braid my hair again. Just sit there, listening to the distant ticking of the old clock in the kitchen and the soft creak of the rafters above me. What is usually a lullaby when I can't sleep grates on my nerves now.

Eventually, I lie back, curling onto my side, the journal beside me. My pendant slips to the spot over my heart, warm against my skin. It pulses, throbs.

Like a heartbeat.

Like *his* heartbeat.

I shouldn't care. I shouldn't.

But the image of him bleeding to send me a warning keeps slicing through me like a dragon's claw through parchment.

Renwick Ravelle. The boy who laughed at my mother's prophecy. The prince who let his father cast us out in shame. The arrogant, stupid boy I swore I'd never forgive.

Yet in the dream, in Longmere, he wasn't that boy anymore. He's older. Tormented. Like he carries the weight of a kingdom alone. I guess he does now. Maybe he's even...regretful. But I don't know if I can believe that—not yet.

I peek toward my window at the stars. Is my mother one of them, looking down on me?

My chest aches, the fire curling tighter beneath my ribs—resentment, worry, and something I don't want to name smoldering there. It hasn't gone out. It never really does. Not since I remembered Drakenholt. Not since I began this cursed quest that keeps pulling me toward the crown prince without a throne, no matter how hard I resist.

The wind brushes against the glass panes of the window, and I breathe deeply, watching those stars so far away. I try not to think about Jairton. About the riddle. About what I'll say to Father in the morning.

I try not to remember the way Ren looked at me in the ballroom ruins—like I was his last hope.

My eyes drift half-shut. The faintest trace of jasmine teases my nose. The pendant pulses.

And then—

A flicker on the backs of my eyelids. A warmth that spreads from under my ribs to my lungs, my heart. A whisper brushes against the edge of my drifting thoughts. Not words—just a presence.

*Mom?*

No. It's not my mother.

It's Ren.

My eyes fly open. I sit up. There's no dream pulling me under this time. No liminal fog. There's darkness, and the journal humming beside me. But the connection—my bond to the dragon prince—is there. Faint, but real.

He's close. Or he's in pain.

If he's reaching for me, I have to find a way to reach back.

I drag the journal into my lap, breath snagging on the edge of hope. Maybe the riddle wasn't all. Maybe there's more—something hidden, something meant for my eyes alone.

The lamplight flickers as I open it. At first, nothing is different. The page is still stained where the drop of blood sank into the paper. I reread the riddle, hearing my mother's voice in my head.

As if I conjured her or maybe Ren, the page vibrates. In the margin, near the edge of the parchment where the leather binding stretches thin, new ink begins to curl.

Hope soars in my chest. I smile. *Yes. Talk to me...*

A word appears. Just one, and as the letters form it, my smile falters.

*Danger*

It's jagged, written in the same desperate hand as Ren's message. The moment it dries, the ink smokes at the edges, twisting up like burning leaves before vanishing entirely.

Gone.

*Erased.*

Like his name from the stories. Like his kingdom from the maps. Like everything that once mattered.

"No—" I press my fingers to the spot, as if I can pull the word back. Pull *him* back. "Don't go. Tell me what's happening."

Only silence answers.

I race to my desk and grab a quill, dipping it in ink. *Ren,* I write. *What's happening to you? Talk to me. Please.*

The pendant at my throat throbs. No ink fills the space under my plea. I swallow hard. Ren doesn't want me to come. He's there, tracking the Story Thief, but he fears what the thief might do to me.

*Danger*... Calliope and Father won't want me to go, either, even though they didn't see this last missive.

And yet, I'm going. Even if I have to face my father's wrath. Even if it means defying everything that's expected of me. Even if Ren doesn't want me there.

Because it's not just about saving only him anymore, or Drakenholt.

It's about saving Evermere and all the other kingdoms the Story Thief seeks to erase. I must save *the story*. Ren's, mine, ours—before it vanishes forever.

# CHAPTER THREE
## DESSALYN | TWO SISTERS, ONE HEART

*All quests steal something first—the ordinary, the expected, the quiet rhythms of before.*

THE ROOSTER CROWS BEFORE the sun crests the eastern hills. I swing my legs out of bed and wince at the stiffness in my spine. Sleep came in fits, full of half-dreams and smoky thoughts. Ren's warning still echoes in my mind.

The morning air has a bite to it, carrying the earthy scent of dew and hay through my cracked window. I dress quickly, forgoing a braid for a simple ponytail, and pull on my garden boots before slipping out of my room.

The house is still, my father, sister, and Falena, our fairy-tale-princess-without-a-story guest, asleep.

I grab the feed bucket from the porch hook, already rehearsing what I'll say to Father. How I'll explain everything—Ren's messages, Vellicor's riddle, Mom's message, and the call of the quest that won't let me stay.

The screen door creaks open. I glance back.

Calliope, wrapped in a shawl and blinking blearily, steps outside and hugs herself against the chill. "I couldn't sleep. I'm betting you didn't either."

Morning duties typically fall to me. I don't mind. I enjoy the quiet of the early hours. But today? I welcome her appearance.

I drop a pointed look at her feet and arch a brow. "You planning to feed the chickens barefoot?"

She looks down. "I hate shoes. You know this." She doesn't go back inside. Just trudges across the dirt with me, yawning into her sleeve.

"You don't usually do farm girl duty," I say, trying for lightness. "Too rustic for a poet and dreamer."

A pained look crosses her face. "I need to move. Sitting still with that riddle in my head is inviting madness."

"You love riddles."

Her fingers graze a morning glory vine along the fence. "Not those that come from Mom's quill, or that might be tainted by evil."

If only we knew which. Hope and fear war inside me. The quill hasn't moved or scribbled a single word since the night before Mom faded into the woods, her eyes wide as if she were glimpsing something beyond our physical world.

We pass the herb beds, dew glittering on the lavender and sage. At the chicken coop, the hens cluck softly, rustling in their straw as

I unlatch the door. Calliope takes the scoop from me and scatters feed, not bothered by her bare toes. The grain tinkles against the coop floor, and the hens flutter and squabble as they scramble for it.

Memories of Mom's passing try to take root, but keep fading away as fast as I latch onto them. It's always the same—as if I can't come to grips with the details, so they stay just out of reach.

"Dessa?"

I realize I've paused, mind drifting, while reaching for a hen's nest of eggs. Blinking, I glance back at her through the small door of the coop. "Yes?"

"I've decided something." She shakes out the last of the bucket's contents. The greedy chickens are a quilt of red, yellow, black, and white feathers. The rooster stomps around, head high. "If you're going to Jairton, I'm going with you."

I leave the eggs and straighten. "What?"

"You heard me."

I'm relieved, even though this is a bad idea. I must protest. Father and Falena need her more than I do. "I know you long for adventure, but you hated traveling to Longmere."

"I hate getting attacked by monsters and having to flee for my life. That's not the same."

The cow lows in the barn, a sleepy protest. I sigh and head that way, knowing she'll follow. "Calli, you don't have to—"

"Yes, I do. Think about it—Father might be more open to allowing you to go if I go with you. He knows how protective you are of me. You won't do anything impulsive or too risky if I'm with you. Appeal to his logic, sister."

I glance over my shoulder. "You think I'm impulsive?"

"Hardly. If anything, I'm the impulsive one. You're...*passionate*." Her expression softens. "And sometimes reckless when it comes to protecting the people you care about. Like this Renwick."

I bristle. "I don't care about him. Not in the way you're suggesting."

Her lips quirk. "Mm-hmm."

"I don't. But he's in need, and it's my duty to help him. We have to stop the Story Thief."

"We don't even know who that is, or why he's erasing kingdoms."

Just like her penchant for figuring out riddles, understanding the why behind something is important to her. I'd like to know, too, but no matter, it won't change my plan to stop the Thief. Fables and lore expound that greed and the hunger for power are at the root of most evil actions.

"I would never want to leave Father in a lurch, but I'm old enough to make my own decisions. If I have to force the matter, then I will, and you need not be caught in the middle of it."

"Always looking out for me." The smile returns. "I appreciate your concern, but I'm also old enough to make my own decisions. If you're leaving, I'm going with you."

We fall into the rhythm of milking Marigold—me handling the bucket, Calliope smoothing the cow's flank and murmuring nonsense poetry to keep her calm.

"I'm not going just to keep you out of trouble," she says after a moment. "I want to see it. Jairton. Drakenholt, whatever might be left beyond the fog you mentioned."

I look at her, unsurprised. I may be *passionate*, but she is an adventurer at heart. "Looking for your own quest, sister?"

"A change of scenery would do me good. I don't deny that I dislike travel, but I do long for something more beyond Fablehollow."

The bucket's nearly full. The goat bleats for attention. I clean Marigold's teats. "Do you really believe Father will say yes?"

She shrugs and then adjusts her shawl. "I think he'll be adamantly against it, but in the end, he'll realize he can't say no to both of us."

I huff a laugh, and the cow flicks her tail at me.

"Still," Calliope continues, brushing hay from her skirt, "we need to offer him a solution. Falena has learned how to stock the shelves, and he trusts her with the quest scrolls. Aileen can help with the rest. She's a hard worker, and her crush on him is cute."

Father has never loved anyone but our mother. Still, he deserves kindness, and Aileen does treat him like a king. I only hope she doesn't get her heart broken, because I doubt he'll ever return her feelings. "She might ask too many questions."

"Then we lie," Calliope says sweetly. "Or bend the truth into a prettier shape. He'll manage. He always does. Besides, we won't be gone long...right?"

I don't answer as we move to the goat and lug the bucket of milk out of the barn.

We enter the kitchen with our breakfast. Calliope hums a half-forgotten lullaby, her shawl trailing hay as she sets the basket of eggs on the counter. The familiar smells of wood smoke, sweet oats, and cinnamon fill the air.

Father stands at the stove in his usual dark blue pants held up with suspenders, his socks sporting holes in the toes. His shirt is striped, the cuffs frayed, the fabric wrinkled. Mom used to sew all his clothes, and while he could afford to replace the ones that are worn out and holey, he won't, because every stitch carries her memory.

His back is to us, stirring the oats in the iron pot. He's been up longer than we thought.

He doesn't look up when he speaks. "The cow complained less than usual. What did you bribe her with?"

"Calli's poetry," I say.

He chuckles and shoots my sister a wink over his shoulder. "Well, no wonder then. No man or creature can resist that."

He freezes when he sees our faces, his gaze bouncing between us—my boots, muddy hem, the way Calliope's toes are covered with dirt. Something flickers in his eyes. A small crease appears between his brows.

"Father?" I set down the pail. Did he somehow overhear our conversation? Can he suddenly read my mind? "What is it?"

He blinks, and the crease disappears, along with that look. "Nothing." He swallows hard and returns to stirring. "You're both up early."

It's not *nothing*. "I know it's unusual for your youngest daughter to be up this early." I playfully elbow Calliope. "But you look like you've seen a ghost."

The spoon stops, and his shoulders droop. "In a way, I guess I have."

My sister and I exchange a glance. She shrugs.

I go to him and place a hand on his back. "You're scaring me. Tell me what's wrong."

He gives a half-hearted smile when his eyes meet mine. "There are just times when I look at you two and see your mother."

My heart twinges. Memories from the dream last night assault me. Her face. How beautiful she was in that dress. The ribbon from her hair. I wrap my arm around his shoulders and lean my head onto one of them. "That must be hard for you."

He abandons the spoon and pats my cheek with a rough hand. "Don't be silly. It's wonderful. I'm grateful every day for you two girls."

*Girls.* That's what he still sees when he looks at us. I'm sure he always will.

Which makes what I have to do even harder. I decide to wait until after we've eaten. Some things go better on a full stomach.

Falena joins us just as we sit down to eat, her youthful personality commanding the conversation. Today, she wears one of Calliope's dresses with a full skirt that she can barely tuck under the table. It's too big in the bodice and hips, but she's used a sequined sash to tuck it in around her waist. Her blue eyes are full of cheer, and she delights in the brown sugar Father has added to our meal. "I read the most enlightening tale last night," she says.

We listen to her recount it over our breakfast of eggs and oatmeal, and it eases the nerves in my stomach enough that I can at least get some of it down.

Father leaves to open the store, and the three of us clean up. Calliope asks Falena to wash the dishes, and the princess sighs but nods. "Can I borrow another book from the scriptorium for tonight?"

"Of course," my sister and I say in unison.

We fall into our usual routine of waking the mercantile while Father prepares the cashbox and checks over the account ledgers. Like Vellicor and Butin, our shop has its own magic, its own personality. Hidden hands move things around at night; displays rearrange themselves.

Minutes before we open, I grab my chance to speak to him. "Father, can I talk to you?" Calliope gives me a tiny nod, letting me take the lead. I inhale to steady my nerves. "It's about my quest."

His expression tightens. He sets the quill in his hand down, as if bracing himself. "What of it?"

"Last night, I had a message from Vellicor." I wait for him to ask about it. His brows rise, but he doesn't say a word. Fear is evident in the way he tenses, though. "I'm going to Jairton."

That crease appears again, deeper this time. "Why?"

"I know you're worried about the risk, but the Story Thief is real, and so is the danger he poses. Vellicor's word is the Language, and the Language cannot be denied. I believe Prince Ravelle is there, and that's where I'm meant to follow."

Father crosses his arms, silent.

"There was a riddle." Calliope fiddles with the rolls of quest parchments in their bin. Vellicor gives them to us, and folks who are meant for them find their way to our shop. "We think it's from Mom. It also directs Dessa to Jairton."

At the mention of Mom, his lips thin. He picks up his quill again, not believing our mother has spoken from the Fade, where all Fae go at death. "No."

My focus drops to the floor. My shoulders droop as his did earlier. I knew this would be a fight, but it's still disheartening. "Ren is in trouble. He needs me."

Father scratches something in his ledger. "The prince should be capable of taking care of himself. He doesn't need a girl to save him."

My fists ball at my sides, and I step forward. "I'm not a girl! And you know as well as I do that the Story Thief is erasing him. He needs a Lorekeeper to save his story and his kingdom. He needs *me*. You can't deny me this."

Calliope steps forward. "We've talked it through, Father. I'm going with her."

He exhales sharply, shaking his head and smacking his hand on the counter. "Calliope—no."

"Yes." She lifts her chin. "We're not children anymore. You raised us to be brave, clever, and kind. All of that matters, and it matters right now with this decision."

He removes his reading glasses and tosses them on the open ledger. "You don't understand what you're stepping into. This Story Thief is using old magic. Magic this kingdom has never faced."

"And if we do nothing?" I demand. "How many more stories will he take? Yours? Mine? Mom's? How many more kingdoms will forget themselves? Vellicor's message stated that another kingdom bordering Drakenholt is about to be erased. It could be ours."

He looks at me, really looks at me, and for a heartbeat, I see his defenses falter. His eyes flicker the way they did in the kitchen when he saw Mom in Calliope and me. "You sound like her," he says. "Like your mother, when she took up the quill. There was no stopping her."

I step closer. "Then let me do this for her."

He paces a short circle, running a hand through his hair, streaked more with silver than I remember. "This is a dangerous, dangerous quest. I won't stop you, although everything inside me demands I do so, but I can't give you my blessing. I'm your father. It's my duty to protect you at all costs."

Each quest has some level of danger. We all know this. "It is dangerous," I concede, "but I will not fail. I can't. Too much rides on it."

I go to him and hug him. The shop goes silent, broken only by the arrival of our first customers on the other side of the door, talking and laughing while they wait to be let inside.

After a long pause, he nods once. "If you're going to do this, then do it wisely. Take the maps. Speak to Halden at the old ferry—he still owes me a favor. And promise me one thing."

My pulse races. "What?"

"If the road turns against you—if something feels wrong—don't press forward out of pride. Come home."

Calliope and I exchange a look. "We promise," she says for both of us.

He presses his hand to his eyes, then rubs his jaw. "Falena stays. I'll make arrangements if I need more help than that."

I throw my arms around him before my courage slips. For a moment, he's stiff as driftwood—but then he crumples into me, as if he can't hold his grief any longer. He holds Calliope next, and I see the tear he wipes away when he turns back to his ledger.

At the door, I flip the sign around and unlock it. I'm eager to set off, but for this morning, I'll stay and help him.

It may be for the very last time.

# CHAPTER FOUR
## RENWICK | GHOST AT THE BORDERLAND

*Quests may lead to ruins or victories. Sometimes both.*

SHE'S COMING.

I feel it in my bones—and that's precisely why I bled the warning across the page. But whether she read it or not, whether it was enough, I can't know.

The border town of Jairton unfurls before me like a story half-erased. Roads are veined with cracks. A fountain has gone dry in the square, arms of ivy climb around the stone like forgotten handwriting. An unnatural silence presses against my eardrums.

I walk the final stretch to the center of town, cloak pulled tight. My boots scrape old cobbles worn by generations. The people here move like ghosts through fog—slow, unfocused, hollow-eyed. A girl sits on the steps of what used to be a bakery, cradling a wooden spoon like a doll. She hums an out-of-tune lullaby.

I start with the apothecary. My magic is fraying, my dragon riding just underneath my skin. It heals some wounds quickly, while others won't heal at all.

The shop sign hangs crooked, the painted mortar and pestle faded by time and sun. Inside, a bell should ring—but doesn't. A man stands behind the counter, polishing a jar of lavender that's already clean. His gaze slides right past me, unseeing.

I clear my throat. "Excuse me—do you carry goldenseal and hydros root?"

He blinks twice. Then sets down the jar and reaches beneath the counter. For a moment, I think he's heard me. Instead, he pulls out a candle stub, stares at it for a long beat, and asks, "Do you know where the bees have gone?"

I don't answer. He doesn't wait. He moves on to wiping down the next jar.

Outside again, I pass a woman sweeping the same spot on her stoop over and over. Her broom hits the same loose cobble with a soft thud. Her eyes are wet, but she's not crying.

A boy sits on the edge of the dry fountain with a fishing pole. No line. Just the stick, bobbing over empty stone. He grins at me as if he's caught something. "I think it's a good day for trout," he says.

My skin prickles a warning. My broken pendant vibrates against my chest. This isn't forgetfulness, illness, or enchantment. It's erosion—memory unraveling thread by thread. I witnessed the same in Drakenholt.

Jairton is being erased, and no one remembers the original version. This is why I came. But if I'm too late, Jairton won't be the last to suffer this fate. Dessalyn, her family, and all of Evermere will disappear, too.

Below a chapel here lies a sealed Lorekeeper vault, forgotten even by those sworn to protect it. If the Story Thief finds it first, the names, maps, and truths too dangerous to rewrite will be lost. Maybe forever.

I need to find it before he does. I swore I'd do it alone, because if Dessa comes, I could lose more than I have left to give. I suspect after Longmere, the Story Thief is using her to track what he can't find on his own—me.

But the vault's truth could damn me in more ways than one. If she discovers what I've done...

*No.*

I don't need her help for this. All I need is to retrieve the information hidden inside. I'm sure of it. I can stop the unraveling of this border town and find the first key to give her to restore my kingdom.

Because deep in my heart, I know she's the only one who can.

The chamber I seek isn't marked on any map. It never was. I follow the remnants of old glyph work carved into the alleyways—symbols I recognize only because a certain Fae Lorekeeper taught them to me before she ever spoke the prophecy to my father.

The way winds narrow and steep, until I reach the crumbling remnants of a once-sacred scriptorium tucked below a chapel. A place long since abandoned, it draws no eye. Most walk past the weeping stones without a second glance, not only because of the place's appearance, but because of the wards.

But I remember the words Serenelle whispered when she helped me hide my greatest shame. "Some stories must be buried—not because they're lies, but because someone might believe them."

I press two fingers against the warded arch. The air shivers around my hand, my gold cuffs warm. Dragon magic throbs beneath my skin in response. I'm drained, but the power still responds. Scales flash on the backs of my hands, my fingers.

The wards are strained but intact. I blow out a relieved breath.

It dies quickly, though. The corruption of this place, this town, feels the same way it did in Drakenholt before everything collapsed. It's happening here. Though the wards sting like nettles and try to turn me away, I close my eyes, grit my teeth, and press through them.

The pews are scattered, some overturned. The dais is empty, save for broken candelabras and ripped up hymnals. I find the stairs and descend.

It takes the last of my strength to push through the spelled magic shielding the vault. I stumble across the threshold to the inner sanctum. Mildew and the scent of old wood fill the air. The walls are lined with shattered scroll racks. Most are empty—already unraveled by the Story Thief, perhaps, or lost to time.

But at the center, the raised stone dais remains untouched. Glyphs spiral across its surface in a language Serenelle and I both understood. My pulse thunders beneath my ribs. The guilt I've kept buried claws its way back to the surface.

The original Chronicle of Drakenholt is sealed inside—a complete telling of the kingdom's founding and its origin with dragons. The lore my ancestors swore to protect. But this version differs from the accepted history that was taught in the academies of Drakenholt before the Story Thief came.

And while damning, that's not why I'm here.

I was fifteen, and the kingdom was under great strife at the time when I wrote a story in the Dragon Language that changed everything. A false tale I inserted into the Chronicle.

I was desperate to be seen—not as a burden, not as a political pawn—but as someone who mattered. Who would eventually lead. So I conjured my own fable. A beautiful lie, threaded with enough truth to make it convincing. It was meant to be symbolic. A balm. A rallying cry in a time of unrest. With the written words of the Dragon Language, I gave myself great purpose. A destined enemy. His glorious fall at my hands. A happily ever after.

But the magic of any Lore Language—be it Dessa's Fae version or mine—is that it does not care about intentions. It preserved the lie, and in doing so, attracted the attention of the Story Thief.

Now, he's using it to twist all the stories. To contaminate them. What began as a dozen pages of fiction has become a foundation for his rise.

Lady Serenelle found me the morning I brought it here. She saw it in my eyes before I confessed. She didn't punish or lecture; she simply helped me place it in the vault and weave the wards to protect it. She warned me never to speak of it again.

Now the seal is cracking, and if Story Thief gets to it first—

I press my palm flat to the dais, teeth gritted. "I'm going to fix this," I whisper to the tomb of this forgotten place. "Before Dessalyn has to know."

The glyphs beneath my hand flare once, then fade. I inhale sharply and call on my fire—crackling behind my ribs, wild and raw. It floods my limbs like acid. My gold cuffs warm once more, and the dragon sigil inked into my wrist writhes.

The glyphs flare again, but wink out just as quickly. The vault does not open.

Why? I study the glyphs inscribed around the lock, and the reason becomes clear. Two magics are required: one of dragon fire, one of a Lorekeeper's blood.

I nearly groan aloud. How could I have forgotten? Serenelle insisted on this safeguard after hiding my damning fable away.

I can't open this without a Lorekeeper. Of which, I know of only two—Dessalyn and her sister.

Is it safer to leave it here, then? Can the Story Thief break this lock?

Can I take the chance that he might?

He's already destroyed my entire kingdom. What else is he capable of?

I broke a sacred code, and Serenelle, gods forgive her, broke one too by helping me bury the fate-binding story. No matter how noble my intent is now, the unraveling of Drakenholt—all of this—started with me.

And now Dessalyn is walking into my mess.

No matter how much I wish I didn't need her...I do. She's the only one who can open this chamber with me. The only one left who remembers Drakenholt *and* bears the Lorekeeper gift.

I caress the obsidian pendant and feel it purr like a cat under my fingers. On the far wall, a mural once showed the first dragon riders taking flight. Now, only fragments remain—half a wing, the edge of a helm, a smear of flame. The rest has been devoured by time...or something worse.

Needing to regroup, I reluctantly leave the chamber and the chapel. Slipping out like a shadow, passing the ruins of the crumbling building and its graveyard, I mix in with the townsfolk in the market. My wounds throb, worse after calling on the dragon fire. I need rest, food.

The tavern is as dismal as the rest of Jairton. Half the lanterns are cold, their oil long burned away. Only a few patrons haunt the corner tables, sipping drinks that no longer steam, chewing food with blank expressions. One man has drunk his fill and sleeps it off by the hearth, where no fire burns. It probably hasn't been lit in weeks.

I drop onto a stool at the bar. The barkeep says nothing—just pours a dram of something cloudy and amber into a chipped glass and slides it my way without meeting my eyes.

It tastes like old vinegar and burned pine, but I drink it anyway. I need the burn. I need something real.

The stool beside mine creaks. I don't look. Not at first. But then I hear it—the scrape of a gloved finger against the counter. A low chuckle, too quiet for anyone else to notice. A whisper brushes my ear—too real to be wind. "You always did prefer to chase your mistakes in solitude."

The voice is familiar. My grip tightens on the glass. I turn, slowly.

Marrow Greyfen leans against the bar as if he belongs here. Hood pulled low, face half-shadowed, the glint of a bone ring catching the tavern light. He hasn't aged a day—though neither of us should, not with magic twisting in our veins. Yet, I feel older than this ancient town.

But there's something different in him now. An absence. A kind of emptiness that mirrors this place. That mirrors me.

Once, he was a friend. A dream shifter with a gift for navigating memory as others do maps. We studied glyph work together to enhance his dream walking abilities. Flirted with the same girls, testing each other's prowess. Even then, he was drawn to the darker things.

"You've made it worse, you know," he says casually, reaching for my drink and taking a sip without asking. "Coming here. Stirring the ashes. You're like a moth to the flame, Renny."

He has the ability to slip through time and space, his dream magic able to transport him between the living and waking. One of the rarest of magical skills and the most dangerous. He can appear and disappear in a breath. I glance at the man in the booth, sleeping away. Marrow's transporter. What dreams does he cling to? "What are you doing here?"

He shrugs. "A man's gotta eat, right? My latest employer sent me to keep watch on this place." He leans closer, smug. "And look who I've found."

My stomach drops. "Why are you watching Jairton?"

"I always watch the places he plans to unmake."

I come off the stool, forcing him to lean back. "You're working for the Story Thief?"

"His name is Solander Cimarron, and he pays well."

My dragon stirs. I grip his lapels and shake him. "He's ruined my kingdom. He's ruining this place."

He sets the glass down with a soft clink and raises both hands in mock surrender. "Still playing the hero, I see. At least, in your own story."

"If you're helping him, you are now my enemy."

Marrow smiles, cruel and vindictive. "I always was." He knocks my grip loose. The shadows cling to him like vines, twisting around his arm, up his neck. "Time's running out, Renny. For you. For her. And for every kingdom that still dares to remember their names."

Her. My stomach drops, but he's gone before I can draw breath—just a whisper disappearing between the waking and the dream worlds.

I stay standing long after, my dragon wanting to emerge and burn the world down to stop him. Solander Cimarron—who is he? I have no recollection of the name. No idea which kingdom he hails from, if any at all.

*Time's running out.*

I shake my head in frustration. I told the only person who can help me stop the Thief—Dessalyn—not to come, but this is exactly where I need her to be. If she doesn't come, all the stories left to save may die.

# Chapter Five
## Dessalyn | Tethers of Home

*The first steps are the hardest—not for the road ahead, but for the roots that hold you back.*

The morning air is sharp with dew, the kind that beads on lashes. I tug my cloak tighter, the strap of my pack already digging into my shoulder as Calliope practically skips ahead of me down the narrow woodland path.

"Can you believe it?" she whispers as though the trees might overhear and scold us. "We're finally off on the next stage of your quest. This is exactly like one of Mother's tales."

Her joy is so bright it almost hurts. At last, we're moving. After a full day and night of pacing and rereading the riddle, I am *doing* something. My blood hums with purpose.

The sun is only a pale suggestion on the horizon, but already the ache in my chest lightens. Finches and bluebirds in the trees call out sweet songs while chickadees scold and crows caw. Jairton may be two days on foot, yet every step forward is freedom.

Calliope spins in her cloak, her hair wild in the dawn breeze. "Do you think we'll see bandits? Or more Storyspawn?"

The last is said with trepidation. I've outfitted us with knives Mother enchanted, and Father taught us how to use to defend ourselves. "My guess is the most excitement we'll have is blistered feet."

The path bends downhill, muddy in places where last night's rain has collected in shallow ruts. Bracken crowds the verges, and the forest presses close, the white pines whispering in the breeze like a thousand secrets being traded. Here and there, cart tracks cut into the muck—evidence of earlier morning risers who've passed through earlier.

A farmer trudges by leading a shaggy mule, a bundle of firewood strapped to its back. He tips his hat without a word, gaze focused on his task. Calliope waves cheerily, oblivious to the vacant look he gives her in return. Times are hard here. The work to simply survive is often more than some can do.

Once he disappears around the bend, she turns back to me, mischief sparking in her eyes. "So," she begins, drawing the word out. "Aside from all of the doom and gloom about Drakenholt, what do you think of the prince?"

I nearly trip over a loose stone. "What?"

"Renwick." She says his name with a dramatic sigh. "Your tall, blond, and glowering dragon prince. While I don't remember him from before the Story Thief erased his kingdom, I did see him in

Longmere. You can't deny he's handsome, and he was so protective of you." She fans herself.

Heat pricks my neck. Ren's face flashes in my mind. At court, he was well-groomed. Short hair. Fierce blue eyes. Clothes of the finest silk and velvet. Now, his blond hair is longer and unkempt. His body has filled out. Those fierce eyes are still defiant and arrogant, but they hold so much more than they did during his teen years. Grief, sorrow, and a determination that stirs something inside me.

I focus on the path, the crunch of gravel underfoot, the cool bite of the wind through the trees. "A pretty face only hides the truth underneath. He's arrogant, self-absorbed, infuriating—I don't find those qualities attractive in the least."

Calliope smirks, quickening her pace so she can walk backward in front of me. Her skirts swish. "Regardless, he's part of your quest, and many romances have been built on less. He needs you, and who can resist that? A royal crown prince in need of his princess! You think about him and all the ways you can help him, right?"

A princess. The very idea makes me break out in hives. "I think about him the same way I think about a thorn in my boot." I swat a low branch out of my way. "He's annoying and must be dealt with, and once this quest is done, he'll return to his kingdom. I'll return to the mercantile." My chest tweaks at the words. "To him,

I'll be nothing more than a Lorekeeper who rewrote his story, and he'll be nothing to me but the crown prince of Drakenholt."

"Mm-hmm." She grins, unbothered. "You can pretend, but I saw the way he looked at you in Longmere. Like a hero spotting the girl fated to—"

"Stop." My voice echoes in the still woods. "I'll never forgive him or his father for what they did to Mom. I'm not a princess—I'm a story keeper. A demi-fae with a gift of the Lore Language. I'm quite content to immerse myself in the stories of our realm and help others with their happily-ever-afters."

"Don't you deserve one, too?"

Everything inside me tightens. For a moment, silence stretches between us. The only sound is the sigh of the pines and the distant caw of a crow.

Calliope softens, her grin fading. "I didn't mean—"

"I know." I force my shoulders to relax and adjust the strap of my pack. "Just...don't go writing a fairytale that isn't meant to be, Calli."

She nods, though I catch the ghost of a smile tugging at her lips. Romance may fuel her, but bitterness fuels me. And I will not let her turn this quest into some foolish story about princes and love.

We've barely gone a mile when the morning peace fractures—

"Wait!"

The voice echoes down the road, and I turn to see a figure running hard from the direction we've come. Cloak askew, hair tumbling free of its pins, Falena stumbles as she climbs the hill toward us, her breath tearing from her lungs.

Calliope gasps. "Falena?"

Has she run all this way? By the time she reaches us, she falters, and I catch her. Her cheeks are flushed crimson, and she bends double, clutching a stitch in her side. "Your—your father—" she pants, lifting wide eyes to mine. "He's taken ill."

The words spear straight through me. My voice comes out razor sharp. "What do you mean?"

"He collapsed not long after you left, complaining of severe stomach pains. Aileen sent me—she begged me to fetch you back. He won't let her call a physician."

Calliope doesn't hesitate. She whirls around, skirts flying as she takes off back toward the cottage. "Come on, Dess!"

I stand frozen in the road, pack heavy against my shoulders. What has just happened to my quest?

I peer at the road ahead. Any step away from Jairton feels like betrayal, like time spilling through my fingers. Ren could be injured. He could already be—

"Please." Falena's hand grips my sleeve, her face pinched with fear. "He keeps asking for you."

Duty cleaves me in two. Father. Ren. Family. Kingdom. For a heartbeat, I stand caught between futures—the one that leads home, the one that leads to answers.

Then I exhale, bitter with guilt, and follow my sister. My boots pound on the path, each step heavier than the last. I tell myself there will be time tomorrow. There has to be.

But as we speed home and the cottage roofline reappears on the horizon, the whisper in my chest turns hollow. When the three of us reach the cottage, Aileen waits at the door, wringing her apron with pale hands. "Thank heavens," she whispers, her eyes shining with worry. "He's so stubborn. Maybe you can talk sense into him."

She's closed the mercantile, and a few customers loiter around asking if we can help them. I instruct Falena and Aileen to open the shop and do what they can for them, while Calliope and I see to Father.

My chest knots. Inside, I shove my pack aside and remove my cloak before I follow my sister to his room. The air is dim, shutters drawn against the morning light. The scent of sweat mingles with the tea Aileen has made him, which he hasn't drunk.

Our father lies in bed, propped against pillows. His skin looks ashen, his breathing shallow. One hand trembles faintly against the coverlet. When his eyes find mine, they're glassy but tender. "Dessalyn," he rasps.

I'm at his side in a blink, sinking onto the chair Aileen's pulled close. "What happened? Falena said—"

"It's nothing." He gives a weak shake of his head. "A stomachache. A foolish weakness. But I would not...risk it becoming more."

I take his hand, chilled but steady beneath mine. "You should see a physician."

"No." His tone hardens for just a breath, then softens again, threaded with fragility. "I'll be better soon. Just stay with me for a bit."

My sister eases onto the mattress and takes his other hand. "Of course we will. I'll make you some soup. You'll feel better in no time."

I should insist he see the doctor, for his sake and mine. If this is only a common stomach ailment, it will pass soon enough. But he looks so frail, so breakable in the half-light. What if it's something more serious? I press a kiss to his brow. "Rest now. We'll be here."

His eyes flutter closed, relief etched across his face.

I sit in silence long after Calliope has gone to fetch water and start the promised soup. My hands twist in my lap, torn by the knowledge that every hour I spend here is another hour Ren—and Jairton—bleed into shadow.

But when Father shifts in his sleep and murmurs my name, guilt claws deeper. So I whisper back the only promise I can manage. "I won't leave you." The words feel like a chain tightening around my throat.

By midday, I'm running the mercantile while Aileen tends to Father. Falena and Calliope help me and her.

The bell on the door sings with each customer, and I smile, weigh flour, and measure ribbon. Customers trickle in, their chatter soft and routine—whether the miller's daughter has chosen a suitor, if the autumn rains will come on time.

My hands do the work, but my thoughts refuse to stay tethered. They drift to the road—what mile Calliope and I would have reached by now, whether Ren even still breathes. My mind is anywhere but on the jars of honey or the bolts of linen set out for trade.

The counter blurs before me, jars doubling until I realize I've poured two measures of salt instead of one. The customer chuckles kindly, but heat prickles my cheeks. I'm not careless, rarely so distracted. Throughout the afternoon, I nod at all the correct times, but my fingers twitch around the scales, weighing barley that won't balance, measuring thread that knots itself into snarls.

Calliope spends her break on nurse duties to give Aileen a rest, reading Father ballads while he falls into a restless slumber.

When the shop finally empties, I retreat to the back room and sink onto the bench where my still-packed satchel waits. I shouldn't even have it here, but I couldn't bear to unpack it. I open my quest journal, fingertips trembling over the last entry.

The ink that forms the riddle is stark against the parchment. I trace the letters with my finger, feeling it tingle. Maybe I've been a fool all along, and I'm not meant to go on a quest. That all of this is somehow...wrong. That the Story Thief has erased more than a kingdom—he's also ruined my story. The quest that seems so clear to me is really an illusion. Or he's pulling the strings to prevent me from completing it.

Contemplating that wrinkle, I itch to head to the scriptorium and use the Lore Language to straighten out this chain of events. To rewrite what my quest *should* be.

But the sacred language of living narrative magic is a syntax of symbols, sound, and intention that binds, unbinds, and alters the fabric of stories. Using it for personal gain—mainly to save yourself or someone you love—comes with a cost. The more you change your fate, the less of it belongs to you.

As I stare at the page, ink bleeds outward, forming new letters.

*The longer you linger, the sooner he fades.*

A chill explodes at the base of my spine and sweeps up to the back of my skull. I jerk to my feet. This isn't Ren's hand—it's Mom's again.

For a tense moment, I can't let myself believe it's her. It's too painful and makes no logical sense, no matter how my heart wants it to be true.

The Fae believe souls go into the Fade when they die, and that those souls are reincarnated into the world around us. They become the air, the water, the trees. It's not possible for Mom to reach out to us like this.

*Is it?*

The message, which seems both a taunt and a warning, brands itself into me until I snap the journal shut, pressing my palm flat to its cover as if to silence a voice that isn't there. Although I'm not in the scriptorium, this feels more like Vellicor's whisper, or something darker, riding the bones of my quest journal.

The bell jangles, and Falena calls my name. I return the journal to my satchel, paste on a smile, and head back to my duties. A farmer waits patiently with eggs to trade, while inside my chest, the words still echo.

*The longer you linger, the sooner he fades.*

I glance once toward the hallway, where Father lies ill behind his door. Guilt twists me in two, but I know what I must do.

After the final customers leave and we tend to the animals, I beg off supper. I'm not hungry. My room is stifling, the walls closing in around me. I try to read, but I can't focus. I pace the floor and repack my satchel. The quest demands I move forward, and I'm going to, but should I sneak out like a criminal or face my father and leave with my head high? I'll insist Calliope stay, so I'll be leaving him in competent hands.

Eventually, the cottage grows quiet, only the creak of the beams sounding too loud in the hush of the night. Sleep won't come as I wrestle with the right thing to do. The latest riddle gnaws at me, restless as a splinter under my skin, and the memory of Renwick's face in my dream keeps threading through the shadows.

At last, I light a small lantern and slip barefoot down the hall. The boards groan beneath my steps, but no one stirs. I open the scriptorium door, its hinges sighing like an old man reluctant to rise.

Inside, Vellicor waits on its pedestal, and Bulin ruffles his feathers, as I set my quest journal on my desk and return to stroke Vellicor's spine. "Once upon a time," I whisper. My voice sounds too thin in the cavern of the room.

Vellicor groans, then falls silent. Bulin's dark eyes stare unblinking.

"I need advice," I say to both owl and book. "What am I supposed to do?"

Neither responds.

I stroke Vellicor's spine. "Please. Tell me a story. Tell me *my* story."

The eye in the center opens, glares, shuts again.

My throat tightens. I press my hands to the cool wood of the lectern. *Why won't you tell me? Why won't* someone *tell me?*

Voices filter to my ears, but not from this all-knowing source. No, these come from outside the room, familiar. I freeze, snuffing the lantern with my palm until only moonlight spills through the high window. Grabbing my journal, I peek out.

Father's door is ajar at the far end of the hall. Aileen's hushed voice seeps out. "She'll want to leave again tomorrow. What shall I tell her?"

A long silence. Then Father's voice—steady, strong. "Tell her what you must. If she goes on that quest, she might never return. I can't lose her." A pause. When he speaks again, the strength cracks, grief bleeding through. "I already lost her mother to visions and prophecies. I will not lose Dessa to them, too."

I clutch the journal to my chest. It feels heavier than before. It now carries both my mother's ghost and my father's lie.

He isn't ill.

*I can't lose her.* He's done this out of love, yes, but it's still a lie, and the betrayal cuts deep.

I retreat silently, the lantern cold in my hand, and slip back to my room. The ache in my chest burns sharper than any wound. For the first time, I feel the full divide between the daughter Father wants to protect and the Lorekeeper I am.

# CHAPTER SIX
## DESSALYN | THE LEAVING

*Every quest demands a price—sometimes it's the ones you love.*

THE COTTAGE IS TOO quiet when I slip back into my room. The walls themselves seem to be listening, waiting for what choice I'll make. The beams creak in their familiar way, the faint sigh of the wind seeps through the shutters, and still it feels like all of Fablehollow is holding its breath.

My satchel waits on the bench, right where I left it, straps neatly buckled. Even when I promised Father I'd stay, some part of me ached to leave. The bag sits there like an accusation, or a reminder—*your story isn't here, not anymore.*

I sink onto the edge of the bed, hands twisting in my lap, and the ache is sharp enough to double me over. *He lied.* In all of my years, I don't think my father has ever until today. My chest feels split clean through, the wound raw and throbbing.

This room has been my anchor since I was a girl. I know every flaw in these walls...the patched leak above my bed, the ink stains

63

on the desk, the shelf stuffed with journals that have tried—and failed—to hold my mother's absence. To walk away from this is to walk away from Father, from Calliope, from the safe and steady rhythms of home.

And yet...

What he's done presses harder on me than the weight of ten packs. I want to confront him—to shout—but what argument is there against love? He did it to protect me. Wouldn't I do the same for my own child?

The thought twists like a knife. *Is* this the first betrayal, or only the first I've uncovered?

Lies won't bring peace—lies are chains. They strangle a story before it can even begin.

I clutch my mother's pendant, its familiar shape biting into my palm, the chain tugging faintly at my throat. Calliope's laughter, Father's steady voice, the scent of ink in the scriptorium—each memory tethers me tighter.

Tears sting my eyes. How can I leave them?

Worse—*how can I stay*, when every moment here risks letting Ren and his kingdom fade beyond saving? Not only that, Evermere may be next.

I pace the room, each turn from bed to window a silent argument with myself. Forgive Father and stay. Continue helping Calliope to keep the shop running, fill the gaps Mother's death has left behind, help Falena find her story, and hand out quests to the people who show up for them. I'd live an ordinary life, surrounded by those who love and care for me.

But safety has teeth, too. I know that now. It bites deep, and once it has you, it never lets go. And if the Story Thief is erasing another kingdom, no one is safe.

I open my satchel and remove my journal. My mind flashes to Renwick, bleeding across a page to reach me. His desperate hand clawing words into the pages. Along with his plea is the riddle, the one from Mother, her voice spilling across the veil to guide me.

How can I ignore either of them? How can I let a kingdom—*an entire kingdom*—disappear because I chose warm porridge and hearth fire instead of the path I'm meant for?

I rub the pendant again, rocking it back and forth as if the chain itself can decide for me. "What would you do, Mom?" My voice cracks in the quiet. "Would you stay? Or would you go?"

The silence answers like it always does. Empty. But a breeze causes the shutters to tremble. Outside, the call of an owl splits the night and raises gooseflesh on my arms.

My gut twists, and I know exactly what she would say. She'd call me stubborn, tell me to stop asking for easy choices when the hard ones are the only ones worth making.

The scales tip. A breath shudders out of me. I drag my satchel onto the bed, fingers fumbling over the buckles. I remove a few extra clothes and stuff in food from the kitchen—a loaf of bread, two apples, a flask of water. Calliope was supposed to handle provisions, but without her, I need enough to last until the next village.

My cloak is still damp at the hem, but I pull it on and secure the ties. The wool smells faintly of smoke from the hearth. My knife, the runes etched by Mom's hand, slides into its sheath at my hip. The hilt feels worn where my palm has gripped it hundreds of times, and for a moment, I remember her bent over the blade, her hair falling loose as she carved the marks into the wood. The blade feels pitiful, inadequate, and yet it's all I have for protection.

Except for my father's love.

The last thing is my quest journal. That goes with me, always.

At my desk, I pull out a piece of torn parchment. I hover over the page, quill poised. How do I tell my sister I'm leaving her behind? That the one person who's shared every part of my life won't step into this next chapter with me?

The words come slowly.

*Calliope—*

*Forgive me. I can't stay. The quest won't wait, and neither will I. Father needs you, and Falena, too. I know you'll hate me for this, but I trust you'll understand someday. Take care of him. Take care of our home.*

I rewrite the last line three times, scratching out words too sentimental or too final. The one I settle on feels unfinished, but maybe that's right. What goodbye ever feels complete? *And know that every step I take, I carry you with me.*

I almost add a line about Father's betrayal, but decide against it. That wound belongs to him and me alone, and someday, we'll have it out. I blot the page before my tears can smudge it, fold the note, and prop it against the stone carving of a star Calliope keeps on the hall windowsill. She'll find it when the sun rises.

My chest tightens so fiercely I can barely breathe. This is worse than leaving Father. Worse than leaving the mercantile. Leaving my sister feels like tearing my heart into halves and walking away with only one piece.

At the back door, I pause. My hand presses to the frame, the wood worn smooth from years of our comings and goings. Calliope's slippers sit by the door, one heel crushed from how she always kicks them off. The sight nearly unravels me. "Goodbye, Calli," I whisper. My voice cracks. "Don't follow me this time."

For a moment, I consider leaving Father a note as well. But the thought curdles my stomach. He would find a way to use it against me, another anchor to bind me here. Better to let silence be my goodbye.

Traveling alone is risky. Traveling alone at night is ten times more so. Ignoring my heart that's beating too fast, I shoulder my pack higher and slip out into the night.

The temperature has dropped. The air hits me like a plunge into cold water—bracing, unrelenting. Stars blaze overhead, sharp as cut glass, and the moon sits low, pale and watchful.

The path out of Fablehollow is a ribbon of pale stone bordered by shadow. The cottages are dark, shutters drawn, smoke long dead in their chimneys. Only the hoot of the same owl follows me, a benediction.

Or a warning.

Every step feels both heavier and lighter. Heavier, because I'm leaving everything I've ever known. Lighter, because I am finally stepping into the story that's been clawing at me since Ren began haunting my dreams.

And then—

A flicker. A warmth, faint but unmistakable, coils low in my chest. Not mine. Not entirely.

*Ren.*

It's a tether that brushes against me when I least expect it, faint as candle smoke. His presence pulses in my chest, like a heartbeat too far away to hear but close enough to feel. I freeze, the cold air tight in my chest, fingers clenching around the strap of my pack.

*He's alive.* Hurting, maybe—but alive.

The connection fades as quickly as it comes, leaving me hollow and shivering. But it's enough. More than enough.

I draw the cloak tighter and keep walking, fire once more coiled under my ribs. Not dragon fire—Lorekeeper fire. Whatever waits in Jairton, whatever waits with Renwick Ravelle, I will face it.

Because this is my quest, and I won't let anyone—father, sister, or Story Thief—keep me from it.

# CHAPTER INTERLUDE
## CALLIOPE | THE NOTE

I AWAKE TO THE sound of birds chirping their bright tune outside my window. Marsh curls against my feet, a warm comfort that's always there. With a yawn and a stretch, I shove off the blankets and stand, my bare feet hitting the cold floor. A shudder runs up my spine. The cat leaps down, tail flicking, ready for breakfast.

I need to check on Father, to make sure he's all right. I shuffle to the kitchen, still trying to come awake, to make tea and maybe some toast with jam to take to him if Dessa hasn't already done so. Marsh gallops ahead of me, meowing.

On the way there, something catches my eye. A folded bit of parchment with my name scrawled across it in familiar script. It's propped against the carved star in the windowsill.

I hear no sounds of her bustling about, preparing for the day. A glance out the window shows she's not in the garden or near the barn. I finger the note, a sinking feeling in my stomach. *Oh, gods, Dessa. What have you done?*

With my heart in my throat, I unfold it with trembling fingers. Her script is hurried. Not as neat as usual. And I know she wrote it in the dead of night while the house slept. While she plotted her departure.

*Forgive me. I can't stay,* she writes.

She's left on the quest without me, her determination burning bright and hot inside her. I know her all too well. I know she can't resist the call. Nor should she.

I wouldn't.

*Couldn't.*

Still, hurt slashes through me. Betrayal. No small amount of fear. All of it churns inside me like a wild miasma I cannot control. I want to crumple the note in my fist in a fit of frustration, but I don't. What if this is the last I'll ever see of my sister's handwriting? A sob catches in my throat. I can't do it. I've suffered enough loss. Losing her would be too much.

Tea and toast forgotten, I rush to Father's room and come to a halt. He's propped up on his pillows, his eyes closed, dozing. When he hears the door clatter open, he wakes. His gaze lands on me, a smile tugging at his mouth as though he's glad to see me. He looks stronger than he did yesterday. Less frail and pale. Which is a relief. But I don't have time to acknowledge that.

He senses immediately that something is wrong, and his face pinches in concern. "What is it, my girl?"

I lift the note in my hand and wave it in the air. "She's gone. Dessa's left us. How could she when you're sick?"

His face twists. Guilt washes over his features in a brief moment before he manages to compose himself. His eyes flick toward the window in his room where the faint morning light presses against the panes, and then he drops his face into his hands. "Oh, Dessalyn. Why are you tempting the gods? Why didn't you let me keep you safe?"

Suddenly, my senses shift, and I know...something is off. "Father?" My voice is on edge. "What's going on?"

His hands fall to his lap, his eyes downcast. His fingers knead the bedding crumpled over his legs, and he tugs at a wayward string on the quilt. "I thought if I fell ill...I thought it would keep her here."

"If you *fell ill*?" My heart claws its way up into my throat as I peer at him from the threshold, the note still clutched in my hand. "What are you saying?"

He refuses to meet my gaze as he continues to focus on twisting the string around his forefinger, then releasing it, then twisting it again in a rhythmic movement that seems to both soothe him and keep him from telling me the truth.

"Father," I say, my voice terse, "tell me what you've done."

Finally, he looks up, meeting my gaze. His is watery with despair and something that teams with regret. "It was the only way to keep her from going. To keep you both safe."

I stare in stunned disbelief. "You're not sick?"

His hand now snakes out toward me. "I was only looking out for you. For her."

He lied. I can't believe it. He lied to keep us both here and to keep Dessa from answering the call of her quest.

And I wonder then—would he do the same to me if I were first? To what lengths would he go to keep me from following the quest Vellicor gives me? I understand his desire to protect us. I know he loves us and wants no harm to come to us. We're all he has left after Mom died.

I spin from the room, seething under my skin. Dessa must have figured it out. If so, it makes more sense why she left. Even so, the betrayal cuts deep and leaves me with raw, unfettered anger. I cannot help the dismay that courses through me.

"Where are you going?" Father calls after me.

I head to my room. "She needs me."

"Calli—"

"I'm going after her." I fling my bedroom door shut, trying to collect my scattered thoughts. To figure out what to do next. I need to dress. To repack my satchel. I need to hurry before the distance grows too great between us. Before it's too late.

"Calli, please," Father calls through my door as I pick up my discarded bag and shove clothes inside. "You must understand why I did it. I never meant to hurt you or Dessalyn. It was only to shield you from what's out there. What's coming…I don't think we can fight it."

The overwhelming emotions in that simple statement are like a ten-ton weight. My shoulders droop, and my chest tightens. Panic prickles over my skin.

*No.* I can't think of anything but getting to my sister. Going down a rabbit hole of dread and doom serves no one but the Story Thief. It only gives him more power.

I spin about the untidy room, looking for my cloak, my shoes. I grab my journal and pen and shove them into the bag with my balled-up clothes. My shoes are under the bed. I tug them out, slip them on, fling the cloak over my shoulder.

When I open the door, Father is there looking forlorn and lost. I want to be sympathetic, but I'm too angry. At him. At her. At everything.

I charge into the kitchen with him on my heels. "I know what I did was wrong," he says. "I shouldn't have done it, but I had to. You two are all I have left."

I snatch a meat pie left over from last night's meal—the one Dessa didn't eat—and a half-eaten loaf of bread off the counter. I wrap them in an oversized towel. Even as I do it, my stomach rumbles.

"I forbid you to go. This won't end well. You can't stop what's happening, and you'll..." He grips my arm. "You'll break my heart."

Mine lurches at his desperate tone. I pause, close my eyes, and take a deep breath. Finally, I turn to him. He looks smaller in his rumpled nightclothes, his face haggard and lined with worry. I hate what I have to do.

"You can't stop us from being who we were born to be, Father." My words are a knife. He flinches. "She's my sister. I'm going to find her."

And with that, I don't look back as I stride out the door.

# CHAPTER SEVEN
## RENWICK | THE VAULT'S HUNGER

*The past never stays buried. It digs its claws in and drags you down.*

THE CHURCH AND THE vault below wait like a grave when I return.

The building looms darker than it should in the morning light, its silence pressing heavier than armor. I slip back through the warped arch into the courtyard, my boots crunching grit, my hands restless.

Foolish to come here again. Dangerous. But I can't leave the seal untended. Not when Marrow's warning rings in my ears. Every shadow seems to twitch, waiting to bite. My dragon stirs, as restless as my fingers, its fire searing in my veins.

Teeth gritted like before, I force myself through the wards and down the spiraling stone stairs to the underground hiding place. Here, the outside world ceases to exist. The sigils on the walls never see sunlight, yet emit a glow. Like always, the dais sits in the center.

It, too, emits a light that I suspect only those of us attuned to it can see. A glow that mocks my shame.

The glyphs spiral across its surface in an ancient language older than my bloodline, older than the bones of this ruined chapel. I kneel, fingers trembling as I trace the grooves I carved with arrogant hands all those years ago.

A new hairline crack spiders through the warding. What has happened since a few hours ago? Have I caused this?

Or has Marrow?

Dust scatters where the stone itself has begun to split. My throat tightens. The lie I buried is bleeding through. I press my palm flat against the cold surface, ignoring the sting as the glyphs thrum back at me. Should I force more magic into the cracks and see if I can open the vault?

If the crack widens, I could get inside. I could destroy what I wrote before the Story Thief twists it further. But if this isn't my doing, then he's already here.

Or, at least, his agent is.

Shadows curl at the edges of the room, faint as smoke but sending a warning buzz through me. Something has gnawed at the ward. Not broken it yet, but is trying. Testing.

I eye the shadows, wondering if Marrow watches me from them. That's when my resolve to open the vault shifts. It's too risky now. Instead, I must keep it intact.

I dig my nails into the stone through my gloves, breath ragged. "Not yet. You will not unmake me yet."

The temptation claws at me, though. If I pour enough dragon fire into the crack, I could unseal the vault. Burn the lie out of existence. Maybe then Dessa would never have to know.

Removing my gloves, I slam my hands on the top. Heat gathers in my chest, climbing my throat like molten glass. My scales flash across my knuckles, claws half-sprung.

The stone drinks it in—

Then spits it back.

I gasp as the fire rebounds. Shadows spill from the edges of the room, oily and writhing. They snake around my arms, burning cold where fire should shield me. I try to tear my hands free. My magic recoils, sputtering against the pressure, but I hang on.

"No," I rasp, forcing more power into the glyphs. My boots scrape on raw stone as I shove harder, fire lashing the vault's surface.

A whisper slides through the darkness. *Renwick Ravelle...liar prince.*

The shadows surge, wrapping around my torso, driving into the bruises already there, stealing the breath from my lungs. I thrash, clawing at them, but my hands can't find purchase.

Pain sears down my side as one coils around my waist and yanks. My spine cracks against the dais. The glyphs burn into my skin, a brand of my own shame.

"Not yours," I choke. "This story is not yours to take."

The shadows laugh—a sound like rusted hinges shrieking—and drag harder. My boots skid on the stone, my vision darkens.

For a heartbeat, I think I hear Dessalyn's voice, far away, calling through the dark. *Hang on. I'm coming.*

The last thing I taste is iron as the shadows crash over me, swallowing the light. They tighten, crushing my chest, threading into my veins like ink into water. My vision tunnels, the dais blurring.

The change happens in a heartbeat, from one breath to the next. My dragon rises.

With a roar that scorches my throat, I tear the fire from deep inside where the oldest part of me resides, the bone and flame of my bloodline. It bursts free, wild and unshaped, exploding from my ribs in a storm of white-gold heat.

The chamber screams, and the shadows shriek, shriveling and clawing at the stone as the fire sears them back. The crack in the dais pulses red, then gold. It bleeds and melts the seals tight enough to hold.

For now.

I collapse, coughing smoke, my palms blistered. The smell of charred air clings to me, foul and acrid. The glyphs glimmer, but the corruption lingers. I've bought time—nothing more.

Dragging myself upright, I stagger toward the stairs. My knees buckle twice before I clear them and arrive in the nave. The morning light spears my eyes like knives. The wards spit me out, stinging, as though they know I've failed to mend them properly.

Will it be enough? My boots catch on rubble. I crash into the grass outside, rolling to my side. The world tilts, shadows flickering at the edges of my vision, but at least they aren't crawling into my skin anymore.

Every breath tastes coppery. Wispy smoke still emerges with every breath. My ribs burn, my side throbs where the shadows dug deepest.

I push up on shaking arms and gain my feet. Sheer determination is all that keeps me stumbling toward the tree line. The chapel grows smaller behind me, hollow and hungry, its stone dripping with the memory of what I unleashed.

The woods blur before me, green and gray melting together. I stagger into them, each step heavier, each breath harder. Can I make it to my horse? My satchel? Can I leave Dessalyn a note?

The last thought I cling to, ragged and desperate, is her. *Dessalyn. You must not find this place before I fix it.*

# CHAPTER EIGHT
## DESSALYN | THE HALF-ERASED VILLAGE

*The closer you walk to the border of a story, the more you risk being forgotten by it.*

BY THE TIME THE sun lifts pale and thin over the horizon, my legs feel like stone. I've been walking all night, the strap of my satchel grinding against my shoulder, my boots sodden from the dew. Each step is a battle against the weight of fatigue pressing me down, but stopping isn't an option.

The hamlet appears out of the mist like an illustration half-sketched. A crooked row of cottages, smoke seeping from chimneys, a bell tower leaning against the sky as if it's too tired to stand upright. Relief stirs in me—a place to rest, maybe even a hot drink and bread still steaming from the oven—but unease follows close, sharp as a splinter.

Why? Is it simply because I'm exhausted? Because I've rarely been this far from home? Or because I know that Father and Calliope are waking about now, realizing I'm gone?

I pause at the edge of the square, breath clouding in the chilly air. At first glance, everything seems ordinary enough. A woman hangs damp laundry on a line strung between two houses. A dog barks once before retreating under a cart. Somewhere, a rooster crows.

But then the details jar. The woman's motions are slow, deliberate, like she's pulling the cloth through water. She pins the same shirt twice, then starts again as if she never touched it. The dog doesn't growl, doesn't sniff—just lies down and stares at nothing, eyes flat and unblinking.

I tug my cloak tighter, scanning the square. At the heart, a hulking structure sags on broken steps, ivy crawling its facade. Pillars half-eaten by rot lean as though about to collapse. The air smells faintly of soot, though no fires burn nearby.

My pulse escalates. There's something wrong here. A pair of boys chase each other across the cobblestones, laughing, but their voices sound hollow and brittle. One trips and falls hard—but he doesn't cry. He just climbs up again, repeating the same laugh he made before, like an echo caught in a loop.

I swallow against the tightness in my throat. I glance around, trying to find anything normal. Anyone not in a fog. Each person I see, every stray wandering the alleys, repeats the same actions over and over.

Is this an unraveling of their story? If so, it's spreading faster than I imagined. And if it's already reached this far into Evermere...what hope is there for Jairton?

I didn't eat supper last night, and I finished off the loaf of bread I brought with me during the long hours, trying to keep up my stamina on the road. I force myself toward the market past the building. My legs feel stiff and reluctant as exhaustion gets the better of me. The cracked cobbles shift under my boots, and the closer I get to the stalls, the more the air feels thick and heavy. An approaching storm?

The smell of fresh bread hits me, warm and yeasty, enough to make my stomach growl. A baker stands at a stall, loaves arranged in a neat row.

"Good morning," I say, offering a smile. I glance over the items displayed. "How much for a loaf?"

The baker blinks. His gaze drifts to my satchel, then to my face, then back again as though each detail is new. "Good morning." He uses the same tone. Offers the same pause. "How much for a loaf?"

I frown. "That's what I asked."

He smiles faintly and places a basket on the counter. "That will be three coppers."

The basket is bare. Just woven reeds, splintered at the rim. No bread inside.

I glance at the loaves stacked behind him—solid, golden brown, crusts dusted with flour. Real. But the basket he offers is just a basket. My hand hovers over it, but I can't bring myself to touch it. "I don't—"

His eyes go distant, his face slack. "That will be three coppers."

My pulse hammers. I back away, nearly colliding with a pair of women who pass by arm in arm. They murmur to each other in low voices. "The rain's coming early this year," one says.

The other echoes her. "The rain's coming early this year."

Neither looks at me, and they continue to repeat the phrase, back and forth, over and over.

I walk away from them and see a child crouched by a fountain's dry basin, a girl of no more than six, her hair tangled, her knees scraped. She's drawing something in the dust with a stick. I move closer to see what—a broken crown.

She lifts her head as I freeze above her. Her eyes are wide, too solemn for her age. "The longer you linger," she says in a singsong whisper, "the sooner he fades."

The words punch straight through me.

My breath catches, ragged. "What did you say?"

She peers past me as if I don't exist and hums. Without looking, she begins drawing again, her stick scratching the same fractured crown into the dust.

I feel dizzy and steer away to another block, my throat tight. This must be the Story Thief's doing. His corruption. His reach.

What can I do to stop it? Use the Language? Write something to protect the final fraying of this town?

I pull out my journal and quill, opening the book to see if Vellicor might reach through it with a message. *Give me the words to fix this story*, I plead.

Nothing happens. *Please*, I whisper. *Isn't this part of my quest? To save innocent people?*

The quill doesn't vibrate. The page remains blank. No tug pinches my chest.

The Lore Language is bound by its own rules—it only shapes stories destined to be written, and on occasion, reshapes those that need rewriting. It does not bow to the desperate pleas of a Lorekeeper too afraid of failing. To use it against its nature, to twist it for personal will, is to risk breaking more than it saves.

Mom always warned, "The more you alter fate for yourself, Dessalyn, the less of it remains yours to live." If I try to force the Language and create a story, I might do more harm than good.

Stifling a sob of defeat, I return the quill and journal to my pack. I wish Calliope were here to offer advice, or at least sympathize with my predicament. In my mind, I hear her voice: *You shouldn't have left me. I'd at least be there to help you conspire a plan.*

On another side street, an inn stands before the rising hillside, its lanterns burning despite the rising sun. Night seems reluctant to leave this place. My stomach twists with hunger, sharper now that the smell of roasted meat drifts from the chimney. I push open the door and step inside, hopeful for anything normal.

Warmth hits me first, a welcome embrace. A fire crackles in the hearth, throwing shadows that dance across rough-hewn beams and the stone floor. Laughter rises from a corner table. Tankards clink. For one blessed heartbeat, it feels ordinary.

Then I look closer.

A man raises a fork to his mouth. It's empty. His jaws work slowly, chewing nothing, swallowing nothing. Across from him, a woman smiles around her spoonful of air, nodding as though savoring the taste. At another table, a boy licks his fingers as if coated with honey—except his hand is clean.

The fire crackles, but the logs don't blacken, don't turn to ash. They just hold their shape, as if pretending to be on fire.

Defeated, I grip the strap of my satchel, forcing myself to cross the room. My boots echo on the warped floorboards, but none of the patrons glance up. They just eat their invisible meals, laughing, murmuring, living half-lives in a story fading from reality.

Before I reach a table, my steps falter. Near the hearth, etched deep into the stone, a mark glows in the firelight. The spiral of glyphs is one I know as surely as my own name. A Lorekeeper sigil.

My breath sticks in my lungs—that symbol belongs to Vellicor. It's his alone, sacred, inked into his spine, bound to his breathing. To see it here feels like blasphemy.

I've been taught since childhood that such marks belong only to him. That no other book, no other place, should carry them. And yet here it is, burning softly in the hearthstones of a border inn where no one seems to notice their food has vanished from the world. It shouldn't be here. Not carved into some tavern wall in a half-forgotten hamlet.

I step closer, inspecting the details. Perhaps I'm wrong. I've barely left Fablehollow in my twenty-four years, and Father never let me stray far on my errands. Is it feasible that others use it as a secret code? Perhaps it isn't forbidden.

My hand hovers, fingers trembling. Is this Vellicor reaching for me? Guiding me?

Or is it the Story Thief, spinning a trick to draw me in? Has he somehow learned to mimic the book? To rewrite stories or erase them, he must have some version of Lorekeeper magic. Does it link him to Vellicor?

The closer I get, the more I sense it. A hum beneath my skin, familiar as a heartbeat. I glance around. Can anyone else see it? Feel it? Or is it waiting solely for me?

The question claws at my insides. If Vellicor wanted to speak, why not through the quest journal? That should be our tether, my lifeline to Renwick's story and the riddles meant to guide me. Why here, in a place I might have passed by without a glance if not for my exhaustion?

Every part of me longs to touch it. It seems like a living, breathing thing, drawing me in.

My hand trembles as it hovers over the sigil. Heat radiates from the stone, as if it's alive. I whisper to myself, half a prayer, half a plea, "Vellicor, if it's you, show me."

The moment my fingers brush the grooves, the world snaps.

The tavern dissolves. No crackling fire, no hollow patrons. Only darkness—black as spilled ink, stealing the breath from my lungs. For a heartbeat, I think I've made a mistake. That I've given myself to the Story Thief. The thought tears through me. My lungs seize. My heart stutters. Every instinct screams to pull back, but my hand won't move. It's caught, glued to the sigil as the dark folds around me tighter, suffocating, drowning me in silence.

Something slithers at the edge of the void. Shapes twitch, half-formed, shadows with too many arms and mouths that open without sound. Icy tendrils race up my spine, and I swear I feel them breathe against my skin, cold and damp as grave dirt.

I open my mouth to scream, but no sound comes out. The dark wants to swallow me whole. Wants to erase me the way it erased Drakenholt.

And then—

A spark.

Small, but enough to sear through the ink and shadows. It grows, spreading into a shape I know even before the features sharpen.

*Ren.*

His form coalesces from the dark like a memory dragged through mud. He's on his knees, cloak torn, hair damp with sweat. His hand clutches his ribs, blood seeping between his fingers. His eyes—those defiant sapphire eyes—find me.

"Dessalyn." The sound of my name in his voice nearly undoes me, the syllables ragged as though dragged from his lungs. His voice is hoarse, breaking, but real.

Relief crashes over me—*he's alive.* But it curdles just as fast, because the shadows writhe around him, dragging at his legs, clutching his arms, whispering in voices that make no sense.

I reach for him. My hands meet only smoke. The shadows tighten, yanking him backward. He jerks like a puppet, straining against invisible strings. One coils up his throat, silencing him mid-word. Another claws across his chest, leaving a smear of darkness that bleeds into his skin.

"No!" I lunge forward, but I can't move. My feet are rooted, my body paralyzed, as if the Story Thief himself has bound me here only to watch.

Ren fights, teeth bared, dragging one hand free of the murk. His fingers stretch toward me, shaking. "Don't—" His voice splinters. "Don't come—"

The shadows roar, their laughter echoing in the void, mocking. They surge higher, swallowing him by inches: his face, his chest, his outstretched arm.

"Ren!" I scream, useless against the dark.

For one searing heartbeat, our gazes lock through the swirl of ink and pain. His eyes are fierce, desperate, begging me to understand. Then the blackness swallows him. The vision collapses.

I'm back in the tavern, gasping, knees weak, palm pressed hard against the glowing glyph. The patrons chew their invisible food as though nothing has happened. Laughter bubbles, empty and wrong. The fire still flames but doesn't burn.

But the mark is branded into my skin. My palm is blistered where I touched it, as if the shadows tried to drag me down, too.

# CHAPTER NINE
## DESSALYN | HUNGER'S PRICE

*Every step of the quest rewrites the story you thought was yours.*

THE MARK ON MY palm still throbs, heat burrowing bone-deep, long after the sigil's glow has faded. I stumble back from the hearth, breath ragged, vision swimming. The air feels singed, scorched, as though I've brushed too close to dragon fire.

My legs give out. I collapse onto the nearest bench, wood rough beneath my palms. My satchel slips from my shoulder, thudding to the floor, and I sit there with my hand curled tight against my chest. The image of Ren—his body dragged under by shadows—replays until I almost retch.

Suddenly, the air shifts. I feel eyes on me. Across the room, someone is watching.

The man sits in the far corner, alone, his hood shadowing his face, and his gloved hands steepled on the table. He doesn't eat. Just observes. When our eyes meet, a prickle runs the length of my spine. I jerk my gaze away, feigning interest in the warped boards beneath my boots, but his attention lingers.

*I can't stay here.* The urge presses on me, insistent. *Move on, get to Ren.*

Exhaustion swamps me even harder. I haven't slept for over twenty-four hours. A blister is forming on my left pinkie toe. Every step since dawn has rubbed it raw.

My hunger gnaws viciously, twisting my gut. The innkeeper is wiping down the bar, over and over, as if the diners don't exist. Behind him is a door to the kitchen.

I glance back at the figure across the way, but the man has disappeared. With the last of my strength, I push to my feet and weave toward the kitchen door. No one stops me. The innkeeper doesn't even glance my way.

The kitchen is cold. A half-chopped onion stinks up the air. Knives are scattered on the counter as if someone stepped away mid-task and never returned. A single loaf of bread lies forgotten on a shelf, hard at the edges but fresh enough. Nearby, the mold on a fruit pie is blue-black, blooming across the lattice top. My throat aches at the sight of the food.

Hands shaking, I help myself to water from a nearby pitcher, thankful for the cool wetness. A second drink fills my belly some and clears my head. I splash more on my blistered palm.

I grab the bread, along with an apple, from a woven basket on a table by the back door. I glance at the pie, but it's too far gone to be safe.

I've never stolen anything in my life. I don't intend to now. I dig two coppers from my pocket and set them on the counter where the innkeeper might see—if he ever truly sees anything again. "Forgive me," I whisper, though I don't know to whom.

Clutching the food, I refill my water pouch, then slip out the back door into the thin morning light. The door sighs closed behind me, shutting away the stranger's stare, the empty laughter, the ghostly feast.

The road waits. Ren waits. I just need to keep moving, regardless of my exhaustion, blisters, and fear.

I leave the inn behind, bread clutched in one hand, my stomach still raw with hunger that even the few bites of bread and apple I choke down don't soothe. The road forks at the far end of the hamlet, and I linger by the signpost, watching for any traveler who might be heading toward Jairton.

A wagon rattles past, wheels wobbling, the driver slack-faced. I wave. "Do you go north. sir?"

He stares straight ahead, reins slack in his hands. The mule plods on, eyes glazed, until the cart vanishes into the mist.

Another figure approaches—a woman driving a smart cart that leads a goat, gaze fixed on some invisible point beyond me. I try again. "I need to get to Jairton. Are you headed that way?" I hold out several coins. "I can pay."

She blinks once, twice. A semblance of normalcy flashes through her dark brown eyes. "Sorry, this is my final stop."

For a heartbeat, I want to tell her to run. To get out of here. She has no idea that those words could be true on many levels.

The warning doesn't make it past the lump in my throat. I step aside as she brushes past, once more seemingly oblivious to reality. The goat glances back at me and snorts. It hasn't yet succumbed to the unraveling fog its mistress has fallen under, and I briefly consider saving it and leading it out of town. It's too small for me to ride, however, and I can barely feed myself at this point.

I grit my teeth and keep walking. If there are travelers sound enough to give me a ride, they're not here. Everyone is fading.

The road curves past a low stone fence, where fields open wide on either side. An enormous house and paddock sprawl ahead. The grandness of the mansion takes my breath away. While I know that I have been in a royal castle and seen its grandeur, I cannot recall any memories of homes with so many rooms, so many windows, such beauty. In Fablehollow, no one has need—or even imagination—for so much space.

Even the lawn is spectacular, with lush green grass, giant trees, and a formal garden. The long, winding drive splits the house and yard from the horse barn.

Horses stamp in the dew, their coats flashing chestnut and gray in the pale sun. They look solid. Real. Alive. Tools lean against the fence—rake, pitchfork, a half-mended harness.

A boy of no more than twelve trots back and forth from the barn to the paddock, his hair sticking out from cowlicks, arms full of hay. He tosses it into a trough, whistles a jaunty tune, then disappears again into the barn.

I stop at the gate. My pulse stutters. For a breath, I can't move, my boots rooted to the packed earth. A plan takes shape unbidden, but sharp as a thorn.

One mount could shorten my journey by a day. A day could mean the difference between Ren breathing or being erased, between Jairton standing or disappearing forever.

I curl my burned palm into a fist against my chest. Is it theft if the quest demands it? If it's the only way to save a story? A kingdom?

The question hammers in my skull. Lorekeepers are meant to bend stories only where it heals or preserves the truth. Is aiding my quest also preserving a future for the people here, in this town, as well as our entire realm?

My blistered toe aches, and I relish the idea of riding rather than walking. My heart also prefers the idea. Like the goat, these animals will be lost to the Story Thief along with their masters if I do not make hard choices quickly.

Father raised me to honor work, to pay what is due. I've never taken what wasn't mine—not even a ribbon in the market when I was small and tempted by its shine.

But kingdoms don't hinge on ribbons. And the longer I linger...

Ren fades. This hamlet and these people fade.

My fingers hover over the gate latch. Cold iron presses against my palm, rough where rust has eaten into the metal. For a moment, I stand there, frozen—then I lift it. The hinge squeals, faint but sharp in the still morning.

The horses raise their heads, ears flicking toward me. The nearest, a bay mare with a white blaze, snorts once and stamps but doesn't shy. She only watches.

The drive is the straightest way to reach them, but I would risk being spotted by someone inside the house. Instead, I slip into the trees, taking me yards out of the way, but giving me cover.

The dew seeps through the worn leather of my boots, chilling my toes until they feel carved from stone, and each step is heavier than the last. Tree by tree, I work my way toward the horses, branches snagging my cloak.

Ten yards. Five. A noise startles me—wood creaking, a clatter of metal. I jerk back behind the trunk of a giant oak, its roots tangled in a carpet of newly turned leaves, red and gold. Pulse racing, I hold my breath.

The boy's shadow stretches across the doorway as he hoists a pail. He returns a moment later, then hauls out a leather saddle, securing it on the dappled mare. Someone inside the house must be going for a ride, or perhaps the boy is going into town for supplies.

Desperation claws higher in my throat. I think about retrieving my knife, but the thought of threatening someone, especially the boy, makes me sick to my stomach.

Instead, I tug out my quest journal, quill, and ink bottle. If this mission should go sideways, I need to let Ren and anyone who might find my journal know what has happened. What I'm attempting to do.

I uncap the ink with my teeth and set it on a stump to my right before I brace the journal on the tree trunk as I keep an eye on the barn and house. With trembling strokes, I make a quick diary entry of what's happened since I entered the town. My options, though few, are stark on the page as I list them. I place a check mark next to *steal a horse*.

When the quill scratches out the word *steal*, my stomach lurches. I can't believe I've written it, much less marked it.

Finally, I add a message to Ren. I don't know if he'll see it. If he's even still watching his own journal that is the receiver of this one. *I'm coming. Hold on.* I stare at the four words, wondering if he can sense my desperation. My determination. They seem far too weak to convey everything I'm feeling. I scrawl one more word—*please*. It looks frail, pitiful on the page, like begging a god who has already turned away.

The ink gleams wet, hungry for a reply. I wait for long, tense moments, mentally praying for some sign that he's still alive.

Nothing. Only the sound of the boy whistling, the soft whiney of the horses.

I close the book and repack my belongings. To the left, I see an apple tree with many of its fruits lying on the ground. Staying in the shadows, I gather a few that aren't full of insects and rub their red and pink skins on my pants to remove dirt. The whistling moves off toward the back of the grand house. This is my chance.

I creep closer to the dappled mare, each breath shallow. She lowers her head as I stretch out my hand with an apple offering. Her breath fans warm across my skin, softer than silk, sweeter than the scent of hay. Her dark eyes, liquid and steady, meet mine.

And that's when the guilt strikes, sharper than my hunger, heavier than my exhaustion. It drops like a stone in my gut, threatening to drag me under before I've even mounted. Mother's voice echoes through memory, steady and merciless. *The more you alter fate for yourself, Dessalyn, the less of it remains yours.*

What if she's right? What if this isn't aid but theft of my own destiny? What if stealing this horse dooms the very quest I mean to save?

The mare's velvet nose nudges my palm. Trusting. Innocent. I press my lips together, fighting tears. What kind of Lorekeeper betrays trust so quickly? Not just a horse's—but the trust of the stories themselves?

The mare noses the apple from my palm and crunches it, sweet juice dripping over my fingers. Her soft lips brush my skin again, searching for more. I glance toward the barn—empty. Toward the house—still.

My throat tightens. I shouldn't. Every part of me knows I shouldn't. My fingers close on her halter anyway.

The leather is warm, solid, familiar. She lets me tug, stepping obediently from the paddock's edge. Her hooves clop once against the packed earth, and the sound ricochets like thunder in my ears.

"Quiet," I whisper. It's not her fault, and I instantly regret sounding harsh. My heart pounds so hard I fear she'll hear it. We inch forward, each step agony. The harness jingles faintly, and I freeze, holding my breath, but no one emerges from either house or barn.

I keep moving. Because Ren can't wait, Jairton can't wait. And every moment I hesitate feels like another story strand unraveling. The mare presses her head against my shoulder as though sensing my desperation. I stroke her neck, muttering nonsense to keep us both steady. Step. Breathe. Step. *Don't look back.*

I'm almost to the trees when the hair at the back of my neck prickles. The same sensation that someone is watching me makes me freeze. Is it the man from the inn? Has the boy seen me and snuck around to ambush me?

The mare tosses her head and snorts, ears flicking back. In one motion, I release her halter, spin, and snatch my knife from its sheath. I lift the blade and turn in an arc, searching for my adversary. "Who's there?" I mutter.

A twig snaps behind me. The presence I sensed is suddenly at my back.

Whirling, I raise the knife higher and strike.

# Chapter Ten
## Dessalyn | On the Run

*Some bonds break with lies; others only sharpen when tested.*

I WHIRL, BLADE RAISED, breath ragged in my chest. The knife flashes down—

—and Calliope shrieks, stumbling back just out of reach.

"Stars above!" she yelps, eyes wide, cheeks flushed.

Horror floods me so fast my knees nearly buckle. I lower the knife, arm trembling. "Calli?" My voice cracks on her name. "What are you—"

She doesn't let me finish. She throws herself at me, arms tight around my shoulders. I nearly drop the blade as I clutch her back, burying my face in the curve of her neck. Relief slams through me so fiercely I can't breathe. *She's here*. She came. Father must be beside himself.

"I nearly stabbed you," I whisper into her hair.

She squeezes harder. Her voice is muffled, stubborn, steady. "You didn't."

When she pulls back, her grin is half mischief, half exasperation, her brown eyes shining. "Stealing horses now? I leave you one night on your own, and you're already turning outlaw?"

Nervous laughter bubbles up inside of me. The mare jostles her head, nodding, as if in agreement. She blows out a breath between her lips and then nudges me, looking for another apple treat.

"You shouldn't be here," I say, scanning my sister and her traveling clothes. My chest still rattles with the thought of the blade in her, not in the air. "Why *are* you here? And how did you find me?"

"You're about as good at sneaking off as you are at wielding that blade." She strokes the horse's neck. "When I found your note, I uncovered Father's deception. It was wrong of him, but he's miserable about it."

"Good." I tilt my head away when the mare's nose bumps me. "He and I have a lot to talk about when this is over."

A shout cracks across the air, sharp as a whip. "Stop! *Thieves*!"

The words shatter my relief. I jerk toward the drive. A man barrels down the slope from the house, his face red, a pitchfork brandished in one hand. His fine riding clothes and polished boots mark him as more lord than farmer. His bellow rattles the quiet morning. "Get away from my horse!"

The mare startles, ears flat, shying back from us. Calliope grabs my arm, eyes wide. "Dessa—"

"No time." I seize her hand and start running, pulling her with me toward the gate. My satchel bounces against my hip. The knife is still clenched in my fist. My boots slip in the wet grass, but I push harder, my pulse thundering louder than the man's shouts. "Run, Calli!"

We burst through the squealing latch, wood rattling as the gate slams back. The owner's fury follows, closer now, his curses slashing through the morning haze.

"Over here!" Calliope cries. She yanks me toward the road.

A horse is tied under a low tree, stamping impatiently. Not the sleek bay mare I nearly stole, but a rangy, sway-backed mare with a gray muzzle and kind eyes.

Recognition jolts through me. "Calli, what did you do?"

Her grin is wild, breathless. "Aileen owed us after aiding Father."

This explains how she caught up to me so quickly. She took Aileen's horse.

The pitchfork-wielding farmer is almost upon us. There's no time to argue, no time for guilt. I shove Calliope up onto the horse's back, then swing after her, my satchel thudding as I land behind.

The mare surges forward with a squeal. We're jolted into motion, mud flying beneath her hooves, the wind ripping through my hair. The man's shouts fade, swallowed by the trees, but my heart doesn't slow.

"Layla's not much to look at and can't be pushed too hard," my sister calls over the sound of the horse's hooves, "but she'll get us to Jairton faster than our feet will."

I choke on a laugh, absurdly grateful for the scrappy beast—and my sister. I almost betrayed myself with theft, and yet Calliope—my impossible, reckless sister—has saved me from it.

Several miles pass, the road growing narrower in spots where trees shedding leaves of gold and rust crowd close. The path bends into a dip, Layla's hooves thudding lighter as she slows of her own accord. Her flanks heave, foam flecking her bit, and Calliope pats her neck, damp with sweat. "Easy, girl. You've done enough."

We clatter to a halt near a stream cutting alongside the road, water flashing silver in the dappled light under the tree canopy. I swing down first, landing with a graceless thump, before Calli follows. She guides Layla to the bank, and the mare drinks greedily, her ears flicking in relief.

My legs shake from the ride, and my backside is already sore. I'm unaccustomed to riding.

My cloak has kept the chill of the morning off my bones, but as the sun climbs higher, it's suffocating me. I pull the strings and free myself from its weight, brushing my hair back from my face as birds trill overhead.

A beautiful moment, alone here in this forest. If only I could enjoy it.

I stretch my calves as Layla snorts into the burbling stream and drinks her fill. My sister kneels to splash her face, cheeks flushed pink, curls plastered to her temples. "Stars, Dessa. You nearly gave me a heart attack back there." She glances up, half-smiling. "But I suppose that's what I get for chasing after you."

I sink onto a mossy rock, staring at my raw palm. The sigil's burn is an angry, red brand. "I'm sorry I didn't say a proper goodbye," I murmur, "but I had to leave immediately. I'd already wasted too much time, thanks to Father's ruse." I cup water in my burned palm and then let it trickle through my fingers.

She grabs my hand and inspects it, brows furrowing and eyes widening. "What happened?"

The words rush out before I can stop them. About the hamlet where people repeated phrases like broken clockwork. The baker who sold me an empty basket. The child drawing a broken crown. My voice hitches as I describe the inn, the Lorekeeper's mark etched in stone where it shouldn't be. And then the vision.

Calliope's eyes widen even more as I try to explain what I saw. Ren, his face pale, his body dragged down by shadows clawing at him.

Her hand curls my injured one into a gentle fist, and she sets her other on top of it. "You're sure it was Vellicor's mark? That the book gave you this vision?"

"I don't know. It could have been the Story Thief himself, twisting the Language to torment me. But it felt real. Too real." My throat locks, and I force the words through anyway. "The crown prince is alive. I have to believe that. And he's suffering. If I don't reach him soon..."

The water gurgles, a Blue Jay call rents the air from deeper in the forest. My sister's voice is soft but steady. "We'll reach him soon. Together."

Tears sting my eyes, quick and unbidden. I blink hard, swallowing the knot in my throat. "You don't understand. Every time I use the Language, every time I answer this quest, I feel the Story Thief's shadow pressing closer. What if he's baiting me? What if this vision was a trap?"

She squeezes my hand gently. "What if it was Ren telling you he still fights? That he's not gone yet. You can't throw away hope just because it hurts to carry it."

Her words hit home because they're true. Layla lifts her dripping muzzle, water streaming from her whiskers. She stamps once, impatient. I drag my sleeve across my eyes, pushing down the swell of fear. "Then we ride. However far this old girl will carry us."

Calliope grins, brushing back her damp curls. "Now that's the sister I followed halfway across Evermere to join on her quest." The smile turns sly as she releases my hand. "Let's ride. We need to save your dragon prince."

Heat climbs my neck. "He's not *my* anything."

She only laughs, light and teasing. "Mm-hmm. You keep saying that, but I've read enough stories to know how this one goes."

I mount Layla first, then hold a hand down for her. "Then maybe you should start writing a new one."

Her smile softens as she leverages herself up. "I'm busy working on my own romance, if you must know."

I've seen the romances she reads. Heard her share the gossip about a man visiting Fablehollow who sails the realm's seas. "With a pirate?"

Layla plods back onto the road, and I keep her pace slowed to a steady jog. Calliope settles her hands on her thighs, her chin brushing my shoulder whenever the mare jostles. "Why not? Why can't my quest be searching for buried treasure—and having a handsome pirate help me find it?"

Our banter continues, light and amusing. We pass a pair of merchants trundling a cart, the wheels thick with mud. They nod in greeting, but their eyes slide past us—vague, unfocused, as if seeing only half of what's real. *Just like in the hamlet.* I swallow the unease that resurfaces and nudge Layla on.

Calliope sighs against my ear. "I can't believe Father lied. It's just...not like him."

I tighten my grip on the reins. "He thinks he's protecting us. Protecting me."

"That doesn't make it right." Her tone reminds me of Mom. "He of all people should understand. He had his quest when he was seventeen. Seventeen! Barely a man. You've heard the stories as often as I have. He tracked that river beast for weeks. Everyone thought he'd die out there, but he didn't stop. Not until he finished."

I bite the inside of my cheek. "And now he fears finishing mine will kill me."

Calliope brushes something off my back. "Maybe he's forgotten how it feels when the Lore pulls you, and nothing else matters. Or maybe he's too afraid to remember."

Our father is human, not Fae. But like all in our kingdom, it does not matter to the Great Story. All are equal when it comes to receiving a quest.

The saddle creaks under us. "He knows better than anyone how important this is. If he doesn't let me do this—if he tries to stop me again—I'll…" The words fade, unfinished. What will I do? Defy him again? The thought should terrify me, but instead my heart answers with a thudding, undeniable *yes*.

"You'll do what you have to," she says softly. "Find the story and live it, no matter who tells you not to."

We ride in silence for a time. Layla's hooves beat a rhythm into the earth. My lids grow heavy. Calliope and I share bread and apples. She's also brought cheese and boiled eggs. The road narrows again between a line of trees, shadows stretching across our path. I urge Layla on, eager for open ground.

A sudden flurry of crows bursts from the trees, black wings tearing through the leaves and sending a shower over us. Their loud caws tear at my ears and sound like a warning.

"It's just some birds," Calliope says, patting my shoulder. "We must have startled them."

A sharp crack snaps my head back to the road—a branch snapping underfoot up ahead on the right. My heart skitters as a figure steps into the road, face swathed in a ragged scarf that hides everything but the glint of his eyes.

Two more emerge from the trees on the other side, one hefting a cudgel, the other with a bow strung and ready.

"Good morning, ladies," the first one drawls, though the sun is nearly at noon. While the rag covers his mouth, I can tell he's smiling. "Fine horse you've got there. Hand her over, and maybe we'll let you walk away."

Calliope stiffens against me. "What do we do?" she whispers.

I tighten my grip on the reins, pulse spiking. "Stay calm."

But inside, I'm anything but. We're too far from the village, too far still from Jairton, and far too empty-handed for bribes.

Which means the only thing left is to fight.

# Chapter Eleven
## Dessalyn | Bandits

*The sharpest blade is useless if you don't see the strike coming.*

THE CUDGEL COMES FIRST.

The man wielding it doesn't speak, doesn't warn—just lunges at me and swings. It's a brutal, ugly arc aimed straight for my head.

I shriek, yanking Layla's reins to the left, but the mare rears in panic. Calliope clutches me tight, screaming in my ear, and then the world tilts. The reins rip from my hands, the saddle vanishes from beneath us, and we crash into the mud.

The breath is knocked out of me. The shock of cold earth, the stink of rotting leaves, the taste of iron on my tongue—suddenly it's all too real.

I gasp, raising a hand. "We don't have anything worth taking. Please—we're just travelers—"

The cudgel-wielder drags his ragged scarf down and grins. His teeth are broken, his eyes flat with hunger. He advances, each step bearing down on us.

"Calli!" I yank her up even as the cudgel swings again. My knife flashes instinctively, catching the wood before it can crack my skull. The force shudders down my arm, numbing my fingers.

Calliope scrambles up beside me, her skirts muddied, hands trembling. "We have no coin!" she cries. "We've nothing for you!"

"Don't lie," the bowman sneers, string taut, arrow notched. "Everyone's got something."

My pulse spikes, terror ricocheting through me. Three of them. One with a cudgel, one with a blade, one with a bow. No mercy in any of their faces.

I force my voice steady, though my heart is a thunderclap. "Take the horse. Take whatever you want, just don't hurt us."

The third man moves in, knife gleaming. His voice is lazy, cruel. "You've got more than most. Pretty cloaks. Sturdy boots. A horse. We'll take it all."

My pulse hammers, deafening. They mean to strip us of everything. Leave us bare and broken on this road. I cannot—*will not*—let that happen. "Our cloaks and boots are worth nothing to you," I say, forcing steadiness into my voice even as it shakes, "but this blade might serve you well." I lift the knife toward the man who is holding much cheaper steel. "It's better than yours. Take it."

He sneers, but I've caught his attention. I'm about to hand it to him, hoping that this deal will save us, and knowing it is severely lacking, when the man with the cudgel swings again, a harsh shadow against the sky. For a moment, I freeze, sure this will split my skull. This is the end…

—until a prickling fire surges down my spine. *Left.*

I stumble aside just in time. The cudgel smashes the ground where I'd stood, dirt exploding upward. The man snarls, furious.

I stare, stunned, my knife trembling in my grip. I didn't know I should move. I felt like someone shoved the thought into me just in time.

Mom? Ren? Vellicor?

Calliope grips my arm, sobbing. "Dessa—"

I grit my teeth, plant my feet, and raise the blade between them and us. My hand steadies. "Leave us be."

The bowstring sings.

Instinct screams *down* before thought can catch up. I throw myself sideways once more, knocking into Calliope and pulling her down. My knees slam into the damp earth as the arrow hisses past my ear and splinters against the tree trunk behind us. The sound is so sharp it feels like it slices through me.

Calliope's voice is high, ragged with terror. "Are you okay?"

I nod, gaining my feet, as she stumbles past me, scrabbling in the weeds until her hand closes on a thick branch lying on the ground. She hefts it and steps in front of me to shield me.

The cudgel-man pounces at her this time, spittle flying from his lips. But before his weapon can harm me, she slams her branch into his shoulder. The crack is sickening, wood against bone. He roars, staggering sideways, surprise flashing across his face before it folds into fury.

"Stay away from her!" Calliope shrieks, voice breaking. She swings again, wild, reckless. "Get away from us!"

The man jerks his weapon up to block her blow, and the two forces smack together with a thud. The bowman already has another arrow notched, eyes cold as stone. His hand draws back, string creaking.

"Don't!" I cry, voice cracking. I can't think—I can only react. The prickling returns, crawling over my skin. Another whisper, urging, *Move right.*

I lurch to the side just as the arrow looses. It tears past my shoulder so close it tugs a strand of my hair loose, embedding itself in the same tree trunk with a dull thunk.

My chest heaves. The knife shakes in my grip.

The third man with the cheap blade circles closer, grin jagged and sharp. "Pretty birds with claws," he drawls. "Let's clip 'em."

Calliope's branch cracks against the cudgel again. Sparks fly. The man grunts, shoving her back, and I surge forward, putting myself between them, blade raised.

"You'll get nothing from us but blood," I snarl, though terror quakes in my bones. I don't even know where that came from. This fight has awakened some inner beast inside me, and I am *furious.*

*Adrenaline*, I think wildly. That's all. Just adrenaline.

The man with the blade attacks. I see the arc before he makes it, as if time has stretched thin and let me glimpse the strike ahead of his actual swing. My body ducks before my mind registers the motion, and his knife cuts only air.

"Dessa!" Calliope's voice is high, panicked. "Behind you!"

The bow man is circling. He snarls, and my lungs burn, but I don't falter. Somehow, I know exactly where to plant my foot, how to pivot so his next arrow misses this time by inches. It's not training. Not instinct. It's something else.

Luck. Or something that feels like it.

Calliope screams as the knife-wielder seizes her and yanks her into a hold. I whirl, vision clear. "Let her go!"

Luck deserts me. The cudgel crashes into my side. Pain explodes up my ribs, white-hot, stealing my breath. I collapse to one knee, the world tilting. My knife slips in my grip.

*I'm not strong enough. Not fast enough. We're going to die.*

Something pulses in me again, loud as a bell in my head. Energy surges. My knife steadies, my vision sharpens. That fury, that adrenaline, has me thrust at the bandit holding my sister.

He curses as my blade slices his arm, forcing him to release her. Calliope scrambles to my side, clutching her branch. Her wide eyes meet mine.

For one suspended heartbeat, I believe we can win.

But the cudgel-man rushes us again, teeth bared, only this time, his swing goes wide. The cudgel tumbles from his hand, and he snarls, staring at his fingers as if they've betrayed him.

The bowman curses as he, too, fumbles with his weapon. An arrow falls uselessly to the ground before he can notch it. His hands twitch, and he glances at his friends with a look that seems to say he's forgotten the motion he's made a thousand times.

The knife-wielder circles back toward Calliope, only to stumble on a root. He crashes to one knee, his blade flying out of his hand and into the weeds.

My chest heaves, my ribs blaze, and I blink in disbelief. What in the stars...?

For an instant, it feels as if the story tilts in our favor—threads tugged by unseen hands, weaving mistakes into our enemies' strikes.

"Dessa," Calliope gasps, keeping her branch at the ready. "What's happening?"

I shake my head, knife raised, the horrid pain in my ribs making it impossible to draw a deep breath. Blood tickles from my temple—I don't even remember how I cut myself. "Stay sharp."

She nods. The thieves glare at us, at their weapons, at each other. They each try to launch another assault, but they've lost all control over their movements.

A sudden shift in the air wraps around us, a cool breeze wafting past my cheek and sending gooseflesh over my skin. A figure bursts from the shadows, cloak flaring, moving with the kind of certainty that leaves no room for hesitation. He brandishes a fine sword and forces them all to step back. When the one with the cudgel tries to swing it, the man's wrist twists, and the sword knocks it away with ease.

He's handsome and cuts a striking figure, cloak snapping as his blade arcs through the air. He moves with the confidence of someone who's faced death a dozen times—and laughed every time.

The other two bandits hesitate, eyes flicking between the newcomer and us, but the new visitor is already on the move, swift as a shadow. His sword flashes again, cutting a line across the nearest bandit's arm, and the man yelps, clutching the wound before he stumbles backward.

The bandit with the bow hesitates, and the stranger's voice cuts through the tension. "Go before I shred you to ribbons."

The archer hesitates, his fingers still struggling to grip the string of his bow. The man charges forward and, with a single, swift motion, knocks the bow out of his hands. The bandit trips over his own feet as he scrambles away and disappears into the trees.

The cudgel-wielder makes a move to charge, snatching up his fallen weapon. The stranger's blade snaps up, the tip hovering inches from his throat, causing him to freeze. The man raises his hands in surrender, weapon thudding to the forest floor, his eyes wide with fear. The dashing newcomer turns the tip of the sword the tiniest amount, drawing a slim drop of blood.

The bandit cries out, lurches back, and turns on his heel to flee in the same direction as his friends.

Without another word, the man sheathes his sword with a smooth motion and turns to us with a smile. "Good day, ladies. While it appeared you had the situation under control, I hope you don't mind my intervention."

There is something rakish about him, from the tilt of his hood to the flourish of his sword. My sister's smile is a welcome sight, and I swear she sees him as if he's stepped straight from the pages of one of her beloved romances—cloak, sword, and all.

# CHAPTER TWELVE
## DESSALYN | BLADES AND BANDAGES

*False names can open true doors.*

THE STRANGER'S HOOD CASTS his face in shadow, but I catch the glint of dark eyes and a tilted, rakish smile.

"Devlin Montague," he says with a slight bow, a gloved hand sweeping out as if this dirt road were a ballroom floor. "At your service."

Calliope is still clutching her branch, but her lips curve, relief and admiration softening her features. She dips a slight curtsy, soil clinging to her hem. "Calliope Lorewyn. And this is my sister, Dessalyn. We're grateful for your assistance."

I shoot her a look sharp enough to cut. We don't know him. We can't afford to share more than we must.

"The Lorewyn sisters?" He tips back his hood, and his grin widens. "Of Fablehollow?"

Calliope raises her chin. "The very ones. You've heard of us?"

He strides forward, hand on the hilt of his sword. "I have, my lady. Those who are blessed with the Lore Language are famous in these parts."

Calliope glances my way, lifting a brow. No one calls us *ladies* back home. A steep cliff she is falling down.

"The Fates must favor my journey today," he continues, "to have come upon you just now."

Calliope sets the end of the branch on the ground and leans on it like a crutch. "The Fates have favored us, as well. Again, I thank you for your assistance with those awful thieves."

Another bow. "My pleasure." He motions at the road. "You're a long way from home. Where do you journey to?"

Before she can tell him, I cut in. "We're making several stops before returning home." My ribs burn with the effort to breathe deeply, and my voice is thin and reedy. "And you? Where is your home?"

Calliope frowns at me, puzzled, but doesn't speak.

"Jairton. I'm headed there now," Devlin says smoothly, as though he hasn't noticed the frost in my tone. His gaze lingers on me a fraction too long, and then my knees give out. I slide down the nearest tree trunk, back hitting the bark with a jolt that sends fire through my side.

"Dessa!" Calliope drops beside me, hands fluttering uselessly before she grabs my shoulder. "Where are you hurt?"

My breath saws shallow, sweat breaking across my brow. I gesture weakly toward the forest. "Worry about the horse—our satchels." The thought is worse than the pain. We've lost our ride, our clothes, food, and, most importantly to me, the quest journal. My only connection to Ren and my future. "We must find Layla."

"Don't trouble yourself." Devlin adjusts his cloak. "I'll retrieve your horse. And ensure those wretches didn't carry off your belongings."

Before I can protest, he's turning toward the woods, cloak snapping behind him as he disappears into the shadows.

Calliope kneels beside me, her skirts dragging in the grass, eyes wide with worry. "You're pale as parchment. Where does it hurt?"

"My head." I don't know when my head sustained an injury, but everything happened so fast. "And my ribs." The words hiss out through clenched teeth. "But it's nothing, only bruised, not broken."

"You don't know that." She presses her hands to her lap as if to keep from reaching for me. Her voice trembles, though she tries to hide it. "You doubled over when you hit the tree, and you're still gasping."

I shake my head, regretting it when the world tilts. Fear claws at my mind. Frustration presses hot behind my eyes. I try to stand, fail. Biting back a sob, I refuse to cry. "We've bigger problems. Our food, our clothes—my journal. Everything is gone with Layla."

Calliope studies me, stubbornness hardening her expression. "And Father thought you weren't ready for this."

I glare at her, though it's weak at best. "Apparently, he was right."

"Don't be ridiculous. You fought like a warrior just now."

Warrior, right. I appreciate her trying to lift my spirits. She takes my knife and goes to a nearby willow tree, slicing off a slender branch. "What are you doing?" I ask.

She strips the leaves and then gathers a plant near a rambling bush before handing all of it to me. "Chew these. They'll dull the pain."

I stare at the offering like it's poison. "Tree leaves and weeds?"

Her eyes flash. "Willow and woodwort alleviate pain and reduce swelling. Now chew."

Reluctantly, I do. The bitterness floods my tongue, sharp and acrid, worse than spoiled milk. My stomach lurches. "That's vile."

Calliope smirks despite the worry in her eyes. "Better vile than in pain."

I spit a shred onto the grass and grimace. "If this kills me, I'll haunt you."

Her laugh is shaky, threaded with relief. She squeezes my hand, her thumb brushing over my knuckles. "Better haunted by you than losing you."

The underbrush stirs. I tense, snatching back the knife instinctively—until Layla steps through, reins in the gloved hand of the stranger. Behind him follows a chestnut stallion, sleek as shadow, tossing its midnight black mane.

Relief crashes through me so hard my back sags against the tree once more. "Layla."

The mare's ears flick toward my voice, her gray muzzle damp with sweat but otherwise unharmed. I want to weep with gratitude. My satchel is still strapped to her back.

"She's a docile one," the man says with an easy smile, tugging both horses forward. "And the bandits seem to have left her alone."

Calliope beams, springing to her feet. "You're a miracle! Dess, look. Our things are safe."

I nod, unable to summon more than a rasp. My chest spears with every breath, the residue of the chewed leaves still bitter on my tongue.

The man studies me, his expression sharpening. "You're injured."

"I'm fine," I croak, trying to rise. The effort ends in a gasp as pain lances my side. The world fades in and out, the trees sway, and I crumple back to the ground.

Calliope grabs my arm. "You're not fine. Stubborn, yes. Fine? No."

The stranger steps closer, crouching, careful with his movements. "I've some skill as a healer. If you'll permit me, I can help."

"No." My protest is weak. I blink to try and keep him in focus.

Calliope glares at me, then turns to him. "She'll let you. I insist."

I close my eyes, furious at them both, but unable to argue. My ribs feel like broken glass shifting inside me.

When I open my eyes again, the man is unrolling a bundle from his saddlebag. Vials of tonic, a length of clean cloth, and a small case of herbs. Everything about his motions is practiced, assured—yet strangely graceful, almost courtly.

"Let's start with the head wound," he says.

I stiffen, but Calliope kneels at my other side and presses my hand. "It's all right. Let him."

He tips the liquid of one vial onto the cloth and reaches for my temple. "Hold still," he murmurs.

I flinch when the cool touch finds the cut at my hairline. A sting flares sharp, metallic, but I hold in my hiss.

"I know it's unpleasant." He rewets the cloth and dabs at the cut again. "It's all right to show it."

I clamp my lips together.

His lips twitch in an almost smile. He steadies me with a hand at my jaw, gloved fingers firm but not rough, and finishes wiping away the trickle of blood.

"It's not deep," he says, matter-of-fact. "Head wounds bleed more than they deserve. Are you dizzy? Lightheaded? How's your stomach?"

He thinks I have a concussion. "I'm lightheaded because I haven't had enough to eat, and I've never been in a fight before. The adrenaline overload was unexpected."

"Hmm." A glance at my sister. "I'm a believer in the theory that the patient knows best most of the time, and your pupils appear normal, so perhaps you're right."

"I am," I mutter, though my voice wavers. I don't have time for a concussion or all of this henpecking.

He doesn't respond—just tips my chin and inspects the wound again before lowering the cloth. "What else?"

"Her ribs," Calliope volunteers.

"No." I cross an arm over my side. The thought of him pressing where the pain is worst, of his hands mapping my body—it's unbearable. "It's nothing."

Calliope folds her arms, face stern. "Dessalyn."

She sounds like Mom. I glare at her, but the next attempt to draw a deep breath ends in a sharp gasp, my eyes stinging. Betrayed by my own body, I wilt against the tree.

The man crouches lower, his voice calm. "I'll be quick. Just answer me." His gloved fingers hover, waiting.

Giving in once more, I give a jerky nod.

"Here?" His hand presses lightly below my right ribcage. A dull ache radiates. "Yes," I grit out.

"And here?"

The next press is sharper, fire lancing through me. I hiss, clutching his wrist before I can stop myself. A curse flies from my mouth.

He stills, eyes flicking to mine. "Not broken," he says softly, as if soothing me. "If it were, you wouldn't be speaking."

I release him, embarrassed, heat flooding my face. "You're sure?"

He digs in his satchel. "It's bruised but manageable with care." From within, he produces a small vial of amber liquid. "A tonic for the dizziness, and it will help you mend quicker. Bitter, I'm afraid."

"Wonderful," I mutter, but I swallow it when Calliope takes it from him and presses it into my hand. The taste is sharp, herbal, fiery—it burns all the way down, but steadies the spinning world. "Is that bourbon?" I spit out.

He winks. "With medicinal herbs added, I promise." Then he pulls free a long sash of clean cloth. "For support," he explains. "To keep you from tearing yourself further when you shift around."

I blink at it, realizing what this means. "No."

"Dessa," Calliope warns again.

He glances away politely but holds the cloth ready. "You'll have to lift your arms. Unless you prefer to collapse again?"

Humiliation sears hotter than the pain. Calliope is already tugging at the clasp of my cloak. Between them, I am outnumbered. I lift my weak arms enough for him to wind the sash under my breasts and across my ribcage.

His movements are professional, practiced—yet the closeness is unbearable. The cloth brushes across the tender area, forcing me to swallow hard as he binds me. Once, his gloved hand steadies my back, and the contact nearly undoes me.

When he ties the knot firmly, the pressure locks my breath, shallow but steadier. I lean against the tree once more, dizzy with relief.

I suck down another swallow of the medicinal liquid, welcoming the burn in my throat and chest this time.

"There." He adjusts the knot, tucking the ends neatly. "It will ease with time. You'll need rest."

"Rest," I scoff, though my voice is thin. "I'm walking to Jairton."

"Not walking," he corrects smoothly, his gaze flicking to Layla. "Riding. And with care."

"I can't ride!"

He points at the sash. "That will hold you secure. Just stay upright, allow your sister to brace your back, and keep the mare at a slow pace."

I shake my head. Calliope tugs my arm and pulls me to my feet. I complain, and even with the sash and tonic, I sway, vision dotted with specks.

He steps closer, offering his hand. The gesture is courtly, a touch of mockery in the bow of his head, but his grip is firm when I take it. He steadies me as though I weigh no more than a reed.

"Easy," he murmurs. "It will be uncomfortable, but you'll manage."

Calliope beams at him. "Thank you. Truly."

My cheeks burn. "I didn't need—" I start, but the ground heaves and falls under my feet, forcing me to grasp his arm until the dizziness passes.

"You needn't prove anything to me," he says kindly.

He and Calliope help me to Layla. She nickers and holds still, patient as if she knows how fragile I am. With their hands guiding me, I haul myself into the saddle, biting back a cry as the movement jostles my torso. Settled at last, I lean forward, gripping the pommel so I don't fall back off.

The mare shifts under me, but is steady and solid. Relief loosens the breath I'm holding. Montague then assists Calliope up behind me and instructs her on how to place her hands on my sides to brace me.

He mounts his stallion with a fluid motion, the beast gleaming like a living shadow. "You said you're going to Jairton, yes?" He points northeast. "Might I accompany you?"

Calliope's voice cuts across mine, bright and earnest. "Of course. We'd be delighted."

My stomach knots. I start to shoot her a look, but I can't turn. She pinches my side as if daring me to contradict her.

Montague smiles. "Then it seems our paths align. I'll see you safely there."

Against my wishes, my quest has gained a new companion.

# CHAPTER THIRTEEN
## RENWICK | SNARE OF SHADOWS

*The strongest flame can be trapped if the cage is woven tight enough.*

SOMETHING WET BRUSHES MY cheek.

I jolt upright, hand flying for my sword. A fox leaps back with a startled yelp, fur bristling, its amber eyes wide. Our eyes lock. For a breath, it looks ready to bolt—then it freezes, nose twitching as it catches the truth beneath my skin.

*Dragon.*

With a sharp whine, it drops low, belly to the leaves, tail curled tight. Submission. Recognition.

Its body answers to mine in the oldest language of bloodlines. A dragon doesn't need to bare his teeth to be obeyed.

My pulse hammers, body aching, but I wave the small animal off with a weary flick of my fingers. "Go." My voice is a rasp, more gravel than sound. It slinks away, vanishing into the underbrush without a backward glance.

The woods hum with evening's lull. Crickets rasp from the underbrush, frogs belch by some unseen pool, the steady rhythm of creatures settling for nightfall. Yet the rhythm falters when I move, the whole forest listening, waiting to decide if I belong.

I did once.

Twilight presses between the branches, heavy and purple. The ground is damp where I collapsed, leaves plastered to my cheek. Every muscle protests, a chorus of aches threaded with fire, as I shift to my feet. My palms are raw where dragon flame spilled through them, the skin cracked and blistered.

A stream gurgles close by, and a horse with no saddle or bags picks up its head from grazing to stare at me as I draw near. I stagger toward the water, drop to my knees, and plunge my hands into the cool current. The sting is blinding, sharp as teeth sinking into me. I welcome it.

I cup the water and drink. The water is no feast. My body longs for fire, not streams, but it clears the soot from my throat enough to remind me I still breathe. I splash more over my face, washing away blood that's dried stiff in my hair.

My dragon stirs, restless and wounded, thudding dully in my chest. I coax a spark to life in my palm, but only a flicker comes, pitiful, dying in the blink of an eye. The failure guts me. Without my fire, I am less than half a man.

That cuts sharper than the wounds still weeping across my skin. Dragon fire is not just flame. It is heart and breath, the pulse that binds sinew to bone. A dragon without fire is a bird without wings, a wolf without teeth. My veins ache without it, my body a husk that barely belongs to me.

Fire is my inheritance. My bloodline. The mark of every Ravelle prince since the first oath was spoken in Drakenholt's name. Without it, I am no heir—no dragon lord at all. Just another man with calloused hands and nothing to offer but broken stories.

Worse, inside me resides the last ember of my kingdom. Each time it sputters, I feel Drakenholt's silence pressing closer, the weight of every voice already swallowed by the Story Thief. Fire is their echo inside me. If it gutters out, then so does every chance of their return.

Most dangerous of all? *Dessalyn.*

Even when I would cage it, her name strikes sparks in me. When I see her face in memory, in dreams, the blaze claws higher, refusing to be smothered. Without it, I cannot reach her, cannot shield her, cannot be the prince she deserves. Without it, I am less than the man she deserves, and less than the one who still hopes to earn her forgiveness.

I sit back hard on the bank, chest heaving. The vault's shadows still linger in memory, gnawing at my dragon essence. Marrow's voice slides in unbidden, a whisper... *Time's running out.*

My jaw clenches. I won't let it run out. Not for me. Not for Dessalyn.

I drag in a breath, shaky and sour. The woods blur as if the shadows followed me here, whispering. I brace a hand against the damp earth, but it's not enough. My ribs scream, my palms burn, and still the thought roars louder than pain.

*She's coming.*

I saw her in the vision. Her face pale in the inn's firelight, eyes wide as mine bled across the mark. I felt her terror, her stubbornness. The Lore is weaving her into this cursed tangle, whether I want it to or not.

"No." The word grinds out, an oath. Even though I need her to access the vault, it's too dangerous. "She can't."

I know it now. If she reaches Jairton, she'll walk straight into Cimarron's clutches. She'll see what I buried with her mother's help, what I should have destroyed years ago. And she'll pay the price for my lie.

A new plan forms in my mind. I stagger upright, ignoring the pain and weakness that cause my legs to shake. I lock my knees, my spine, and force myself forward. If I can reach her *before* she makes it to Jairton—turn her back, send her home—perhaps the Story Thief won't notice her yet. Perhaps I can still shield her.

My dragon snarls, the pendant warming. It wants her near, wants to kindle a bond with her, bend her to its will. I tell myself it's only protection, not dominance or manipulation. But deep down, I know better. An entire kingdom is counting on me. And that means I must do whatever it takes to bring them back. If my story cannot be destroyed, I must rewrite it.

But first, I must retrieve what is already in the vault.

At war with myself, I rip a strip of linen from my tunic and bind my blistered palms. I think of allowing Dessalyn to come here, lying to her to coerce her into helping me open it. And then what? How will I keep it—and her—from Cimarron while I compose a new version?

The prince in me refuses to put her in danger. Sacrificing her life for mine, for my people, is no way to write a happy ending. "I will not let you walk into this trap," I murmur.

The forest falls quiet again around me, as though waiting to see if I mean it.

I do mean it, even if the next step breaks me.

The outskirts of Jairton stretch before me like a corpse half-buried. Huts sag against one another, timbers rotting, thatch gone to seed. I limp through mud that stinks of mildew. Every step jars my injuries, but I keep moving.

Cold bleeds through the street, seeping beneath my skin. The shadows stir, becoming writhing tendrils. I brace, suspecting they're the same ones I fought in the vault, but they're not. These are laced with a spider's magic.

The bell tower soars above the square, crooked as a snapped bone. Its bronze tongue is long gone, the arch vacant. A figure steps from the ruins, cloaked in gray, as though the stone itself has taken form.

He grips a staff as tall as he is, etched with runes that glow a sickly crimson. They look like letters, but wrong—shattered versions of the Lore Language, twisted and void of meaning.

His hood cloaks his face, but when he lifts the edge, I see eyes like caverns. Black voids veined with threads of silk, widening until they seem to swallow me whole.

"Renwick Ravelle." His voice rattles the air. "The Story has been expecting you."

My hand finds my sword hilt. "Who are you? What do you want?"

The mage tilts his head. Those silky spider threads leak from the edges of his hood, curling and reaching. "Want? I want nothing. I only serve." His staff thuds once against the ground, and the runes blaze bright.

The air convulses. Bands of black tendrils coil from the staff, writhing serpents of magic. They snap tight around my wrists, my chest, my throat.

My dragon roars inside me, fire clawing through my veins, my muscles, begging to be unleashed. I bellow, forcing the flames into my palms, a spark trembling to life. For one searing heartbeat, light flares, burning back the dark coils.

But the mage's staff drinks it in. The flames in my hands are siphoned straight into those broken lore letters, devoured like meat sucked from a bone.

Agony tears through me. What little fire I managed is ripped out, my blood boiling as if the staff drains the very essence of me. I stagger, knees slamming down onto the cobbles, breath shredded to smoke.

The Story Thief has sent another of his minions. I snarl, spitting blood, forcing myself upright against the bindings. "You can't have it. You can't have me."

The mage's eyes widen, voids swirling faster, hungrier. His voice drops to a hiss. "Then burn yourself trying, dragon. My master wants your flame, and I will deliver it."

The coils cinch tighter, crushing my chest until stars bloom across my vision. My knees threaten to buckle, but fury roots me to the ground.

*You are a dragon*, something deep and primal reminds me. *Not prey. Never prey.*

I dig inward, past the pain, past the emptiness of drained flame. Past the shame. And there, buried in my bones, I find the ember that refuses to die. The ember that is *mine*.

I drag it up with a roar. Fire explodes from my lungs, searing through the bindings. The mage reels back as his spider silk unravels in the destruction of light. The stink of it scorches the air.

I lunge forward, sword blazing as if forged for this moment. The steel sings, fire racing along its edge. I drive it into the mage's staff. Sparks shriek as the two magics clash.

He stumbles, smoke pouring from his cloak. For the first time, his void-eyes widen, startled. "Impossible..."

I press harder, every muscle shaking, every wound screaming, but my sword holds. "Tell your master," I snarl, teeth bared, "Drakenholt does not bow."

With a guttural cry, I wrench free. The fire lashes out one last time, knocking the mage back into the rubble of the tower. Stone splits. Dust plumes. Silence follows.

He should be broken. Defeated. Yet his laughter echoes low and cold. "You burn bright, prince. But even the brightest flame can be doused."

I freeze, blade still blazing.

He rises amid the ruin, blood streaking his mouth. "Marrow walks beside her. Even now, she trusts him."

The power falters. My lungs seize. "Lies."

The mage smiles. "Threads entwine them. And when she sleeps, he will be there. Watching her in her dreams."

My sword nearly falls from my grasp. The ember inside me sputters, not from weakness but from fear. *Dessalyn, no.*

The mage crumples at my feet, staff split down the middle, its runes sputtering into silence. Smoke rises from the earth, the stink of charred moss and ash clinging to my throat. My chest heaves, ribs raw, every breath a ragged tear.

"You won't win," he wheezes, cracked lips curling. His eyes swim, threads of his spider silk spilling down his cheeks like tears. "You've lost her, dragon prince, just like you've lost your kingdom."

The words sink hooks into me. My blade shakes as fury lances through my veins.

Lies. They must be lies.

But the certainty in his tone—the relish—scrapes bone-deep.

Marrow. With Dessalyn.

A growl rumbles up, dragon-deep. I stagger back, the world shifting under my feet. My fire gutters, but it hasn't died yet. Not completely.

"If he touches her..." My voice shreds into the night. "If he so much as breathes on her, I'll burn him to ash."

The mage laughs, broken and thin, until I silence him with a kick that sends him sprawling into the weeds.

No more waiting. No more sealing cracks, no more hiding shame.

As fast as my feet will carry me, I shove through Jairton's outskirts, past the hollow-eyed villagers repeating their broken lines, and the growing night enveloping them. The road waits, stretching dark and endless into the trees. Somewhere beyond, she's walking it. Alone. With him.

My very bones burn. I taste blood in my mouth. I welcome it all. Pain means I'm still alive. Fire means I can still fight.

"Hold on, Dessalyn," I mutter, breath ragged. I tear open a stall's gate and throw myself onto the nearest stallion, barely broken, wild with longing. He bucks hard, but I drive my heels into his flanks, and we are gone. "I'm coming. And I swear by Drakenholt's flame—he won't take you from me."

The shadows try to cling, whispering doubts, but I tear through them.

Because this was never just Dessalyn's quest. It's always been mine, too.

# CHAPTER FOURTEEN
## DESSALYN | THE FIRE BETWEEN

*Every dream is a story trying to write itself.*

THE ROAD TO JAIRTON stretches in front of me, pale and endless, though no moon lights it. My clothes cling damp and soiled to my skin, my hair tangled in knots, my palms raw with blisters that look like open mouths. How did I burn myself?

The dream's floating sensation makes my stomach churn. I don't remember. I don't remember starting this walk, either. While some things are familiar, like the road and the forest, I know it's not reality.

Even so, one thing I'm sure of is this—if I stop, I'll be swallowed whole.

Ahead of me lies my quest journal in the center of the road. It rests there as if it were dropped only moments ago. I lunge for it, but the instant my fingers almost brush it, the book appears farther down the path, out of reach.

"No!" The word rips out of me, ragged. I give chase, lungs heaving, legs burning. Each time I get close to it, it disappears and reappears farther away. It's as if the road itself is pulling it from my hands. Teasing, taunting.

Ahead of me, a low, rolling growl that doesn't belong to any beast rips through the air.

I look up and gasp.

The horizon is gone. In its place, a wall of solid black cloud billows upward, roiling like ink spilled across the sky. It's massive, spanning everything—sky, stars, road—swallowing whole trees and hills as it surges forward. It devours them, everything disappearing in its wake. Just...gone, as if they never existed.

This is no dream. It's a nightmare.

The sound grows louder, deafening, and I realize it isn't growling.

It's *bellowing*. Triumphant. It's hungry, and everything it consumes feeds it.

Under the noise are screams. Voices. People and their stories crying out as they're unmade.

"No—no, please—" I stumble forward, desperate, clawing at the ground, scrambling for the journal before the cloud reaches it. My blistered palms slip on the graveled path, searing with pain as I scrape them raw.

The journal flickers like a mirage. The black mass swells closer, so close its edges lick at the road, threads of stories unraveling.

*If it eats the journal, it eats me.*

I hurl myself forward with everything left in me, choking on tears. The roar of the cloud shakes my bones, shakes the world. I fall.

A thunderclap splits the noise, and a stallion bursts onto the road ahead, hooves striking sparks. It carries a cloaked rider with a drawn blade. The horse skids to a halt, throwing its weight back on powerful haunches. The rider raises his sword high as the horse's front hooves paw the air.

The word he shouts tears through the night in a language I don't know—rough, guttural, searing—and the blade erupts in fire. Flame whips up the steel, spilling outward, forming a wall of blazing green.

The black mass recoils. It slams against the wall, hungry, furious, but it cannot cross.

I stumble to my feet, chest heaving, the heat of the fire kissing my face. Is it Montague commanding this flame?

No, this is not his horse, his cloak. Who, then? Who has saved me and my beloved journal from the roiling black mass?

The stallion rears again, mane ablaze with reflected flame, and the rider's hood falls back.

I gasp. My throat closes.

*Renwick.*

He looks carved from fire itself, jaw hard, eyes fierce, every line of him alive with defiance. The gold cuffs around his wrists flash. A dragon sigil forms in the air before him. He swings from the saddle, boots hitting the stone, and strides toward the journal that still lies just out of my reach.

He snatches it up. Turns. And then he's striding toward me, the green wall blazing behind him, his stallion shadowing him like a living sentinel.

"Ren—" The word tears from my chest in a sob. Relief floods my limbs so hard that my knees buckle.

He presses the journal into my hands, closing his own over mine as I clutch it to me.

Before I can speak, before I can thank him, his arms come around me. Solid, steady, real. I bury my face in his chest, the smoke and heat of him filling my lungs.

The fire. The journal. Him. All of it anchors me, steadies me. There's a tug in my chest, drawing me to him.

He holds me close, and something cracks through me—not flame, not Lore, but something older. My bones *know* him. My blood recognizes his. The journal may bind our quests, but this—this moment—binds us.

It shouldn't. I don't want it to. I still remember the night his father humiliated my mother. I still remember the fury that scorched me. But my fury bends in the face of this connection. His presence is a tether, and my body answers as if it has waited lifetimes for it. For him.

For a heartbeat, I believe the nightmare is over.

But then—

The dream shifts.

The fire dies. The black mass vanishes, smoke on the wind. Ren fades, crumbling to cinders in my arms. His weight, his heat...gone.

"No!" I'm on the road again, alone, the journal heavy in my hands. Another sob leaves my mouth.

Movement stirs to my left. A man leans in the shadows of the trees, cloak falling rakishly from one shoulder. *Montague.*

He quirks his head, eyes glinting with amusement. One hand rises, tipping an imaginary hat toward me. Then he's gone.

I jolt awake with a gasp.

The road is cold beneath my bare feet, gravel biting into them, and for a moment, I can't clear my thoughts. The journal is nowhere to be seen, but my palms are blistered and raw like in the dream. The pain is real. I'm awake, but...

Moonlight drifts in and out of cloud cover, silvering the world in fragments. Behind me, the shell of the old house looms—broken walls and collapsed rafters, long since abandoned. A few stones cling to their foundation, stubborn as old bones.

I remember this place. We stopped for the night. A dying fire flickers low in a hastily made fire pit between one wall and the road. Calliope sleeps curled near it, her satchel for a pillow, her cloak a poor excuse for a blanket.

But Montague is nowhere to be seen.

My chest tightens. I'm sure the dream has followed me. My gaze darts to Layla, still tethered nearby. She lifts her head and snorts, calm, unbothered. Relief thuds through me. At least she hasn't been stolen.

This is where we stopped at sundown and made camp. My ribs ache, as do my thighs. The dream caused me to sleepwalk, and now I'm here, shivering, the dream replaying over and over with this scene as the backdrop.

The fire may have died to embers, but I still feel the heat of Ren's arms around me, phantom warmth clinging to my ribs. It lingers, taunting me, as if the dream carved itself into my flesh and won't let go.

I rub my chest, heart hammering, certain I'll find a scorch mark there. Certain that if I close my eyes, I'll feel his breath again.

Where's Montague? I scan the landscape and take a shaky step toward the firepit and my satchel. I have to be sure the journal is safe. If the dream followed me this far, if Montague has abandoned us, I must be sure I have not lost it.

That's when I hear hoofbeats.

Not the soft shuffle of Layla's sure-footed pace. These are harder, sharper. Bearing down fast.

My breath spikes. My heart slams into my ribs. Bandits? Has Montague returned from some midnight ride? I whirl, bare feet slipping on dew-wet gravel, searching the dark.

A rider breaks through the tree line, cloaked, faceless under the clouds. The horse is tall, muscled, but unfamiliar. Not Montague's. Not any mount I've seen before.

I stumble backward toward the ruin, throat raw with a cry building. I'll wake Calliope, grab the knife—

"Dessalyn!"

The voice stops me cold. It tears through the dark, hoarse but commanding. It's one I know.

My knees weaken. My hands fly to my chest, as if to cage my wild, pounding heartbeat now trying to break free. The fated tug I've tried to deny—low in my belly, sharp as hunger—lances upward, catching fire in my ribs. It burns in my chest as if my soul itself recognizes him before my mind does. Heat ripples under my skin—phantom fire, *his* fire, echoing the dream.

The night closes in. Every breath, every heartbeat says the same impossible truth—*he's here.*

It's impossible, and yet...

Every cell in my body yearns for him. My heart, my belly, my mind know him. Without thought, his name spills from my lips, raw and reverent, as if the Lore Language itself has come to life. "Ren?"

The rider reins in hard, the horse skidding in the gravel, breath pluming white in the night air. The hood slips back as he lifts his head. And there he is.

Prince Renwick Ravelle. In the flesh.

Not a dream. Not a vision.

His face is cut in stark lines under the moonlight, drawn with exhaustion yet as fierce as ever. His sapphire blue eyes burn like twin embers under storm-dark brows. Blood stains his temple, and his cloak is ragged. His boots are caked in mud.

But none of that matters. Because *he's here*.

I blink, but he doesn't disappear. My knees buckle for real this time. The pull to him in my chest tightens, hot and inexorable, as if my very bones have been waiting for this moment, aching toward him across every mile and every word shared between us.

His gaze locks on mine, and in that instant, the world falls away—the road, the ruined house, the night itself. There is only him. Us.

"Dessalyn," he rasps, and the sound of my name on his lips makes the thread between us tighten so much I can hardly breathe.

# CHAPTER FIFTEEN
## DESSALYN | BLOOD AND FIRE

*A secret burns brighter once it's set free.*

RELIEF RIPPLES THROUGH ME like a tide I can't control, a hundred crashing waves against my body, as Ren and I walk toward the ruin where the fire has sunk to embers.

The early morning air bites sharp in my lungs, cool as river water, but beside me, his presence is a heat all its own. The rasp of his boots on the grass steadies me more than the ground itself.

Ahead of us, Layla lifts her head to greet his stallion. The gorgeous charger snorts and bobs his head. Ren steadies him, murmuring something under his breath in a low, rough voice that curls through me like smoke.

My chest aches. I still can't believe it and want to reach out and touch him to prove it to myself. He's here. *Flesh, breath, blood. Not a dream. Not a phantom vision.*

The fact that I threw myself into his arms a moment ago causes heat to rise in my cheeks. The fact that he wrapped his arms around me makes them grow even hotter. Most would say we don't know each other. In my heart, I know that isn't true.

While we haven't been together physically, we've been together in this quest. Time and emotions move differently in quests. The heart overrides logic. Destiny upstages the best laid plans.

The embers in the firepit are nearly out, throwing weak shards of light across my sister's sleeping face. As we draw closer, she stirs at the sound of our steps and the stallion's whinny. She pushes herself up on her elbows, curls spilling loose over her shoulder, and blinks into the gloom. Her gasp splits the quiet. "You!"

Ren gives a slight tilt of his head, his cape and hood making his large frame seem even bigger to me. Or maybe my memory of him in Longmere is faulty. Even in my dreams, I don't recall him being so...substantial. I've never stood so close to him, though. It feels as if he's a shield against the world. "In the flesh." His voice is hoarse but firm, as though he's daring anyone to deny it. "For now."

I swallow the instant lump in my throat at the thought that the Story Thief might succeed at any moment and erase him from my life. "He's still the crown prince," I remind my sister. "He should be addressed as such."

If I'm being honest, this is a weak attempt to put distance between us again. To remind myself, more than Calliope, that he's royalty, and no matter the circumstances, there are protocols to follow. To him, I say, "I apologize for our poor manners, Your Highness."

A corner of Ren's mouth quirks, and he peeks at me from the corner of his eye. "I appreciate that, but let's sweep formalities aside. I prefer you call me Ren. I like how it sounds when you say it."

The heat in my cheeks flares again. At this rate, I may self-combust.

Calliope scrambles upright, cloak falling from her shoulders, eyes wide. "How—what—?"

"It's a long story," Ren cuts in, his light tone turning steely. He looks from her to me, shadows pooling beneath his eyes in the dim morning light. "Where is the man who joined you on the road?"

How does he know about Montague? I glance around, but Devlin has not reappeared. The mention of him stirs the dream memories, and I feel a sinking sensation in my stomach. "He was here when I fell asleep last night, but I haven't seen him yet this morning."

Calliope whirls in a circle, searching for him in a near panic. "He's gone?" She stops and smooths her wild curls. "I bet he just went to catch fish for breakfast. There's a stream nearby," she tells Ren. "He's been so kind and helpful."

My bare feet are freezing, and I make my way to my boots, hissing at the pain in my ribs as I pull them on. "Do you know him?" I ask Ren.

The prince drops the reins and allows his horse to wander over to Layla. He folds his arms over his chest. "His true name is Marrow Greyfen. He serves the Story Thief."

The words hit me like the lash of a whip. "What?"

"No." Calliope shakes her head. "No, that can't be. He's been a total gentleman. He saved us from bandits on the road."

"I saw him," I blurt out, the memory of him in my dream, the jaunty tipping of his invisible hat, causes my stomach to knot. "He was in my dream. It caused me to sleepwalk. That's how I ended up on the road."

Ren's head snaps toward me. His expression shifts. "You *what*?"

"I dreamed of this terrible storm, devouring the world. He was there." I point to the road. "You were in it, too, and my quest journal. A horrible black mass was coming toward me, consuming everything in its path. You..." I falter.

"I what?" Ren demands.

"You stopped it with your fire. You saved me." My voice comes out soft. Small. I glance at him and see what looks like pride on his face. I offer a smile. His lips turn up with a ghost of one in return.

"And Marrow?" he asks, his tone gentler.

I replay what I can remember, the edges of the dream already fading. "He was watching. Smiling. He—" My voice falters. "He said nothing, just tipped his hat and vanished."

Ren's jaw locks. For a heartbeat, he looks more dragon than man, fury and dread sparking behind his eyes. The embers in the fire pit turn into actual flames. "Marrow is a dream walker. He weaves through mortal minds like threads on a loom. But he cannot cross into Fae or dragon Lorekeeper dreams unless…" His voice drops, his face darkening. "Unless he has your blood."

The air turns thin. My chest heaves. "That's impossible."

But the words tangle as memory slams into me. Montague—Marrow's—hand pressing the cloth to my temple to clean the gash.

What did he do with that cloth? I'm not sure, but I think he slipped it into his satchel.

It's a good thing I'm already seated. My legs go weak. "He—" I choke, furious with myself as I point to my head. "He doctored my wound. And he kept the bloodied cloth."

Shame scalds hotter than my burns. *Foolish. Naïve. Stupid.* The terms pound against my skull.

Ren swears under his breath, a dragon's curse in a tongue older than fire.

"No," Calliope insists, voice rising. "You're wrong. He fought the bandits, wrapped Dessa's ribs, and then he offered to ride alongside us to keep us safe from others who might do us harm."

"How badly were you injured?" Ren asks me.

"Bad," my sister cuts in before I can answer.

I wave her off and shake my head at him. "I'm sore but fine." His gaze travels down my body, assessing. Everywhere his gaze lands, I feel a spark. I pull my cloak tighter.

He quickly glances away and clears his throat. "He staged the whole thing." His voice is sharp enough to sting. "It's an old trick he's used many times. He feeds on trust. He pays cutthroats to attack, then swoops in as savior so you'll follow him anywhere."

"Stop it!" Calliope's face crumples, hurt and defiant all at once. "He wouldn't do that."

"Calli." I rise on shaky legs and step between them, pulse hammering. "Let's hear Ren out."

The prince takes a deep breath, shoulders rigid, then scrubs a hand across his jaw as though leashing himself. When he speaks again, his tone is patient. "You couldn't have known. We grew up together. He was one of my court. A rare and gifted individual whom I used to trust, too."

Calliope's defiance melts, leaving only grief etched across her face. She turns away, blinking hard. My heart wrenches for her. For me. For the way Marrow's lies have tangled around us so easily. "How do I break the connection?" I ask.

Ren sighs, a sound of weariness. "Other than to burn the blood he took, I don't know. Until we can find him and that cloth, he'll be able to tap into your dreams. Possibly even your visions."

I clench my blistered palms into fists, the pain setting off a vow already taking root inside me. I'll find a way to sever him. To cut him from my dreams and burn the tether he's forged. *He won't use me again.*

Calliope busies herself with stoking the fire, movements brittle. "Yes, well, first, we need breakfast. We can't hunt him or the Story Thief until all of us are in better shape."

"Let me," Ren says, and when she moves aside, he holds out his hands, and the flames turn into a proper fire.

She flicks a glance at me. "Impressive. I'll see what I can gather for us in the garden. There might still be a few vegetables." She sets off to an overgrown patch of ground behind the house's ruins. I ache for her, but I can't soothe her grief when my own is raw.

I reach for my satchel, relieved to find my quest journal inside. Ren crouches near me, close enough that his cloak brushes my leg. His voice drops to a murmur only I can hear. "I can help your wounds. The burns, the ribs." His hand takes one of mine, and he examines my blisters. That's when I notice his palms are also covered with them. "Dragon fire heals swiftly, if you'll let me."

His touch causes a shiver to roll through me. My throat tightens, and I turn his hand over to compare our wounds. They're a mirror for each other. "How did this happen?"

"In Jairton, I was trying to repair a cracked ward on a vault. Cimarron's shadows attacked me."

"Cimarron?"

A nod. "At least Marrow was good for one thing—he told me his name. The Story Thief is Solander Cimarron." He peeks at me through a lock of hair. "Do you know him?"

I turn the name over in my mind. "No, do you?"

"I don't." His thumb strokes over the pulse point on my wrist. "How did you receive your burns?"

"I saw the shadows attacking you." At his raised brow, I tell him the story of the vision I had. Of the sigil burning my palm. Of more blisters appearing in the dream-nightmare. "We're connected in many ways, it seems."

"This is my fault." He takes my other hand, holding both now. Mine are small compared to his. "Please let me heal you."

I peer at his temple and the wound there so like mine. "Why not use it on yourself?"

His gaze flicks to the ground, rueful. "Dragon fire cannot heal what was born of dragon blood. My fire burns too hot in my own veins. To use it inward is to consume myself. But on another..." His hands squeeze mine gently. "It can mend what would otherwise linger."

The thought of his hands on me, fire coursing through my skin, makes my heart flutter, a startled bird beating against my ribcage. "Will it hurt?"

"Yes." His honesty is blunt, but his voice softens. "For only a breath or two. Then the pain will fade."

The choice hangs heavy. Pride wars with need, with the ache chewing my ribs, the blisters making even holding the journal a challenge. His gaze holds mine, and in it I see kindness. Solidarity. My heart gives that tug. "I trust you."

He shifts even closer, his warmth flooding the air between us. Once again, I'm amazed at his size. His massive shoulders, his solid chest, his thighs that look carved from granite. He releases my hands, only to position the palms upright before he hovers over them. "Ready?"

I bite my lower lip, finding myself lost in his eyes. The sun's first rays lighten the heavy purple-gray of the night and cut through the forest. It's just enough to see the blue in them. The color is clear sapphire, filled with his inner fire, I suppose.

"Breathe," he whispers.

Fire flares through me, sharp and consuming, pain lancing like a spear. I bite down on a cry, but his hands grip mine, anchoring me to him so I don't pull away.

It's over in a heartbeat, leaving me winded. He cradles my hands in his, continuing to murmur words of comfort. The heat from his large hands begins to supersede the heat from the fire, until all that's left is a gentle buzz.

"Now, for your ribs," he says.

His touch is careful, reverent, like I might shatter under it. The intimacy of the moment is awkward, but he catches my eye, and I refocus on those beautiful blue orbs. As his fingers undo the cloth wrapped around me, a shudder runs through me.

"I'll make it as painless as I can," he offers.

I nod. "Just do it. I can handle it."

"It might be better if you lie down."

On top of my cloak, I try to find a comfortable spot. It's useless. Although my tunic is between his hand and the skin covering my ribcage, it feels as if there's nothing there, that I'm bared to him. His hand comes to rest just under my breast.

His eyes never waver from mine. "Try to relax. Let it in." *Let me in.*

He doesn't speak the last words, yet I hear them as if he has. For a breath, I wonder if I'm being naive again. Stupid. Foolish. Marrow's deception has undermined my confidence and natural intuition.

But the tug, our connection, won't quit. I can't resist it any more than I can resist the call of my quest. It coils through me, and my body trembles with recognition.

Ren hesitates. Blinks. Did he feel it, too?

*It's the quest*, I assure myself. It's letting me know I'm on the right path. That's all. Nothing more.

The fire tears through my ribs, and I arch up off the ground, crying out. It surges through my entire chest, causing my heartbeat to stop, then restart with a hard thud. White-hot agony burns the bones and tissue, and I clamp down my teeth to keep from issuing another cry.

And then it ebbs. When I blink up at Ren, his forehead is beaded with sweat. His full lips have thinned into a line. His eyes are closed, and a divot has buried itself between his brows.

The ache in my ribs dulls. My temple no longer throbs. My lungs expand without tearing. I release a quiet laugh of relief. "Thank you," I whisper.

His face hovers above mine, still drawn tight with concentration as he opens his eyes. They are alight with dragon fire, and something else that seems just as dangerous. Concern for me is evident in his gaze, the tic under his eye, and his clamped jaw. "It's my pleasure."

For a long moment, neither of us moves. His hand remains on my ribcage, his focus dropping to my lips. I lift a hand to caress his cheek, and then Calliope returns.

"I found wild onions, and Devlin—or Marrow, whatever his name is—left the fishing line in the stream. We caught more fish without trying." She pulls up when she sees me lying on the ground with Ren hovering over me. "Am I interrupting something?"

The moment over, I scramble to sit up. Ren tries to help me, but I brush off his efforts and clasp my journal as if I were writing in it. Which is an obvious lie. "Ren healed my injuries." I scoot away from him a bit and find I can't look him in the eye. "Thank you," I say again.

He tries to hide a grin. "I can see it helped. Eat something salty. Dragon fire burns water out of you."

Realizing I sat up without discomfort, I glance down at my ribs, then lift my head and smile. "That's amazing. I feel good as new."

Better, even.

Calliope clucks and sets the fish onto fry. Ren clears his throat and mutters about taking his horse to the stream to get a drink.

When he's out of earshot, Calliope lowers her voice as she cleans off the onions and adds them to the pan of fish. "What just happened?"

I fiddle with my journal, my satchel, my cloak. "I told you, Ren used his dragon fire to heal my wounds."

Her look suggests she knows I'm not telling her the full truth. "And?"

"And what?"

"Did he kiss you?"

"What?" I stand and fasten the cloak around me, dusting off the grass and soil. "Of course not. Why would he do that?"

"You're blushing. Something happened."

I wave her suspicion away. "Don't be ridiculous." But I hasten toward Layla and lead her to the stream as well. I must escape my sister.

Ren is cleaning the dried blood from his face and neck.

I knot the reins onto the saddle and give Layla her lead. She sniffs at the stallion, making him lift his head, but he stands absolutely still until she dips her head to drink. "How far is Jairton?" I ask.

Ren stiffens, eyes shuttering. "It doesn't matter. There's nothing there for you."

I study my palms, no longer blistered. Not even a scar mars the skin. "But the quest is sending me there."

Ren stands and searches through the saddlebags on his horse. "It was pointing you there because I was there. That's all."

Now, he's here. With me. What's our next step to stopping the Story Thief and rebuilding his kingdom? "Are you sure? If we were both directed to Jair—"

He cuts me off, pawing through the satchel. He pulls out a waded up shirt, scrunches up his nose, and tosses it aside. Next comes a leather pouch with jerky. He tucks that back inside. "I'm sure. There's nothing there for us."

He's too adamant, and still won't look at me. I pat the stallion's neck. "What aren't you telling me, Your Highness?"

His hands stop. "Please don't call me that."

"Please be honest with me."

His silence makes my frustration surge hot, nearly as sharp as my vow against Marrow. I think of Father and his tricks to keep me safe. Is that what Ren thinks he's doing? Keeping me from Cimarron and whatever dangers he presents?

Leading Layla back to the firepit, my frustration only grows. I pull my satchel close, tugging free the quest journal. Ink and paper won't lie to me, not the way men do.

My hand trembles as I write: *What's in Jairton? Is it still my quest to go there?*

The page stays blank. My heart feels like it might collapse under yet another disappointment.

Calliope glances at me from under her brows as she places breakfast in front of me. "Is everything okay?"

Before I can reply, faint strokes appear on the parchment, curling and stark.

*Go to Jairton. Your destiny awaits.*

The words blaze, sure as fate.

I grip the journal tight, my stomach twisting, Ren's warning pounding in my ears. The quest or the prince...

Which do I heed?

# CHAPTER SIXTEEN
## DESSALYN | THE STUBBORN HEART

*Each choice is a thread—pull the wrong one, and the whole story unravels.*

THE MORNING TURNS THIN and gray, the kind of light that makes every shadow stretch longer than it should. The ruined wall casts a crooked silhouette across the clearing. Smoke still snakes from the fire pit, but it smells more of ash than of fish and onion now. We've eaten what little Calliope managed to squeeze together, though the taste of it turns to dust in my mouth.

Ren hasn't spoken much. He sits apart, with a knife and whetstone from the satchel, sharpening the blade with long, deliberate strokes. Each rasp of steel against stone grates along my spine. Calliope hums as she tidies up, but even that feels forced.

"How did you know Marrow traveled with us?" I ask.

Ren's hands move with slow precision. He hesitates for a moment before he replies. "When I left Longmere, I went after a lead on the Story Thief." His eyes stay fixed on the edge of steel. "I found more than I expected."

The rasp of stone on metal continues to ravage my nerves. "What?"

He pauses, then lifts his gaze. "Marrow."

My stomach knots. "He was there?"

"Briefly. He told me the Thief's name, but not much else. Later, a mage attacked me. He's also working for Cimarron. The mage carried a staff that drained fire and nearly broke me. But before I finished him, he told me something I couldn't ignore."

Calliope leans forward, her curls spilling over her shoulders. "What?"

Ren sets the sword aside, his expression tightening like a trap springing shut. "That Marrow had already wrapped his dream-threads around Dessa. That he was walking her dreams."

My throat goes dry. I force myself to whisper, "That's why you came."

He nods once. "I couldn't stay in Jairton knowing he had his hooks in you. If he can slip into your visions, he sees what you see. He can glimpse any future you stumble into. He'll carry it straight back to the Thief."

Calliope's lips part, horror blanching her face. "He knows we're helping you."

"Yes," Ren says grimly. "And that's why I had to find you."

The words fall heavy, and for a heartbeat, all I hear is the weak crackle of embers and the pounding of my own heart. I can't carry it any longer. The journal's words blaze in my mind no matter how I try to smother them. *Go to Jairton. Your destiny awaits.*

I draw a breath, steadying myself. My chest aches, not from the injury that Ren has healed, but from what I'm about to do. "I'm going on to Jairton." My voice doesn't shake, though my palms dampen.

The whetstone stops mid-scrape. Ren lifts his head, eyes narrowing like storm clouds. "You can't."

Calliope looks between us, her hands diving into the pockets of her skirt. "Why?"

I shake my head, squaring my shoulders. "The quest has spoken. I don't have a choice."

"You always have a choice," Ren counters. "This one may cost you everything."

"The journal has spoken." I hold out the journal. "It's the next step. It's my destiny."

Calliope clears her throat, trying for lightness, though her eyes shine with worry. She takes the journal before Ren can and opens it, reading the last entry. A soft sigh escapes her lips. "You must then."

Ren's jaw tightens, a muscle ticking there. "I don't care what that journal says. Cimarron is waiting. He wants you, Dessalyn. You can't go."

Calliope hands the book back to me. "Sorry, prince. Everyone knows what happens to those who ignore their quest. They can never find their happily ever after."

He rises to his full height, cloak shifting with the movement, and I swear he seems more dragon than man, more shadowed. "And we know what might happen if you walk straight into the Story Thief's hands."

The words dig under my skin. Do we truly know? Or are we only guessing?

Torture? Death? Or worse—being forced to write for him, to twist stories until the world crowns him king of every tale. The not-knowing gnaws at me more than certainty ever could.

Maybe Ren is mistaken.

For a moment, I almost fold. Ren's presence, his certainty, presses against my chest, daring me to back down. He believes so fiercely that it makes me want to believe him, too.

But I can't.

I pace a few steps away, boots crunching in the already trampled grass. How do I make him understand? Just like with Father, destiny isn't enough for him. He's reacting out of fear and a need to protect me. I know he believes in prophecies and that he wants more than anything to save his kingdom, yet he fears the Story Thief and what he might do if he catches me more.

But, it's not only Cimarron who might be there. Marrow might be, too. If he is, I must break his hold on me and my dreams. I stop pacing and face Ren. "Did Marrow leave us to go to Jairton to meet up with the Story Thief then?"

Ren starts to answer, stops himself. "It's possible."

It's more than possible by the look on his face. "Then I have no choice. The connection he forged with me has to be severed. If I do nothing, he'll walk into every dream I have. Every vision. He'll see everything, including you."

Ren's eyes flash, a fire sparking there, but he says nothing.

"You said it yourself," I press. "He took my blood. He'll use it, and me, to help the Story Thief. If Jairton is where he's gone, then Jairton is where I end this."

Calliope comes to stand next to me. "She's right. If we don't stop him, Cimarron will always have the upper hand. She can't control her dreams and visions any more than I can control the weather."

Ren looks between us, gaze heavy. His jaw works, a dozen words locked behind his teeth.

I lift the journal, flipping it open to the page where the words wrote themselves into the parchment. I hold it out like proof, like law. "This is where my quest leads, and mine is inexorably entangled with yours. Whether you come or not, I'm following my destiny."

He stays silent. Glares. I glare back, but the silence gnaws at me. His shoulders are rigid, his jaw set like stone.

Fine. If he won't say anything, I will. I tuck the journal tight against my chest and take a step toward him. "What else do you have to do, Ren? Tell me. Your kingdom is still in ruins, and every step you've taken on your own has failed. Cimarron is always a step ahead of you." My voice quavers, but I push harder. "I'm a Lorekeeper. If you could do it on your own with the Dragon Language, you'd have done it already. You need me to restore what he's taken from you, don't you?"

His eyes flare, the blue catching the weak light. I think he might roar back. Instead, he folds his arms and glares down at me. "This isn't about what I need. It's about keeping you safe."

Ah, there it is. "You don't know what Cimarron is planning for me. You're simply assuming he wants me because of what Marrow did." The words sting as they leave my lips, because part of me knows they're not true. "What I need is to finish my quest. To follow the Lore. And I need you to stand beside me, not in front of me, trying to block the road."

Calliope lifts her chin from where she's crouched by the fire pit. "Quests don't bend for anyone, not even princes."

Ren's cloak shifts as he turns away, but not before I catch the tightness in his throat, the battle playing out there.

I step into the space. "Come with me. Use your sword. Use your dragon fire. Protect me, if that's what you think you must do. But don't you dare tell me to stay behind while you fight this war alone."

The air between us sizzles. His chest heaves, his fists flex. For a dizzying heartbeat, I can almost feel the dragon inside him, straining against his ribs. "You're the most stubborn woman I've ever met," he mutters.

I lift my chin. "Get used to it."

Calli snorts.

Ren's glare lingers, simmering like banked fire. He looks ready to argue again, but I'm done waiting for him to come around. I turn on my heel and stride to Layla. My ribs don't protest the movement—thanks to him—but my pulse hammers hard enough to make up for it. I yank my satchel off the ground and march straight to his stallion.

His voice cracks across the clearing like a whip. "What are you doing?"

I throw the satchel over the stallion's back and cinch the strap. "Getting to Jairton faster."

His boots thud on the ground as he follows. "That's my horse."

"Not anymore." I grab Calliope's satchel and toss it up beside mine. "If you refuse to ride with us, then he'll carry me."

"You can't just take him." Ren looks as shocked as his voice sounds. "He's not a cart horse for you to load with your baggage."

I spin, cloak whipping behind me. "Watch me."

For a moment, we lock eyes—his blazing with fury, mine with defiance. The tension buzzes between us like a struck chord.

Calliope, bless her meddling heart, pipes up behind me. "Honestly, you two sound like an old married couple. Just get on the horse together and argue on the road."

Ren chokes, mutters something that sounds very much like a curse.

I whirl toward my sister. "Absolutely not. You'll ride with me."

But she's already tugging Layla's reins and mounting up. "Nope. I'll follow behind. You two clearly have...issues to work out."

"Calliope!" My voice cracks with outrage.

Before I can argue further, Ren stuffs the knife and whetstone in his satchel and steps in close. His large hand clamps around my waist, and with insulting ease, he hoists me off my feet and sets me astride the stallion.

I gasp, clutching at the saddle. "What do you think you're doing?"

He swings up behind me in a fluid motion, all heat and solid muscle pressing against my back. The world narrows to the scent of smoke and steel clinging to him, the tickle of his breath brushing the back of my neck. My heart stutters.

And then it happens—that tug. The one that's haunted my dreams and has been active since he arrived. Low in my belly, sharp as hunger, shooting upward to lodge hot and insistent in my chest. It isn't just the rush of riding double or the intimacy of his body against mine. It's something older. Stranger. A force that feels written into my bones, binding me to him.

My breath stumbles, catches. I don't want it to be real, don't want to admit what my body already knows. The Lore guides quests, not hearts. This pull...this can't be destiny, too. Can it?

His thighs bracket mine, his hand steady at my hips. Our connection thrums, undeniable, as though the Lore itself is binding us together in this saddle.

His breath ghosts my ear. "You said we're going to Jairton. You'd better hang on."

He snaps the reins. The stallion surges forward, the clearing and Calliope's smug face blurring behind us as we hit the road.

# CHAPTER SEVENTEEN
## DESSALYN | THE SPACE BETWEEN HEARTBEATS

*The road carries shadows; some ride with you.*

THE STALLION WANTS TO fly. Every muscle under me trembles with the strain of it, and each time Ren reins him in, the motion jolts me harder against the prince's chest.

My back presses flush to him, my shoulders brushing the solid wall of his chest. His thighs frame mine so perfectly that it feels like I've been carved to fit here.

I try not to notice. Stars above, I try. But every sway of the saddle, every lean into the curve of the road presses me closer still. His breath warms the loose tendrils of hair at my neck, and the tug in my heart—the one I refuse to name—burns sharper each time.

The road winds east through a forest still heavy with morning breath. Mist clings low around the roots of the trees, curling like smoke over moss and bracken, while the canopy drips from last night's dew. The air smells sharp with pine and damp earth, tinged with the faint bite of chimney smoke from villages hidden behind hills.

Somewhere deeper in the woods, a jay shrieks. I jump, and the stallion's ears flick in annoyance. I can't blame him. The whole forest feels too awake, too watchful, as if even the shadows are keeping tally of our passing.

The horse moves like a creature bred from shadow and fire, hooves biting into the dirt, head tossing at the slow pace. I sympathize with his impatience. I, too, am longing to race ahead, but Layla can't keep up.

She and Calliope plod behind us, the mare stubborn as ever, her hooves clopping steady as a drum. Calliope leans forward over her neck, whispering encouragements, but the mare ignores her as only an old horse can.

Ren reins in the stallion with an easy hand, much like he lifted me into the saddle. He sits balanced and fluid, his body answering the horse before the stallion even makes a move. It's infuriating, how natural it is for him—like the leather and steel are part of him, like the horse was forged to obey his command.

The prince was born for the saddle. He's at home in one, while my thighs ache from gripping too tightly, and my spine jars against every uneven patch of road. One moment, I'm chilled from the cool forest air, and the next, the heat of Ren's body seeps through my cloak and tunic until it feels impossible to tell where his warmth ends and mine begins.

I try to steady my breathing, to find a rhythm that's mine alone. It's impossible. Even his heartbeat feels as though it's entwined with mine.

The forest whispers around us. Birds trill from the canopy, wings flashing silver as they dart through slants of light. Squirrels skitter along the branches, knocking the occasional acorn to the ground.

Beneath it all is the occasional murmur of other travelers. The creak of wagon wheels, the clop of hooves, the hum of voices carrying through the mist remind me that we're not alone.

A peddler trundles past, his cart loaded with bolts of faded cloth. He raises a hand in greeting, but I pull my hood lower over my brow. Calliope, ever friendlier even after Marrow's trick, smiles back as she urges Layla along a few paces behind.

"Morning to you," the man calls. His voice is bright, but his eyes—his eyes are vague, unfocused, the same dazed look I saw in the hamlet. The sight twists my stomach.

Ren only gives the man a curt nod, utterly unbothered. I turn quickly away, my hand tightening around my quest journal in my lap.

That calm grates at me worse than the saddle. How can he sit there so steady, so unshaken, while every passerby makes my pulse spike? Marrow looked harmless, too. He was dashing and compassionate. Helpful. He fooled me once. He won't do it again.

A group of farmers appears next—baskets strapped to their backs, children trailing with wooden hoops and sticks. Some gape at us—at Ren and the stallion, at least—and a few wave. They look ordinary, harmless, but what if the Story Thief has written them that way?

The thought needles at me until I have to bite my lip. Ordinary is a story, too. A mask, if the Thief wants it to be.

*Is* he able to create stories from nothing? I'm doubtful of such a power. If he could do so, he would create an entire army. Instead, his power comes from erasing what's already there.

If only I understood why.

Ren's thigh brushes mine, a quiet reminder of his nearness. He doesn't so much as glance at the farmers, his attention fixed on the road ahead. Am I having any effect on him at all, like the way he's affecting me? Isn't he worried about Marrow appearing? Or some other minion sent by Cimarron, like the mage he told us about?

Maybe that's it. He doesn't fear because he trusts his own strength. Because if another attack comes, he believes he can handle it.

I want to be like that. To be confident in my abilities. What will that take?

I shift against the saddle, trying to ease the ache in my thighs, and nearly groan when it only presses me closer to Ren. The warmth of him is maddening, distracting, dangerous. If I keep letting myself notice it, I'll lose my mind.

So I do the only thing I know to do—I open my journal.

Its familiar weight steadies me. Ink and parchment never lie, never betray, never confuse me the way people do. I rest it between the pommel and my lap and pull the ink bottle and quill from inside my cloak. I balance all of it against the jolt of the horse's stride, and force my focus onto the page.

"What happened when your kingdom first began to disappear?" I ask Ren. "Who did it start with? How fast did it spread?"

He peers over my shoulder. "What are you writing?"

"We need to get down to business." I jot down the questions as if recording them for the Lore itself. "The details are crucial to understanding how Cimarron operates."

Silence stretches between us, filled only by the steady clop of hooves and the soft hiss of the stallion's breath. Then I remember. "You can't speak about it, can you? Not directly to me? That's why you choked up in Longmere. Why you could only tell me your story through the journals."

He nods. "Cimarron cursed me to keep me from seeking help."

I must work around it, then. "Give me your pendant."

"Why?"

I shift and hold out my hand. "Trust me."

He lifts it from around his head and hands it over. I dip the quill's nib into the ink and close my eyes. The Lore is not to be tampered with or corrupted for one's own gain, but breaking a curse on another is acceptable if the curse interferes with their story. In my mind, I tap into the Language, asking Vellicor's permission. The stallion clips along. The birds continue to sing. I hover my quill over the broken dragon and wait.

The quill vibrates. My request is granted. I lower the nib to the back of the pendant and draw. A sigil forms. Ren makes a quiet huff. I hand the necklace back. "There. Let's see if this works."

He slips it on, fingers the pendant. "It started small—a village in the north. People woke with names missing, stories half-remembered, their histories vanished."

When he pauses, I glance back at him. "Are you okay?"

He massages his throat. "I don't know what magic that is, but it's amazing."

"The Lore Language is filled with rules and restrictions, but a simple curse breaker rune is as much Fae magic as it is Lore."

Joy lights his face. "You are handy to have around."

I blush and fiddle with the quill. "Go on, tell me the details about the erasure."

"Like I said, it started small. Within a month, the entire place was blank."

A shiver trails my spine. "And no one looked into it? Tried to stop it?"

I feel more than see him shake his head. "How do you fight what you can't see? By the time we realized it wasn't sickness or madness, it had already swallowed towns whole."

I scratch furiously at the page, ink blotting from my haste. "Why your kingdom?"

He doesn't answer. I glance over my shoulder, and our faces are close enough to touch. "I don't know," he says. "But the old stories claim it was the first to be born into this realm. Maybe the first kingdom to be born is the first one you need to erase?"

My gaze lands on his lips. The stallion jars, and our mouths nearly brush. My pulse spikes as if the quest itself means to stitch us together. I whip my head back around, cinching my thighs tighter on the beast, and heave a great breath. "That...uh...makes sense. If Drakenholt is the foundation of the realm, removing it makes the other kingdoms unstable. More vulnerable. Like the main seam in a tunic—unravel it and the other threads are easy to pull out."

A heavy silence descends. He releases a sigh that causes the strands of my hair to shift and sends a heated blush over the back of my neck. "It was midsummer." His voice takes on an edge. "The bells had just rung for the equinox festival. We were at the table—my father, my mother, my brother, and I. My parents were trying to pretend everything was still fine. They'd called in their finest scientists, their smartest advisors, to work out what was happening and fix it. Laughter still hung in the rafters when I noticed a toy slipping from Rordan's hand." His breath rasps like a sword dragged from its sheath. "Not because he dropped it. Because his fingers weren't there anymore."

My stomach plummets.

"He looked at me," Ren continues, sadness tightening his voice, "and his eyes held mine as if begging me to do something. I tried, but...I didn't know what to do. His face blurred, his tiny voice cried out, and then..." His hands flex on the reins, his chest bumping my back as he heaves a hard exhale. "Then there was nothing. Just an empty chair and a toy on the floor."

The words dig into me. The stallion's stride feels too steady, too normal, when the memory is anything but.

I scrawl notes, my eyes blurring with tears. "Ren... I'm so sorry."

"My father roared as if he could call him back. My mother wept into silence. And I—" He breaks off. "I swore then I would never let another be taken while I drew breath. I yelled at them. My parents. The advisors and the scientists. I railed at them. I begged them to bring him back. It did no good. None of them understood what was happening."

The words strike at me as the scene plays out in my mind. My chest aches with the weight of it, with the weight he's carried alone. I want to turn and reach for him, but I grip the journal instead.

I think of losing Calliope. Father. "I can't imagine—" My voice cracks. The urge to press my palm over his heart tugs at me. "How awful."

"Mother went next. The midsummer bells turned into death knells. That's when I begged Father to summon your mother. He said it was impossible, but by then, his mind was confused. Clouded. He was grieving and yet didn't register why. I believed he thought it impossible because he was confused. I didn't realize he knew your mother was...dead."

My heart squeezes. "You knew Mom's prophecy was coming true."

He leans closer, his breath brushing my ear. "If only I'd listened to her. I might have been able to save them."

I want to deny it's true, but it may well be. My quill hovers, blotting the same spot until the parchment bleeds. "Why is Jairton important to him? There must be a reason."

He hesitates. "Some say it was once part of Drakenholt. Maybe he thinks it still holds power."

His tone is dry, flat. I glance back at him. His gaze is locked on the road, unreadable. The muscle ticking in his jaw reveals there's more. "What is it?"

"What?" He doesn't look at me. "Nothing."

I decide to try a different tactic. "My biggest question is, why is Cimarron erasing kingdoms? If he wants to rule them, he'll need subjects."

"Drakenholt has—*had*—too much power for him to rule us. I think we were a threat to his plans. Erasing us was the only way to remove that threat."

"But he hasn't managed to erase you." I sketch the outline of a dragon in the margin. "There must be a reason."

Again, I sense his hesitation. A woodchuck sits in the ditch, chewing on an apple and watching us pass. "I suppose he hasn't found the story I'm tied to."

I scribble that down, tap the end of the quill against my chin. "What story is that?"

"I don't know."

The reply comes a bit too quickly. He may not know the answer, but he knows something.

"The erasure is bleeding over into Evermere. What threat could our peaceful kingdom pose to him?"

"Not your entire kingdom. You. Your Fae heritage—what do you know of it?"

"Mom was Fae, and she passed on her Lore Language abilities to Calliope and me, although my sister's connection to it isn't as strong as mine. It hasn't seemed to have awakened fully in her. But she also has skills with animals and herbs. I have visions."

"Your Language sings differently in your blood than the Dragon Language sings in mine. I hear it when you speak. I feel it when we communicate in writing."

I stiffen. "What about that makes Cimarron want me?"

His thigh presses lightly against mine as the stallion sidesteps a rut. "Another story we must investigate. Cimarron has marked you for a reason, Dessa. Perhaps your heritage is part of it."

My quill scratches harder against the parchment as I make a note. I hate that he might be right, but it isn't only his words that unmoor me. It's the shadow in his voice when he speaks of his baby brother, of his mother, of the festival bells turning to a death knell. It's the way his hands grip the reins like they're the only thing keeping him from unraveling.

Renwick Ravelle, crown prince of Drakenholt, wielder of dragon fire—he is also a man who lost his brother at the dinner table, a son who watched his parents dissolve into silence.

I feel it in my bones—that emptiness carved into him is the same shape that could one day be carved into me if Calliope were taken. The same grief waits for me if I fail.

The journal trembles, ink bleeding in loops I can't quite finish. Because for all his power, for all his dragon fire, Ren is fragile in ways I never expected, and more so in ways I recognize.

The tug in my chest—sharp, undeniable—twists deeper. This is about him, a kingdom, and the bond threading between us, one I don't yet understand but can't ignore.

And stars help me, that bond makes me want to keep him safe as much as he wants the same for me.

# Chapter Eighteen
## Renwick | The Weight of Secrets

*Fire cannot burn away the truth forever.*

THE STALLION TOSSES HIS head as we break through the trees into a clearing. Sunlight spills across open grass, gold and honey over a patchwork of late-day shadows. At the far end, a spring bubbles from the rocks, tumbling into a shallow pool rimmed with cattails and rushes.

It looks peaceful. Peace is so rare for me these days, I soak it in.

The stallion prances, impatient for water. I swing down first, and when I turn, Dessa is already shifting in the saddle, her journal pressed tight to her chest. She's determined to dismount on her own, of course—she always is—but her boots hesitate against the stirrup. Before she can slip, I reach up, grip her waist, and lift her down.

She stiffens at the contact, but her body fits against mine like we've done this a hundred times. For a breath, I hold her, every line of her pressed against me—her cloak brushing my arms, her breath catching, the faint scent of ink clinging to her.

"Thank you," she whispers, her gaze flicking away, cheeks tinged pink.

I let go reluctantly, cursing myself as if I've been caught stealing. The dragon inside me rouses at it. The man does too. I want to protect her with every ounce of fire I have left, even though she has every right to hate me.

I force myself to step back, to gather the reins. "Careful. He's restless."

She nods, already scanning the clearing with those wide, relentless eyes that see everything and forgive nothing.

We lead the horse toward the spring. The water gurgles, bright and cold. I crouch to cup it in my blistered palms. My skin still stings, but I barely register it. I healed her, and that's what matters.

Layla and Calliope lumber into the clearing.

Beside me, Dessa smiles at her sister, then kneels and trails her fingers over the surface. Ripples shiver outward. "It's beautiful here," she says softly.

"Yes," I answer, though I'm not looking at the water. Her hair catches the late sun, the stubborn lift of her chin, the way she carries both exhaustion and destiny as though they are her birthright.

They are, I guess. "Tell me about quests. In Evermere, how are they given?"

Her face brightens. "They arrive when the Lore decides. Vellicor, our sentient book, relays them to us, and we transcribe them to parchment. Those who are deemed ready receive a nudge from the Fates to travel to our mercantile. Some are excited for their quest, others resist, but all are sent on their way with their destiny in hand."

"How does this book, Vellicor, choose them? Is it enchanted by Fae magic?"

She nods. "It's a tool of the Language."

"How does it decide who receives a quest?"

"Anyone can be chosen. Most in Evermere will be."

"Anyone?" I echo. "Even common-born?"

Her lips purse. "The book draws no difference between royal blood and not. All are worthy of a quest. Why?"

I internally wince at my poor choice of words. My kingdom was built with a system that divides society into hereditary classes. I come from privilege, and yet, my royal bloodline has done me no good in this fight. "In Drakenholt, it's different. Quests are rare. Sacred. Only certain nobles marked at birth are—*were*—chosen." It's hard to remember none are left but me. "To fail was to bring shame not just on yourself, but on your entire bloodline."

Her full lips part, surprise shadowing her features. "That's harsh."

"Cruel even, sometimes." My hand tightens on my knee. "I've seen men twist themselves trying to fulfill a quest. And if they failed…" I cut myself off, the truth of my own false prophecy and failure ripping these peaceful few moments to shreds.

She tilts her head, studying me as though she hears the words I refuse to say. "Our quests are sacred, too, because they are our destiny. Those of us with Fae blood are especially called to desire one. It's a calling, a purpose. Failing to complete one is like cutting off an arm or leg. Our quest becomes a part of us."

I look away, into the water. "Even if it leads you to truths you don't want to learn? That will change your world forever?"

"Even so." Her voice turns curious. She speaks softly, encouragingly. "Is there something you know about my quest that you haven't shared?"

Behind us, Calliope laughs. "She's so stubborn!" We both glance at her, and she points at the horse. "She refuses to drink."

Dessa takes the stallion's reins and leads him to stand beside the mare. "Maybe Firebrand can motivate her."

"Firebrand?" I ask. "You've named him?"

She pats his neck, and her voice is teasing. "Were you going to call him 'horse' forever?"

I smile. Firebrand chooses that moment to whinny and stomp, his dark eyes glued to the water. The late afternoon sun hits the surface, making it glitter like a thousand diamonds.

At first, it's nothing but a ripple. Yet Firebrand and Layla both become agitated. They snort and stomp, and Firebrand jerks his reins from Dessa's grasp.

My gut tightens, and I come to my feet. Scales flash beneath the water like shards of emerald glass.

"That's beautiful," Dessa says. "What is it?"

"Move back," I command, shifting to put myself between her and the pool. My hand drops to the hilt of my sword. "Take the horses," I instruct Calliope. "Take them to the tree line."

Another flash. A tail, long and finned, cleaves the surface before vanishing again. The stallion screams, rearing. Calliope gasps, struggling to keep hold of his reins. He jerks hard, trying to break free as Layla trots off toward the trees.

Smart horse.

Dessa clutches my arm. "Is it dangerous?"

I pat her hand, then give her a gentle shove toward her sister, still wrestling with Firebrand. "From the horses' reactions, I'd say yes."

The water bulges. Inch by inch, something rises. First, a crest of slick hair, long as riverweed, dripping black rivulets. Then a brow plated with scales. Eyes like two lanterns glowing green, brighter than any mortal gaze, emerge next.

Those eyes lock straight onto Dessa.

She staggers back a step, breath hissing from her lungs. "Stars above, what is that thing?"

Calliope gasps, too, her hands flying to her mouth. "That's a...a Mireling." The stallion dances sideways, and she stumbles, nearly falling, but catches herself. Her voice comes out panicked. "But that's impossible. They belong to Seabright and its deep waters. They don't venture inland or reside in springs. They're half-drowned wraiths, cursed with a hunger for Fae flesh."

The creature's lips peel back, revealing teeth like a shark's. It surges forward, dragging itself hand over hand through the reeds. Webbed fingers clutch the stalks, ripping them free. A gurgle bubbles from its throat—words, not quite human, strung together in a wet, choking tongue.

Still, its gaze stays on Dessa.

I draw my steel, the blade singing. "Get behind me!"

Instead, she shoves her journal into Calliope's hands and pulls a knife from her belt. Her chin lifts, fierce and stubborn.

"Dessa!" I bark. "Do as I say!"

"I won't run from it," she says, far too calmly. "If it wants a Fae for dinner, it'll have to fight both of us for the chance."

*By the stars, she's infuriating.*

By the same stars, she's magnificent.

The Mireling bellows, a half-growl, half-rush of water through a cave. Its long body writhes, scales shifting as it slides closer to shore.

"Don't let it sing!" Calliope cries. Her voice is high with panic. "Their voices immobilize you so they can drag you under the water!"

The Mireling gurgles again, throat swelling, about to loose that very sound. I surge forward, sword raised. "Cover your ears!"

Beside me, Dessa doesn't flinch. She raises the hood of her cloak and tightens it firmly around her head. Knife steady, she plants her boots in the mud and stares down the nightmare crawling for her.

I curse under my breath. She'll get herself killed. She'll get *me* killed trying to save her.

But I'll save her anyway.

The Mireling lets out its garbled cry, a sound like drowning lungs. My blade flashes, slicing the air between us. It lunges, faster than any swamp beast has a right to. Clawed fingers rake for Dessa.

"Ren!" she cries, ducking aside. Her cloak snaps, a blur of dark green.

I slam my sword across the creature's forearm. Steel bites scale with a screech. Black ichor sprays, sizzling where it touches the reeds. The smell is salt and rot, as if the sea itself has turned sour.

The thing reels back but doesn't fall. Its eyes lock on Dessa again, glowing brighter. It wants her, not me. *Always her.*

Over my shoulder, Calliope shouts, "Strike the gills! Just below the jawline—left side!"

The Mireling lashes out with its tail, catching me across the ribs. Pain detonates in my side. I stagger, but Dessa rushes forward instead of away, her knife slashing true at the place Calliope described.

The blade cuts shallow. It's enough—the creature shrieks, a choking howl, black blood foaming from its mouth.

My heart lurches at the sight of her rushing into danger. I shove between her and the beast, sword carving downward. The Mireling thrashes, tail whipping, claws raking. One catches my shoulder, hot pain tearing through cloth and flesh.

I snarl and answer. Dragon fire leaps from my chest to my sword, licking along its edge. The blade burns, and when I thrust it into the Mireling's torso, the smell of seared scale and brine fills the air.

The creature convulses, choking on its own song. It flails back toward the water, ichor boiling where the flame touched it.

Calliope yells again, "Don't let it dive! If it returns to the spring, it'll heal and come back stronger!"

Dessa, stars damn her, doesn't hesitate. She darts past me, mud splashing as she plunges her knife into its gill again and again, both hands gripping the hilt. The Mireling shrieks, seizing up, its arms thrashing wide.

I wrench her back before it can crush her in its death throes. She slams against my chest, wild and panting, her eyes blazing. My arms lock around her, holding her tight even as she fights to go forward again.

"Enough," I growl into her hair. "You've done enough."

The Mireling flails, its body collapsing into itself, scales melting to sludge. With one last screech, it crashes back into the spring, the water boiling black before stilling. Only reeds remain, broken and smoking.

The sisters' ragged breaths and the stallion's distant snort fill the air.

Dessa sags in my arms, knife still clutched tightly. Her face is pale but fierce, her chin lifting even now. She looks like victory and defiance all at once.

*She'll be the end of me.*

I loosen my hold, though every instinct screams to keep her there. "You nearly got yourself killed," I rasp.

Her lips curve, stubborn. "I kept it from singing. I killed it." When I grunt, she adds, "With your help, of course."

Heat sparks between us, the same heat I felt when my fire surged through her wounds. I want to tell her she was magnificent. I want to tell her I'd burn a hundred Mirelings to keep her safe.

Instead, I sheath my sword with a sharp whoosh. "Next time, stay behind me."

"Next time," she retorts, still breathless, "we'll work as partners just as we did this time."

# Chapter Nineteen
## Dessalyn | Blades and Shadows

*A weapon writes a story; the question is whether you control its ink or the ink controls you.*

THE MIRELING'S BELLOW STILL rattles in my bones, but the clearing has gone quiet again.

Pulse pounding, blood rushing in my veins, I sheath my knife. The collapse of it into the reeds, the hiss of its body dissolving into brackish water, continues to echo in my mind. I doubt I'll ever forget it—those eyes, that smell, its haunting cry. Another nightmare to add to my collection.

Yet, I'm exhilarated—my heart soaring from the fight. I focus on that, rather than what runs beneath it...a current of fear, dark and cold.

That thing wanted me.

And it nearly had me.

"Dessa!"

Calliope barrels into me, nearly knocking me off my feet. Her arms wrap tight, curls tangling with my cloak. I can feel her shaking. Or maybe that's me. "You terrified me!"

I hug her back, pressing my cheek against her hair. "You saved me—*us*," I murmur. "Your knowledge—your warning about its song. If you hadn't—"

She pulls back, eyes bright and wet. "Don't you dare praise me when you went charging at it like a hunter!" Her voice wavers, half fury, half relief. I can hear the echo of Mom in it—the way she used to scold us when we climbed too high or swam too far. It hurts in a tender way.

I bite back a laugh, though my pride at facing such a fierce creature and surviving bubbles up so strongly it nearly bursts free. "It had to be stopped."

"You were reckless." Her hands ball into fists. "You could have died! It might have dragged you into the water, and I would have never seen you again. You—"

"I'm fine." I squeeze her shoulders until her lips pinch shut. "I'm standing here because of you. Remember that."

She cocks a brow. "You're still here, thanks to your good prince."

I glance at Ren, who grins, wiping his sword in the grass. "At least someone is giving me an ounce of credit."

Ignoring him, I brush damp strands of hair from her face, then peer at the horses. Layla crops calmly at the grass now, as if nothing has happened. Firebrand snorts and paws the ground, eager to be on our way. I gesture at Layla, adjusting my crooked cloak. "Mount up. We should get moving."

Ren steps up to us, broad and immovable as the oaks. He sheathes his sword, his cloak thrown back from his shoulders, his eyes running over me from head to toe as if still checking that I'm in one piece. "Not yet."

I stiffen. "We need to get to Jairton before nightfall."

"You need to learn how to use that blade properly." His gaze pins me as sharply as his sword ever could. "If you're going to throw yourself at dangerous beasts, you'll at least know how not to die in the first three seconds."

"I did just fine!" Even as I say it, my arms tremble from the effort of holding my knife steady. My legs feel like reeds in the Mireling's grip. But I won't give him that truth. I need him to see more than a girl who faced off with death and nearly lost. "Our father taught us just enough to defend ourselves."

His mouth hardens. "You would have died if I wasn't here."

The words sting. Did he not see my bravery? My quick actions? Yes, I was scared—terrified, actually—but I refuse to give him the satisfaction of admitting it. "I'm not helpless."

"No," he says flatly, "but you're untrained. And that's just as deadly."

Before I can argue further, he grabs both horses' reins and strides deeper into the clearing. "Come," he calls. "Away from the spring."

Calliope shoots me a curious glance but follows. I grind my teeth and stalk after him, my knife heavy at my hip.

Beneath a swath of shade, he shrugs out of his cloak and jacket. All that's left is a white cotton shirt, undone at the neck and revealing tan skin underneath. The sight of his shoulders—broad, muscled, moving with effortless control—steals my breath before I can stop it. A dragon sigil at his throat matches the one beneath his gold cuff.

He turns to Calliope. "Do you have a dagger?"

She blinks, then fumbles in her satchel and produces a slim blade. Mom gave it to her eons ago, but she only uses it for harvesting certain herbs. "Will this work?"

Ren frowns and sighs, but seems to resign himself to the fact that neither of us is a soldier or a fighter. "Get rid of the extra layers of clothes. Your cloaks and anything that restricts movement." He studies our skirts. "Those aren't ideal, but if you normally wear them instead of pants, it's important to understand their limitations."

He continues for another few minutes, discussing, of all things, clothing and how to use it to disable an attacker. Calliope and I exchange glances and peel off our cloaks and sweaters. We can't remove our skirts, but it's freeing to shed that weight.

"Line up about three feet apart," he instructs, gently taking my elbow to guide me to the spot he indicates. His large hand warms the skin through my thin tunic sleeve. "Good."

He plants himself in front of us, taking out his sword and explaining the different parts of it as if we're children.

"We know quite a bit about blades," I tell him, hiding my smirk. "We don't have much call to use them as scriptographers, but we are familiar with their anatomy. We sell many types at the mercantile."

"Is that so?" He holds up the sword carefully by its blade. "Describe the parts of the hilt to me."

My sister steps forward. "Oh, that's easy." She points to each part as she names it. "Pommel, grip, guard, ricasso, quillon."

I can't tell if he's impressed or not in the way he nods. She steps back, and he flips the sword with the ease of one who has spent much time with such a weapon so that the hilt now rests in his hand. "Lesson one. Grip. Not too tight, not too loose. The blade should feel like an extension of your hand."

For the next hour, he drills us. Different angles to hold our knives, depending on the damage we seek to do and our opponent's skills. How to plant one leg behind the other to balance our weight, how to shift that weight to add momentum to our thrusts. How to dodge a strike and turn an opponent's blade aside instead of trying to meet it head-on. Places to strike for maximum impact.

The air grows heavy with the scent of churned earth and pine sap. Each time I lunge, dust sprays and sticks to the sweat along my arms. My tunic clings, damp, and the rhythm of our breaths weaves with the scrape of boots in dirt and the low command of his voice.

Sweat slicks my palms and trickles down the back of my neck. Calliope collapses twice in giggles and groans, muttering she'll never survive.

Ren isn't even breathing hard, although his shirt clings to his chest, the linen stretched taut across muscle honed by years of training. His arms flex as he demonstrates a sequence of jabs, whirls, and slices. His thighs anchor him like bedrock.

"My father drilled this into me when I was barely taller than a sword," he says at one point, his tone casual but shadowed. "If you forgot a step, you started over. Again and again until the move was in your bones." Something tightens in his jaw, and I know he's seeing more than dirt and blades...he's seeing ghosts.

Sweat glistens at his temple, sliding down his cheek, then neck to vanish beneath the edge of linen. He looks carved from the same stone as the Drakenholt castle was built with, immovable and enduring, and it infuriates me that my body notices more than my mind wants it to. He moves like fire given flesh, quick, fluid, and unrelenting.

I try not to stare and fail.

"Now you," he orders, positioning my feet. His hand brushes my hip, light but sure, and the touch brands me hotter than the afternoon sun. My pulse stumbles.

Calliope faces me. I try to remember what Ren just showed us, but my brain goes blank. "I...um..."

He takes my hand and guides the knife into the first of his sequences. "Aim for the spot just under the ribs. Upward motion. Sink it in deep."

I perform the movement as Calliope tries to block my advance. I let her, of course, but then go through the steps in the air as if an actual attacker is standing there.

Ren eyes me with a dismal sigh. "You must be quicker on your feet, Dessa. You must think three strikes ahead of your opponent." He sheaths his sword and picks up a stick. He waggles his fingers at me. "Come at me."

I blink away the ridiculous attraction his honed body stirs and will myself to focus on his instructions. I launch myself at his insulting stick, and his face lights up as I complete the sequence, damaging the stick and forcing him back several feet.

"Good!" The surprise on his face lights a fire inside me. He smiles, and my heart flips. "Again!"

I realize five minutes later, as I'm going through another sequence, that I'd do just about anything to keep that smile on his face. The thought rattles me more than any strike or dodge. It's not loyalty. It's not gratitude. It's something more profound, tugging at that place in my chest.

"My turn," Calliope says, and we switch.

Ren grabs a fresh stick. "Remember your footwork," he tells her. "Don't telegraph your thrusts."

Catching my breath, I watch as my sister comes to life under his guidance. We both do.

"Are you as deft with a quill as you are with your dagger?" I blurt, my pulse continuing to hammer as I watch his muscles move.

A grin tugs at his mouth, softening his face in a way that makes my pulse trip. "Better."

Heat that has nothing to do with our workout rises in my cheeks. "We'll see, I suppose."

He gives a mock bow. "I'm at your service, storykeeper."

Calliope collapses at the base of a tree, fanning her face with her skirts. "I need a break."

Turning away from Ren to hide my flush, I sag beside her. The sun hangs low, staining the clearing amber. My body is tired, but I feel stronger. More capable.

Still, a suspicion gnaws at me. "This training," I murmur, eyeing Ren as he wipes his blade, "was it really about our protection—or a delay tactic?"

He arches a brow. "Delay tactic?" A hand goes to his chest. "I'm hurt you would presume such a thing."

Calliope smacks my leg. "What my sister means to say is, thank you. We're far from being warriors, but we do need to know how to defend ourselves."

Before I can retort, the sound of wagon wheels crunches through the trees.

Both horses lift their heads from their grazing. Ren stiffens. Calliope and I come to our feet. In my mind, I see Marrow again, remember how easily he deceived me. My hand finds the hilt of my knife without thinking.

A caravan creaks into the clearing, painted wagons bright against the fading light. Horses snort, children chatter, and the smell of spiced bread wafts from somewhere within. Two travelers—a man and a woman—stride ahead, lifting hands in greeting.

"Merry meet," the woman says. Her skirts are colorful, if a bit worn, and she sports a patchwork jacket, large hoop earrings, and a bright scarf wrapped around her head. "We're on our way south and need a place to camp for the night."

It seems as if she's asking permission. As if we somehow have rights to this clearing.

Ren keeps his hand on the pommel of his sword, even as he covertly motions for Calliope and me to stand down. "South to where?" he asks casually.

"Fablehollow," the man says. He's in tan pants and a loose, bright blue shirt with a vest. He also wears a hoop in his left ear. "It's where I'm—" His gaze lands on me and Calliope, and his eyes widen. "Wait—you're the Lorewyn sisters, aren't you?"

Calliope and I have both already straightened at the sound of our hometown. My sister nods. "Yes. You know of us?"

"It's me!" He beams, nearly bouncing with excitement as he slaps his vest. "Arnaldin Keppers. You gave me my quest three months ago."

His face now seems familiar, although his appearance has changed considerably since we last saw him. Layla nudges my backside, startling me, but I pat her neck and smile. There's no danger here. "Mr. Keppers. It seems your quest has agreed with you."

His smile is full of pride. "You won't believe it. I have to tell you everything that's happened!"

I think of all that has happened to me. To my sister and Ren, too. Ren leans close, his voice a low rumble meant only for me. "It might be safer to stay with them than to search for another camp before dark."

I glance at Calliope's eager face, at the jovial caravan setting up by the spring. Feeling some relief at the brightly colored wagons with their weary-eyed travelers, I reach into my satchel and draw out my journal. "Then please join us. You know I'm always up for a good story."

# Chapter Twenty
## Dessalyn | Threads in the Dark

*Some stories are bargains. The question is, what are you willing to pay?*

Darkness bleeds like ink around me. At first, there is only the sound of a quill scratching—a faint, steady hiss as if someone is writing on endless parchment in the void. Then words begin to shimmer through the black, curling like smoke, only to vanish again before I can grasp their meaning.

Two figures stand ahead of me. One I know immediately—Marrow. His form is unmistakable in his cloak, his swagger still confident but guarded. Why?

He holds a staff loosely at his side, carved runes along it pulsing. Staff. Runes. Like the mage Ren told me about? His eyes flick this way and that, constantly shifting, never still. For a moment, I want to snatch that staff and beat him with it.

The other figure is unknown to me, but my blood chills at his presence. He is turned away, a cloak draping him from crown to heel, his face hidden by the hood and thick shadows swirling around him.

The material is not that of an ordinary garment. The fabric itself seethes with words—stitched in silver thread that writhes and shifts as though alive. Lines of poetry, fragments of history, half-remembered names. I catch glimpses as they appear and vanish again and again, as if the garment breathes.

*Drakenholt.*

*Flame unbound.*

The next two make my breath catch.

*Vellicor.*

*Serenelle.*

My stomach twists. It's as if this stranger is wearing the bones of stories as armor. The bones of *my* stories.

Marrow bows his head. "You summoned me."

Summoned. My brain catches up to what my body already knows.

This is Solander Cimarron. The Story Thief.

Chills race over me. This is no dream. It's a vision...or...something. It's as if I'm eavesdropping on their reality.

Cimarron's voice rolls through the darkness, a deep alto, every word vibrating against my ears. "It is time to push the next piece into place."

Marrow's thumb strokes over a pulsing rune. "Tell me where to begin."

"Fablehollow." The Thief doesn't turn, doesn't need to. His presence fills the space like smoke filling a room. "Find the Lorewyn patriarch, Thand Lorewyn. He holds the key to the scriptorium and to the girl. Get close to him. Earn his trust. Use him to get to the book."

My heart stutters. *Father.*

Marrow's head tilts. "And what of Jairton?"

"I will handle Jairton," Cimarron replies, almost with amusement. "You had your chance and failed. The vault must be unsealed, and the thread that binds the dragon prince de-storied. Once I claim it, Renwick Ravelle will finally unravel. The dragon lore will be fully mine to rewrite. Its power surpasses all that of the other kingdoms, and I will use the girl to reshape this world into my playground."

Marrow bows his head at the word failure. "He used dragon fire to stop the cracks I created. I had no recourse."

Cimarron's cloak stirs, the words rippling across the fabric like water disturbed. "You were supposed to bend his mind to my will!"

A pause. "His mind would not let me in."

"His blood! Why did you not secure it for me?"

The swagger is replaced with steel. "He's not like the others. He knows me. Knows my tricks. There was no way I could make him bleed without risking our mission."

Cimarron snarls, and the cloak ripples again, its folds snapping against each other this time. "I grow impatient with your excuses."

A longer pause, as if Marrow is searching for the right response. "Yes, master."

Two words, but they convey so much more—his own impatience, his fear, his drive to get what he wants from this deal. I wonder what that might be.

The cloak settles. The Thief's voice comes out calmer and deadly serious. "Her protector must be erased, forgotten." Gnarled fingers make a rolling motion in the air. "He will be dust on the wind, and I...I will be master of all, including the Lore Language."

Marrow remains quiet for another long moment. His thumb continues rubbing that one rune. "And the Lorekeeper?" Marrow asks.

A low rumble. "She will be mine."

Something in me quakes. My mouth opens before I can stop it. "No."

My voice slices the air, sharp and defiant, while terror grows in my belly like a living thing. "You will not touch my father. You will not lay a hand on him—or me. I'll destroy you both before I let it happen."

Marrow jolts, his smoky eyes widening as he whirls. "She's here." His swagger slips for a heartbeat, hand tightening on the staff. A pale patch of sweat gleams at his temple.

Cimarron only laughs. It's a horrible sound, like the pages of a book burning. "So bold. So foolish." The words flowing on his cloak speed up, showing me passages from my journal. The gnarled finger points at Marrow. "And you, stupid Dream Walker, letting her use your gift against you." He spits. "Her Fae power is ten times what yours is."

Fae power. Is Marrow Fae?

Slowly, the Thief turns, though his hood still shadows his face. "Do you think you stand apart from my story, little Lorekeeper? You're already ink on my page."

My blood heats with anger. "You're wrong. I choose my own destiny."

"Do you?" He glides closer, the cloak of words shifting faster now, the phrases from my quest journal unraveling into nothingness. Shivers race over my skin. "You will do what I ask, or I will unmake everything you love. Your sister. Your father. Evermere and all of its inhabitants. All will vanish, forgotten. Even you won't remember them."

Fury beats like a drum in my head. "I'll never do what you ask."

The Thief lifts a hand. The air bends, and images surge around me—visions so sharp they cut.

Ren.

Calliope.

*Mom.*

She stands in a shimmering light, her face pale, her eyes as bright as I remember. Her hands reach toward me, lips shaping my name—*Dessalyn.*

It's a trick like everything else he and Marrow do. I blink back the pressure surging behind my eyes. "She would fight you, too."

That laugh prickles over my skin again. "She tried and failed, but she *is* alive. Do what I ask and I'll give her back to you."

My knees loosen. *Alive*? "That's not...possible."

Cimarron's voice coils around me, snakelike. "Oh, but it is. She lives, caught between stories—a page half-written, waiting to be inked again. I can restore her. I can return what was stolen. All you need do is fetch what I want from the forgotten Lorekeeper vault in Jairton. The prince doesn't want you to find it, but you must. Deliver it to me, and your deepest desire will be granted. Your family will be whole."

My throat tightens until I can hardly breathe. "You're lying."

He tilts his head, and though I cannot see his face, I feel the smile—wide, merciless. "Do you dare take that chance? Refuse me, and she will be erased forever. Not even memory will hold her to you."

The cry rips from my lungs. "Don't you touch her!"

"Then obey me, girl. Retrieve the vault's secret. Say nothing of this to anyone. Do not tell the prince, or my offer is void. If you tell your sister, I will wipe her story away, too. She will be gone forever, as if she never existed. But do as I say, and I will show leniency with you."

Mom's eyes—so real, so desperate—burn into me. My heart tears in two. I can barely get out the words. "What is this secret that's in the vault?"

"A story." The cloak settles, the words vanishing. A parchment with Drakenholt's crest appears. "A very valuable story that ties me to your prince. He fears what you'll think of him when you find it. That's why it's hidden there, and why he steers you away from Jairton."

Marrow grins, shifting the staff to rest on his shoulder. "How can you trust Ravelle when he keeps secrets from you, sweet Dessalyn?"

I swallow, ignoring him and staring at the vision of the parchment. Is it true? Is this the real reason Ren has tried to keep me from Jairton?

Mom's face flashes in my mind again. Her pendant heats on my skin. "How do I retrieve it?" I hear myself ask.

The vision fades. The Thief doesn't move, and yet it feels as if he's invading my personal space. A darkness fills my mind, my chest. My heartbeat dulls. I want to step back.

"The ward your mother placed on the vault requires dragon and Fae power combined to open it. You must get the prince to fuse his magic with yours to unlock the ward and retrieve the story. He will insist on destroying it. You must not allow that to happen."

Betray Ren to potentially save my mother? The idea makes me sick.

"Give me your word in the Language," Cimarron commands. His voice is a seductive whisper in my ear. A too loud boom in my ears. "Swear to me you will bring me that story, or I will force you to erase your own family, word by word."

An image is shoved into my mind of him compelling me to do precisely that, using my Fae power and the Lore Language to erase Father and Calliope's very existence.

Any vow or pact sworn in the Lore Language is binding. It cannot be rooted in falsehood, only in truth. The Language itself records and enforces the terms. If either party breaks the agreement, the Lore exacts a price—memories stripped, stories unraveled, entire bloodlines erased from history.

What can I do?

I choke. I can't get the words out, and yet I must. "Prove to me my mother is alive," I demand. "I want to see her in person before I agree to any deal."

A flick of his wrist and I am no longer in his presence. I am in a dark blue void. I hear Mom's voice. "Dessalyn?"

I whirl and there she is, rushing toward me. "Mom?"

We throw ourselves at each other, and her pendant on my collarbone blazes with heat and light. Our embrace is fierce, and hot tears sting my cheeks.

She draws back, looking me over, the familiar scent of jasmine filling my nose. Her hand slips beneath my chin, and she presses her forehead to mine. For a second, the ache of grief that is always inside my chest eases. Despite what is happening, the world feels right again.

She pulls away and scans my face. "What are you doing here?"

I hiccup on a sob and catch my breath. Is this how I could see her in the mirror? She's caught in this in-between dimension of an unfinished story? "The Story Thief. He is a kind of story-keeper who erases kingdoms. He's forcing me into a bargain to erase Prince Ravelle to save you."

She wipes at my tears. "You mustn't let him blackmail you. You cannot save me, Dessa. Do you hear me? Save the prince. He is the only hope the realm has. You must not worry about me. I will find a way back to you. I promise."

I want to believe her. I want to curl into her embrace and never leave. "But he will force me to erase Calliope and Father. I..." I shake my head. "I can't."

She strokes my hair, cups her pendant in her palm for a moment. It's cool, not hot, when she releases it and it falls against my skin once more. "Oh, my poor sweet girl. Cimarron is corrupting many things, but he cannot corrupt you. I promise you that. My pendant will protect you. Do not believe—"

I'm ripped away from her and once more in front of the Story Thief.

"Do we have a bargain, Lorekeeper?" he demands. "Bring me what I want, and your mother lives."

The pendant flares ice cold. I straighten my spine and look into his shadowed face, gripping the only piece of my mother that I still have with trembling fingers. "I will retrieve the story and hand it over to you if you agree to bring my mother back to our family and leave all of us alone and in good health," I say in the Lore Language.

A parchment appears in midair. An invisible quill writes the exact words I've spoken on it. My signature appears at the bottom with the date.

Again, I sense more than see the Thief's smile. "I agree to return your mother to your family and leave all of you alone and in good health, if and when you hand over the dragon prince's story."

Once more, the words appear, along with his signature and the date.

Then the parchment rolls up and vanishes.

The Language accepted it. It was a good bargain. He's telling the truth. The dream-vision collapses.

I wake with a gasp, drenched in sweat. The world tilts between shadow and dawn. The clearing is alive with voices, the creak of wagons, the crackle of fires being smothered. Horses stamp, children laugh, someone coughs. The ordinary noise feels obscene after what I've just witnessed. Of what I've just done.

My hands shake as I push the blanket aside. My chest aches, every breath too shallow. Tears still stain my cheeks.

Ren kneels by our fire, steam curling from a tin cup. "You're up." He smiles, then it falls away as he studies my face. "Bad dream?" Seeing my distress, he instinctively moves closer. "Was it Marrow?"

The truth burns on my tongue. I wipe away the dampness on my face and shake my head. I can still feel Mom's arms around me. Still hear her voice. I can't tell him. Not all of it, anyway. "I'm fine."

He extends the cup, but my fingers tremble too badly to take it. He scrutinizes my face like a man mapping a battlefield. For a beat, he says nothing. The cup hangs, steam ghosting up between us. I shake my head again and stand.

"Calli?" I shake my sister's shoulder. "Wake up."

She stirs, her pretty hair a wild halo, eyes still heavy with sleep. The moment she sees my face, she bolts upright. "What is it?" She searches the area, taking in the caravan, the people, the horses. "What's wrong?"

I swallow hard. The lie forms quickly, but it isn't a complete falsehood. I motion her and Ren into a private circle. "I saw Marrow and Cimarron. He ordered Marrow to get close to Father—to break into the scriptorium."

Ren curses. "That piece of horse dung."

Calliope pales, her hand flying to her mouth. "Oh no! Father..."

Ren paces a few steps away and back, his hand going to his sword hilt.

Calliope jumps to her feet, sleep gone. She seizes my hands. "We must go home. Right now. We must warn him."

I squeeze her fingers, trying to steady her even as my own heart fractures. I must tell them both something, even if it's not the complete truth. "I must go on to Jairton. The quest knows I have a job there to do, and I must save Ren and Drakenholt in order to save Evermere and the other kingdoms, too. If I fail, the Story Thief will erase Ren, and from what I've learned, if that happens, we'll have no chance at all. The entire realm will collapse and become *Cimarron's* story, not ours."

"No, Dessa!" Her eyes brim with tears. She places herself between Ren and me as if she can stop me. "We can't leave Father undefended. Marrow will—"

Ren begins to bank our fire. "Marrow cannot enter your father's dreams unless he has his blood. Or unless Thand loses his senses through wine or sickness. Is he prone to too much drink?"

I shake my head. "Never, and he's healthier than most men his age, but Marrow could trick him, as he did us. Stage something to cause him harm."

"Calliope, you can protect him," Ren tells her. "You know what Marrow looks like. How he works. If you're there, he won't succeed."

Calliope shakes her head, clutching me. "We're stronger together, Dessalyn."

Again, it's Mom's tone that rides her voice. My throat burns. I don't want to send her home alone on this dangerous road. What choice do I have? "This one time," I whisper, "we must be strong in spirit together instead."

Her breath shudders. "I can't leave you."

"You must."

"You can travel to Fablehollow with the caravan," Ren says. "They'll protect you on the road."

She is exasperated. "They're too slow! Layla is too slow. I need to get there now."

Ren glances at the travelers packing up and calling to their children. "I'll speak to Arnaldin Keppers and explain the urgency. His steed is of sound quality. Ride with him. He can get you there in a day's time."

She blows out a breath. I nod at Ren to do it. Once he walks away, I tug her farther from the wagons.

"There's more to the dream," I confess, my voice barely above a whisper. "I can't tell you all of it because of a bargain I had to make. Please don't ask, but trust me. I'm doing what I have to do, and if I succeed..." A frail smile passes my lips. I can't get over how good it felt to be in our mother's arms again. "All will be well."

"You made a bargain?" Her lips tremble. "With the Story Thief? Dessa, I don't like this."

I grip her shoulders. "It's a good one, I swear. I'm doing what I have to do to save us. To save our family and our kingdom. Whatever happens, remember that I love you. Always."

Her tears spill over, and mine nearly do, too. We clasp each other, holding on as though we can stop the world from splitting us apart. On my collarbone, the pendant pulses.

Ren returns with Keppers. I thank him for his help, and Calliope mounts his horse, her face streaked with tears but resolute. He waves at me and climbs up with her. Layla is left to trudge with the caravan.

I watch until they disappear down the road, every hoofbeat stealing a piece of my heart. Calliope looks back once, and I force a smile. Ren stands beside me, quiet, waiting. I sense he knows I'm keeping parts of the dream-vision from him. His nearness should comfort me. Instead, it deepens the storm raging in my chest.

Marrow's words have burrowed under my skin. *How can you trust Ravelle when he keeps secrets from you?*

Even if it damns me—even if it means betraying Ren—how can I not follow through on the bargain I have made?

I touch the pendant and Mom's words follow on the heels of Marrow's. *My pendant will protect you.* Do I dare believe her?

Like a slow, terrible echo, I see the silver stitch of letters on the Thief's cloak—my name, my family's names—unraveling in my head.

# CHAPTER TWENTY-ONE
## DESSALYN | THE STORM THAT FOLLOWS

*The truest words can sound like lies if spoken too late.*

THE WORLD IS HUSHED as Firebrand carries us north.

The stallion's strides eat the road, steady and tireless, his breath puffing in the chill air. The dawn still hasn't fully inserted itself between the trees that line the road. A lavender haze blurs the horizon where night is giving way to morning, and mist clings low along the grass and curls around the horse's hooves.

I sit pressed against Ren's back, the rhythm of the ride vibrating through me, my hands clenched tight at his waist. I tell myself it's the cold. Or the ache of saying goodbye to Calliope. Or the unknown that waits for me only hours away in Jairton.

But it isn't.

It's the dream. The bargain I made.

Cimarron's laugh still rings in my ears. His words coil like snakes around my heart. *Bring me what I want, and your mother lives.*

My fingers find Mom's pendant. I rub it hard enough to leave an impression, as though I can pull some hidden strength from it. As though she wove some of herself into it before she vanished.

Maybe she did.

I close my eyes, remembering the heat of her embrace, the way her voice trembled when she begged me not to give in. *You cannot save me, Dessa. Do you hear me? Save the prince. He is the only hope that the realm has.*

But how?

How can I save him when the bargain binds me? When keeping silent about the truth is the only thing holding my mother's life in the balance?

Worse—how can I trust him when he doesn't trust me?

Anger flares low in my belly. He's keeping important truths from me, putting all of us in danger.

"Dessa?" Ren's voice cuts through my thoughts. I blink, lifting my gaze. His head is turned slightly, his profile handsome against the pale sky. His eyes flicker back to me. "You've been quiet since the caravan. I know you're worried, but I will protect you."

*Her protector.* That's what Cimarron called him.

I don't want a protector, but I'd be insane to believe I don't *need* one. I barely survived the attack by Marrow's bandits. Marrow himself tricked me. The Mireling might have won if not for Ren's fire.

I'm helplessly, stupidly, in need of someone who understands these lands. Who knows how to fight. One who can teach me not to be tricked again.

*Save the prince. He is the only hope that the realm has.*

My fingers grip his cloak tighter. I force my voice steady. "I was thinking."

"Of the dream?"

My breath stutters. He's too perceptive. "Yes," I answer, careful, cautious. The pact won't let me tell the truth—not all of it. "You said Marrow was a childhood friend. A gifted individual who was part of your court, right?"

"Yes. You haven't told me everything, have you? About that dream."

"He..." I swallow. "The Thief is using him. I'm sure he's not without fault, and that he will profit if Cimarron succeeds, but..." I think back to the way he deferred to the Thief one moment, and dared to argue with him the next. "I wonder if he's being coerced." *Like me.* "If it's possible that Cimarron has threatened Marrow, or is blackmailing him."

Ren curses under his breath, his hands tightening on the reins. "Does it matter? Marrow may be the last of my kingdom, but he's turned traitor."

"Maybe he has a good reason."

Tension radiates off Ren. "What reason could he possibly have to destroy all those lives? To erase all those people?"

If I were in Marrow's shoes, would I be tempted to do the same to bring Mom back? It's something I can't stop thinking about. Am I saving my family but obliterating Evermere? The entire realm?

"The Story Thief said my father holds the key to the scriptorium and to the 'girl.' Me, I think. He told Marrow to get close to him and earn his trust so he could get to the book. Why does Cimarron want Vellicor? The book won't work for him. It only works for us." Except, a new thought hits. One I forgot about. "Unless Cimarron is a Lorekeeper, like me and Calliope."

Ren's broad shoulders shrug. "He must have some type of story magic, but it could be from a dragon Lorekeeper bloodline. I searched for any reference to him in what remains of our library archives, but found nothing. That was before I knew his name, but still. If he has you and Vellicor, it's possible he could rewrite whatever he wants, regardless of his heritage or lack thereof."

This doesn't align with what I know. "But the Lore Language can't be used that way. For a story or two? Sure, but there are dire consequences for misusing it. Even if he forced me to erase certain stories,"—I swallow the tightness in my throat at the thought of my sister and father being wiped out of existence by my hand—"I could end up with anything from a memory bleed to complete soul erosion. I wouldn't be any good to him then."

He rides easy in the saddle, yet his back stiffens. His voice is edged with trepidation. "What's a memory bleed?"

"If we use the Lore to make a change in the world, the Lore may take something from our minds. For instance, if I speak the Language to protect myself, I may lose a cherished memory of my mother's voice, or my first love. If any of us tamper with the Great Storybook of the realm, we risk being erased, even without the Thief's meddling."

"Vellicor is linked to the Great Storybook?"

"Yes, directly."

"Then we made the right decision sending your sister home. Calliope will protect Thand, and together, they will keep Vellicor safe."

It goes unsaid that Ren will keep me safe. My logic argues this point, knowing he's keeping some truth from me that could affect everything.

"I'm still worried," I admit. "Marrow is a master manipulator. And what if Cimarron wasn't talking about me? What if he was talking about Calliope? Have I played right into his hands by sending her back?"

Ren's voice lowers, becoming more tentative. "You can second-guess yourself into infinity. I believe you've taken the best measures you can for now to protect your family and fulfill your quest."

My chest cracks open at the thought of my bargain to return Mom to us. If I want Ren to open up about his truth, I must tell him everything I can about mine. "I think my mother is still alive."

He jerks on the reins, startling Firebrand. The horse prances in place as Ren swivels enough to fully look over his shoulder at me. "What makes you believe that?"

I tug the pendant from under my cloak. "This was hers. It's unique. Fae blessed, or possibly Lore charmed. I'm not sure, and I only realized it when it acted differently in the dream. My mother came to me and told me it would protect me from the Thief."

He frowns, studying the jewel and considering my words. "She knew about the Thief long before the rest of us did, but whatever you saw in the dream could be another trick."

My stomach shrivels. "A trick?"

He sees my crestfallen expression. Leading Firebrand to a pretty copse of trees changing their leaves to bright yellows and oranges, he dismounts and pulls me down next to him. His hands stay on my waist, even when I'm solidly on the ground. "I know you want to believe what you saw was real, that she's alive, but Dessa, you can't get your hopes up. Cimarron was showing you what he wanted you to see so he could play on your emotions."

My heart twists with a new surge of grief. Again, I want to bang my head against the nearest tree. Could this be true? Could what I saw in the dream be an illusion?

I fold my arms around me, remembering how good it felt to be wrapped in Mom's embrace. To smell her again. To hear her voice. "No." I shake my head adamantly. "I know it was her. She was real, Ren."

His eyes are deep pools of sapphire. He leans forward, close enough to kiss my lips, and gently rests his forehead against mine. "Dessa, I know that's what you want more than anything in the world, I just don't want you to end up hurt when you realize it's not true."

In those beautiful eyes, I see pity now. A sob lodges in my chest. I refuse to give it a voice. I choke it down and stumble away from his comfort. That pity. I remind myself that the language worked for the contract. It wouldn't have done so if Cimarron couldn't return my mother to me. She *must* be alive. If only it could give me proof. "I feel it in my heart," I say. "She's stuck in some kind of limbo, but she's not dead, and I'm going to free her, just like I'm going to get your kingdom back."

A frown tugs at the corners of his mouth. He tilts his head back and stares up at the sky.

Even though he's met her, I feel like I need to make her real to him in the way that she is to me. "She came to Evermere from the borderlands when she was young. Father said she was a marvel—quick to learn, clever with words, gifted in weaving Lore. She could charm a page into telling its story, or quiet the quills when they grew restless. She…" I grip the pendant. "She loved us fiercely."

Ren is silent for a long time. "That was evident at court. Tell me how she…died."

"She faded right before our eyes." The memory is a blade under my ribs. "Not like your parents. She began aging quickly. She disappeared into the woods more and more. Father was concerned and kept going after her, but she didn't want to come home. She..."

"Went into the Fade like Fae do?"

That's what we all believed. That when she finally disappeared for good at the edge of the woods, leaving only a note behind telling us it was her time and not to search for her anymore, that she had died. For Fae like herself, that meant returning to nature.

Now the Thief has claimed otherwise, dangling her life like bait before me. What's true and what isn't? I stare at the horizon. "That's what we believed, but now, I know differently. Cimarron has her. He took her from us."

Ren opens his mouth to say something, then turns away.

I march over to him and grab his arm. "Why is it so hard to believe I could be right?"

"Because..." He trails off, shaking his head. "It's nothing. I'm paranoid right now, too suspicious of the Thief's actions and motivations."

Again, I feel that tug in the center of my chest. I sense the conflict within him. He wants to share something, but he's holding back. "Whatever it is you know, tell me," I insist. "About my mother. About Jairton. I can't help you if you keep things from me."

Those eyes study my face for a long moment, then he points at the pendant. "You believe that's enchanted to protect you from the Thief, yet it hasn't prevented him from getting close to you."

Once again, he's redirecting the conversation. I worry the pendant between my fingers, and it warms. Mom's voice seems to swirl in my head. *The prince will reveal the truth when the time is right. For now, think. Look. See. Listen.*

I scan the area, listen to the song of birds. Feel the wind on my face, growing stronger. "He sent others to get close to me," I correct Ren. "The dream was the first time I actually saw him. Except, it wasn't a dream. He and Marrow were awake. I was the only one asleep. I'm not sure exactly how it happened—how I managed to... project myself to where they were, since they were both awake."

Firebrand has started grazing in the grass, nosing aside some of the fallen leaves. Ren watches him, considering my words. "Perhaps Marrow was able to pull you to him."

I shake my head and pace a few steps away. "He seemed surprised when I appeared. I don't think either of them knew how it happened, but Cimarron told Marrow he was incompetent for allowing me to *use his gift*." I pace back to Ren, a new thought making me pause. "Is it possible that when Marrow took my blood, it left him open to my Fae powers? That somehow I can now enter into his dreams at will, and also appear wherever he is, if I so choose?"

This idea causes Ren's forehead to furrow. "Have you ever had that sort of thing happen before?"

"I've never had a reason to try. This could turn the tide for us. Give us the advantage."

My growing excitement is lost on him. He shakes his head. "Until we fully understand the link between you and how it works, you need to guard yourself against any of his intrusions. Don't seek out the channel. Promise me you won't take unnecessary risks."

Will he and I always be at odds with each other? His eyes are shadowed now, haunted again. Secrets coil behind them. "A quest is all about risk."

He releases a sigh that tells me he's as exasperated as I am.

"Ren." I lean forward and touch his arm. "The vault in Jairton. There's a story in it that will help both of us, and you know about it, don't you?"

He draws away from my touch and grabs Firebrand's reins. The mount tosses his head as Ren leads him toward the road. "We should keep moving."

I grip his bicep, keeping him in the copse. "The Thief wants what's in that Lorekeeper vault, and I need to know why. Tell me what you know, or I'll take the horse and leave you here."

He knows I'm not strong enough to overtake him, but I am bullheaded and shrewd enough to make good on my promise. His jaw locks, the muscles working. Clouds fill the sky, the shadows growing thick around us. A breeze rustles the leaves, sending dozens more showering to the ground.

He releases the reins and steps away, dragging a hand through his hair. His voice is ragged when he finally speaks. "The vault...what lies in it is my fault. A story I wrote. A lie. A prophecy that should never have been inked."

I freeze. My blood runs cold. "What?"

Ren doesn't meet my eyes. "The original Chronicle of Drakenholt is there. A full telling of the kingdom's founding and its origin with dragons. When I was fifteen, I wrote a story in the Dragon Language that changed things. A false story I inserted into our copy of the Chronicle."

I struggle to find words. "Why would you do that? Even the Dragon Language has consequences if you misuse..." That's when it hits me. I stagger. "You wrote about the Story Thief? You...created him?"

He scrubs his face. "My kingdom was in turmoil, and I sought a way to restore order and peace, so I conjured a prophecy. The story was meant to be symbolic, a rallying cry to our citizens. With the written words of the Dragon Language, I thought to give myself great purpose. A destined enemy." His shoulders bow. "Instead, I gave Solander Cimarron a weapon. A way in to destroy everything I love."

My heart thunders. I put a hand to my mouth, truly unable to speak.

He nods as if he agrees with the damning thoughts racing through my head. "Your mother helped me seal the story away in that vault before it could spread. She said the Lore would demand a price if it remained loose. We locked it in Jairton and buried it under stone and seal. Now, the seal is cracking due to the assaults of Cimarron and his minions. If he gets to it first, he will finally be able to erase me."

I can barely breathe. His confession is jagged, broken, but it fills in the holes of what the Thief told me. A story ties them together—a false prophecy with no tie to the Great Storybook.

And it was buried by my mother? I take a step closer. "This can't be true."

"The destruction of Drakenholt is my fault." He lifts his head at last, and the anguish in his eyes makes my heart ache. "Now you know."

I wish I didn't.

He reaches out but his hand falls back without touching me. "Do you hate me, Dessalyn?"

My throat tightens. Anger boils inside me all over again, but it's edged with something else. Why would my mother keep such a story a secret? Why would she not tell us? Surely, there was a way to undo the magic. To keep the Thief from rising. My thoughts spin, and I feel dizzy. I stagger to the nearest tree, ignoring a leaf that sticks in my hair. The breeze picks up.

The memory of one of my earliest stories flashes through my mind. Vellicor had given it to me, but thinking I knew better, I translated it with my own flourish, changing the meaning of a simple sentence. That was all—one sentence—and yet it affected the entire story. When my mother saw what I had done, she banished me from the scriptorium for weeks. She explained the consequences of doing such a thing. Still, it was the consequence itself that left me with deep regret and solidified my intention never to manipulate the Language again. Because of that single sentence, a child in the village went missing. Our neighbor grew sick. Calliope forgot how to tie her shoes. Mom corrected each of those unfortunate outcomes, and all was well once again, but I learned a valuable lesson.

The heavy weight of his grief mingles with mine. "I don't hate you." How can I? His intentions were pure, even if misguided.

His breath catches, and he searches my eyes. "You don't?"

"I'm angry you didn't tell me sooner," I admit. "But no, I don't hate you. I'm upset with you, though."

The air trembles between us. He closes the distance in two strides. His hand cups my cheek, rough thumb brushing the skin there. "Dessa."

The sound of my name coming from his lips makes my face bloom with heat. The tug in my heart sharpens, coiling. Every part of me leans toward him.

And then his mouth brushes mine.

While I'm unsure of what's real and what isn't, he's steady and solid, pressing me into the anchor of his arms. I welcome his kiss. He's the blaze, and I am the forest, burning.

My pulse thunders in my ears, drowning out everything but the drag of his mouth and the heat of his body pressed to mine.

His lips are desperate, fierce, full of everything he's held back. Mine meet his with the same ferocity, because I am lost otherwise.

Time stretches, elastic. His hand slides from my cheek to cradle the back of my head, fingers threading through my hair, and the pressure of the kiss deepens until my knees weaken. I lean into him, into his strength, into the fire in his chest that feels as if it could melt every shadow.

The tether between us pulls so tight it aches. The pendant sears against my collarbone. A sound escapes me—half sigh, half sob—as though my body can't hold the storm of feeling inside.

Ren groans low in his throat, the sound vibrating into my mouth, and it's the most human, most vulnerable sound I've ever heard from him.

His fire collides with the storm inside me, two forces battling and binding. In that instant, I believe we can stop the Story Thief with this alone—our fire and storm, united.

The world narrows to just us. My bones know him. My blood remembers him. This bond I can't explain thrums with power and need.

I'm flying. The truth he's admitted to sets me free. Free to trust him again, and...

*Boom.*

The sky cracks open. Thunder rolls, long and low, shaking the trees. Firebrand whinnies, stamping nervously.

I wrench back, gasping from the kiss, my heart lurching at the sound of that thunder.

The dream memory comes roaring back—the black clouds devouring the world, my journal slipping away no matter how close I got to it, my screams lost in the gale. And Ren, arriving on Firebrand, using his fire to stop the encroaching darkness. Saving my journal. Anchoring me in his arms.

Now, a similar storm brews on the horizon, black clouds massing, lightning flickering at their edges. "Ren, look!"

He follows my gaze. His eyes harden. "We ride."

I nod, too shaken to argue. He swings onto Firebrand's back and pulls me up behind him. The pendant flares hot, as if urging us on.

The stallion bolts forward, carrying us into the rising wind.

A storm is coming. And I don't know if this time, even Ren can anchor me against it.

# CHAPTER TWENTY-TWO
## DESSALYN | THE CAVE OF WHISPERS

*Some storms bring rain. Others bring omens.*

THE SKY SPLITS OPEN.

Firebrand bolts forward, hooves striking sparks off the stones, his mane whipping wildly in the shrieking wind.

The storm is alive—thunder snapping like the crack of a whip, lightning clawing the sky in jagged silver scars. Shadows writhe in the depths of the forest, taking the shape of things that don't exist.

"Hold on!" Ren shouts. His back is iron under my grip, every muscle braced as he drives the stallion off the road and up a steep ravine. Branches lash at us. Stones tumble under Firebrand's hooves. My breath tears from my lungs, and the pendant sears against my skin like it, too, fears what's coming for us.

"Where are you going?" I yell.

"To shelter!"

Against the sharp bite of the wind, I peer over his shoulder. A cave yawns ahead, black, narrow, and more like a gash in the earth than shelter.

Ren drives Firebrand to the mouth and leaps down, yanking the stallion by the reins. I half tumble from the saddle, skirt tangling around my legs, only to be caught by the prince. His strong hands keep me upright, his eyes meeting mine for a brief moment as the gale lashes at us. The tug under my breastbone flares needy, images of our kiss flashing across my mind.

Time spins out, but then the wind sucks at Ren so hard, he staggers backward. Even Firebrand fights not to lose his footing. It's as if the storm wants to swallow horse and rider whole. His clothes melt against his body as he lurches forward, thrusting me toward the cave. "Inside!"

I stumble in, my boots slipping on slick rocks. Cold water drips down my neck. While the mouth is wide, a few yards in, the walls are so close I scrape my shoulders as I squeeze through to allow for him and the horse. Ren shoves Firebrand in, tethering him to a jagged spur of stone. The stallion fights, eyes rolling, but Ren's voice, calm and commanding, keeps him from breaking loose. Ren strokes his neck, his next words so low I can't catch them over the storm, and the horse settles with a stomp of his forefoot. Dragon Language? Whatever it is, it soothes the anxious animal.

Rain slashes against the cliff outside, the wind howling and driving it into the cave.

Ren strides to me, filling the cramped space with his size. His hair is damp, his shirt plastered to his chest under his open jacket. His muscles shift as he braces his arm against the wall. His closeness steals my breath more than the race up the ravine.

Neither of us speaks. My heart beats with the thunder, wild and frantic. "It's the same storm," I whisper.

Ren glances down at me, frowning and wiping water from his face. "What storm?"

"The one from my nightmare. The fire, the black clouds swallowing everything, my journal slipping away—" My voice cracks. "It wasn't a nightmare. It was a vision." I glance around the dark space as if Marrow might be here, watching, tipping his imaginary hat at me. "And now it's come true."

His jaw tightens. He leans closer so I can hear him over the noise. Our faces are inches apart, his breath warm against my cheek. "Then we endure it, Dessa. Together."

*Together.* The word lands deep, pulling at that tether in my chest. I press a hand to the rock wall, grounding myself, but where earlier his presence anchored me, now it overwhelms me.

Whispers curl in through the mouth of the cave—my name, soft, beckoning. *Dessalyn... come...*

It's not Marrow's voice, but I can't place it. I clap my hands over my ears. "Do you hear that?"

Ren shifts, angling to shield me with his body, but he doesn't know from what. His scent—smoke, steel, something sharper underneath—crowds me as much as his bulk. "I hear nothing but the storm."

The voice continues, joined by others. Feminine, seductive. Words twisting through the gale. *Your mother waits...*

Narrators of my story? Of my mother's fairytale? Either way, they are sent by the Thief, calling to me, tempting and enticing me to walk out of this shelter and into their siren song.

I squeeze my eyes shut, fighting the lure. The pendant throbs like a second heartbeat. I mentally grasp for it, anchoring my thoughts.

"What do you hear?" Ren grips my shoulders. "Dessalyn, look at me. Tell me what's going on."

I fight him at first, too caught up in snuffing out the voices. He grabs my chin between his fingers and thumb and forces me to meet his gaze. His eyes blaze in the dim light, storm-blue and fierce. The roar outside fades, if only for a heartbeat, and the voices dim. "I hear people," I tell him. My mouth is dry, my lips parched. I lick them, trying to get some moisture back. "Voices."

His gaze drops to my mouth, and heat flares low in my belly before his eyes slowly return to mine. "What do they say?"

"They want me to leave the cave and go into the storm." My breath hitches. "They claim my mother is waiting for me."

He wraps me in his arms, our bodies pressing together in the small space. "They're lying, you know."

His heartbeat is under my ear. I listen to its steady rhythm, snaking my arms around his waist. "I know, but..."

"It's the Thief." He rubs my back, stroking my spine to calm me. It's working as surely as listening to his steadying heartbeat. "He's using them to manipulate you. But you're safe. I won't let them or the storm take you."

The storm wants to. I can feel it clawing at the edges of my mind. Dream-threads probe for a way in. Marrow's work? I shiver.

Cimarron wants me to get to Jairton and retrieve the story. Why would he send a storm to delay me and then lure me into it? It doesn't make sense. But Marrow? Perhaps he has his own agenda.

A new thought hits. "What if it's meant to drive *you* into the storm?"

He leans back to glance down at me. "Me?"

He and Firebrand were nearly sucked out of the cave. "The Thief is looking for ways to erase you. To keep you from standing between him and what he wants."

Ren catches on. "So if he draws you into the storm, he knows I'll follow."

I clutch his wet cloak. "You must be careful. You're not immortal. Even if Cimarron hasn't gotten his hands on his origin story, he can still kill you."

Ren's hands linger, his thumbs brushing warmth into my arms. It feels too intimate. My breath tangles with his, the cramped quarters and the noise outside forcing us close enough that our foreheads almost touch.

"I can't lose you," he murmurs.

The words crack me open. I want to kiss him again. I want to believe in him, trust him with everything, even the bargain I've made. The tug in my belly sharpens until it's almost painful. "Promise me," I say. "Promise me you won't jeopardize yourself to save me."

His smile is soft, gentle, and totally lights up his face. "I can't promise that, Dessa." He cups my cheek with a hand, rubbing a thumb along my jawline. "I'll always save you, no matter the cost."

Another shiver racks my body, but this one I welcome. His lips are so close, his body radiating heat, that smile…

If I fall for him, how will I ever find the strength to betray him?

A deafening crack of thunder rattles the cave. Firebrand screams and jerks against his tether. Ren pulls away to calm him, running a hand down the stallion's slick neck, murmuring words again that I can't hear. My heart hammers at what almost just happened between us—another soul-wrecking kiss—and my legs tremble.

Ren keeps stroking Firebrand's neck, but his gaze flicks back to me, dark and unyielding. For a moment, the cave is full of our three frantic heartbeats—mine, the stallion's, and Ren's. He looks like a man balancing on the edge of a blade.

Then releases the reins, and turns to me. Fire dances in his eyes. He says something low, guttural, in a tongue that is not Common.

The words reverberate through the cave, thrumming against the stone, against my chest. I don't recognize the syllables, but the cadence is unmistakable. I know this for it is—Dragon Language.

"Ren?" My voice is a whisper, half in awe, half in terror.

He holds my gaze, drenched hair plastered to his brow, eyes burning. "I swore it once to my kingdom. I swear it now to you." His voice is iron, each word vibrating with power. He drops to one knee. "By dragon's blood and dragon's flame, I will protect you until death takes me."

The vow crashes through the cave like a thunderclap. My pendant sears my skin. The storm outside cries out as though struck, the wind screaming one last time before—

Silence.

The thunder dies mid-roll. The rain ceases, its drumbeat cut off so abruptly my ears ring with the hush. Outside, the darkness lifts, leaving behind only the plop of dripping leaves and the faint hiss of retreating water.

Ren lowers his head, chest heaving, as though the vow itself has torn something out of him.

My heart pounds. "Ren...do you realize what you just did?"

He straightens, and his jaw is set with a kind of reckless determination. "Yes."

Like my Lore Language, Dragon Language binds. It punishes if broken. His vow isn't a simple promise—it's a chain forged in magic and fire. He's tethered himself to me now.

Our eyes lock for endless minutes. For him to do this without my consent is wrong. It is reckless, domineering—exactly the kind of arrogance I swore I'd never tolerate. I should be outraged, horrified, and disgusted by such an act.

Instead, I'm simply shocked.

And a bit in awe. I've never witnessed a dragon binding—certainly never felt one. The words shiver through my veins, fire and steel braided together. My insides are too warm, the hollow terror in me momentarily replaced by a fierce, alien courage that is not wholly my own.

It's his.

Then, heat fires through my chest. My pendant flares again. I jump and yank it out with a startled cry. The pulse of Ren's vow collides with the steady thrum of the charm, the two forces straining against one another, as if my mother foresaw this moment and wove protection into the jewel to keep me from being bound by more than my own will.

"Ah!" I yank the pendant free, clutching it in my fist. The azurite glows, pulsing like a heartbeat that isn't mine. The fiery agony is so sharp it tears a small cry from my throat.

Ren's head snaps around. He's at my side in an instant, his hands closing around my shoulders. "What is it? Dessa, what's wrong?"

I can barely breathe. The vow's power coils through me, binding and suffocating all at once. My fingers tighten around the pendant as if it's the only thing keeping me upright. "You shouldn't have done that."

Confusion flashes across his face. "The vow? It was to keep you safe. To make sure—"

"To make sure I'm yours," I cut in, voice shaking with anger and something else I can't name. "You created the bond without asking me. Do you understand what you've done? What fate you've chained us to?"

His jaw hardens, though his hands don't leave me. "I swore to protect you, Dessa. Until death. That is no chain—it's my oath."

The words tumble out raw, trembling. "You bound me without my consent."

His brows knit, eyes searching mine, but the vow holds my tongue closed on the truth. The pendant pulses again, as if fighting the vow, guarding me against being consumed by it.

I shake my head, torn between fear and fury. "Next time you make a choice like that, Renwick Ravelle, you ask me first."

He looks stricken, caught in his own pride. His expression asks if I'll forgive him—or if I ever can.

A shiver wracks me. Then the clash subsides, leaving me gasping, trembling, my fingers clenched tight around the pendant.

What will this mean to my bargain with the Story Thief? Although Ren created the binding, will it prevent me from betraying him when the time comes? Worse—will it turn the betrayal into something even more catastrophic for both of us?

Cautiously, Ren steps to the cave mouth. "The storm has ended as quickly as it came."

On shaky legs, I follow and peer past him.

The air outside is unnaturally still, the sky washed clean. The silence feels too absolute, like the world is holding its breath. The ground is a muddy mess, rivulets tracking down the embankment and forming a small stream between us and the road.

Without looking at me, Ren loosens Firebrand's reins and leads him outside, the crease between his brows growing deeper with every step.

He was doing what dragon princes do—being a hero. Until now, I haven't considered how his story archetype compels him to act. He's lost his family, his friends, and his kingdom. I'm now the allegory of all three. As such, he is driven to protect me at all costs.

Still, I struggle with this new twist in our entangled fates. My pulse trips over itself. My ears ring—aftershocks of the thunder or the binding he forced between us? My heart is torn between anger and...relief.

Because this binding is empowering. Emancipating, even. Yes, it now creates an unbreakable connection between us, but it's filling me with dragon fire. Courage. A calmness I haven't felt since Mom disappeared.

Ren glances back at me, and his eyes are fiery once more. Gone is the earlier confusion about my anger. In its place is a different kind of uncertainty. He points at the side of the cave. "Look."

Carved into the wet stone just outside the mouth are letters a handspan high, black as ink and still dripping as though they've been etched by lightning itself. A single word that chills me to the bone.

*Hurry.*

Ren and I exchange a glance. Firebrand whinnies. I clutch the pendant, my heart hammering against my ribs.

Who carved it? The Thief? My mother? The Lore itself?

Ren mounts the horse and holds out a hand to help me up behind him. I stare at the word for another moment before I swing up to the saddle, my body already aching from the endless miles and the tension I'm carrying. As he leads Firebrand down the ravine and through the new stream carved by the rain, I'm surprised to find that I feel surer than ever.

The quest is calling, and I will answer—no matter the cost.

# Chapter Twenty-three
## Calliope | The Other Thief

*The danger you see is rarely the danger you face.*

Ren's words echo like a curse all the way back to Fablehollow.

*You can protect him. You know what Marrow looks like.*

But with every pound of the horse's hooves, my gut clenches tighter. I left her. I left Dessa behind. I despised it the moment I climbed onto the back of this horse with Keppers. Even though I knew it was the right thing to do.

I also cannot stop thinking about Dessa's last words to me.

*A bargain I had to make.*

Gods, Dessa. What did you do?

I part ways with Keppers at the end of the road. His brows are creased with worry, but he says nothing as I bid him farewell, throw a jaunty wave, and run as fast as my legs will take me to the cottage.

When I burst into the house, the door bangs against the wall with a loud thump. "Father?"

He hurries in from the kitchen, his eyes wide and round as he clutches a dish towel between his hands.

"Stars above, girl! What are you—where's Dessa?" His voice cracks, and in that single crack, I hear all his worst fears.

I rush inside, dropping my satchel, and flinging myself at him. He hugs me, his arms tight, and for a moment, all my fears and worries drift away. I'm home. He's here. He's fine. The Story Thief has not yet come. Thank the stars.

When I pull back, my arms are shaking, my legs ache, and sweat runs down the side of my face.

Relief softens his face, but worry never leaves his eyes. He's already bracing for bad news. "Dessa?"

"There is much to tell you." I grip his hand and lead him from the kitchen to a chair in the small living area.

When he sits, his face is pale, and I realize then he must fear the worst. I bite my thumbnail and launch into the story, the words spilling out of me in a quick rush. I tell him everything that's happened from the moment I left here to find my sister, to the moment Dessa and I parted on the road. I tell him about finding Ren. I tell him about Dessa's vision—that Marrow is coming to Fablehollow to use him to break into the scriptorium and reach Vellicor.

When I say this, he stiffens and frowns. "By all the stars, he will not get Vellicor." At that, he jumps up and heads to the scriptorium. I follow on his heels, my heart finally returning to normal after my jaunt up the drive.

"Where are you going?"

"To check."

When we enter the scriptorium, things are just as they are supposed to be. Calm. Quiet. The book sits in shadows. As always, Bulin's eyes glint in the half-light but he is silent.

But Father doesn't go to Vellicor. He goes to one of the bookshelves and pulls off a hefty tome with a faded green cover. He plops it down on one of the desks. When he opens it, the cover cracks.

I move closer to see what book it is and peer over his shoulder. The pages are yellowed, the ink faded.

"What is that?" I ask.

"You said something about a vision—that this Marrow was in her dreams?"

The thought of it sickens me. "Yes."

"I'm looking for a way to block him."

"But he could do that with Dessa because he has her blood."

He taps the book. "Well, he's not getting mine." There is a determined edge to his voice that makes me smile.

He flips through the tome with frantic precision, lips moving as he scans. The faded green cover creaks with every turn of a page. Dust rises in faint motes, catching the lamplight.

"Here," he murmurs, stabbing a finger at a block of faded script. "On the nature of Dream Walkers."

I lean closer, breath held, as he reads aloud.

*"They were born of twilight, straddling the seam between waking and dreams. Their gift was a burden—to carry the stories of worlds not their own, to walk the corridors of thought and memory. Some kept the balance, shielding the living from horrors that should never touch them. But others broke faith. They wove false bargains, fed on secrets, and bound souls with ink and shadow."*

The words feel heavy, each one sinking into me like a stone.

Father turns the page, more urgency in his voice now. "Listen to this part. *To guard against the Walker's intrusion, one must bind the person so the Walker cannot gather the dreamer's blood. Even so, bind the dream. A talisman of vervain and the angisina sigil, sealed with an oath, may ward the mind from their touch. Salt across the threshold of the sleeper's chamber may bar their entry, though only while the ward remains unbroken. Yet beware. The Walker needs only a crack, a single unguarded thought, to slip inside."*

He rubs a hand down his face. "This is what I'll do. Oaths, wards, whatever it takes. He doesn't have my blood, and he won't get any."

My chest tightens. I want to believe him. I want to believe a few lines of ink and salt will stop Marrow. A fluttering noise catches my attention. I glance up to see Bulin ruffle his feathers.

Suddenly, Vellicor comes alive. The cover ripples, and the single eye opens.

The Lore Language floods me, hot and urgent, pounding in my veins until I can barely breathe. My feet are moving before I can stop them. I peer down at the empty page. "Once upon a story…" I breathe.

I freeze, my breath caught in my throat. Words bleed across the page, urgent, as if the book itself is desperate to warn me. The blood drains from my head.

*The thief of dreams walks with another. A dealer of stolen tales.*

Father hurries to my side. "What is it?"

The letters smear, twist, reform. Slowly, an image takes shape on the parchment—shadows thickening until they resemble the outstretched wings of a bird, talons poised mid-strike.

A hawk.

But the image is rough, blurred—a shadowy silhouette rather than a true rendering. Not the crisp lines of a tattoo, but something half-formed, shifting as if the Lore itself refuses to give me the shape. It's not a mark I could ever recognize on someone's skin. Only a symbol. Only a warning.

Even so, a cold certainty settles in my bones. Someday, I will.

Beneath it, more words bleed through like fresh wounds.

*Marked in ink. When the hawk glows, the story is
already his.*

Father's jaw tightens as he stares at the page. "This Marrow doesn't work alone."

But dread knots in my stomach. Because I already understand—Marrow isn't the true danger.

The inked thief of the stolen tales is.

# CHAPTER TWENTY-FOUR
## RENWICK | A VOW IN ASHES

*Stories are often bonds that demand protection.*

CLOUDS DRIFT LOW AND heavy across the midday sun, bruised gray and purple, as if reluctant to leave. A thin drizzle still falls, cold drops spattering my face and running down the back of my neck beneath my collar.

Ahead, a rockslide sprawls across the path, stone and soil heaped in a jagged mound. The air smells of raw earth where the slope tore away. I pull on the reins, slowing Firebrand to a halt, my hand tightening until the leather bites into my palm. He snorts and sidesteps, restless, tossing his head as though he remembers the wind trying to tear him from the ground.

The storm has passed, but the one inside me hasn't. It grinds in my chest, heavy as the clouds above, raw with the memory of Dessa's lips, of her trembling in my arms, of the vow that ripped from me with dragon fire.

I swing down from the saddle, boots sinking into the muck. My shoulder brushes Firebrand's as I steady him, murmuring low to soothe him. The stallion is sweat-slick and edgy, but he follows as I lead him toward the rubble.

Behind me, Dessa shifts, her skirts whispering against the saddle. She's quiet—too quiet. A Lorekeeper's silence is rarely empty; it's filled with thoughts sharp as quills. I can feel them now, brushing against the edges of me through the bond I forged between us. It's not her voice in my head, not quite, but an echo—her tension, her suspicion, the hot flare of her anger when she remembers what I did without asking.

She no longer clings to me while riding. Not now.

Her hands rest lightly on the saddle horn as I lead Firebrand around the mound of rocks and mud, her back stiff, her body angled away as though even touching the same horse is too much closeness. And yet, when Firebrand stumbles on a loose stone, she gasps, clutching the leather tight, her fear pouring into me like a jolt of lightning.

The bond carries it. Her emotions are their own storm inside me, mixing with mine.

I grit my teeth, force myself to keep moving, guiding our steed step by step around the worst of the debris. The stones shift under his hooves, sharp edges scraping, but we find a narrow line where the ground holds steady.

I glance back. Her face is pale, lips pressed thin, her eyes fixed on me with something between accusation and...fear.

The kiss. The voices. The vow. All of it still lies between us like the broken branches on the road—sharp, unavoidable, dangerous to ignore.

It feels like we're riding through the aftermath of a battle. In truth, we are.

I can still taste her. The memory of her lips brands me hotter than the dragon fire in my blood. She kissed me back—that's what undid me. Not pity, not fear, but want. In an instant, I forgot the storm. I forgot the voices that clawed at her, dragging her toward ruin. For that one breath, there was only her, only the tether between us.

A warning rumble rolls down from the slope above. "Ren!" Dessa shouts.

A boulder, slick with rain, breaks free from the bank and rolls straight for us, picking up speed as it bounds down the hillside.

"Hold on!" I jerk Firebrand hard to the right. The stallion lunges, his shoes slipping on the mud. Dessa's cry cuts the air as she pitches off balance, her fingers clawing for a hold.

I grab for her waist and brace. Firebrand rears, then skids, mud splattering over my legs as the boulder slams into the road where we were a heartbeat before. Shards of stone spray a wash of icy water over us.

The hiss of my curses and the thunder of my own pulse fills my ears. Firebrand trembles next to me, nostrils flaring. My grip on Dessa tightens, her breath coming fast and sharp as she locks eyes with me.

She didn't hate me after I confessed to writing the story that gave the Thief the opening to do all of this. It was everything.

She twists slightly in my hold, her fingers prying at mine. "Let me down," she says, voice tight. "I'll walk."

The bond throbs between us. I release her, and she slides off the saddle, landing lightly despite the mud. She steps behind Firebrand, eyes fixed on the ground, shoulders rigid.

I guide the stallion forward, my boots sinking with every step. The vow hums in my chest, answering her retreat, pulling me back to her even as she tries to put distance between us.

I bound myself to her. Without thought. Without permission.

I had no right, and yet I couldn't stop myself. Seeing her shaken by the voices that made her flinch, watching her fight them alone—it tore something out of me. The vow rose from my chest like it had always been there, waiting for her. The Dragon Language answered, searing me from the inside out, wrapping her fate into mine.

If she dies, so do I.

If I fail her, the fire will consume me.

I don't care. I would do it again. But her eyes afterward—it wasn't relief I saw in them. It was shock. And something akin to betrayal.

She keeps her distance now, walking near the stallion's haunches, one hand on his flank for balance. Her jaw is set. She's not demanding answers about the bond, but her silence is a demand all its own.

My dragon demanded I act, just as her quest demands she go to Jairton. I've never felt such a pull before. Not even for my kingdom. Not even for my own life. This is new to me—this bone-deep compulsion. This need to protect at all costs, to be near her. This vow feels older than either of us.

I glance back at her. Mud streaks her hem, and tendrils of damp hair cling to her cheeks. Her eyes are dark and unreadable as storm water. The pendant at her throat glints when she adjusts her cape. I feel its heat from here—like a heartbeat echoing mine.

She lifts her gaze and catches me looking. The bond thrums bright between us—her suspicion, her hurt, my guilt—all of it laid bare without a word.

She looks away, jaw tightening, and the tether slackens.

She hasn't told me everything about that gift from her mother, just as she hasn't told me everything about her dream. She thinks I don't know. But I do.

I keep my gaze on the path. I have my own secrets, and they rot in me like poison.

She now knows about the false story. She knows I wrote the prophecy that gave Solander Cimarron his foothold in our world, the one Serenelle helped me seal in Jairton. I expected rage. Condemnation. Gods know I deserve it. Instead, she looked at me as if... as if she understood.

Why?

Because of her mother. Dessa believes she still lives.

The truth twists in my gut. How do I tell her that my father might be the reason her mother vanished? That I might carry the stain of that curse in my own veins?

The road curves. Firebrand snorts, clambering over a fallen branch. The air is thick, heavy, damp with the storm's retreat. My heart is no lighter.

I want to demand she tell me the truth about that dream, about why she clings to her pendant like it's the only thing keeping her alive. But every time I try, I choke on my own guilt.

So instead, I say nothing.

Fate. Fire. Bargains and bindings.

The road to Jairton is paved with all of it, and I have no idea if either of us will survive what waits at the end.

The sound of Firebrand's hooves squelching through mud fills the silence. Dessa's voice cuts through the hush. "Ren."

I glance over my shoulder. Her eyes are fixed ahead, but her knuckles are white where she grips her quest book. "Before we reach Jairton, I need to know what we're walking into. Tell me about the town."

I let Firebrand's hooves answer for a long moment, their steady squelching through the mud almost a balm to my heart. Part of me wants to keep my jaw shut, but the look in her eyes—unyielding, determined—won't let me.

"Jairton is complicated." My voice sounds rough even to my own ears. "A border town, small but lively. Caravans came through from Seabright with salt fish, silk, and ironwork. Miners from the northern slopes brought ore. The market square was always crowded—bright banners, children underfoot, storytellers on every corner. It once smelled of spice bread." A ghost of a smile touches my mouth before fading. My throat aches at the memory—like I can still taste the spice on the wind, only now it's ash. "That was before."

"Before?" she presses.

"Before the vanishing began." I guide Firebrand around a large boulder, my hand firm on the reins. "Jairton is just across the border from Drakenholt. I didn't realize the erasure had spread to it. But when I was there, I saw the same hollow look in people's eyes. The way some of them kept repeating nonsense words. Acting like they were eating when there was nothing on their forks..."

"Calliope and I witnessed the same in several places. It's like...it bled into our kingdom."

"Now, Jairton is half a town—a place of near silence. You'll see the buildings, but they're husks. A handful of souls remain, clinging to scraps of memory. The rest are shadows. Already forgotten."

Her breath hitches, and I feel the spike of her grief through the bond. "And the ward?"

"The vault lies beneath the old worship hall. Your mother and I sealed it deep—stone, iron, Lore Language, and dragon fire together. The ward feeds on both. That's why it hasn't broken, even under Cimarron's assault. But..." My throat tightens. "That ward is weakening."

She sounds steady, but inside, her emotions sear me through the bond. Suspicion. A thread of fear. "And you know how to open it now that you have me to help?"

"It's your mother's ward. I suspect you'll be able to figure it out. All I know is you need my blood to mix with yours in order to reverse it."

"Our blood?" Her aversion slices right through me. "Are you sure that's required?"

"Actually, no. Now that we have a bond between us, it may not come to that. But I know when your mother set it up, she did it so it requires the blending of our magics. Of our two languages."

"The bond might be enough?"

I don't look back, but I feel her gaze on my shoulders. I should tell her about my father's curse. About how I know her mother cannot be alive because of it. But first, just for this moment, I want to explore what's between us. "You can feel it, can't you?"

A pause stretches long enough that my chest tightens. When I finally do glance over my shoulder at her, she quirks a brow. "Yes, okay? I can feel it. I feel..." She waves vaguely at me. "Your emotions and I sense your thoughts. It's quite overwhelming, to be honest. But if it helps us stop the Thief, I'll consider it worth it. Just...don't do anything like that again without my permission."

My actions have not been accepted yet, but she's practical above all else. I turn away before she sees my smile. "I promise."

"If the vault breaks open, Cimarron wins," she continues. "If we rescue the story first, we win."

Such simple sentences. Yet, it is the difference between life and death for me. Possibly for her as well. "The vault was built to store Drakenholt's oldest records—stories no one else should ever touch."

Through the bond, I feel the quicksilver spike of her emotions—curiosity, determination, and still some anger—all at once. Her mind is racing ahead, cataloguing, calculating—as if her quill is poised over the world itself. "Why there? Why are those stories not stored in your archives?"

"The histories in there tell a different story than those in Drakenholt's archives about how my kingdom came into existence with the dragons that once ruled the skies."

"A different origin story?"

I nod. We are finally past the last of the storm's wreckage. I bring Firebrand to a halt so I can face her. "It was something I uncovered during my apprenticeship. Something no Ravelle had knowledge of, as far back as our line goes."

Her fingers worry the edge of her journal. "What is it?"

A slice of sun peeks through the clouds. A part of me is relieved to share this knowledge, knowing that if I disappear, if the stories hidden in the vault are destroyed, Dessa will know of it. She can record what I tell her. "The original lore states that in the beginning, dragons—fierce beasts—ruled Drakenholt. Humans were their slaves. It was only when a ruler, prophesied by a storykeeper like yourself, rose against them, that the dragons were eventually overthrown. Their blood was mixed with the new ruler's using a magical bond. His family's, too, and thus was born the lineage of dragon royalty."

She considers this, and I feel her mind working it over. "And the stories in your archives?"

"They tell of the dragons and humans getting along from the start. That the dragons wanted to protect and help the humans, and that's why they bonded with them. That the dragons selected the first royals based on their high intellect and prowess to lead the kingdom."

"A sweeter story people would swallow."

"Yes." The blade of sun cuts across her face, lighting up her green eyes. I can't take my gaze off of her. "One that made the first royal family sound as if they were picked for their superior qualities, giving them and their successors"—I point at myself—"an advantage over others."

She steps forward and touches my arm. "It's time for the true story to be returned to your kingdom. A new starting point for Drakenholt."

*And for me.* If I'm to save it, I must rebuild it on the truth. The thought terrifies me, but it also feels like air filling my lungs for the first time. "Yes. If we can open the vault, I'll take all the stories and carry them back to the place they belong."

Her fingers squeeze my arm. "We'll do it. Stop the Thief and rewrite your future."

I want to kiss her again, but offer a smile instead. "Shall we?" I gesture to the road and then to the horse. "The final leg of this journey awaits."

She steps back to allow me to mount, pocketing her journal, and then accepts my hand to help her up behind me. Her hands settle on my waist, and I'm pleased to feel her lean against me as I flick the reins and we take off.

# CHAPTER TWENTY-FIVE
## CALLIOPE | STRANGERS AND QUESTS

*Beware those looking for stories under the guise of wanting a quest.*

FATHER AND I FALL into a rhythm with an undercurrent of worry. Every morning, I awake with dread balled in the pit of my stomach as I wonder about Dessa—where she is, what she's doing, if she's all right.

In her absence, Falena helps by feeding the chickens and the goat, milking the cow, and even lending a hand in Fable and Grim when needed, though she tires of routine quickly. She chatters about nothing and everything—perhaps to fill the silence we're all too afraid to break.

I wonder, though, if someday our roles will be reversed. If I'll be the one on a quest, and Dessa, Father, and Falena will be the ones fretting about my well-being.

As I prepare for the day in the mercantile by restocking the shelves behind the counter, the door chime sounds.

I glance up, expecting one of our regulars—maybe Mrs. Bramble with her rheumatism tea or the courier with parchment deliveries. Instead, a stranger fills the doorway.

He's tall, broad-shouldered, and sun-kissed—looking like trouble wrapped in sea mist. His navy coat is salt-stained at the cuffs, the silver buttons dulled by sea air. Wind-tossed hair brushes his collar, and stubble shadows his jaw. The grin he gives me is lazy, roguish, knowing...and something about it carries the faintest touch of sorrow, as if he's used to hiding sharp edges behind smooth charm. He smells faintly of wind and spice.

But it's his eyes that strike me most—bright green, almost aqua. Yes, that's the color.

"Morning," he greets, his voice a low rumble, warm enough to melt butter.

My heart skips—an involuntary flutter, like a thread has been plucked somewhere deep inside me. My palms go warm.

"Morning," I say, finally finding my voice.

He strolls in, unhurried, his boots scuffing along the floorboards. The stained glass from the transoms paints him in shards of color—amber across his jaw, blue across his coat sleeve, green splashing at his feet. His gaze lingers along the mismatched shelves with curiosity, but there's something sharper beneath it. Purpose. A man searching for something he shouldn't want.

"Is there something I can help you find?" I ask.

Falena is in the back, and Father is somewhere in the house, but a shiver crawls along my spine. Instinct. Wariness. Or maybe intuition—something old and knowing rising in me.

He turns his brilliant gaze to me and grants a knee-melting smile. My gut quivers as if struck by a soft blow. "I was told this little shop sells a bit of everything—potions, charms, maybe even a good story or two."

"We offer what most travelers need," I say, watching him warily as he picks up a jar of dried lavender. "And yes, we have books."

Quests, too, though I don't tell him that. He doesn't appear to be the type looking for one. Rather, the quest looks for him. My pulse thuds in agreement.

"Books are crucial," he says, grin deepening. "But a good story..."—the word lingers in the air, making my hackles rise—"now that's worth more than gold these days."

A wash of heat rolls through my limbs. Something in my chest tightens. The air feels...charged. Too aware. Too bright.

My nerves jitter. "I suppose that depends on who's telling it."

He chuckles, a rumble deep in his throat. He replaces the lavender and makes his way to the counter, pausing to stand directly across from me. When he leans on one elbow, his eyes catch mine—and something electric leaps between us. My pulse jumps. My breath thins. "I'm looking for a magical relic, and I was hoping you had it. A bit of lost treasure that has an important story tied to it. Small, might fit in the palm of the hand."

He opens his hand. His fingers are callused, and the salty scent of the sea invades my senses. A vision flashes—rigging whipping in the wind, sails billowing, a storm-dark horizon. I blink, startled. I never have visions. That's Dessa's ability.

"Word is," he continues, a flicker of tension crossing his expression before he smooths it over, "it might've washed up around here."

Is this the pirate I've heard gossip about? Fablehollow is far from the nearest major port, but the Evermere River leads to Silver Cove on Silvermist Bay. Across the bay is Tidewatch-by-the-Bay, one of Seabright's busiest ports. We get some of our best water-resistant parchment from there.

My pulse skips again. "We don't deal in relics or lost treasure."

"Of course not." He flashes that too-easy smile again—too quick, too practiced—and moves away from the counter. He picks up a jar of resin, turning it over in his hands like he's measuring its weight...or distracting himself. "Just thought I'd ask. You'd be surprised what ends up in shops like this."

He sets it down gently. Tips his head in a playful salute. "Well, lass, if you do happen to come across any lost treasures, you'll let me know?"

"How will I get in touch with you?" I ask, trying to sound indifferent. My cheeks betray me, warming traitorously.

He grins wider, clearly noticing. "A message in a bottle, of course."

He leaves a small shell on the counter. The moment it touches wood, a soft tingling spreads through my fingertips.

"I look forward to our next transaction—and perhaps you'll have a story for me then, too."

The chime jingles as he leaves, the scent of salt and clove lingering behind him. I exhale slowly, realizing my hands are trembling. My heartbeat stutters against my ribs as if something unseen has plucked a chord inside me.

I stare at the seashell, wondering if it's enchanted...or if I am.

Father shuffles in from the back. He glances from the door to me. "Everything all right?"

"Fine," I lie. Because how do you explain a stranger who walks into your shop and leaves the air crackling, as if he's stolen something invisible?

My gaze drifts to the shelf he stood beside—and I freeze.

One of the bottles—the one he held with the silver stopper—is glowing faintly.

The light pulses once, soft as a heartbeat.

And I can't tell if it's calling to me...

or to him.

# CHAPTER TWENTY-SIX
## DESSALYN | CLOSING IN

*Quests can free you...or devour you.*

I RIDE PRESSED AGAINST Ren's back as twilight descends. Firebrand's stride is steady beneath us, but my thoughts are anything but. They twist tighter with every mile, drawing us closer to Jairton.

The pendant at my throat weighs heavily on my collarbone, faint heat threading into my chest. A reminder. A warning. A tether to a bargain I never should have made.

*Bring me what I want, and your mother lives.*

The Story Thief's words spread through me like poison. I see Mom's face when I close my eyes and feel the warmth of her arms. My mother, alive, waiting. If I save Ren, I lose her forever. If I save her, Drakenholt is lost, Ren erased. Evermere may be next.

And Calliope? If our mother is erased, if her story ends...what does that mean for us, her daughters? For our bloodline? The Lore is merciless in its corrections. Does it strip us from existence as well? Or leave us hollow, shadows in a world that no longer knows our names?

The thought makes me clutch Ren's cloak tighter, though I tell myself it's just the cooling night air seeping into my skin.

The spire of a worship hall spears the horizon ahead, pale against the deepening dusk. *Jairton*. My chest lurches.

From this distance, it appears normal. The road widens toward a set of stone gates, and rooftops huddle beyond them like children around a fire. Warmth glimmers faintly in windows. A banner stirs in the wind. "It's almost beautiful," I say.

Ren, who's been silent for the past hour, grunts. "Don't be fooled. Danger waits for us around every corner."

Firebrand clatters through the gates. There are no guards. No chatter from those closing up shops and returning home. No final hammers ringing from the forges, or inns welcoming travelers.

The banner I thought was waving hangs in tatters, unmoving. The light in the windows is nothing but the last reflection of sunset, already fading. Carts stand abandoned in the streets, market stalls deserted. A child's ball rests in the gutter, waterlogged, and a doll has been left on a doorstep, limbs askew.

The air tastes stale and thick. I tighten my grip on Ren's waist. "It looks—" My voice cracks. "It looks forsaken."

His shoulders are rigid, his spine locked. "Just like in the castle, the town, all of my kingdom." His voice drops with sadness and despair. "The erasure is nearly done."

Firebrand's hooves echo too loudly on the cobbles, as if even the stones are hollow. A chill trickles down my spine, colder than the twilight air. Something shifts at the edge of my vision. A shadow glides across the roofline, too fast, too fluid to be human. I twist in the saddle, heart slamming against my ribs. Empty windows gape back at me.

Then I hear a scraping—nails on stone.

"Ren," I whisper.

He's already slowing Firebrand, one hand dropping toward the hilt of the sword at his hip. His head tilts, listening.

The scrape comes again, closer this time, followed by a low growl that vibrates through the street. My throat closes. I know that sound.

*Storyspawn.*

The wolf-creatures Calliope and I encountered in Longmere haunted my sleep for weeks afterward. Shadows stitched into flesh, eyes burning with a light that wasn't fire, teeth dripping ink instead of blood.

One leaps from the alley ahead, claws skittering across stone as it lands, facing us.

But this one is worse than those in Longmere. Its body warps and jerks, as though its story was rewritten mid-sentence. There are too many joints. A muzzle that stretches too long, tearing at its own skin. It pants, tongue lolling black and slick.

Another drops from a roof. Then another slithers out of the shadows behind us.

We're surrounded.

My quest book is a weight inside my cloak, heavy against my side. My hand trembles toward it.

Ren's voice cuts the air, low and sharp. "Hold onto me."

The first spawn lunges. Firebrand rears, screaming. I cling to Ren's waist, heart in my throat as his sword arcs through the dark. Ren's blade sings, cleaving through flesh. Fire flares in his eyes, smoke curling from his mouth with each ragged breath. But the pieces of the spawn knit back together, shambling upright as if mocking him.

"Ren—!"

His frustration lashes through the bond, hot enough to burn. "I see it." His voice is grim, his body iron as he wrenches Firebrand to face the next attacker. "But they don't want to kill us. Not you, anyway. Not yet."

He's right. The Story Thief wants to erase him, not me. But he needs us both to unlock that vault. I rip my knife from its hiding place. "They're not killing either of us."

Through the bond, I feel his fury, his determination to fight. Beneath my own skin, a darker certainty whispers...they won't touch me. Not because I'm strong, but because *he* won't let them. The Story Thief is pulling the leash.

What are my options? Desperation claws at me. My hand finds the edge of the journal, and words of Lore slip from my lips, too fast, too sharp. I don't even think about the consequences. I must *do* something. I raise my voice as the words fly from my mouth. The air shudders. For a heartbeat, the spawn dissolve into ink and wind.

But then...

They return. Whole. Hungrier.

The Thief's laughter scratches the inside of my skull.

The spawn circle tightens, eyes kindling—coal-bright, unnatural. Their bodies flicker at the edges where fur gives way to smoke and back again, like a sentence being written and erased, written and erased.

They don't rush us all at once. They...press. One veers left, jaws snapping close enough to make Firebrand flinch. Another goes right to block the alley where a ribbon of shadow coils away. A third slinks behind and huffs a wet breath against Firebrand's hocks, forcing him to sidestep into a narrower lane.

"They're herding us," I whisper.

"I see it." Ren's voice is flint. He turns Firebrand in a tight circle, keeping the largest of them at the sword's reach. "Keep your knife up. If one takes you, I burn this town to the bedrock."

I try for bravado and am surprised when my voice rings with it. "You won't need to."

MISTY EVANS & MICHELLE MILES

The nearest spawn lunges, and Ren meets it with his steel. The blade slices the creature from jaw to sternum. Black ichor fans across the cobbles, eating at old mortar with a hiss.

It knits back together.

Not perfectly. Worse. A second jaw forms within the first, teeth crooked, ink-dripping. It grins, delighted.

Cold threads through my veins. "They're wrong," I breathe. "Like a child copied a wolf from memory and put the pieces in the wrong places."

"They're not wolves," Ren snarls, feinting left, killing right. "They're stories given flesh." His sword takes another head. It tumbles, rots to letters midroll, and the letters crawl back into a skull.

Firebrand wheels beneath us, foam lacing his bit. The spawn behind us snaps again—deliberate, restrained. Not a killing bite. Another nudge.

"I don't understand," I say, a bit of panic now shaking my voice. "If Cimarron wants the story, why send these abominations to make it harder for us to get to it?"

"A test," Ren says. "Or he's not fully in control of the monsters he's created."

That thought sours my stomach.

The worship hall looms ahead, pale stone gone sallow in the last light. A bell tower juts like a finger pointing at the sky. The doors—twin slabs of oak bound in iron—are closed. But I can feel the pull from beneath, faint as breath in a crypt. The ward my mother wove thrums under my skin, answering something in my blood—and in Ren's—like a heartbeat underground.

I drag in air. "Left," I choke. "Take the next left—don't let them funnel us to the square."

Ren kicks his heel. Firebrand surges...and three spawn drop from the roof, hitting the stones in front of us with a meaty slap. Their claws rake grooves across the cobbles, drawing lines like tally marks. Their eyes glow. The middle one opens its mouth and, stars above, a voice spills out that isn't a voice. *"Dessalyn...at last."*

"Faster," Ren says, not to me but to the horse, to himself, to the dragon burning behind his sternum.

We don't go faster. We go narrower. The street pinches to an elbow of alley hemmed by shuttered windows and sagging balconies. Laundry hangs like abandoned flags.

Ren jerks Firebrand right to avoid teeth. I lean left to avoid a rusted lantern. A claw scores the hem of my cloak, and I slash instinctively. My knife bites, and for a heartbeat the creature's paw splits into individual letters—C, L, A, W—before snapping back into place.

"They're words," I gasp. "But they're not holding their form. You're right...he's losing control of this story. If we—"

"Hold." He saws the reins, twists, and cuts. One spawn leaps for his throat. He ducks and drives the pommel of his sword up under its jaw. Bone—no, consonant—cracks. It collapses with a wet cough. Two more take its place.

My hand flies to my cloak. The quest book is warm, alive with the same dread that grips me. I yank it free, every instinct screaming that this is a terrible idea, and flip to a blank page. Ink blotches already pool at the margins.

"Dessa—what are you doing?"

"Buying us a breath." I chew the inside of my cheek until I taste iron. "Cover me."

Ren doesn't argue. He becomes a wall—blade, shoulders, fire. The bond surges. I feel his focus like a shield—fierce enough to bruise. I brace the book against my thigh, the horse's movement turning my letters into desperate slants, and whisper three syllables of Lore that should scatter a tale like dust.

Everything goes into slow motion. As the words land, the spawn unravel. Fur turns to frayed script, bodies smear to ink, eyes pop like punctuation, and run in rivulets down the gutter.

The street empties.

My breath breaks free. "It worked—"

They flow back together.

Faster. Worse. The one I split with my knife now has multiple mouths, each whispering a different line from a different story. A fairytale and a recipe. A hymn and a ledger. Nonsense that makes no sense.

The Thief is watching. I feel it like a draft on the nape of my neck. But...does he realize he's no longer writing this story?

Through the bond, Ren's frustration cracks like lightning. "Clever trick." His voice is quiet, deadly. "Needs fine-tuning."

My fingers shake as I snap the book shut. "I was trying to see if they were bound to him."

"And are they?"

I swallow. "Yes, but the bond is...like a child's story. There's no cohesiveness. No true plot or structure."

We burst into the square. It's empty of people. Full of absence. A ribbon someone once won at a harvest game flaps from a post, the ink of its name faded to a pale ghost. The worship hall squats on the far side—stone, iron, ward humming under my skin. The oak doors are shut, but shadows gather along the jambs as if listening.

The spawn spread out, forming a ring. They pant in unison—a chorus without a conductor.

"Get down," Ren snarls. "If we're doing this, we do it with our feet on the ground."

I slide off the horse, knees soft. Firebrand stamps, ears pinned back. Ren swings down after me in one smooth motion and shoves the reins into my hand. "If one gets through, you run for the doors."

"What if they won't open?"

"They'll open for you." His jaw sets. "I'll make them."

I want to say I won't leave him. I want to say I can't. Instead, I nod, because my voice is a fallible thing and there's a bargain trapped in my throat.

The first spawn pulls the circle tighter. Ren steps forward to meet it.

He fights like a story told around a winter hearth—inevitable, right, older than the walls that hear it. Steel sings. The dragon in him stirs—I see it in the flare of his eyes, feel it in the heat that licks along my skin through the bond. He doesn't breathe fire—he bleeds it, in sparks along the blade, in smoke that curls from his teeth when he snarls. He cuts a creature in thirds. It splits with a sound like tearing vellum...and congeals at his back.

They're learning him.

"Behind you!" I shout. He pivots without looking, sword already there. The spawn leaps onto the blade, body mottling into wet letters that slide down his arm. It laughs soundlessly, without a mouth, until he flicks it off, sending it skittering across stone.

The ring compresses.

They nip at Firebrand's flank, teasing, taunting. When I slash one, it recoils, then presses forward again, lips skinning back to show those extra teeth. They want us between the horse and the door. They want—

"Inside," I whisper to the ward below the hall, a prayer, a plea. The hum answers. Faint. Waiting. Like my mother's voice just before a bedtime story—*begin*.

The largest spawn yet pads into the square. It isn't a wolf. Not anymore. A stag's antlers sprout from its skull, branching letters tangled in the tines. A second set of legs has torn through along its ribs, knees backwards, hooves splitting to claws. Its eyes are blank pages. It lowers its head and scrapes an antler along the cobbles until sparks jump.

"Look out," I call.

Ren lifts the sword. Flames lace the blade, the hilt.

The stag-thing charges.

The impact shudders the ground. Ren's sword takes it, his knees bending, boots scraping. The antlers drive him backward. Firebrand screams as two lesser spawn try to hamstring him.

I jerk the reins and drive my knife down, feeling the blade sheer through shadows into something that bites back. Ink splashes my wrist. It burns.

"Dessa!" Ren barks—warning, command, apology all at once.

"I'm fine." I'm not. My arm throbs. I yank the knife free and stab again at a chest that isn't a chest. The spawn splits into clauses, reforms, and bites. Teeth catch my sleeve and rip. The bite pushes me a step closer to the doors.

"Stop it," I spit, throat raw. "You don't get to choose where I go."

It blinks, bewildered.

Ren snarls and wrenches the stag-thing's head sideways, shoving flaming steel between antlers. Bone-letters crack. The blade jerks free—and the creature rears, crashing down hard enough to spiderweb the stones.

"Enough," I hiss. My pendant pulses, scalding. I'm done being prey. I'm done being herded. I'm done letting Cimarron's leash decide the measure of my steps. He's no storyteller. He's a hack playing games.

I flip the quest journal open, but I don't write. I speak. A story as old as riverbeds. Dangerous as floodwater. Lore rushes out of me. "Storyspawn freeze."

The square takes a breath and holds it. The spawn pause, as if the sentence of their bodies has hit a comma and is waiting for the next clause.

Ren's head snaps toward me, shock and wild pride flashing through the bond. "How long?"

"I don't know." My voice shakes. "A breath. Maybe two."

He grabs Firebrand's bridle, shoving the stallion forward. "To the doors."

We run.

The pause fails. A tail twitches. A claw digs. A throat clears ink. I can feel the Lore slipping from my fingers, trickling away like water through a sieve. The stag-thing turns to look at us, its blank-page eyes finding me and beginning to form the first letters of my name.

We reach the worship hall. The oak is cold under my palms, iron bands slick. The ward below beats, impatient now, insistent—like a heartbeat knocking at the underside of the world.

"Open," I whisper.

Nothing moves.

Ren slams his palm next to mine. Heat surges along my skin, bond snapping taut. His dragon fire hums against the ward, two songs recognizing each other.

"Open," he says, and his voice is smoke and vow and inheritance.

The seam shivers. Iron groans. The doors shift a finger's width—

—and slam back shut.

The pause breaks.

The square erupts. Spawn throw themselves at the steps, claws scoring stone, antlers raking sparks, teeth straining for the tendons at Firebrand's hocks. Ren wheels between me and the pack, sword a line of light. A prince holding a line made of nothing but his own body.

I press my forehead to the oak. The pendant sears. *Mom*, I think, like a child. *Help me. Help us.*

What if the bond is the key? Not blood in a bowl. Not cut skin on iron. The joining. The way our Lores mesh when he touches me. The way mine fits like a key in his lock.

"Ren!"

"I'm a little busy," he grunts, driving steel through a jaw to the hinge.

"Give me your hand."

He doesn't hesitate. He shoves his left hand back without looking, palm up. I seize it, slam both our hands flat to the iron.

Heat roars. Not his dragon fire alone. Not my Fae Lore alone. Both, braided. The ward answers. The iron bands flare to a dull, buried red. The seam exhales, a breath of old stone and beeswax and something like sunlight under the earth.

Behind us, the stag-thing screams.

The doors part.

Ren yanks me through the widening gap. Firebrand shoulders after, eyes rolling white, barely clearing before the doors heave and crash shut. A dozen claws hit on the other side. Teeth scrape iron. Antlers slam against the band. The wood groans but holds.

I sag against the inside of the door, lungs burning, heart ricocheting. A hall stretches before us—pews skeletal in rows, the altar bare.

Ren stands with his back braced against the wood, sword lifted, chest heaving, smoke curling faintly from between his teeth. He looks at me like I'm the only thing in the room that's real.

My fingers are still fused to his. The pendant pulses like a second heartbeat. The bond thrums hot and bright, fierce as victory, fragile as glass. Now that I'm here, I feel even more conflicted. This is it. What decision will I make? "Whatever happens, know that I…"

I can't say it. What I'm thinking. What my heart feels.

He squeezes my hand and gives me a sad, crooked smile. "I know."

Outside, the claws rake. The oak still holds.

Beneath us, the ward shivers again, welcoming and wary.

*Dessalyn Lorewyn...*

Somewhere under the skin of this dying town, a story that will change my future calls my name.

# CHAPTER TWENTY-SEVEN

## DESSALYN | THE VAULT OF SECRETS

*The quest beckons one to salvation...or ruin.*

RAINWATER DRIPS THROUGH HOLES in the roof, pattering against rotted beams and stone tiles slick with moss. The wind rattles through the empty window frames, and outside, claws continue to scrape against the stone—storyspawn prowling, circling.

Firebrand stamps and snorts, tethered inside with us, his ears flat, whites showing in his eyes. His bulk presses close, his warmth filling the ruined aisle where pews lie splintered like bones.

Ren leads him deeper, one hand firm on the reins, the other resting on his sword. His broad back is a wall in front of me, his shoulders tense, every line taut with control. The bond warms between us.

Both of us and the horse are covered in inky ichor. I wipe my hands on my already ruined skirt before I touch the pendant, hot as a coal against my skin. The weight of it is unbearable in this place.

*We shouldn't be here*. The wards rake over my skin and dig into my gut. They push at me to leave. Flee.

Yet this is precisely where the quest has led me.

Firebrand shifts uneasily, nearly crowding me against the wall. My palm skims the slick stone. My voice escapes in a whisper before I can stop it. "Why didn't you do it?"

Ren halts, half-turning. His face is shadowed, the dwindling light from a crack in the roof casting a hard line on his jaw. "Do what?"

"You know." My throat tightens. "I saw you shift in Longmere. Your dragon was...beautiful. It burned the spawn like they were nothing." I glance toward the door, where shadows writhe against the threshold. "Why not now when we needed it?"

His silence is a blow. Firebrand shifts again, hot breath landing on my shoulder.

Ren reaches out, and flame dances from his fingers, lighting a wall torch. The flicker of it catches in his eyes—blue, but rimmed with weariness and strain. "I tried."

My pulse stutters. "Tried?"

His fingers tighten around the reins. "The fire came. But the shift..." He shakes his head once, sharply, as if disgusted with himself. "The dragon wouldn't answer."

I don't understand. "Wouldn't...answer? Has that ever happened before?"

"Never. It's like something pulled me back. Held me here." He makes a fist and smacks it against his chest before he meets my gaze, his voice raw with emotion. "Maybe it's from the bond. Maybe Cimarron's corruption is leeching into my Lore. Or maybe—" He cuts off, jaw clenching. "Maybe I feared I'd burn you instead."

That tether between us snaps tight with his frustration, his shame, his fear that he could harm me. He doesn't need to say more.

I step closer before I think better of it, my hand brushing his forearm, then resting there. His skin is warm, muscles tight. "Ren," I whisper, his name catching like a flame in my throat. "You're not less because the dragon didn't answer."

His eyes flick down to where my fingers rest, then back, searching mine. "You don't understand," he rasps. "The dragon is my birthright. My weapon. Without it—"

"Without it, you still fought for me." My voice grows stronger. "You still brought me through those beasts. Dragon or not, you're the prince who stands between me and the dark." My heart hammers. "You're still enough."

The muscle under my palm flexes as if my words have struck deep. He exhales, ragged, causing the bond to flare. This time, it's not with his guilt but with something warm and alive like a spring morning. Something that makes my chest pinch, because what I'm about to do will break that bond forever.

His free hand lifts, hesitates, then cups my jaw. The callused pad of his thumb brushes my cheek. "Dessa…"

My name sounds like a vow and a plea all at once. It steals my breath. I want to lean in to him, to close that last inch, but my own guilt binds me. I wonder if he feels it, and I try to snuff it out. I search his eyes, seeking some sign that he can read my mind, read my emotions, and sense the betrayal I'm considering.

His eyes darken, but I can't tell if it's because of that or because he's about to kiss me. Panicking, I raise up on my toes, wrap my arms around his neck, and kiss him instead.

His lips are warm and soft. He groans against mine, and the sound ripples through my body. He releases the reins and tugs me to him, pressing his body into mine.

I welcome his warmth and his strength. I welcome the way his strong hand sneaks underneath my hair to the back of my neck, and his lips turn greedy. "I will always protect you," he murmurs against my mouth.

My lips part. His tongue sweeps inside. Heat washes through me, and I tug him closer, pressing against him, wanting to suck all of that heat up and not ever leave this moment. I don't want to think about the next one or the next. I don't want to think about choosing my mother over him. Choosing my family over his kingdom.

I don't want to think at all. All I want to do is feel.

He cups my jaw, his thumb brushing lightly along my cheekbone. The bond hums—warm, insistent—as if it recognizes something I don't want to admit.

I have secrets that will break him. I should step back, but I can't. Not when his eyes hold mine like I'm the only thing keeping him tethered to this world.

"Dessa," he murmurs again, breaking the kiss. His voice is softer this time, as though my name itself is fragile. The space between us is my chance to stop this. To end it before it goes any further.

But the sound of him saying my name cracks my heart open. Everything between us feels unbearable. My pulse roars in my ears, nerves sparking with the awareness of his body so close, his warmth so intoxicating.

If I continue down this path—if I let myself want this—it will make the choice waiting for me at the vault impossible.

My mother or him.

A future with her...or one with him.

The bond drums hard, dizzying, and before I can think better of it, I tilt my face into his palm. A breath hisses from his mouth. Our foreheads nearly touch, close enough that if I move an inch—just one—our mouths will meet again.

And stars help me, *I want it.*

I run my fingers through his damp hair. His eyes close for a breath as if he's waited for my touch. When they flick back open, the blue in them is nearly black. He presses me against the stone wall, one hard, muscled thigh parting my legs, his broad chest anchoring me there. He lifts my chin, and I lick my bottom lip, a thrill blazing through me when his intense gaze zeroes in on it.

The growing shadows crowd around us, ignoring the torchlight. I trace the scar over his left brow. The flicker of light touches the broken pendant he wears.

"Why me?" I ask softly. I fear it's because I'm the only person who can save Drakenholt. That if he didn't need me, he wouldn't look twice at me. "Did you only bond with me to keep me safe long enough to rewrite your kingdom?"

A flash of hurt crosses his face. "Of course not." His voice is raw, edged like steel, and soft as smoke all at once. "Do you think I would bind myself—risk myself—just for duty? For a crown already turned to ash?"

His hand slides from my jaw to my throat, not pressing, only cradling the fragile column, as if my very breath matters. "I felt the pull to you long before I made the oath. In Longmere, when I saw you ready to fight the storyspawn with nothing but your wits and your will. When you read my entries in your journal and didn't turn your back on my pleas for help, even after the way my father and I treated your family. When you left your father to come to me." His mouth tilts in something that isn't quite a smile. "When you looked at me like I was still a man and not just a cursed dragon prince."

My chest heaves, the place between my legs hot and aching. I want to believe him. With all my heart, I want to.

"You're more than the key to my kingdom, Dessa. You're..." His throat works, his thumb now brushing against the frantic pulse in my neck. "You're the only thing that's made me feel alive since Drakenholt died."

His words slice me open, tender and brutal all at once. *Alive.* I make him feel alive.

I want to laugh and weep in the same breath, because that's what he's done for me. From the moment he strode out of the fire in my nightmare, he's been a tether I didn't ask for and can't cut away.

"I don't..." My voice cracks. I slide my hand from his hair to his cheek, the rough stubble rasping against my palm. "You don't know what you're saying."

"I know exactly what I'm saying." His gaze pins me, dark and unflinching.

The bond ignites again between us, low and insistent, and my heart rebels against my mind. Against the bargain with Cimarron. Against the knowledge that if I choose Ren, I might lose my mother forever.

"I don't want to be your kingdom's crutch," I whisper. "Or your cage. I want to be...me. I don't know if that's enough."

His forehead tips to mine, and the words I don't say burn like coals behind my teeth. *If I save you, I might doom her.*

His breath warms my lips, his hand is firm at my waist as if he would hold me here forever.

Before I can untangle the mess of words and wants clawing in my chest, a new sound breaks the air.

*Crack.*

Not thunder, not stone settling. It's sharper, deeper—like ice fracturing on a winter lake. The vibration runs through the soles of my boots, rattling the torches in their brackets. Firebrand stamps nervously, tossing his head.

Ren jerks away from me, his hand flying to his sword. "The vault," he says.

Another fissure splits the silence, this time louder, echoing up through the floor beneath us. The ground itself pulses faintly with heat, as though dragon fire still lingers deep below.

My heart stutters. The cracks he told me about. The ones he sealed—are they failing? "The ward?"

"Cimarron is pressing harder. He wants what's inside."

Or someone else does. The Thief knows I'm here. That our bargain makes me the one who will give him the story he needs. There's no reason for him to bring a magical storm to slow our progress, to then carve *hurry* into the side of the cave. No reason to send Storyspawn to attack me and rebuff my attempts to retrieve the very story he so desperately wants.

Again, I wonder, could it be Marrow? For what purpose?

The shadows dance violently on the walls, elongating into grotesque shapes, twisting like hands reaching. The air tastes of iron and ink, as if the Thief himself has slipped a breath into this ruined church.

Ren grabs my hand—his palm hot against mine. "Come. We don't have much time."

He leads me across the nave, past toppled pews and the collapsed altar, to the stairwell yawning downward into blackness. He grabs a long-dead torch from its holder, and I feel a different sort of tug on the bond—his magic. The end ignites in flame.

I gasp, stumbling at the sensation that surges through me. His magic floods the tether between us, white-hot, pure power—a poker drawn straight from a forge and pressed into my chest. It's heat and weight and heartbeat all at once, too much to contain, too intimate to endure.

It's not just flame I feel. It's him.

My pendant sears my skin, its heat mixing with his. The bond or a warning?

Does it matter? I can't turn away. My quest, my bargain, my mother—all of it points me here.

Ren glances back, his eyes catching the flicker of torchlight. Fierce. Determined. But not afraid. "Stay close, Dessa."

We descend into the dark.

# Chapter Twenty-eight
## Renwick | The Fire Between Us

*Some truths burn hotter than dragon fire.*

As I GUIDE DESSA downward, the torch in my hand sheds light that bends and warps against the walls.

The dragon fire stirs inside me, restless and hungry, but when I glance back at her, the pulse steadies. She's my anchor to something human.

At the bottom, the vault waits. The air is heavy, almost suffocating. Magic presses against my ribs. I sense an extra heartbeat that doesn't belong to me. Hers through the bond? Or something else?

Firebrand's hooves echo above us as he paces, unhappy. My body aches. Every muscle sings with fatigue from the fight. I can still feel the sting of shadow-claws along my arm, the acid hiss of the storyspawn ink when it splattered my skin.

Beneath it all lies a deeper yearning—the connection with Dessa humming through my veins, tuned to her.

I keep glancing back to make sure she's okay. My sword is raised and ready, but I can't protect her front and back. The place appears deserted, yet I must not take chances that trouble waits in the shadows.

The torchlight gilds her hair in molten gold. She shouldn't seem so calm after everything we've faced tonight, but her spine is straight, her chin high. I can sense it now—the rhythm of her Fae blood. While she is aggravated over my vow and the bond it created, her magic has threaded itself with mine.

I should be thinking about the vault, about the cracks in the ward, and the stories we came to protect. But all I can think about is her hand in mine in the dark, her breath warm against my lips. The memory of our kiss is a wound that refuses to close.

"Are you sure you're strong enough for this?" she asks quietly. "I know your strength has been waning, and you just fought hard."

I huff out a short laugh. "I've survived worse."

Her steps falter, and I glance back at her again. She knows I'm lying. My strength is fading, and we both feel it through the bond.

"I'm okay, Dess." I squeeze her hand. "I swear."

A finger strokes under the gold cuff and across the inside of my wrist, touching the dragon mark there. "You will be," she promises.

The stairs spiral until we reach the bottom. The torch flares brighter, reflecting off the half-collapsed arch that leads into the chamber and the dais beyond.

The space grows tighter, the glyphs on the walls twisting in the light as we pass. The dais and the sealed vault draw me to them, and the cracks gleam. My dragon fire still clings to them, barely holding.

Dessa takes a slow step forward. "It's beautiful." Her voice trembles, and through the bond I feel her awe, her fear—and something else I can't name. "And terrible."

Her words stir the chamber. The seal flickers, reacting to her presence, to *our* presence. The bond turns molten like her hair, a current passing from her pendant into mine. "Do you feel that?" I murmur.

She nods, touching the stone on her collarbone. "It's always been our destiny."

I secure the torch in a holder. "This is where it's buried, along with the origin story of Drakenholt."

She glances at me, green eyes catching the light. "I feel Mom's magic." She rubs her arms. "It tingles."

I touch the scorched metal of the vault itself. It's cool now, but the pulse of dragon fire echoes beneath my fingertips. "The seal is barely holding."

She crouches, tracing her fingertips just above the surface. The Lore responds, light flaring in fine threads beneath her touch. "It's alive," she murmurs. "Trying to remember what it was made to protect."

Her hair brushes her cheek, and I resist the urge to tuck it back. "Can you repair it?" I ask.

"I could," she says slowly, "but if I do, we may never get inside." Her eyes raise to mine. "Is that what you want?"

"What are my choices? Leave it here and risk the Thief getting it, or take it myself and..."

"And do what with it?"

I've spent many hours contemplating that exact thing. "Rewrite it. Burn it. Lock it in the Drakenholt scriptorium. I'm not sure."

She straightens and paces. "My Lore Language exacts a price for rewriting a story. Does yours?"

I drop my gaze to the floor. "Yes."

"And that price is?"

"The author loses his gift. The Language rejects him."

Her steps stop, and I feel the weight of her stare. "You're prepared to risk that?"

And so much more. "I am."

"What if it doesn't restore your kingdom?" She's suddenly beside me, her fingers on my arm. "What if there is no way to bring back those who've been erased?"

Does she know something I don't? I've considered this many times as well. "I can't bring them back, even if I don't rewrite or destroy the story, Dessa. You're the only one who can do that."

She walks away again, scanning the glyphs on the walls. Her fingers travel over one then another, as if she's reading them with her touch. "I fear neither of us can."

It's a gut punch. "I thought this was your quest. To save my kingdom and stop the Thief."

She heaves a deep sigh. "What if I'm wrong? What if I do more harm than good?"

The dais quakes. Another *crack* echoes in the chamber. We exchange a glance.

Dust falls from the ceiling onto the vault. "I can sense the Thief's magic is here," I say, hand on my hilt. "If the ward breaks, he will—"

The ground trembles. She stumbles, and I grab her arm. Her body falls into mine, her eyes wide. "I know, but..."

That look on her face twists something in me. The bond vibrates a warning. I feel her emotions. "You're afraid of opening it."

She doesn't deny it. Her gaze fixes on the cracks, her brow furrowed. "There's something odd with the magic, or maybe with what the vault holds. The ward...scratches against my mind."

I keep a hand on her elbow. "Because it's your mother's magic. It knows your blood."

Her breath shudders. "I don't think it's that. I feel her magic, yes, but there's something older, ancient even, that's inside with your story."

That thought chills me. "Like what?"

She pulls away from my hand. "I don't know. It feels like a sleeping beast, curled around the contents. What if we open the vault and whatever it is escapes?"

A beast? Surely, I would have sensed it. "I don't feel anything except the wards."

She bites her bottom lip, averting her gaze. The bond vibrates again. I study her face—the tightness around her eyes, the way her fingers tremble as she turns to the walls and traces another sigil. "What aren't you telling me, Dessa?"

Her head whips around.

"I can feel it," I press. "Through the bond. You're hiding something. Every time you consider opening the vault, your fear spikes."

"I'm not—"

"Don't lie to me." The words come out sharper than I intend. "What is it you're afraid of?"

Her lips part, but she doesn't speak. The silence stretches. The glyphs on the vault glow brighter, reacting to the strain between us.

Finally, she whispers, "You won't understand."

"Then make me." The plea slips out before I can stop it. I step closer, closing the space between us.

Her eyes glisten with tears she won't let fall. "I can't," she says softly. "Not yet."

The bond throbs in my chest—frustration, guilt, longing—all tangled together until I can't tell which emotions are hers and which are mine. I reach for patience. "You'll tell me when you're ready." The chamber shifts again, more dust falling from the ceiling. A crack appears in the wall to our left. "But I fear, my sweet Lorekeeper, we are running out of time."

She steps back from the dais, shaking her head. "We shouldn't open it, Ren."

The floor quakes under my boots. "We must, Dessa."

"Please, don't make me—"

A chunk of rock falls and smashes into the vault. The cracks split into dozens more.

I want to grab her by the hand and drag her to the lock. But I can't force her to do this. "This is your destiny as well as mine. Whatever happens, we face it together."

Her eyes are glazed with tears. "You'll hate me."

There it is again—the bond's warning. It echoes in her words. What has she done?

It's too late now, whatever it is. "Never," I insist. These are strange times. Even though it's clear she's done something that might cause my ruin rather than my salvation, I can't do anything but smile. "Your heart is pure. I know it. Whatever it is, I will not hate you."

Another tremor shakes us. She loses her balance, falling toward the vault and catching herself on the lip of it.

I lunge forward and slam my palms onto the cracking wards. "Ready?" I ask, a plea in my voice.

A tear slips down her cheek. She bites her bottom lip. "What do I do exactly?"

"Just place your hands flat on the center. That's the lock. Tell it to open. Your magic will do the rest."

She gives me one more heart-wrenching look, then slides her palms into place.

The cracks pulse once, twice—then catch fire.

Dragon fire should burn gold. This burns white. The light flares so bright it sears the inside of my eyelids, threads of heat snaking over the stone like veins of lightning.

"Ren, it's—" Dessa's voice catches, but the roar building in the air swallows the sound. The ward recognizes her. It recognizes us.

The cracks split wider, edges glowing as if the stone itself is bleeding light. My dragon mark burns in answer, agony streaking from my wrist up my arm. It lands in my chest, searing my ribs.

I try to hold the fire in check, to keep it from raging out of control, but the Lore doesn't want control—it wants connection.

Pain tears through my palm. My skin splits, blood runs, and drips onto the floor. It hisses where it lands, and the ward responds, hungry. A rumble rips through the chamber, deep and ancient, and I feel Dessa's magic twist through mine.

Her pendant ignites. A second light, it blooms in the darkness—green and gold, pure as sunlight through glass. It catches the dragon crest around my neck, and the two flare together, feeding off one another.

The air shudders. She cries out.

I stagger back, but the Lore doesn't release me. The current rips through the link between us, my power pouring into hers, hers pouring back into mine until there's no difference between dragon fire and Lorelight. No chasm between the Fae Lore Language and my Dragon Language.

The cracks blaze red now, bleeding energy instead of flame. The noise rises to a pitch like metal being torn apart.

Dessa clutches her chest, her face ghost-pale, sweat beading along her hairline. "It's pulling—"

"I know!" My words are lost to the rush of power. My knees hit the stone. The air is being sucked from my lungs, my vision collapsing in on itself. The light is reversing, dragging everything into it.

The world inhales.

The suction is brutal and endless. My body arches, fighting it, ribs straining. Yet, the fire in my veins answers the call. I feel it tugging at my core—at something older than my name, older than Drakenholt itself.

Through the bond, Dessa's pain scorches me. Her heartbeat stutters against my own. I can feel her magic clawing for purchase, the pendant burning a brand into her skin.

Our Lores are working together, not to break open the wards, but to...

Summon. Call. Conjure.

And whatever they're calling through...
It's already here.

# CHAPTER TWENTY-NINE
## DESSALYN | WHEN THE QUEST TURNS

*Stories are always warnings to the wise.*

MY SENSES REEL. THE world under my feet shifts—literally.

Out of the rift between the floor stones, letters crawl—torn fragments of words that form and unform, twisting into a silhouette. Each one sears my vision, runes blinking like dying stars before they tangle together into the outline of a man.

The air in the vault goes brittle.

The shape condenses—ashen skin, hair coiling like ink in water, eyes sunken with a faint, pulsing silver light. His arrival causes frost to spread across the stones, crawling outward like veins of ice beneath our feet.

*Marrow.*

My breath catches. He's not the cocky, swaggering hero of his own story anymore. He's not solid, not whole. Words flake off him like mist, each one unraveling before it hits the ground. A living sentence that can't hold itself together.

"You shouldn't have opened it," he rasps. His voice is roughened by something ancient and broken. "He's using you both."

Ren steps between us, sword drawn, flames flickering along the steel. Blood drips from his hands. "Step back. He's not real."

"Oh, I'm real enough." Marrow's lips curl into a shadow of a smile, though half of it flickers and dissolves into letters. "Real enough to stop you before it's too late."

My chest feels as if it will cave in. Ren is losing power, losing...everything. His lifeblood is draining out of him, dripping onto the stones, this chamber drinking it in.

The bond rises, then fades. Ren's rage, his instinct to protect, boosts it, only to falter because of his exhaustion.

Fear grips me. "Too late for what?" I force my voice to hold steady, while the Lore inside me quivers in recognition of Marrow's presence. His magic has a taste, cold, metallic.

His head tilts, the silver light in his eyes narrowing. "The Story Thief will keep you like a prized toy, Lorekeeper, as the king kept me. He needs to unmake him." His gaze slides to Ren, and the chill deepens. "And he will. Because that's what you were made for."

Ren shifts, his boots scraping the frost. "You lie."

"Do I?" Marrow flickers—one arm distorts into a swirl of letters before reforming. "You think the bond between you was an act of will? You think the Lore didn't plan this from the beginning?"

My pulse spikes. The connection burns with Ren's horror, pulling tight in my chest. He nearly staggers. "What are you saying?"

Marrow's gaze finds me again, sharp, knowing. "You're not his salvation, Lorekeeper. He's your sacrifice."

The word hits me like a physical blow. My throat closes. The stories in my veins shudder and twist, whispering of pasts and futures. Prophesies and bargains. "Mom," I breathe, the sound of a broken prayer.

Ren glances at me, his face blanching. "What did Cimarron promise you?" he demands. "Whatever it was, he lied."

"Not a lie. A promise sealed with a Fae bargain," Marrow tells him. His body grows more solid. "But even a bargain can be rewritten if the one who entered it is chained in blood."

My heart falls. Ren glances at me, then lunges, the sword a blur of fire and fury, but it slices through empty air as Marrow vanishes into smoke. Frost glitters where he stood, and his last words linger, whispering from the cracks in the vault like an echo that won't fade.

Ren exhales hard, lowering his blade. His gaze lands on me. "What have you done, Dessa?"

I can't answer. Can't shake the look in Marrow's eyes. *He's using you both.*

He's right.

The bargain was true, but if Cimarron rewrites my story and binds me to his twisted words in blood...then Ren's fate is sealed with mine.

My mother's, too.

My knees give out. I sink to the floor. The vault is still now, yet it beats between my ears like a heart I can't silence.

Marrow materializes again behind the dais, stretched thin. The frost spiderwebs across the vault floor, tracing the same runes etched into the dragon fire seal. "We're strangers bound by fate, Lorekeeper. You're blood—my blood. Our mothers'. It runs in both of us."

Ren glances toward me, confusion mirroring my own.

*Our mother's.* The chest is too tight. "What?"

Marrow's eyes gleam, silver and sorrowful. "I'm Serenelle's firstborn—the one she buried in dreams and abandoned in a river."

My mind can't make sense of it, even as my body shakes with the truth of it.

Ren stills, as if the flame inside him has turned to ice. "You're saying—"

"Your mother's maid found me in the reeds where Mother left me after she wrote a prophecy. Hesta raised me long enough to discover my rare gift of dream walking—and then she sold me to your father for gold and glory. The king wanted me, a dream walker, to secure his kingdom. I was his weapon, his pet, his proof that the gods still spoke to men. That's why I grew up in the palace with you."

His hand lifts, ghostly fingers brushing the air above the vault. The glyphs pulse once, twice, in answer, as if recognizing him. Recognizing him as they do me, *because he's blood to my mother.* I can't even comprehend it. "No," I say, the word shooting out in denial. "That can't be true."

His voice trembles with fury and grief as he pins me with hate-filled eyes. "It is. I suffered at the hands of the king, while she—*our mother*—built her perfect family elsewhere. You and Calliope, safe in Evermere. Loved. Wanted."

The words cut deeper than any blade. I stagger to my feet, dizzy. My thoughts splinter—Mom's gentle hands, her lullabies of river and forest, her stories of distant places and their heroes.

I also think of the stories that were never shared about her life before she met Father. Before she arrived in Evermere. Anger floods me. I cling to the need to argue. To prove him wrong. "I don't believe you." But there's a part of me that suddenly questions everything. That wonders...

Ren's sword lowers an inch. "All the years we grew up together, and you never said a word."

Marrow's laughter fractures. "Not until I walked Serenelle's dreams when she came to the palace with her family." He spits the last word like it's poison. "In her dreams, I saw everything, including a prophecy about me. She tried to hide it, burying it here in this vault, along with Drakenholt's secrets. I came here to retrieve it and couldn't. When she helped you lock away your story, I begged her to free mine. She refused."

"A prophecy?" I repeat. "About what?"

His lips curve in a corrupt grin. "About the role I would play in your life, sister."

Ren moves to shield me. "I won't let you harm her."

I stand and shift to Ren's side. "She refused to help you, so you made a pact with Cimarron."

"I made a *choice*," Marrow spits. "He offered what she spurned—my rightful place in the realm. Power. Meaning. You think *he's* the monster? At least he didn't abandon me."

Ren's temper flares, fire racing up his arms. "He's using you!"

I stare at him, and for the first time, I see it. Mom's eyes. The tilt of her lips. How could I have missed it before? My whole body trembles. Why didn't she tell us? Why did she abandon him?

The pendant sears my skin with too many emotions to name—grief, guilt, disbelief.

Marrow turns his anguish into a sneer. "He's using *you*," he fires back at Ren. "The bond between you was never love or this quest—it was by design. He twisted the Lore and wrote it into the tale himself."

I can't breathe. The Lore in my veins throbs, resonating with his every word. "No." Another denial rips from my throat. It can't be true. What I feel for Ren is...destiny. *My* destiny. "You're lying."

His gaze softens, twisted by something that almost looks like pity. "Didn't you ever wonder how you could walk in Ren's dreams, sister? How easily his fire recognized yours?"

Ren looks at me, horror and disbelief warring in his eyes. The bond quakes, trying to reject what it knows is true. "You're a dream walker, too." His head falls back as if he might find solace on the cracked ceiling. "I'm an idiot."

I shake my head vehemently. "My dreams are prophesies—visions of what is to come. Potential futures." Even as I say it, I remember those that weren't futures at all—the ones I shared with Ren. They were all from our *past*.

*Gods above, I walked in his dreams.* The realization rips at my heart.

Marrow's voice sharpens. "I wanted my story freed, but now you've made a bargain with Cimarron. If you open this vault, he gets all these stories, and you get your mother back." Venom coats each word. "You get to live happily ever after, and what do I get? To still be an outcast. To disappear. Again."

"You're the one who's been trying to stop us," I murmur. "Just to spite me."

He smiles. "And being the overachiever you are, you have foiled me yet again."

"What is this bargain?" Ren demands. "Tell me exactly what it says."

Does it matter now? I open my mouth to explain, but can't push the words past my lips. "The only reason the Story Thief would purposely bind us together is if he wanted to use me to—" The realization, the truth, hits like lightning—if Ren and I are bonded, and I die...

*He will die too.*

It's too much for me to consider. Too much to bear. I can't even wrap my mind around the fact that I'm staring at my brother across the vault. That he hates me, when I didn't even know he existed.

I grip the edge of the dais, and the vault buzzes, echoing my racing heart.

But something was keeping Ren here before he bonded with me. It was already tethered to him, rejecting Cimarron's attempts to erase him. What is it? Is it the story inside the vault?

Marrow shakes his head, and at first, I think he's reading my mind, but he's still drowning in bitterness and anger. "It's time for me to write my own story."

My stomach twists under the weight of all of it. "At what cost?"

His reply is a whisper that echoes through the vault like thunder. "Every ending demands one, doesn't it, sister?"

The seal flares to life. Letters burst from the fissures like fireflies turning to knives.

Marrow floats back, half-man, half-nightmare. "We'll all pay his price now." He glances at me, his tone almost tender. "But you, Lorekeeper...you can finish it. You can choose how the story ends."

Ren steps forward, defiant. "Tell me what price he'll take."

Marrow's voice fractures with pain. "He already has."

The floor splits. The ward screams open. And through the widening rift, a voice spills out like ink made of night.

*"We have what we need. Come home, my Lorekeeper."*

# Chapter Thirty
## Dessalyn | Ashes and Echoes

*Some stories burn brighter in their ruin.*

The vault explodes.

Runes scream as they tear free from the walls, spinning through the air like shards of glass. The floor splits, vomiting flame and frost in the same breath.

My voice catches, the sound drowned by the roar of magic unbound. "Get the stories!"

Ren and I dive for the contents, the light blinding. I feel paper, leather, fabric—burning with words too alive to hold. Barbs of quills pierce my skin. Fire licks my palms.

"Go!" Ren's voice is rough, half-lost in the thunder of the collapsing stones. He shoves a handful of books and rolled parchments into his cloak, his movements frantic.

"There's more!" I shake my burned hands, tears slipping down my cheeks. "We have to save them!"

"I'll grab what I can. You run!"

The ward's symbols unravel—beautiful, terrible, alive. Words ignite midair before they burn and turn to ash. The air tastes of ink and smoke. I can't breathe without choking.

I grab Ren's wrist to drag him toward the stairwell. The dragon sigil beneath his skin flares to life, scorching my already injured palm. The bond flares too, molten and wild, threading through my veins like lightning. "Not without you!"

He tightens his grip on the salvaged scrolls, eyes blazing gold through the smoke. "Then move!"

The walls weep fire. Frost crawls across the floor like a tide. "Marrow!" I yell, but he's gone, vanished into the haze. His name dies before it reaches the ceiling.

Halfway up, the stairs crack. The vault's ceiling caves in. Story light bursts through the fissures in an explosion of glowing script, raining down on us in ribbons of gold.

For a heartbeat, they cling to my face and hands—words trying to anchor themselves, whispering fragments of the Lore in the vault that we didn't save. One strand lashes out and hits Ren square in the chest. He cries out, dropping the scrolls. The strand of letters coils, reshaping and fusing into a single sigil that burns through his shirt.

A dragon, haloed in gold.

He falls to his knees, gritting his teeth as light pours out of the mark. Our bond surges, convulses, surges again—the heartbeat of not one, but two dying stories.

His.

Mine.

Ours.

"Ren!" I drop my load and lunge for him. He's unsteady, and as the stairwell crumbles, so am I. We stumble.

When I try to gather the stories again, he lifts me. "Leave them," he shouts. "There's no time!"

I twist, reaching for the scattered parchments, but the room shifts. Ren pulls me against him. Heat and pain explode through my chest as his symbol brands its reflection into my own skin, just above my heart.

Everything stops—the fire, the collapse, even sound. The world exhales.

Then the light implodes. We're knocked onto the few remaining steps, the vault dissolving in a roar of stone and smoke. Ren covers my body with his as the vault falls into ruins.

I want to stay there in the protection of his arms. Stay hidden from the revelations that have turned my world upside down. But he won't let me. "Come on, Dessa," he murmurs when the worst has passed. "There's nothing left we can save."

As he scoops me up and begins the slow trek to finish the spiral climb, I glance back. He's right—it's all gone.

The world outside is half-moonlight, half-snow made of ash, drifting in the air. A sob racks my body as I watch the pieces floating around us. The ghosts of every story lost.

We make it through the arched doorway before Ren drops to his knees, but doesn't let go. The ground heaves once, then stills. For a moment, I think the world has stopped breathing. The church is in ruins, its stained glass windows blown to jeweled shrapnel. Starlight—or what passes for it—filters through the smoke coiling around the fractured beams.

I press my hand to his chest. His shirt is torn where the sigil burned him. Beneath the fabric, gold light pulses, keeping time with his heartbeat. Each flicker feels like a countdown.

He shudders. "Everything we needed...gone."

There's only a crater of smoking stone where words once lived. The Lore held in the vault is destroyed. Every prophecy. Every name.

Every line of Ren's story.

A sound tears out of me, half-scream, half-sob, when I realize what's about to happen next. His story—the one we've been chasing—is the tether keeping him here. "Oh, Ren." I pat his body to reassure myself he isn't gone. That he's not being erased in front of my eyes.

He lifts his head, eyes dazed and bright with pain. "It's okay, Dessa." His voice breaks on my name. "We tried."

"Don't you dare give up." I slip from his weakening grip and kneel in front of him. I cup his face in both hands. His skin is hot, fevered. "I will not let you disappear."

He tries for a smile that doesn't reach his eyes. "Maybe I already have."

Something moves at the edge of the ruin—a flicker of black through the haze. My heart lurches. "Firebrand!"

The stallion bursts through the drifting ash, tack half-torn, flanks streaked with soot but alive. Relief punches through me so sharply it hurts. The horse tosses his head and snorts, mane singed but proud, as if daring the broken city to challenge him.

Ren manages a rough laugh, low and disbelieving. "Of course, he'd survive the end of the world. He's too wild not to."

I jump to my feet and press my forehead to the horse's neck for a quick second. His coat is warm, grounding. Alive. My fingers shake as I pull out my quest journal, quill, and ink from my satchel. I will not let Ren's story disappear. He is part of my quest, and...

A spiral of light rises from the destroyed vault like a soul leaving a body. We both whip our heads toward it. My ears ring with the Story Thief's voice—slithering through the smoke.

*You've done well. Come to me, Lorekeeper.*

His voice slides through me like oil on water—every word sinking deeper than breath. The words brush the inside of my mind with cold fingers. The world tilts.

I gasp and clutch at my temples. "Never," I whisper. "You can't have me."

Ren's eyes shoot to me. "What is it?"

I force the words out through clenched teeth. "He's calling me." Did he snatch Marrow or did my brother abandon us of his own accord? What will happen to him now? To all of us? My blood ices. The pressure between my ears increases. "Cimarron is trying to pull me to him. He destroyed all those stories and now..."

"You've fulfilled your part of the bargain," Ren says softly.

The pressure eases. I glance around as if Mom might suddenly appear. She doesn't. Is she home with Calliope and Father? I close my eyes for a brief moment, praying she's alright.

I drop to my knees beside Ren again. "I'm sorry," I say, touching his wrist, his chest. Both sigils react. I grab the ink and quill and open my journal. "I'm going to fix this. I swear. I'm going to rewrite your story."

Ren's jaw hardens. "And risk losing your memory? Those you love?" He shakes his head and stills my fingers. The light flickering under his skin is weaker now, fading with every breath. He tries to stand, falls.

I steady him and press a hand to the sigil. "Don't fade," I whisper. "Please don't fade."

He looks at me, exhaustion softening his voice. "If the vault's gone, my story's gone with it. It won't be long now."

I shake my head, fierce through the tears streaking ash down my cheeks. "It didn't destroy you. The sigil saved you. I saw it—your fire...it *moved*."

His eyes find mine again, full of something I can't name. I can't tell if it's wonder or dread in his tone. "Into you," he murmurs.

The dragon glows faintly through his shirt. I glance down, and beneath my own, its twin answers, pulsing once, twice. The same rhythm. The same heartbeat.

The twin heartbeat thrums between us—ancient, defiant, alive. "Can a dragon bond rewrite itself?" I ask.

He reaches for my hand, holding my trembling fingers. "I don't know. I've never shared one before."

At his touch, the bond deepens its beat. It vibrates through me. *That's it.* That's why he hasn't been erased yet. "Well, I think yours has."

"Then you're my anchor now. My tether to this world."

I think I always have been. I nod, even as fear claws at my throat. Because anchors can break, and the Story Thief knows exactly where to find me.

In the air between us, a single glyph appears. It floats—spinning lazily like an ember caught on the wind and glowing the same gold as the sigil on Ren's chest. When I focus on it, I hear a faint echo.

Another heartbeat.

Calling me. Calling us.

It flickers, then flies up into the air. "What direction is that?" I ask, watching it go.

He blinks with fascination as it hovers, flickering, the moon and a blanket of stars behind it. "South." His eyes light up. "To Klamere?"

The palace.

The dragon sigil tattooed on my chest beats to match the flickering one in the sky. Words tumble through my mind. The quill jumps into my hand. I tear open the journal, and Lore flows from the quill in elegant script—but it's Mom's handwriting.

*The Story Forge waits. Find it. Write a new story.*

Goose flesh races over my skin. My hand stops. "Mom?" I whisper.

Ren leans close, reading the words. "The Story Forge? I thought that was a myth, a legend."

I've heard the myths, too. There were once three great forges that together created the realm. Once the five kingdoms were written into being, the forges disappeared, never to be seen again. "Do you know where one is in Drakenholt?"

His brows draw together. "It's said the palace was built on top of one. That it's inside Fire Mountain."

"Forged in fire," I mutter. "Of course. That's where your kingdom's origin story—the real one—was written."

Mom's pendant heats. The floating sigil flares brighter, whooshing away, then back. Like the stars overhead, it's a light to lead the way.

I close the journal and gather the ink and quill. "The Lore is calling us there." And a new Drakenholt origin story isn't the only thing I'm going to write. I have another plan in mind as well.

Ren grabs my wrist, stopping me. "We don't even know if the forge is real, and to get there, we have to cross the Wraithlands. It's dangerous, Dessa."

I jerk him to his feet. We're both coated in grime. Ashes flake off our clothes, our skin, as we face each other. I wipe soot from his cheek. "Quests are never easy, Ren. Never straightforward." I press a hand over his heart. "If you want to save your kingdom, then this is what you must risk for it."

"You're asking me to risk your life."

"And you'll be risking yours to protect me." Our bond pulses in confirmation. "I don't know if what binds us is fate or the Thief's design, but it's real. We only need listen to it. Follow it."

He blows out a resigned sigh. "Fate or design—it doesn't matter." He brushes a loose strand of hair behind my ear. "I'd still choose you."

As a milky ray of moonlight breaks through the murky air, I stare into his eyes, drowning in their sapphire color. Amidst this horrible monochrome gray, they flash like jewels in the starlight. My voice comes out soft. "I'd choose you, too, my crown prince. It's time to finish what we started."

Only this time, my quest is leading us to the place where an important story was once born...and where one must now end.

# CHAPTER THIRTY-ONE
## DESSALYN | THE NIGHT BETWEEN

*In ruin, the quest remembers.*

NIGHT PRESSES CLOSE AROUND Jairton. Smoke curls through the streets, ghostlike. The moon is only a smear behind it. Light drips onto the cobbles in faint, uneven pools, too weak to chase the dark.

Ren keeps one hand on Firebrand's reins and the other on the hilt of his sword as we move through the city that no longer breathes. Each hoof step rings too sharply, too alive, echoing off walls. My throat burns with every breath.

"No Storyspawn," I whisper.

"Not yet." His voice sounds flayed—raw from smoke, from fear.

The sigil flickers ahead of us like a dying lantern, gold against gray. We follow it past shuttered windows and half-vanished market stalls, past a fountain long dry from the Thief's erasure.

My legs shake with every step. When Ren stops before a townhouse of pale stone and iron balconies, I almost walk into him.

"Here," he says. "A noble's house. No one's left—they won't mind us making use of it."

I want to argue—to keep moving—but my body sags with relief. I can barely lift my boots. We haven't eaten since morning, and after what we've endured, even Firebrand's steps drag.

The gate shrieks open, the sound knifing through the quiet. Ren flinches, then mutters, "Let's get inside and see what we can find."

He leads Firebrand to the rear courtyard. A small barn waits, its doors ajar, the air inside thick with old hay and neglect. "Let me settle him. Then we'll check the house."

"I'll start," I say, reaching for my satchel.

His hand circles my wrist—warm, grounding. "Not without me. Empty doesn't always mean safe."

I nod, too tired to argue. In the barn's half-light, I notice two other horses, ribs faintly visible beneath dusty coats. They watch us with hollow eyes.

While Ren removes Firebrand's saddle, I find a bucket and scatter grain for the others. My legs tremble as I work; the smell of oats and damp wood makes my eyes sting. The white mare with a gray diamond on her forehead noses my palm. I stroke her neck, whispering nonsense—soft words to fill the silence. "They're all alone now," I murmur.

Ren straightens, brushing ash from his sleeve. "We'll turn them loose in the morning."

The thought catches in my throat. "And then what? Who takes care of them?"

He doesn't answer. The wind sighs through the rafters like a grieving thing.

I press my cheek to the mare's warm neck. "You'll be all right," I tell her, knowing it's probably a lie.

At the rear of the house, Ren is about to barge inside with sword drawn, but I stop him with a hand. "What if someone is still inside? We should knock."

He frowns, doubtful, yet humors me. No answer comes.

We ease the door open. I call out, part of me hoping for a re-ply—another part praying for silence. We're alone.

Everything is immaculate—candles burned down but still up-right, carpets clean, a faint scent of lemon. No people. No noise. Only stillness, patient and waiting.

In the kitchen, I light several lamps. Ren takes one to scout the rest of the house. His footsteps echo down the grand hall, up the stairs, and across the rooms above.

I wander after him, feeling like an intruder in someone's mem-ory. I've never been inside such a grand place, except once—his home in Klamere. The thought tightens my chest. I creep through the drawing room, the lamplight glinting off crystal decanters and gilt frames, everything preserved as if time simply stopped.

When he returns, the lamplight highlights his drawn features. As tired as I am, he's battling an even more profound exhaustion.

He gestures toward the staircase. "There's a bath upstairs with running water. Clothes in a wardrobe that might fit you. I'll keep watch down here and check for food."

I open my mouth to argue, but see his determination etched as deeply as his fatigue. "Thank you."

The bathing chamber could belong to a dream. The tub is carved marble, the tiles veined in gold. When I twist the taps, water rushes out, startlingly warm, steam blooming. I almost cry.

Clothes folded in an armoire wait for owners who will never return. I take a linen gown, a soft shirt, and trousers small enough to nearly fit. Once satisfied with my haul, I undress with shaking hands and slide into the tub.

The water darkens with soot and blood. Heat wraps around me, seeps into my bruises, and stings my cuts and burns. My weary muscles surrender; my thoughts drift. I could stay here forever. I let my head fall back and stare at the cracked ceiling. "Everything burns," I murmur. "And yet we're still here."

The bond hums faintly in my chest—a reminder I'm not the only one still breathing.

Sleep tempts me, heavy and dangerous. The moment my eyes drift shut, I jerk awake.

Dreams are no refuge. Dream walkers hunt there.

I still struggle to consider myself one. What does this mean for me now?

Shaking, I drag myself out of the cooled water, dry with a towel that still smells faintly of sunlight, and dress in the borrowed clothes. The gown hangs loose at the shoulders and tight through my breasts, but it's clean.

The kitchen glows when I return, the air rich with lamplight and the scent of food. Ren has been busy.

A loaf of bread, dried fruit, salted meat, and a bottle of honey wine wait on the table. Olives, chutney, and crackers crowd a thick ceramic plate. My stomach growls loud enough to echo.

I tear off a piece of bread and eat standing up, too hungry to care about manners. The first bite tastes like...home. My heart tugs at thoughts of Calli and Father. Our meals around the kitchen table. What are they doing right now, I wonder? Are they safe?

Tears sting my eyes. I miss them so much.

Mother, too.

"Ren?" I call out, cringing at the sound. Even knowing the owners are gone, I can't help feeling like I don't belong here.

Bootsteps cross the wood floor. I look up—and forget to breathe.

He stands in the doorway, freshly washed, hair damp and curling at his temples. The shirt clings to broad shoulders, half-buttoned. The trousers are a shade too tight, the fabric pulling across his thighs.

"You look..." I stop before the word *beautiful* escapes.

He smiles, a flash of weary amusement. "I see you started without me."

I gesture to the spread. "Better be quick. I'm so hungry, I might finish everything before you can grab any for yourself."

He laughs. We sit across from each other, a candle between us, our hands brushing when we reach for the same slice of fruit. The brief touch sends a ripple through the bond, a spark that settles low and warm inside me.

We eat in companionable silence at first, too tired for words. When we finally speak, our voices are hushed, as if afraid to wake the house.

"You need to reconsider this plan," he says.

Outside the sitting room window, that twinkling sigil waits. It wants us to follow it. "My mother's message said to find the Story Forge. It adds up that it's the one under your castle."

He pours me a glass of the wine. "The Wraithlands—"

"—will test us, as everything else on this quest has." The thought makes me want to hole up in the house and never leave. "Yet, we're both still here, stronger than before."

He watches me over the rim of his cup. "We'll need supplies to last four, maybe five, days."

I gesture at the pantry. "Which we can take." I sip the wine, enjoying its sweetness before it warms my throat and chest. "We're taking those two horses, too. I'll ride the white mare. The other can carry blanket rolls and food."

A small huff of laughter escapes him. "You have an answer for everything."

"I'm a Lorekeeper and the eldest sister. It's in my blood."

As he smiles at me, the heaviness lifts. We talk about supplies, routes, and what to scavenge from the house and barn come morning. The ordinary details of survival feel almost sacred as we finish off every bit of the food and drink the last of the wine.

Ren studies me through the candlelight. His voice drops low. "If I fade," he says, "promise me you'll keep going."

The food in my stomach sours. I shove back my empty wine glass. "If you fade," I whisper back, "there won't be a world left worth saving."

Later, when the candles burn low, he leads me to a bedchamber where the sheets are still crisp, and the air carries the faint perfume of roses. Moonlight filters through the windows, painting everything in silver and black.

I hesitate at the foot of the bed, clutching my journal. "If I sleep, Cimarron or Marrow might find me."

Ren sets his sword belt within reach of the nightstand, then points at the high-backed chair by the window. "I'd already planned to sit there and keep watch over you."

The words stir guilt more than comfort. He's swaying with exhaustion, yet still refuses rest.

"You need sleep as much as I do."

"I'll manage."

"You won't," I counter softly. "Not after everything. Sit there, and you'll be half-dead by morning."

His mouth curves faintly. "That's better than letting a dream walker drag you away while I snore."

The image almost makes me smile. If only it weren't so chillingly possible. "You're not staying up all night in a chair, Renwick Ravelle. You've risked enough for me since all this began."

He lifts a brow, the ghost of mischief flickering behind the fatigue. "So you're inviting me into your bed now?"

Heat rushes to my face. "Inviting you to rest," I clarify. "It's a large bed. We can stay on opposite sides."

He watches me for a beat longer than necessary, and something unreadable passes through his expression—a mix of gratitude and restraint. "As you wish, Lorekeeper."

The mattress dips as I climb in first. The sheets are cool, whispering beneath me. When he lies down beside me, the space feels impossibly small. His weight shifts the mattress again; the faint brush of his sleeve grazes my arm. I feel that single touch everywhere.

He stretches one arm behind his head, eyes half-closed. "You shouldn't have tried to save those stories," he murmurs. "When the floor gave way—I thought I'd lost you."

"You didn't."

He turns his head toward me. In the dim light, his expression softens, stripped of princely armor and fire-born pride. "You were brave back there. Reckless," he adds, "but brave."

My throat tightens. "So were you. You saved us both."

He gives a small, rueful laugh. "Not entirely true. I'm alive because of you—and whatever this is between us." His hand moves absently to his chest, over the golden sigil. "When it burned into me, I thought it was the end. Then it..."

"Rewrote our bond." I look away, unable to breathe. "That wasn't me. It was your dragon."

His fingers drift, finding mine atop the blanket. "It's you," he insists quietly. "You're the reason I'm still breathing."

The bond answers—slow, deep, steady. Each beat feels like it's syncing us closer.

I try to focus on anything else. "When you talk like that, I don't know if you're thanking me or blaming me."

"Both," he admits. "You've made my life infinitely more complicated."

I huff a laugh, too tired to hide the affection in it. "You're welcome."

He shifts just enough that our shoulders brush. The contact sends warmth curling low in my stomach.

"If you dream," he says softly, "I'll find you. My dragon will lead me to you."

I turn my head toward him, the space between us filled with moonlight. Dawn is only a few hours away. "And if you fade, I'll bring you back."

His hand tightens around mine. "Deal."

The Lore vibrates in my bones, sending a shiver lacing up my spine. Without even meaning to, I've created a new pact—a Fae bargain.

In the moonlit silence, neither of us speaks. The touch of our joined hands feels like a key in a lock. The world shrinks to this room with the faint hum of Lore between us—his dragon, my quill—partners in this quest.

My eyelids grow heavy, fear loosening its hold. His voice drifts through the quiet, low and rough-edged. "Sleep, Dessa. I'll be here when you wake."

Outside, as I drift off, Jairton too sleeps—its streets hollow, its stories gone.

# CHAPTER THIRTY-TWO
## DESSALYN | FIRE IN THE DREAM

*Quests don't stop for sleep—they burn their way into your dreams.*

THE WORLD BETWEEN WAKING and dreaming feels like a tide pulling me under. Ren's hand is warm in mine, his breathing even. The rhythm of it steadies the frantic beat of my heart, and for a little while, I let myself believe we're safe.

I stare at the ceiling until the shapes blur, exhaustion weaving its spell. I tell myself I'll stay awake. That I'll feel it the moment Cimarron's presence brushes against my mind. But the bond hums low and soft—Ren's heartbeat synced with mine—and the warmth of it pulls me deeper.

My thoughts drift. I see ash turning to snow. A golden sigil pulsing faintly in the dark. Then a voice, familiar and jagged, whispers through the haze. "You shouldn't be here, sister."

My eyes snap open—but I'm not in the bed anymore.

I'm standing in a hall of black stone and fractured glass, where moonlight bleeds through a broken ceiling. Beneath my feet, the floor ripples as if made of liquid words. They shimmer under my boots, whispering as I move.

"Marrow?" My voice trembles, echoing across the ruin.

A figure steps out of the shifting dark. His outline wavers—half solid, half script. The silver light in his eyes cuts through the shadows. "You shouldn't be here," he says again, this time not with surprise, but warning. "This isn't your dream."

I glance around. Recognition flickers. The ruined arches, the faint scorch marks on the pillars—it's Drakenholt, or what's left of it, seen through a veil of memory.

"I didn't mean to come," I say. "At least—I don't think I did."

He laughs, the sound bitter and small. "No one ever means to step into another's nightmare. But you Lorewyns have a way of trespassing where you don't belong."

The bond stirs uneasily, sensing his anger. The idea that I'm a dream walker still hasn't taken root. "Are you sure you didn't bring me here?"

"Why would I do that?" he snaps. "Leave before you see what's left of me."

"Are you fading like this kingdom?" I ask. "Maybe that's why I'm here. To help you as well as Ren."

His expression fractures—pain, anger, something haunted linking all of it. The walls around us shift, peeling back into fragments of memory: a throne room gilded with firelight, a boy kneeling before a king, chains of words binding his wrists. The scent of burned parchment fills the air, and the boy's screams echo faintly before fading.

"You want to save me, don't you?" he asks, a tremor in his voice. "That's what Lorekeepers do. They mend broken stories."

"I want to save us all," I say quietly. "You. My father. Calliope." My throat tightens. "Even Mom."

The air freezes. His face twists. "Don't you dare speak of her to me."

"She must have loved you, Marrow."

"She abandoned me!" His voice cracks, a roar that shakes the hall. "She left me in the reeds and walked away to build her perfect little family."

"I don't know what her reasons were, but I bet it was to keep you safe."

"Safe?" He laughs again, but it's a wretched, broken sound. "The king turned me into a tool. A prophet on a leash. And when I discovered it, I told him. I told him how she'd left me for him to find. That's why he spoke the Severance Decree."

My heart stutters. "The what?"

A sly smirk flashes before he glances up at the starry night. "You didn't know."

"I..." My mouth has gone dry. I don't know what to say. "What is that?"

Marrow strolls to a damaged balcony, the night wrapping around him like a blanket as his boots scuff against the marble. "Ren didn't tell you." His tone suggests this surprises him. A soft, vicious chuckle purrs out of his mouth. "Oh, Dessa, you're so naive. Your mother wasn't simply banished from Drakenholt; she was severed from the realm. Words spoken in the old language and sealed by the king's blood."

The ruins tilt. The horizon trembles. I stumble to find new footing. When I do, my gaze locks on him, my emotions tangled like briars inside my chest. "Why would he do that?"

His fury ripples through the air. The pillars bend inward. The floor buckles beneath me, ink seeping up between the stones. "Think, Dessa! Because he believed she'd planted me as a spy in his court."

A spy. "And you let him believe such a lie?"

The sly smile turns cruel. "Why wouldn't I?"

Disgust wars with heartbreak inside me. I want to punch that smile off his face. The answers to questions I've been carrying around all these years fall into place. "She didn't go into the Fade," I say to myself more than him. "Her story was unraveled. And that's how the Story Thief captured her. He caught a thread in the unraveling."

"My plan worked out even better than I anticipated."

Rage sears in my veins, scorching reason away. The shadows thicken, Marrow's protective blanket wrapping tighter. He expects me to lash out. He's ready for a fight.

I should give it to him. I should take all of my rage and bitterness out on him. What he's done to Mom, to our family. To me.

Beyond the balcony, a golden sigil flashes. The dragon.

Did Ren know of this decree? Did he know what would happen to Mom after it was issued?

The sigil shimmers, demanding my attention. As I glance at it, I swear it morphs into the outline of her face.

She smiles—sad, but encouraging. There's so much in her eyes. I can't unbraid all of it, but I know if she were here, she wouldn't want me to wage war on Marrow. On my *brother*.

Swallowing my anger, I reach for patience and understanding. What would it be like to grow up at the king's mercy with no mother? No family? How would I feel in his place?

I soothe my voice. "You have every right to feel betrayed and angry. But don't let Cimarron use that to remake the world. Help me stop him. Come home with me."

"Home?" he spits out the word. "I have no home."

"Then let us make one." My voice breaks. "Please, Marrow. Don't let him erase what's left of us."

His expression softens—something like grief bleeding through the cracks. Then he shakes his head. "I couldn't help you if I wanted to."

"Why not?"

Before he can answer, the floor ruptures and splits open with a deafening roar. Heat and shadow surge upward, swallowing his next words. Ink erupts from the cracks, boiling like lava. Words tear free from the stone and twist into limbs and claws—into a skull with no eyes. Each letter glows a sick, pale light before burning black.

"Marrow!" I stumble back as the floor collapses between us. "What is that?"

He backs toward the shattered balcony. His cloak of shadows whips around him. "You think I called that thing?"

"It came from your nightmare," I shout over the grinding of stone.

"It came from the kingdom," he snarls. "You shouldn't have come here. The nightmares breed in anyone who lingers in Drakenholt—they feed on your emotions!"

The beast bellows, its voice a chorus of broken syllables. Runes pour from its mouth and sear the walls. One grazes my arm, burning a word into my skin: *forget*.

Pain lances through me. I clutch the wound, but the word keeps shifting, trying to etch itself wherever it touches.

Marrow raises his hands. Streams of silver script coil from his palms and lash at the creature. The blast knocks it back but not down; it slams into him, driving him into a column and splintering the dream like glass.

I shout his name, but the ruins absorb it.

Pinned beneath rubble, he groans. The light in his eyes flickers. "Get out of here!"

I run toward him, dodging the monster's claws as they carve gouges through the liquid floor. My feet splash through phrases and names that dissolve the moment I step on them—are they fragments of Drakenholt's erased stories?

The beast lunges again. Instinct takes over. Without thought of consequences, I reach inside to the Lore pulsing through my blood and let it surge outward. Words ring out from my lips—old ones, half-forgotten—forming a barrier of light between us. The creature recoils, shrieking.

Marrow stares at me, stunned. "You shouldn't be able to do that."

"I must if I am to save you."

The barrier cracks. The monster slams against it, scattering sparks of gold and black. I dive beside Marrow, dragging him free from the rubble.

"What are you doing?" he asks, disbelief and bitterness tangled together.

"Isn't it obvious? Saving you, you idiot."

He grips my wrist, his voice rough. "You're going to die if you stay here."

My blade appears in my hand. The one Ren taught me to use. "No," I say, breathless. "No one is dying here tonight."

The beast rears again, larger now—feeding on the chaos, on our emotions. Runes spiral through its body like veins of black fire.

I stand, weapon ready, drawing on the last of my strength. The Lore inside me ignites—answering the call that has driven my quest. A golden light blazes through the cracks in the floor, pushing back the darkness.

"Dessa!"

Ren's voice—faint, echoing from somewhere beyond the dream.

The bond flares, a ribbon of destiny curling heat around my heart. The golden sigil in the air—his sigil—flares to life above me.

Marrow shields his face, shouting over the storm of light. "He's pulling you back!"

"I can't leave you here!"

"You have no choice!" His expression wavers between fury and fear. His voice cracks and ripples. "Go—before the nightmare ends us both!"

The beast roars, lunging. I swipe at its throat. Blood pours from the wound, and it bellows. Its claws rake across my shoulder as the bond ignites with fire flooding my veins.

In the next blink of my eyes, light swallows everything. I am ripped from the dream's hold.

I gasp and stumble forward onto blackened stone. A storm howls above me, hurling cinders through a blood-red sky. The ruins around me are different now—no marble halls or ink-soaked floors. This is a world built of fire and ash.

A roar splits the air.

I lift my head—and my breath catches.

A dragon towers above the broken battlements, emerald green scales glinting. His wings unfurl, scattering sparks with every beat. The air trembles under the force of him, and yet...I know that shape, that heartbeat pulsing through the bond.

"Ren," I whisper.

The dragon turns, eyes like twin suns locking onto me. Recognition flares—and horror.

He's not in control.

A nightmare creature of smoke and teeth prowls the court-yard below him. Its limbs are made of shattering runes, its mouth a rift of light that devours sound.

When it lunges, Ren's dragon form lashes out, fire pouring from his throat in a blinding torrent. The flames incinerate everything—stone, shadow, memory.

I duck behind a fallen arch, the heat blistering even from here. "Ren, stop!"

He doesn't hear me. His roar shakes the world, a sound of rage and despair intertwined. The beast leaps again, clawing for his chest. Ren slams it into the ground, talons carving into the burning soil.

The bond between us shudders—the wild, primal instinct of a creature lashing out in fear and vengeance. I step into the open, ignoring the scream of the wind. "Ren, it's me!"

He swings his head toward me, teeth bared, fire gathering in his throat.

Behind those eyes, I see the man inside the monster—the flicker of his soul trapped behind the scales—and then the flame surges.

I leap.

The fire strikes the ground where I stood, exploding in a ring of fire. The heat scorches me. I hit the stones hard, the dream fracturing at the edges, but I can't leave him.

The nightmare beast rises again, lunging for me this time. Its claws rend the air, each strike leaving trails of fractured words. I roll, slashing with my blade, but the steel melts in my grip.

Ren roars again—a sound that's both warning and fury—and the world ignites. A stream of flame bursts from his mouth, engulfing the monster. The creature shrieks, disintegrating into ash and smoke that whirl away.

When the fire fades, I crawl from the rubble, coughing. "Ren?"

The dragon stands at the heart of the ruin, chest heaving, smoke curling from his jaws. His scales ripple, green shifting to gold, then crimson and back again.

I rise slowly, palms out. "It's over. You did it. It's gone."

He growls low in his throat, a sound that vibrates through my bones. The bond quakes—fear, remorse, longing—all tangled together.

I take a step closer. "You didn't mean to hurt me. I know that."

He lowers his massive head, eyes bright with anguish. The heat rolling off him should burn me. Instead, it feels like standing too close to the sun and being welcomed by it.

Another cautious step. I let him scent my hand. I run gentle fingers over his snout. "It's me. I'm safe. So are you."

The rumble in his chest softens. He closes his eyes and exhales. Through the bond, I hear him—not words, but the shape of them, rough and human.

*Forgive me.*

"I already have," I whisper.

He nudges me gently, lowering his massive body until his wings fold around us like sheltering walls. Then, with a slow motion, he crouches lower. I feel the connection nudging me—an invitation.

"You want me to...ride you?" I ask, breathless.

His eyes flash with a trace of wry amusement that's pure Ren.

I don't know where to put my feet, how to grasp his scales. Somehow, I manage it after two tries. The scales are warm and smooth under my palms. The moment I settle, he launches skyward.

A cry tears from my throat as I grasp his neck. The world explodes into light and wind. We rise above the ruined city, above the wind, and through layers of smoke and starlight. The air here tastes different—cleaner, untouched by despair. Far below, the land glows with veins of gold where the Dragon Lore still burns under the castle's remains.

*The Story Forge.*

Not a myth. It's *there.*

For the first time in what feels like forever, I laugh. The sound spills out of me, wild and unrestrained, and through the bond I feel Ren's answering joy.

He flies me over mountains, dips into valleys. We skim vast plains and follow the edge of the forests to the sea and back. It steals my breath. Tears stream from my eyes. It feels like something holy, sacred.

Like freedom I've never known.

When we finally land again, the dream changes. The fires are gone, the ruins dark. As soon as my feet touch the ground, he shifts in a burst of light.

He stands before me in human form, shirtless, sweat and soot streaking his skin. The sigil on his chest glimmers.

"I nearly burned you alive," he says, voice rough with guilt.

I shake my head. "You saved me."

His hand comes up, fingers brushing my cheek. The warmth in his touch is gentle, steady, and real.

"I thought I'd lost you," I whisper.

"Never."

He kisses me—soft at first, then fierce, as if the fire of his dragon heart has found its match in mine. I surrender to it, willing to push everything else aside. Giving him what he seeks, I wrap my arms around his neck and let our connection fill me up.

He backs me against a pillar, pillaging my mouth. His hands trace down my sides, land on my hips. His grip is firm, possessive, and my body answers before thought can catch up.

The bond flares. Heat spills through every vein, gold light flickering beneath our skin. His breath brushes my throat, a low growl rumbling in his chest that sends shivers racing through me.

"Dessa…" My name breaks from his lips—a question.

I tilt my head back. "You're burning."

"So are you." His forehead rests against mine, sweat and smoke mingling between us. "Tell me to stop."

"I can't."

His laugh is rough, unsteady. "Good."

The pillar at my back warms as his magic seeps into the stone. I feel it everywhere—the echo of wings unfurling behind him, the faint scent of rain and flame. The world narrows to his heartbeat and the way his hands cradle my face, reverent now, as if he's reminding himself I'm real.

When our lips meet again, the kiss turns slower, deeper. His power thrums against mine, gold and silver threads weaving together until I can't tell where one ends and the other begins. The fire of Drakenholt feels distant, replaced by a gentler blaze that consumes without pain.

The dream around us shimmers, bending to our joined magic. Pillars become stars; the floor beneath our feet dissolves into light.

He murmurs against my mouth, "If this is a dream, don't wake me."

"It's ours," I breathe. "Let it last."

He gathers me against him, and the dream obeys—folding us into warmth and light, the two of us suspended in the glow of a love that feels as if it could last forever.

My hands explore his chest, his moan sending waves of satisfaction through me. I'm infatuated with his muscles and the strain I sense under them. He's holding back.

I don't want him to.

He slips the neckline of my gown off my shoulder, his hot lips trailing down my neck and over the sensitive skin there. A thumb brushes my peaked nipple through the fabric.

It's my turn to moan. I arch into that light touch, even as I sink my nails into his back and draw him closer, urging him on.

# CHAPTER THIRTY-THREE
## DESSALYN | LOST IN THE NEEDING

*What's found on a quest can never be forgotten.*

THE DREAM DOESN'T END, only changes form. His lips trace upward, leaving sparks where they touch, and the air between us trembles as the fire of the dream follows us into waking.

My heartbeat stutters. I open my eyes.

We're no longer in the ruins of Klamere but in the bedchamber in Jairton. The sheets are tangled beneath us, our bodies pressed together as if the bond itself refused to let go.

His skin is warm, slick with sweat, his heartbeat wild beneath my palm. The golden light that lingered in the dream still clings to us—soft ribbons glowing faintly over our joined hands, our chests, our mouths.

"Dessa," he whispers, half-asleep, half-awake. "You and I..."

"It's real." My voice catches. "We're destined for each other. Even in dreams."

He smiles faintly, the kind of smile that can undo me. He rises above me on an elbow and brushes hair from my face. "Is this what you want?"

I answer with a kiss—hungry, searching. The line between dream and waking disappears completely. He responds with equal ferocity; every brush of his lips lights me up, makes me hungry for more.

I taste smoke and desire, the ghost of the dragon's fire still inside him. His hand finds my waist, fingers curling just above my hip. I feel the tremor in his touch, the restraint. He could crush me, burn me, but he doesn't. He gentles the flame, worshipful, as if I am the story he's been chasing all his life.

My own control falters. I trace the edge of the sigil on his chest, feel its heat echo beneath my fingertips. "You're burning again," I whisper.

"So are you." His voice is a growl of devotion. "It's not fire—it's…"

"Love?" I supply.

The bond hums, answering for both of us. Magic flares through our skin, gilding every inch it touches. My pulse pounds where his mouth follows—throat, collarbone, the swell of my breast. The air smells of heat and wildness, of rain about to break.

My fingers tangle in his hair, leading his lips where I want them. The world narrows to his touch, the press of his mouth. My breath and heartbeat stutter as his fingers skim the neckline of my shirt, then bare more of my skin.

He lifts his head just enough to look at me. The emotion in his eyes—raw, tender, terrified—makes my throat ache. "Tell me this is real."

"It's real," I breathe. "You're still here, and I won't let you go."

He kisses me again, deeper this time. His hand slides under my gown. The room tilts when he cups my breast, the bed sighing beneath us as the golden light from our bond spreads through the sheets. I arch into him and the edges of everything blur—our magic, our hunger, the space between wanting and having.

His muscled thigh slips between my legs, the ache there responding. I welcome him, shifting to open my knees as I grab the hem of his shirt and tug it over his head.

As he rises to toss it aside, I see him in his glory. His bare skin. The mark on his wrist. The dragon shimmering over his heart.

"You're beautiful," I say.

His smile is wicked as he tugs me up to remove the gown. "We have much to learn about each other, starting right here, right now." The garment joins his on the floor, and one lazy finger sketches a line between my breasts as his gaze envelopes me. "And when it comes to beauty, yours far outshines mine."

Heat rushes to my cheeks at his words, at my nakedness. I dip my head, only to have him take my chin and gently raise it so I'm forced to meet his eyes again. "Where did you just go?"

My mind panics, pulse racing. A memory from the dream pushes past the truth—that I'm unaccustomed to such flattery and don't know how to answer—giving me a reprieve. "Did you know about the Severance Decree?"

His hand falls away. "How did you...?" Confusion is replaced with comprehension. "Marrow."

I've ruined the moment and feel raw, exposed. I reach for the sheets, but his hand stops me.

"I only realized it after you told me Serenelle was dead." His eyes are vivid, burning with a different fire. "I swear to you. I never knew before then."

I hold his gaze, a new boldness steeling my backbone. "That was days ago." It feels like a lifetime since I walked into his dream-memory of that night. "Why didn't you tell me?"

He closes his eyes for a heartbeat. His emotions roll through me—sorrow, guilt. "I planned to when we reached the vault, and then Marrow showed up. Everything spun out of control."

"Another thing you've kept from me."

He drops his gaze to the bed. "Just like you kept your bargain with Cimarron from me."

The blow strikes my heart. "I was working on a way to save you and my mother."

Those vivid eyes rise to meet mine. "Secrets will break both of us, and give the Thief leverage."

He's right. I touch his wrist. "I'm all out of secrets."

He leans in and caresses the back of my head. "Me, too."

I smile and pull him down on top of me.

The rest of our clothes disappear, and we're skin to skin. Our bodies fit together with ease, and I revel in the feel of him moving against me. His fingers and lips explore every inch of my body. In turn, I explore his.

With every touch, every kiss, his dragon breathes inside me, solidifying the bond. Ren feeds me flashes of memories, and the sensation of flying catapults me through time and space again as he enters me and I cry out.

He stops, hovering over me. "Are you...alright?" he asks with lidded eyes and rough voice.

I'm more than alright. I'm soaring, every nerve in my body on fire. "Move," I order. My legs are locked around his waist, my nails once more dig into his back. "Or I'm going to die."

A low rumble of laughter shakes him. It vibrates in my chest, deepening the ache between my legs. "As the lady wishes."

Hips press, bodies rock. His mouth locks on mine even as his eyes hold my gaze. The heat builds, the rhythm demanding my surrender. The bundle of nerves at the apex of my thighs is so taut, I whimper.

The sound drives his dragon mad. I sense it writhing, even as he tenses. "Dessa..."

The sound of his guttural plea makes me explode into a thousand shimmering lights. My name again leaves his lips, but this time, it's a yell. His body arches, and I feel him go over the edge with me, every muscle in his body tight with his pleasure.

In the aftermath, we slumber. I curl on my side, him at my back. He pulls me close, whispers in my ear.

This time when I sleep, I don't dream.

Light is low as it comes through the lace curtains when I rouse. Ren is in a chair nearby, cleaning his sword with a glow in his eyes and a smile on his lips. He hums and whistles, stopping abruptly when he notices me watching him.

He sets down the sword and crosses to me. "Good morning, Lorekeeper. Or I should say, good afternoon."

I accept his kiss, my body aching in all the right places and all the right ways. "How long have I been asleep?"

"There's still enough daylight to cover some miles on the way to Klamere."

"You should have woken me sooner."

His lips are warm. The linger on mine again, the heat from earlier resurfacing. "You needed the rest. This will be a grueling ride."

I want to enjoy more time with him in this bed, but I already feel the ticking clock goading me to get up and dress. I toy with a lock of his hair, unbound and grazing his naked shoulder. "As long as you're with me, I'll be fine."

"You're sure you don't want to stay another night?"

The look in his eyes makes me hesitate. "I would love to, but time is of the essence."

He helps me from the bed with an aggrieved sigh. "Everything is ready to go. I'll let you dress."

I snag the shirt and pants and drag them on. He returns with food, and I dig in, famished. We discuss the dream and the nightmare monsters. "Marrow said they're part of Drakenholt's erasure. That they feed on emotions, and anyone who lingers there too long is vulnerable to them."

He nods, finishing off a slice of bread with jam. "I encountered them on my way here. They always set off my dragon."

A flicker in the corner of my eye catches my attention. I glance that way and notice a mirror on the wall. A shadow falls across the room. In the reflection, a shape solidifies standing inside the glass, watching.

Marrow.

I freeze.

Ren feels it instantly; his body tenses, eyes snapping to follow mine. "What is it?"

"The mirror." My voice barely works. I leave my seat and stand in front of it. "He's—Marrow's here."

My brother's reflection tilts his head, expression unreadable. The glass ripples, as if water moves beneath it. A hairline crack cuts down the center—slow, deliberate.

"Dessa," Ren stands and moves for his sword.

The mirror fractures. The sound—sharp, crystalline—echoes like the shattering of a thousand dreams.

Ren steps between me and the shards, protective instinct in every line of his body. "What does it mean?"

I shake my head, voice unsteady. "I don't know...but it's not the first time. Every mirror at home has done the same thing. It's me. I seem to be something the mirrors can't bear to reflect."

He turns to me, takes my face gently in his hands. "Or maybe you burn too bright for glass to hold."

The bond trembles, softer, comfort instead of fire. He brushes his thumb over my lower lip, and the world feels still again—fragile, but whole.

"Come," he says quietly. "We ride for Klamere."

# CHAPTER THIRTY-FOUR
## RENWICK | THE WRAITHLANDS

*Between the ashes of what was and the silence of what's forgotten, even light forgets its name.*

DAWN NEVER TRULY RISES in Drakenholt now.

It drifts—a slow unfurling of dim silver across a land that no longer remembers the sun.

The Wraithlands stretch before us like the ghost of my kingdom. Once, these hills rolled green and gold beneath the banners of Drakenholt. Fire-flowers lined the roads, and the air shimmered with heat from the forges. I remember it as it was—bright, alive, unbroken.

Now, color has seeped from everything. The fields are as gray as the clouds, the trees ash-white. The wind sounds hollow, exhaling through the reeds.

Firebrand's hooves clop against the fractured road as we trot. The sound seems to fall into the ground instead of bouncing back, swallowed by the void. He tosses his head, uneasy. I can't blame him.

Behind me, Dessa rides the white mare. The beast moves with ghostly grace through the morning mist, her mane a streak of moonlight. The sight of them—Dessa's hair braided loose, her cloak fluttering around her in this washed-out world—makes my chest tighten.

"You've gone quiet," she says.

I glance back, trying for a smile. "It's the land. It remembers me, yet its welcome home is lifeless."

She scans the horizon, where the mist thickens over broken towers and half-buried walls. "And what does it remember?"

"That it once had a king who didn't listen. A prince who didn't believe. A story that not even dragon fire could keep bound into existence."

Her gaze finds mine across the distance between our horses. The wind steals her next words, but I read her lips—*You're still here.*

Our connection hums warm and alive inside my chest. My sigil glows. It's the only color left, a heartbeat of gold threading through the gray.

I let myself believe that's enough—that her light alone could hold me in this fading world. "Flame towers lined that ridge ahead. You could see them from Klamere's tallest tower—a crown of fire stretching for miles. Travelers used to call it the Ember Road."

She studies the empty ridge. "All gone now."

"Yes, it's a grave."

We ride in silence for a while. The mist curls thicker, veiling the ruined spires and the skeletons of bridges that once carried caravans into the capital. Fragments of script shimmer faintly in the air, dust caught in sunlight. Words untethered from their stories drift until they fade.

"This is where you came through," she says quietly. "When you went to Jairton."

"A brutal trip." I shift in the saddle, gloved fingers tightening on the reins. "The wraiths nearly took me then."

A low rumble echoes through the air. The horses slow, uneasy.

Dessa leans forward to soothe the mare, her voice a soft melody that cuts through the silence. Even the land seems to listen to her. I watch her lips move, the gentle rhythm of her hands. She doesn't realize what she does—how her presence mends all of us.

If only the Wraithlands will bow to her.

But this place doesn't bow. It feeds.

The miles drag on. As we draw closer to the valley, I feel something inside me falter. My left hand—still holding Firebrand's reins—flickers, the edges of it dissolving.

I blink, flex my fingers. The world shimmers. The hand solidifies again.

I close it quickly, hiding it beneath my cloak. I glance at Dessa. Her head is down, her eyes half-closed as she hums. At least she didn't see what just happened.

The last thing I want is for her to look at me with the same fear I feel—the fear that the Wraithlands are doing to me what they did to Drakenholt. Erasing me. Word by word.

The bond vibrates, as if it senses my deceit. I tell myself it's my imagination. The lie can't echo through magic. But the warmth in my chest pulses with a harsh disbelief.

I slow Firebrand ever so slightly so that Dessa catches up. Her cloak trails behind her in the wind, that single line of forest green cutting through a world that has no color. She looks like she belongs here and defies it all at once—Fae-born, Lore-bound, a spark walking through shadow.

"Ren," she murmurs. "Do you hear that?"

I listen. There's nothing but the whisper of the field grasses brushing against themselves like paper on paper. "I hear only what isn't there," I say.

She glances over, her brow furrowed. "It feels like the land's waiting for something."

"It is," I admit. "For us."

We crest a ridge, and a great plain opens wide before us. What was once farmland now lies drowned beneath a silver fog. The remnants of a village poke through—chimneys like grave markers, a half-collapsed windmill bent in prayer. The river that once glittered gold under the sun now runs black and sluggish, reflecting no light at all.

"The ink river," I tell her, slowing Firebrand. "It flows from Klamere itself. The forges all along this route used to burn so hot that the water shimmered red at night. You could smell the metal in the air."

Dessa studies the dark water as we ride parallel to it. "Now it smells like old books."

Her words hit something deep inside me. "That's exactly what it is. Every tale that died here bled into the ground. The Story Thief turned the once golden water to black ink."

The fog thickens, wrapping around the horses' legs. It's warm as breath. The curl of it against my skin makes the hair on the back of my neck stand on end.

Dessa notices it too. "This isn't natural."

"Nothing in the Wraithlands is."

A faint whisper threads through the air. It's so quiet I almost dismiss it as the wind. Then I hear it again—sharper this time, shaped like a word I know too well.

*Ren...wick.*

I stiffen. Firebrand snorts, stamping his hooves. The white mare jerks her head.

Dessa straightens in the saddle. "Who said that?"

"No one." I scan the fog, hand going to the hilt of my sword. "Keep riding. Don't listen."

Her voice trembles slightly. "It said your name."

"It always does."

Because that's what the Wraithlands feed on—the names of those who still have stories left to tell.

I press Firebrand forward, leading her toward a stretch of higher ground where the fog thins. The air grows colder, bitter, as if trying to cut its way into my lungs. Shapes, faint as breath—people made of silver ink—walk through the fog. A woman carrying a child flickers and vanishes. A man hammers at an invisible forge. Their faces blur, reform, disappear.

Wraiths. Echoes of what once was.

"They look so real," Dessa whispers.

"Don't be fooled." I keep my gaze forward. "They're illusions. Stories without endings. They'll try to make you finish their tales."

Her horse shies as one turns its head toward her. "What happens if I do?"

"You bring back something half-formed, I think. Not truly alive."

The silence deepens. My hand slips on the reins. I think it's due to sweat, but when I glance down, my fingertips have turned translucent again. I curl my hand into a fist before she sees.

But the bond tightens, a chain on my growing secret. She looks over, suspicion flickering behind her concern. "Are you all right?"

"Yes," I lie, and the Wraithlands echo me with a hundred ghostly whispers—

*yes... yes... yes...*

Dessa's gaze pins me. "You don't sound normal."

Before I can answer, the fog swirls upward into spirals of glowing script. A low rumble shakes the ground beneath our horses' hooves.

The stillness breaks like a held breath. Even the wraiths turn their blank faces toward the horizon.

The first gust tears through the plain, scattering the wraiths like smoke. The words in the air turn bright gold, then crimson.

The mare whinnies and jerks her head to the side. Dessa tugs on the reins. "Ren—"

"It's an Echo Storm." I draw my sword. Its edge flickers, light bending wrong around it. "We need to find cover."

The wind turns against us. It comes not as air but as sound—a thousand voices tearing loose from the fog. Words shatter mid-syllable, breaking into light and shadow. Firebrand rears, eyes rolling white, and the white mare dances sideways, nostrils flaring.

"Where do we go?" Dessa's voice is half-swallowed by the roar.

"I've got you." I wheel Firebrand around, guiding him close enough for our knees to touch. The storm uncoils above us, a whirl of script made from every story the Wraithlands has devoured. Sentences whip through the air like ribbons of light-ning, each one glowing for a heartbeat before it unravels.

Letters strike the ground and explode into sparks. "Keep your head down!" I shout.

She lowers herself against the mare's neck, cloak snapping in the gale. The gold thread in her hair catches the storm light, reminding me of the dragons carved into both of our chests.

I grit my teeth. The storm is a living thing, twisting its attention toward that glimmer of color. Toward her.

"We have to ride!" I urge Firebrand into a gallop, Dessa following. The horses plunge through a haze so thick it feels like wading through smoke.

My dragon stirs under my skin, restless, warning me that this place hungers.

Lightning splits the sky above. I catch a word inside the flash. *Forget.*

It hits the ground ahead, carving the word into stone before the wind scatters it.

Dessa gasps. "Did you see that?"

"Yes." My voice sounds hollow. "Don't read them. Don't even look."

The storm feeds on meaning. One glance, one spoken syllable, and it takes something from you.

The wind rises again. This time, I hear my own name break apart and scatter.

*Ren. Renw—*

It dissolves before it can finish.

A tug behind my ribs makes my breath stop. My vision dims, shapes blurring. My hand slips on the reins, and when I glance down, the fingers are half-gone again, translucent as smoke.

"Ren!" Dessa's shout cuts through the noise. She's beside me, eyes wide with fear, and I know she's seen it. The hand. The fading.

I force the reins steady with my other hand. "Ride! Don't stop!"

The storm bellows, echoing my defiance. Words pound into the ground around her—*stay, stay, stay*—burning themselves into the earth.

A flare of gold explodes beside her. She cries out, clutching at her head. I see it—the light swirling around her in the shape of a crown. The sigil on her chest glows through her cloak, answering the storm's fury.

A murmur of voices teases our ears. Then they shape into a single voice. Soft. Female. Familiar.

*Dessalyn.*

Dessa's head jerks up. "Mom?"

The world lurches. The wind stops.

Every letter, every spark of light freezes midair.

The voice comes again, clearer now, rolling through the silence like a tide.

*The forge waits, Dessalyn. Find it before the thief unwinds the heart of Klamere.*

I pull Firebrand to a halt, the horse trembling beneath me. Dessa turns toward the sound, eyes unfocused, lips parted. She's listening with every part of her soul.

"Dessa!" I leap from the saddle, catching her arm. "Don't answer!"

"She's calling me," she cries. "She's alive."

The storm stirs again, hungry for her hope.

"She's trapped," I say, shaking her. "You know this. Don't let the storm lure you!"

She blinks, dazed. "You don't understand—she's telling me where to go!"

A wave of words crashes over us in a wall of light. I drag her from the saddle and wrap my arms around her, shielding her as glowing script rains down. Each word that strikes my back burns, branding the shape of language into my skin.

*Forge. Fire. Heart.*

The storm screams the last word so loudly it cracks the sky.

Then everything bursts apart.

I hold her tightly, whispering the words of my oath into her ears, blocking out any echoes of the storm that linger. The wind dies. The fog sinks back to the earth.

Dessa sags against me, trembling. I realize I'm holding her too tightly. I loosen my grip but don't let go.

Her breath brushes my throat. "Ren..."

"I'm here."

When she looks up at me, storm light glows in her eyes, threads of gold flickering through the green.

I cup her face in my fading hand, and for once, I don't care if she sees. The truth is already there between us—this land is unmaking me, and only she can hold me together.

Our connection pulses once, a slow heartbeat shared between us. She presses her palm to my chest. "You're still solid," she whispers, as if saying it might make it true.

"Only because of you," I murmur.

The world around us is nothing but ruin, but here, in her arms, I can almost believe Drakenholt still remembers me.

# CHAPTER THIRTY-FIVE
## DESSALYN | WHAT THE HEART FORGETS

*Between what's lost and what endures, the heart becomes a*
*forge.*

THE WORLD HAS GONE still again.

Ash drifts from the sky like snow, soft and slow, whispering against the earth. It gathers on the edges of the ruined
stones and the curve of the horses' manes, glinting pale in the
half-light.

We've taken shelter beneath what's left of a stone arch—a
fragment of some old shrine, its runes long since worn smooth.
The air smells faintly of rain and metal, but the storm has
passed. For now.

Ren paces the edge of this small camp, sword sheathed but
never far from his reach. His movements are careful, deliberate.
The way he keeps his left hand hidden beneath his cloak tells
me what he doesn't want me to see.

He's fading.

I turn back to my journal, shielding it from him with my body as I write. The purple ink gleams gold in the candlelight. Mom's pendant is warm on my collarbone.

Encouragement for what I'm doing or a warning?

Most likely, both.

Each line I write steadies Ren a little more. I can see it. My anxious breathing calms. I can feel it through the bond, that quiet hum of life returning to his pulse.

But the price is mine. Each line sears behind my eyes, a phantom heat that leaves my fingertips numb. I've tried not to let him notice. He deserves one less worry in this broken place. I sway slightly, slamming down a hand on the cold stone floor to keep myself from falling over.

Ren's boots scrape against the stone. His strong hands steady me. "You should rest."

"I will," I lie, pulling away, even though that's the last thing I want to do.

*Fire cannot be unmade. Only reborn.* The Language shimmers on the page, reflecting back at me, but I close the book enough that he can't read it.

He moves to sit across from me. "Dessa." His voice is roughened by exhaustion. It carries the tone of disapproval. "I know what you're doing."

I freeze, the quill hovering over the parchment.

"Don't." His tone softens, pleading now. "Every time you use the Lore, it takes from you. You're trembling."

I force a smile that I often use on Calliope when I'm lying. "Maybe I'm just cold."

"You're not," he says quietly. "You're burning yourself away to keep me alive."

The truth hangs between us, fragile as glass.

"I can't stop," I whisper. "If I do, the Story Thief will finish what he started."

He kneels in front of me, the movement slow, deliberate. "You think I'd rather survive at the cost of your life?"

"It's not your choice."

"Then whose is it?" His voice cracks. "You're writing me back piece by piece, but every line you carve into that book, it's carving you out."

The quill trembles in my hand. "It's *my* quest. I must use the skills and abilities I have to complete it."

"You're not a sacrifice."

My patience snaps. "I'm the reason you're still breathing."

His jaw clenches, his eyes glinting with the faint light of his dragon fire. "You think I can live knowing you're dying to keep me whole?"

"A quest requires courage to do the hard thing." I close the journal all the way, the glow of the ink dimming as it seals. "You won't have to. At the Story Forge, I'll use the Lore and your Dragon Language to fix everything."

He exhales, sharp and angry. "That's not courage, Dessa. That's madness."

"Maybe." I rise, facing him. "But it's the kind that saves kingdoms."

He rises, too. The space between us goes electric. His dragon fire stirs the air, singeing the edges of my breath. "You think I'll just stand here and let it happen?"

"I think," I say softly, "you'll have to trust me the way I've trusted you."

Something in him falters. His hand lifts, hesitates, then brushes my neck. The touch is feather-light, as if he's afraid I'll vanish beneath his palm.

"You're stubborn," he murmurs.

"And you're being erased. You would do the same for me if our situation were reversed."

He huffs a quiet laugh, but his eyes are sad. "We make a fine pair of disasters."

I lean into his hand, letting the warmth of his touch linger. "Empires are rebuilt from ruins."

For a tense moment, neither of us moves. The fog drifts around us, the silence of the Wraithlands pressing close—but within that silence, our bond glows bright and defiant. His thumb traces the skin beneath my eye, memorizing me as if afraid I'll vanish.

He stays near while I pack my journal. His movements are quieter now, watchful, as though afraid that even breathing too loudly might shatter what's left of my strength. "I can take first watch while you rest," he says, breaking the silence. "We'll ride again once you've—"

"We'll ride now," I interrupt. "The faster we reach Klamere, the sooner this ends."

"You're too weak to ride."

"I've been shaking since we left Jairton," I admit, fastening the clasp on my satchel. "If I stop now, I might never start again."

He studies me a moment longer, clearly debating whether to argue. At last, he sighs, running a hand through his hair. "Stubborn Lorekeeper."

"Half-erased dragon."

The faintest smile curves his lips, but it doesn't quite reach his eyes.

I turn toward the arch, tracing the runes carved into its weathered face. Most are worn smooth, but one line of script glints faintly as the wind shifts. I brush away the ash coating the stone. Beneath it, offerings remain—a few dried flowers, a cracked bowl filled with gray dust, and a metal disc with a dragon's head. The design catches the meager light and throws it back at me. The floating sigil flashes, as if in acknowledgment.

I wave Ren over. "Look."

He joins me, the chain around his neck glinting as he leans over. The broken dragon pendant glows suddenly, and a pulse of gold flickers from it.

He inhales and fingers his pendant. "What's this, now?"

I crouch, brushing away more ash. Beneath the disc is something buried deeper. A small iron box, sealed with melted wax and stamped with the same dragon insignia as his necklace. When I touch it, the metal is warm despite the cold air. Heat shoots up my arm and into my chest.

Ren touches the same spot on his own chest. "I felt that."

I glance up. "It's reacting to us."

He hesitates. "Why?"

I shrug, Lore flowing from my mouth. "The Lorekeeper and the Dragon Prince—the same magic bound twice." I dig the box free. The earth around it steams. "Whatever this is, someone left it here in offering to the dragons." I shake it lightly and hear a soft metallic clink from within.

Ren extends his hand. "Let me." The moment he touches it, his pendant flares with light—the jagged edge along the break glowing.

The shrine's runes drum, just once, but it's as if they recognize their prince.

We look at each other. The dragon on his broken pendant calls my attention. "What happened to it?" I ask. "How did it break?"

"It's the last element of the True Flame. The Dragon Flame. It broke the day the kingdom forgot its name," Ren says, tracing the cracked stone.

"Were there other magical artifacts?"

"When the Story Thief devoured Drakenholt's story, every magical object tied to the realm was unmade—except for things anchored to living souls."

"That's why it's still here," I say, "because it's anchored to you."

The pendant half lifts, pulling toward the box. "It's calling to it."

My pulse quickens. "Can you open it?"

He tries, but the seal won't budge. I hand him my dagger. "Pry it open."

"Dessa, we don't know what it is."

I nod at the box. "Do it."

All attempts that follow fail. Minutes later, we are both sweating and irritated. The sun is getting low on the horizon. "Bring it with us," I say, heading for the horses.

He hums, twisting it in the light. "Removing an offering is..."

"Sacrilege. I know." I stuff my journal into my satchel and mount White Ash—the name I've bestowed on my pretty mare. "But it's part of the Dragon Lore. I can feel it, and so can you."

He gives me that look—the one that sits between frustration and reluctant admiration. "You're impossible."

"But right," I counter.

He huffs out a laugh. "That too."

"No one is here to care, Ren, and it could be a key to your future." *Our future*, I don't say.

If I even have a future with him. I'm starting to doubt my quest goes any farther than the Story Forge.

He tucks the box into his saddlebag with a muttered prayer to the old dragon gods. We finish breaking camp in silence, the air between us threaded with unspoken worry. As we lead the horses from beneath the shrine, I glance back. The runes along the arch glimmer as if saying goodbye. A chill ripples down my spine. I press a hand to my chest where the pendant burns faintly against my skin. "We're close," I murmur.

Ren swings into Firebrand's saddle. "Klamere is still a day's ride away."

"To the truth," I amend, kicking White Ash into a gallop.

He urges Firebrand forward, and together we ride into the waking fog—our path lit not by sunlight, but by the faint, stubborn glow of two half-broken souls refusing to disappear.

We ride for hours over broken ridges and through dry ravines, the horses becoming as sluggish as we are. We crest a ridge, and below, a narrow spring winds through the rocks—gleaming with bluish-gold light.

"Lorelight," I whisper. "What is this place?"

"A memory pool." He clicks his tongue at Firebrand to get him moving again. "The waters here held memories once. Now?" He shrugs. "They're corrupted like everything else."

I tug my reins in its direction. "I need to see it."

"Are you sure?"

But I've already left him. It only takes a moment before he and Firebrand catch up. At least he doesn't try to talk me out of it.

He dismounts near the pool's edge, helping me down with a grip that lingers a heartbeat too long. "Careful," he says. "Places like this can trap you in what they show."

The water looks impossibly clear under the night sky, its surface rippling with the reflection of the first stars appearing overhead. As I watch, the reflections morph into old runes of the Lore Language, words half-inked. I step closer despite Ren's hand closing lightly around my arm.

I pull out of his grip. "I have to see."

I kneel beside the pool. The moment my fingers brush the surface, the light surges outward. Cold shoots through me and straight to my bones.

A vision blooms. I'm in a forest, and Mom is there, pressing a wrapped bundle to her chest as she hurries past boulders and giant tree roots. I follow, sensing her distress, her urgency. Every so often, she stops to peer over her shoulder. Does she sense me or whoever she's running from?

The forest dissolves into reeds. In the moonlight, I see what she cradles—a small boy swaddled in gray cloth. She presses her lips to his forehead, whispering something I can't quite hear. Then she sets him in a boat of reeds and sends it adrift, tears bright on her cheeks. "*He'll prize you above all others.*" Her tears flow freely. "*You'll be safe behind the palace walls.*"

At first, I think she means the king will prize him. Then cold understanding riddles my bones.

The Story Thief—that's who she means.

"*Forgive me, my son,*" she whispers with a choked sob. "*One day, your sisters will find you.*"

The boy floats toward the shadows. The water shimmers again, and I glimpse him later — older, wild-eyed, his hands stained with ink and fire. Marrow.

My throat tightens. The truth unravels inside me. She didn't abandon him. She hid him from Cimarron. Even as far back as Marrow's birth, she must have foreseen what was to come. At least, she saw some version of it. She believed being inside the dragon court would keep my brother safe.

I pull back my hand. The glow fades, leaving ripples of light that slowly sink into the depths.

Ren drops beside me. "What did you see?"

I look up at him, tears stinging my eyes. "My mother and Marrow. She thought she could protect him from Cimarron by placing him behind your castle's walls. That by being inside the court, he would be safe."

He studies my face, his expression softening. "She didn't abandon him. Not the way he believes."

"No," I murmur. "With his rare gift, she thought he'd be cherished and nurtured by your father. Not...enslaved."

He rakes his fingers through his hair. "Visions and prophecies can be unreliable."

"Only when a tainted Lorekeeper messes with our stories. It's the Thief's tampering that has changed the threads of all of them."

The pool shivers again. I see our reflections—his and mine—ringed in the same light that had surrounded Mom. Flame and memory, bound together.

A breeze stirs the surface, scattering the image. Ren reaches out, brushing his fingers over mine. "Still, what the pool shows may not be accurate."

"It is," I insist. I touch my pendant. "I just wish it had shown me who Marrow's father is."

Ren's gaze drifts toward the darkening horizon. He picks up on my thoughts. "You think it's...?"

My gut ties in a knot. "It would explain much, wouldn't it? How Cimarron found a way to corrupt the Lore without consequence? Between his own Fae powers, my mother's gifts, and then discovering Marrow, a gifted dream walker with his own blood, he defiled the Language and began erasing the world."

The words hang in the air between us.

Thoughts of my mother and Cimarron together batter my mind. I glance once more at the pool. The last of the light sinks beneath the surface, but the memory lingers—my mother's tears, the boy in the reeds, the vow she whispered to him. *Your sisters will find you.*

The echo of it sparks through the bond. Ren pulls me close, steadying me as exhaustion claims my strength.

The valley goes dark, but the truth we've uncovered burns in my heart.

# CHAPTER THIRTY-SIX
## DESSALYN | THE HEART OF THE MOUNTAIN

*Between what's written and what's lost, creation and destruction each demands a price.*

THE WRAITHLANDS BREAK AT last. Monochrome plains give way to the jagged rise of mountains, their black slopes streaked with veins of red stone. They remind me of the color of embers smoldering in a hearth. Wind funnels through the ravines, carrying the scent of smoke and something older... metal, dragon-fire, memory.

Klamere.

The capital of Drakenholt. The heart of a kingdom that's been erased.

The ruins sprawl across the mountainside like the skeleton of some magnificent creature—its towers empty, its bridges snapped, banners burned. The once black marble has gone the color of bone.

Ren reins Firebrand to a stop. His breath fogs in the cold air, but he doesn't move. For a long time, he simply stares. Through the bond, I feel the ache twisting in his chest, sharp and wordless. Grief braided with guilt. Shame that runs so deep it has no name.

My heart clenches. I want to touch him, to comfort him, but what is there to say?

A few of my own memories of the light and laughter that once filled this city mix with his. Most of it is gone, blanked out. Only the dreams and the vision I had of Mom in the mirror back home are solid. Others tease at me, but don't truly form.

Somewhere deep within the ruins, loose stone shifts, echoing with a sigh. He dismounts, boots sinking into the ash. His hand trails along a toppled column, fingertips brushing soot from the carved reliefs of dragons in flight. "I used to stand here at the festival of fires," he murmurs. "You could see banners from every kingdom rippling along the terraces. Music from the forges...people cheering when the first flame was lit." His voice falters. "I thought we were invincible." The last word breaks in his mouth like glass.

The words slice into me. I slide off White Ash and reach for him, but before my fingers touch his sleeve, he turns away—shoulders rigid, jaw clenched. His pain is too raw to share.

I let my hand fall. "We'll bring it back," I say. "We'll bring you back."

Firebrand snorts. Ren touches the stallion's neck, his gaze drawn toward the palace's west wing, where the mountain rises as a backdrop. Sturdy and unchanged, its ragged peaks resemble the end of dragon tails daring the sky.

The half-broken pendant at his throat flickers. At the exact moment, the sealed iron box in his saddlebag begins a low-pitched whine. A golden light radiates from its seams, steady and rhythmic, as if something inside is calling to the ruins.

Ren lifts his head. "It's pointing us that way."

I feel a magnetic pull. The tug is unmistakable, drawing us straight into the shattered arches of the long halls that once led to the infamous library my father helped the king design. I nod, swallowing the lump in my throat. "That's where the quest wants us to go."

Together we lead the horses toward the palace gates, following the light of two relics that still remember what Drakenholt once was—and what it might yet be again.

The gates of Klamere resist us at first. Iron twisted by centuries of fire leans at odd angles, fused into the stone like bones into scar tissue. When Ren braces his shoulder against the arch and shoves, the hinges shriek—a sound almost human. It echoes through the courtyard, startling a dozen birds from their perches. They scatter into the pale sky.

Inside the walls, silence reigns. No voices. No footfalls. Only the slow drift of ash swirling through light that filters weakly from the broken dome above.

The courtyard once opened into a grand avenue. Now the bricks are split, choked with washed-out weeds. The fountain at the center overflows with gray dust, the statue of the first dragon king shattered in two.

Ren leads me through the debris and finally kneels beside a stone tile, brushing away the soot with careful fingers. "This is the mark for the Sacred Fire Library," he murmurs.

The emblem is faint but unmistakable—three intertwined flames circling a dragon's eye.

Bringing the box with us, we leave the horses and follow the narrow path that curves behind the courtyard, our boots stirring up dust. Columns flank the way—some cracked, some toppled—but enough remain to guide us to a pair of doors twice our height, carved from blackened bronze.

Even through the decay, the artistry steals my breath. Dragons coil up the panels, their scales shaped from script, each etched in a combination of both of our Lores. Two languages intertwined—story and flame bound together.

Ren's hand hovers above the carving. His voice drops to a whisper. "I learned my first Dragon Tongue here before it became the central library. My father used to bring me to watch the scribes weave fire into words."

I touch the lower edge of the door, tracing a faint flourish at the corner—a looping spiral carved beneath the dragons' tails. Recognition prickles my skin. "That's my father's mark."

"He left it that final day, after the addition of the scriptorium, before everything went so wrong."

My throat tightens as I imagine him standing here—alive, proud, hands coated in ash and ink, shaping beauty into metal. "He always said that building a master library and scriptorium was its own kind of quest."

Ren glances at the door's hinges. "There isn't much left."

The artifact's whine intensifies, ringing in my ears. "But we're on the right track."

Together, we push. The bronze doors stick, groaning like something half-asleep. Then, with a breath that sounds eerily like a sigh, they open inward.

The Dragon Library unfolds before us.

It's a cathedral, its rows of shelves rising like cliffs into darkness, their contents long reduced to dust. Only the bindings remain—ghostly shells of books, their words scorched away. The floor glimmers with specks of ink dust, glowing blue-white like stars fallen to earth. The scholarly tables, sitting areas, and fireplaces are all in disarray.

Each step sends a ripple through the haze. When I breathe, I taste the sweetness of old parchment mixed with the metallic tang of dragon fire.

Ren moves at my side, silent, reverent. The light from his pendant reflects in his eyes like twin flames. "I loved it here even when it was a simple, everyday library," he says, voice barely more than breath. "Every storykeeper from the royal line began here."

"And this..." I step forward, brushing my fingertips along a broken lectern. The carved base bears the same sigil from the archway: *Here, flame learns to speak*. "Was this where your lessons took place?"

He nods. The bond quivers with emotions that are too deep for words—loss, love, a kind of quiet awe. They quiver inside my chest. The box's glow deepens to gold. Its hum matches the pulse of Ren's pendant. The twin lights pierce the dust, illuminating the far wall, beating back the darkness. "What's back there?" I ask.

He leads me to a collapsed stairway that descends into darkness. His voice drops to a hush, reverent and uneasy. "The entry to the scriptorium."

I remember now. My mother and father had spoken endlessly of this place—how the king wanted a single sacred scriptorium to unite all who studied Dragon Lore. One heart to bind every forge, every story.

I stare into the darkness. "The mountain's heart lies beneath it, doesn't it?"

His expression is grim, resigned. "It does, but there may be more than the scriptorium waiting for us."

I tighten my grip on my satchel, the weight of the journal against my hip both a comfort and a curse. I try to lighten the mood. "I'll protect you."

He snorts, although his eyes are still somber. "Then let's see what stories the mountain remembers."

As we descend, the warmth of the surface fades, replaced by a chill that isn't cold so much as emptiness—an absence of breath, of life. Even our footsteps are swallowed, muted by the weight of the mountain.

I want to linger in the scriptorium, to admire my father's work, but the stories are gone. The desks for translations are toppled. There is no grand dais for a book like Vellicor, yet I sense there should be.

"It was grand," Ren says, watching me take it all in. "There were thousands of works, many translated from other realms for us by the scholars. Art, history, medicine, engineering...I wanted to study it all."

The empty shelves are a deserted graveyard. A chill races over my skin. All those words, all those subjects—so much knowledge, gone forever. I sway, lightheaded. Ren grabs my arm to steady me. "We should keep going," I say.

Our boots echo off the stone floor as we cross through the deserted place. At the very rear, there is an unmarked door. It's locked, but Ren easily snaps it with a blow from his sword handle.

When he opens it, a dark, foreboding staircase awaits. He grabs a lamp and lights it before we descend into the tight space.

The walls close around us, slick with veins of black crystal that shimmer faintly from lamplight. Draconic runes curl across the stone like veins of fire frozen mid-burn.

Ren leads, the artifact cradled in one arm. The sealed box glows steadily, casting golden reflections over his jaw and throat. His pendant mirrors it, light spilling from the crack that splits it in two.

I hear whispers, sighs. I feel like someone is watching me. "It feels...alive," I whisper.

He glances back. "Every legend about it claims the dragons forged this place with their own flame. Some say their breath runs through its veins even now."

His voice carries a quiet awe that makes me ache. This was his world once—his inheritance. All the beauty and burden that comes with a kingdom's soul.

We pass through a narrow corridor carved with our two languages intertwined. The stone warms beneath my fingertips as I trace them. "These are old," I murmur. "Older than either of our tongues."

Ren nods. "When the dragons first allied with the Lorekeepers, they carved the first Story Forges here, binding flame to word." Halfway down, he stumbles. The glow from his pendant flickers, dimming almost to nothing.

"Ren." I catch his arm. His body feels wrong—thin at the edges, blurred. My stomach twists. "You're fading again."

He straightens, jaw tightening. "It's the mountain. It remembers the prince who lived, not the ghost who came home."

The bond tightens. A rush of heat flares through it—then falters, weaker than before. My heart hammers, desperate to keep its rhythm matched to his.

"Let me write," I say, reaching for my satchel.

He catches my wrist, shaking his head. "No. You're already pale. I can feel what it's doing to you."

"Then we'll both die before we reach the Forge."

"Better that than watching you burn yourself away one line at a time."

I pull free, swallowing the lump in my throat. The story I've already been rewriting is as much to blame as anything. I must not share it with him, though. Not yet. I hate keeping another secret after I told him I had none left. This one, though, will fix everything. "It's not your decision to make."

He exhales roughly, raking a hand through his hair. "Please, Dessalyn."

Two words. But in them, everything. "Fine. Let's go."

We descend the final steps in silence, our argument hanging between us. The words I'm hiding pulse beneath my ribs, alive and dangerous.

The staircase opens into a vast chamber. The air here is warmer, pulsing with its own breath. Lava veins thread through the obsidian floor, casting red-gold reflections that dance across the high ceiling.

At the center of the cavern stands a stone platform—a circular, shallow forge, its rim carved with thousands of runes. The writing is again in both languages--the Lore's silver curves and the Dragons' angular flame.

"The Story Forge," Ren says softly. His voice trembles, reverent and afraid. "I've never seen it before. My father insisted it was a myth."

For something that shouldn't exist, it feels heartbreakingly familiar. I step closer. Faint heat radiates from it. "It's stunning."

He touches it, and I feel a surge of white-hot heat blister my own skin. He jerks his hand back. "It's...hungry," he replies.

The artifact in his hands whines louder, answering the Forge's silent call. The sealed wax cracks; light spills from the box in slow, radiant waves. A faint sound follows—something like a heartbeat echoing against the stone.

Ren's eyes darken. "You were right—it's meant to be here."

My pendant flares, a brand against my skin. The quill in my satchel stirs, trembling as if something beneath the world is breathing again.

I nod, unable to tear my gaze away from the forge. The air above it ripples, shimmering between gold and crimson. Images flicker within the light—memories, stories, fragments of what was written here long ago.

A crown of flame.

A boy kneeling before a king.

A woman with silver hair writing words that bleed light.

*Mom.*

The vision vanishes as quickly as it came.

Ren touches my shoulder. "Dessa?"

I force a breath. "I saw her."

He doesn't ask who—he knows. The hum deepens, resonating through my bones. Whatever lives in this place—whatever power waits—it's awake now. Watching. Listening.

And it wants a story.

Good thing I've brought one.

# Chapter Thirty-Seven
## Dessalyn | The Price of Language

*When two truths burn as one, creation must choose which voice to keep.*

The glow from the runes dims to a steady light, as if the mountain is listening, waiting for us to speak the right words to wake the forge.

Ren circles the platform. "It's dormant," he murmurs, tracing the carved lines with his fingers. "Like a dragon sleeping beneath its own flame."

The artifact's whine lowers to a murmur, purring. Its light flickers, gold shifting to silver and back again. I move closer, drawn by the rhythm pulsing between the runes and the box. "It's as if it's waiting for something."

"Or someone," he says quietly. "These are Lore Language sigils along the inner ring. But these outer ones"—his touch hovers above the sharper, angular marks—"are Draconic."

My pulse quickens. "I've seen it everywhere since we arrived—the Lore and the Dragon Languages—carved together into archways and doors."

"Who do you think came first? The dragons or the Fae?"

"Even the oldest of our parchments doesn't give us that answer. Maybe they came into being at the same time. Evolved together."

"Dragons always claim dominance."

There's a cheekiness in his tone. I glance up at him. "Yet, the dragons themselves are all gone."

"Fair point. And the Fae are alive and well throughout the realm." He juts his chin toward my quest journal, tucked close at my side. "Who was the first Lorekeeper?"

"There were two." The story is one every storykeeper knows. "Gadrick and Painia. They wrote the realm into being with the Great Storybook."

"You believe that?"

"It's a better creation story than a dragon hatching humanity from an egg."

He snorts at my poking fun at that dragon legend. "But all the Story Forges are said to be fueled by fire."

I caress the inner ring of sigils, feeling them vibrate under my fingertips. "Fire born from words." I tap the inner ring. "Words first, then fire." I gesture toward the lines curling across the platform, the symmetry so deliberate it's unmistakable. "Look at it.

Lore shapes creation, and flame brings it to life. Alone, they're one half of a whole. Together, they create worlds."

His frivolity fades, and his jaw flexes. "Or unmake everything."

Before I can reply, the artifact's whine deepens even more. The lid bursts open. A surge of light explodes outward, flooding the chamber.

We both stumble back, shielding our eyes as heat ripples through the air. The sound it makes isn't a voice but a resonance—like a thousand pages fluttering in a storm.

When the light fades, the box lies empty—except for a single object resting inside.

A quill.

Its shaft gleams bone white, the point tipped in gold. Faint veins of red pulse along its spine, and at its center, the filigree of a dragon's scale is imprinted in the metal. The air around it bends, trembling.

My pulse skips. "The Heart Quill." Another story every Lore-keeper knows. "It's real."

Ren stares, reverent and wary. "What's the Heart Quill?"

My voice shakes, and I can't keep the smile off my face. "It's the first quill. The one Gadrick and Painia used to write the Great Storybook."

He strokes the nib. "It's forged from dragon bone."

"And Fae gold." My throat tightens. "They're...combined. Just like the Languages."

He kneels beside the box, light from the Forge reflecting off his face. "It's meant to bridge the two lineages, dragon and Fae. Fire and story, bound by blood."

His words sink into me, heavy as prophecy. "Blood," I echo.

The Forge stirs. The Lore marks brighten. The quill shivers. The pulse beating inside the mountain quickens until I can feel it in my own heart. The quill rises like a dancer and spins.

Ren glances up, his expression grim. "What's it doing?"

"It wants to write a story."

"Does it need ink?"

The truth curls cold and certain in my gut. The Heart Quill won't answer ordinary ink, not for something born of both tongues. It needs a medium alive enough to carry their magic. I shake my head. "No. Not ink."

Ren seems to realize the same thing at once. "No." He rises, backing away from the box. "Dessa, don't even think—"

The dragon on his chest glows with a fierce light. My twin echoes it.

"It's not calling me." My voice trembles despite my resolve. "The anchor to Drakenholt is...you."

His eyes flash, but the shadows deepen despite the light flooding the chamber. They snake around him, and his form goes transparent for a heartbeat. "And I'm here."

*Not for long.* I swallow the words. We're running out of time. "Your blood." The words are bitter in my mouth. "Your blood is the ink the Forge must have, or it will never awaken."

As a true hero, ready to sacrifice himself, he sticks out an arm. "Take it. As much as you need."

I swallow, understanding the Fae inscriptions now in a way I didn't before. "It will require all of it, Ren." My voice becomes a whisper. "Every last drop."

His hand falters. "What?"

I can't hold his shocked gaze. Mine drops to the ring of Dragon sigils. I can't read them, yet I search for any way to work around this horrible detail.

He strides toward me, fierce, desperate, gripping my shoulders. I'm forced to look up at him. "I've given everything—my kingdom, my people, my fire. Isn't that enough?"

"Your fire isn't gone," I whisper, laying a hand on his chest. "It's just waiting to be written anew."

He releases me and shakes his head, stomping away. "You don't know what it will cost to do that. You said the Lore exacts a price if you write something not given to you by that damned book."

"It does," I say softly. I'm caught in a web of my own making. "The Lore always demands what you love in exchange for what you want."

He flinches, shoulders sagging. "Then we need to find another way."

His form ripples again. I'm running out of time. "There isn't one." I take the quill out of the air. It's warm in my hand, and a whisper fills my ears. Words not my own, ancient and aching.

*Write. Breathe. Burn.*

Ren closes the distance, his hand covering mine, stopping me. At least, I can feel it—and the tremor in it. "It could cost Calliope. Your father."

"Maybe," I say, meeting his gaze. It won't. It will cost me him. "But if we don't use this, the Story Thief will unmake everything. Every tale. Every name. Including yours and theirs."

His expression fractures—anger and fear, love and despair colliding behind his eyes. "You think I'm worth that?"

"Yes," I whisper, then raise my voice. "*Yes.*" I know the following words are true, even if they rip my heart in two. "My quest requires sacrifice. Yours requires the same."

The Forge answers with a low, resonant throb. The quill flares to life between our joined hands, its gold tip glowing brighter, hungry for the story I'm about to give it.

A column of light rises from the forge, spiraling upward. The runes ignite—silver and gold, Lore and Fire—twin flames.

Ren steps back, his arm shielding me. "What's happening?"

The quill quakes. I grip it more firmly. "I don't know."

The light thickens, and from its center, a shape begins to form—a woman's silhouette, hair streaming silver, her gown made of shifting script.

My throat tightens. "Mom?"

Ren stiffens beside me as she materializes fully. Her eyes shimmer silver, her expression soft but unbearably sad. "My brave girl," she says, her voice carrying both warmth and sorrow. "You've done well. You found the Story Forge that can remake the world."

Ren dips his head in respect. "Lady Serenelle," he says quietly. "I'm sorry for everything."

She glances at him, her gaze tender and haunted. "The dragon prince who lived when the kingdom did not."

He flinches at that, but I continue. "Are you free from Cimarron's hold? The bargain was voided at Jairton. The story he wanted went up in flames, but not by my hand."

She smiles faintly. "My heart still beats, but I'm not free. Not yet."

A mix of anger and disappointment makes me tremble. "Then how are you here?"

"You brought me here by waking the Old Language and unlocking the quill. I'm bound by blood to both, as are you."

I glance at the quill. "I am?"

"The blood that runs in my veins and yours is from the Originals. They built this place, binding dragon to Fae and Fae to dragon. Two languages, two dynasties, bound together to create this realm."

Ren peers at me, jaw dropping. "You're Fae royalty."

I blink, feeling anything but. "No, that's—"

My mother speaks over me. "The Forge wakes because the two tongues—and their bloodlines—have found each other again and shaped a new bond. Lore and Flame—the written word to create, the fire to seal it. But what you see here," she gestures to the glowing runes, "is not only a forge. It is a weapon. A rewriting engine. Every word written and burned upon it reshapes existence."

I'm still trying to wrap my head around the fact that I'm directly descended from Gadrick and Painia.

"The possibilities are endless—and terrifying," Ren says.

I shove my wandering thoughts aside. "That's why it's hidden. To keep those like Cimarron from destroying our world."

Her gaze dims at his name. "The Forge demands life. To write upon it is to feed it your soul, your story, your breath. Gadrick and Painia sealed it, hoping it would sleep forever."

Ren's voice hardens. "But Cimarron found it."

Mom shakes her head. "Not the forge. He found me."

The air chills.

My chest constricts. "You mean—"

"His quest was to reshape the world—or so I believed when I met him. He told me he was from Evermere and showed me a parchment with his quest written in the Lore Language. It was only later, once he began corrupting stories, that I discovered he was a shadow weaver."

Goose flesh races down my back. "From Thornveil," I murmur. "The kingdom of shadows and twisted tales."

She nods. "I showed him the way to the first Lorekeeper sanctums. I thought he knew the Language, that he was one of us. Instead, he used me to twist it. When I saw what he'd become and the opening your story gave him,"—she glances at Ren—"I tried to stop him."

"But it didn't work," Ren says.

She shakes her head, tears spilling down her luminous cheeks. "He found other ways to erase stories. Small things at first. He went after dream walkers, and I..." Her voice trails off.

My legs tremble. "Marrow. You tried to save him. Protect him. Is he Cimarron's..." I can't say it out loud. It's too terrible to consider.

"Marrow is not his child—no." She sees my relief. "But he's now bonded to him, and that bond is as strong as blood. I never meant to abandon him. I cloaked him with my magic to hide him from Cimarron, but it wasn't enough."

Her words crash through me like breaking glass. My brother, my mother, the thief—all bound by her sacrifice. "Who is it, then?" I dare ask. "Who is his father?"

Before she can answer, Ren grabs his chest. His pendant flickers. His form ripples.

"Ren!" I grab for him, but my hand goes right through him.

He staggers and falls. I rush to kneel beside him, terror clutching at me. "What should I do?" I yell at Mom.

She points to the quill in my hand. "Because the Forge is awake, the price is already being drawn. Your bond feeds it."

I stare down at the Heart Quill, its glow pulsing wildly. "Then tell me how to stop it."

She steps closer, cupping my face in hands made of light. "You can't stop it, my love. You can only finish the story."

"What does that mean?"

Her eyes soften. "The Severance Decree still binds our family. Until it's undone, none of us can truly be free. Not you, not Ren, not even Marrow. To rewrite it, you must write upon the Forge itself—with the Quill, fire, and blood."

Ren stiffens. "You're asking her to—"

"I'm asking her to choose," Mom says. "The Decree severed us from the world's memory. If it remains, the Thief will always have power over our bloodline. But if she rewrites it..." Her voice falters. "...Dessa will vanish. The world will remember what was lost, but not who restored it."

My stomach drops. "What?"

Ren's voice cracks. "There has to be another way."

Mom peers down at him. "You would give your life for hers. But would she let you?"

The bond hums between us, aching and raw. A new wave of anger floods me. "I won't let either of you decide for me," I say, standing. "If the price of saving everything is my story, then I'll pay it."

*And I'll take Cimarron with me.*

Mom's eyes fill with tears. "My daughter, always the brave one."

The chamber trembles. The Forge flares hot, blinding us. The mountain groans, and for the first time, I feel the Story Thief's presence pressing against the edges of the light here.

Ren draws his sword, his fading hand gripping the hilt tight. "He's coming."

Mom glances toward the darkness gathering along the far wall. "Then my time is over."

She places her hand over my heart. Warmth floods through me, pure and comforting. Her pendant sparks. "My power is yours now. My story ends so yours can begin."

"Mom—no!"

Light bursts from her chest, scattering into a thousand glowing glyphs that spiral upward and fall like silver rain upon the Forge. Her pendant burns white-hot, then shatters. The warmth of her soul fills me.

And then she's gone.

The chamber falls silent except for a last echo of her voice.

*Write wisely, my heart. Save the prince. He is the world's destiny.*

# Chapter Thirty-eight
## Dessalyn | The Story Thread

*When a story breaks, what remains is not silence—but the scream of what refuses to be forgotten.*

The last of Mom's light fades into the air like falling stars.

Silver motes drift down and settle on the Forge's rim, glowing faintly before they sink into the stone. The silence that follows is unbearable.

Ren kneels beside the platform, breathing hard, one hand clutching his chest where the pendant burned through his shirt. He looks...half there. Fading at the edges, his outline softening like smoke.

I clutch the Heart Quill to my chest. "She's gone," I sob.

He lifts his head, eyes shining gold in the gloom. "No one's ever truly gone when their story still lives."

The reassurance should comfort me—but it doesn't. Not when her words echo in my skull. *Write wisely, my heart. Save the prince. He is the world's destiny.*

A low tremor shakes the ground. The Forge responds to something unseen, its runes flaring bright and angry. Red light gathers in the air, swirling, condensing—then collapsing inward on itself.

Ren motions at me. "Get back!"

But I don't move. The air between us tears like paper, and from that opening, something crawls out. Ink pours across the floor—thick, dark, alive. It spreads like a shadow given form, then reshapes into a man's silhouette. A breath. A heartbeat. Eyes opening—gray and burning at once.

"Marrow," I breathe.

He staggers, his body flickering in and out of existence. Letters crawl beneath his skin, glowing and fading in erratic rhythm. He looks like the brother I saw in the memory pool and yet not—older, haunted, half-shadow.

"Dessa." His voice cracks. "What have you done?"

"I'm rewriting our story," I whisper.

He looks past me toward the Forge, horror flooding his face. "You woke it."

Ren steps between us. "You've got one chance to tell us why you're here."

Marrow's laugh is hollow. "You think I wanted this? He called me." He grips his temples, grimacing. "The Thief...he's inside everything now—the stories, the stone, even me."

The runes around the chamber flare. The air darkens as if something vast presses closer from beyond what we can see.

Ren lowers his sword slightly. "You're tied to him."

"Not tied—used." Marrow looks at me, desperation burning through the ruin of his face. "He made me his quill, Dessa. His vessel. Every word he writes, I bleed it into being."

I shake my head. "That's not possible—"

"It is," Marrow says, a bitter smile twisting his mouth. "You think I wanted to be the Story Thief's scribe? He promised to free me from the shadows, to give me a story of my own. Instead, he hollowed me out."

Ren's jaw tightens. "Help us stop him."

Marrow's laughter is sharp and broken. "Stop him? You don't stop a story once it's begun." He takes an unsteady step toward me. "Isn't that right, sister? Just like a quest, it must always move forward."

The Forge pulses at his words, runes blazing.

Marrow flinches, pressing a hand to his chest. "He knows I'm here," he whispers. "He's coming."

A ripple of darkness spreads across the chamber floor, swallowing the light from the lava veins. The shadows twist and rise like a storm given shape. A figure coalesces within it—tall, robed, eyes like twin voids spilling starlight.

Solander Cimarron.

The Story Thief.

His voice rolls through the chamber, velvet and venom. "Ah," he says, almost tenderly. "My Lorekeeper, and my favorite mistake."

Ren steps in front of me, his fading form flickering even as his dragon fire ignites in his veins. "This ends here. Now."

Cimarron smiles, the motion cold and inhuman. His gaze locks on mine. "On the contrary, Prince. It's just the beginning of a brand new story for all of us."

The mountain groans. The Forge's glow surges like an awakening sun. The Heart Quill burns in my grip, and runes crawl up my arms like chains of light.

I realize the truth too late—Mom's sacrifice didn't seal the Forge.

It opened it.

And now, all of us are standing on the edge of *its* story.

The chamber shivers like it's caught between two heartbeats. Cimarron's presence fills the space. The shadows around him crawl and twist. Where they touch stone, the runes gutter and die.

"Run," Marrow cries. His voice breaks on the word. "He'll devour anything that remembers itself."

Ren steps forward, sword raised, his fading body haloed in firelight. "This is my kingdom. I will not run."

Cimarron laughs—a slow, indulgent sound that slides down my spine. "Still pretending you can fight the inevitable?" His gaze slides to me. "Shall I finish the job properly this time?"

Ren lunges. Dragon fire flares, gold against the black. His blade strikes true—but it passes through Cimarron's body. The Thief catches the steel bare-handed. Words emerge, melting the steel.

Ren reels back, clutching the hilt. "He's rewriting reality."

"That's what he does," Marrow utters. "And he's using me to do it."

I clutch the Heart Quill. Its tip burns hot against my palm. "No more. I'll end the story he's writing."

Cimarron's head tilts toward me. "Ah, but you've already begun, haven't you? Trying to pen a tale where you win."

How does he know? I ignore him; I have to stay focused. I open my journal and—

He gestures, and the air fills with torn pages—ghostly stories fluttering, each one screaming as they attack me. "Every rebellion begins in ink and ends in silence."

I beat back the pages. Marrow staggers between us, shaking. "Stop—" He presses a hand to his chest, and his eyes blaze with twin sigils—one of shadow, one of silver. "Dessa, he's inside me. I can feel him ripping me apart."

Ren grabs him by the shoulders. "Fight him!"

"I can't!" Marrow gasps. "He has control of my story." His gaze snaps to mine, flicks to my journal. "But you...you can erase me. Rewrite the story...without me."

The words hit like lightning. "No—I can't do that. It will destroy you."

He smiles—a weary, human smile. "You're not destroying me. You're freeing what's left."

Ren starts to protest, but Marrow jerks free. "Do it, Dessa. Before he takes me completely."

Cimarron spreads his hands. "By all means. Let's see if the apprentice can outwrite her master."

The Forge roars. The mountain's veins blaze gold. The chamber becomes a storm of fire and story. I lift the Heart Quill, its point catching light from both tongues. The air hums with the weight of every word ever written.

Ren's fading hand covers mine. "Together," he says hoarsely.

I nod. My throat aches. "Together."

We draw a single sigil across the air—a word older than time, the first story unmade. The quill burns, the Forge screams, and the shadows convulse.

Marrow throws his head back and shouts in the Draconic tongue—one I don't know but somehow understand. "*Remember me.*" Then he dives straight into Cimarron's darkness.

Light and shadow explode. The impact knocks me off my feet; the Forge cracks down the center, spilling fire like blood.

When the light clears, Marrow is gone. Only his voice lingers, a whisper that curls through the smoke. *Finish it, sister.*

Cimarron staggers, his form flickering—half solid, half void. For the first time, the Story Thief looks afraid.

Ren pulls me upright. His outline wavers, translucent. "He's weakened. This is your moment."

I stare at the glowing fissure that splits the Forge—the quill trembling in my hand, the runes waiting for the final word. I raise my journal. "Time to write The End."

The walls tremble as if the world itself can't bear what I've proclaimed. Heat spills through the cracks in the Forge, a river of gold and shadow twisting together, blood and ink.

Cimarron rises from the smoke, half his face burned to light, the other half pure void. His voice fractures, a hundred stolen tongues speaking at once. "Do you think this will stop me? I am the story."

"No," I say, lifting the Heart Quill. "Not anymore."

He dives at me. Ren intercepts him, sparks exploding when they collide. The impact throws us both backward. He's weakening fast—his edges shimmering like glass under too much heat.

"Dessa—finish it!" he shouts, his voice echoing from somewhere between this world and the next.

I stumble to the platform. The Forge pulses like a wounded heart, its light feverish and unsteady. Is it tied to Cimarron's?

My hands shake as I raise the quill. The words come to me—not from thought, but from the Lore itself, old and heavy with truth.

*To steal a story is to unmake a soul.*

*To return it is to burn one's own.*

Tears blur my vision. "I can't just erase him," I whisper. "That's not the point."

I flip through the pages of my journal. My rewrite of Cimarron's tale—the one I began in secret, never meant to be read—stares back at me.

Ren's pendant flickers. "Dessa—what are you doing?"

I meet his gaze. "Finishing what Mom started."

I place the Heart Quill atop the platform, its point glowing white-hot, then I toss the journal into the Forge's magical flames. The pages catch instantly, curling and blackening. The air fills with the smell of parchment and something sweeter—like wild honey and lightning.

Cimarron screams. The sound splits the mountain. The shadows whip around him, unraveling. Wind lashes the chamber, beating against me. Words pour from his body—stolen names, broken fates—each one flying free as the ink burns from his skin.

Ren staggers toward me. "You're doing it—you're rewriting him!"

"I'm not rewriting him," I call. "I'm remembering what he stole."

The quill lifts of its own accord. The blood-red vein along its spine flashes. My hand closes over it, and pain sears through me. Blood pours from my palm, and I dip the nib in it before I write the final line across the air itself, each letter burning into existence above the Forge:

*Let the thief be forgotten, but the stories remembered.*

The runes explode into brilliance. Cimarron's scream becomes silence, his form collapsing before vanishing entirely.

For one perfect heartbeat, everything holds still. The wind dies. The flames settle.

The air tastes clean again. The mountain exhales.

Then the light turns inward.

I feel it pulling—through the quill, through the bond—into me. My heartbeat stutters, matching the rhythm of the Forge. My skin glows with words, every one I've ever written rising from beneath the surface.

Ren's arms catch me as I sway. "Dessa—no. What...what's happening?"

"I have to finish the story," I manage, voice thin. "My life for yours."

He shakes his head, his golden eyes wet with fury. "I won't let you."

I lift a trembling hand to his face. "Quests exact a price."

He grips my hand, pressing it against his heart. "Yes, my blood, remember? Me. I'm the sacrifice."

The Forge erupts. Flame and Lore spiral together, a cyclone of creation. For one shining instant, we are one—fire and ink, word and will. Images flash through my mind—my memories, my mother's light, Marrow's last plea.

Ren.

He's no longer fading. His grip on me is firm. The beautiful sapphire blue eyes are mesmerizing.

The bond tugs. Once, twice...

My heart stops.

"Dessa!" he screams.

The beautiful light swallows me whole.

# CHAPTER THIRTY-NINE
## RENWICK | THE LAST FLAME

*Ashes—like stories—remember the one who made them.*

Silence.

Real silence—no whispers from the Lore, no heartbeat from the mountain, no breath from her.

Dessa's body lies in my arms, her skin pale as marble, her hair streaked with soot. The glow that once rippled beneath her skin has gone still. The runes around us have dimmed, their golden fire turned to ash-gray veins that no longer pulse. The mountain is spent.

So am I.

Her head rests against my shoulder, weightless and too heavy all at once. The Heart Quill lies beside her, bloodied and cracked down the middle.

I can't feel our bond. Not the faintest echo. The silence of it is worse than any pain.

"Dessa," I whisper, rocking her. My voice sounds broken, foreign. "Open your eyes."

Nothing.

I press my forehead to hers, fighting the sting of tears. Her scent—wild ink and rain—lingers, mocking me with its warmth.

I choke. "You said you'd finish the story. You didn't say you'd—"

My throat closes.

The Forge hums faintly, a dying ember of sound. Then, a crack. Light slips through a seam in the stone.

I lift my head. The lines of the Forge blaze, slow but sure, tracing the rim of the platform like veins reigniting after long sleep. The sigils glow. It beats, once, twice, three times. My heart echoes it. The mountain echoes it.

"No," I whisper. "Not like this. Not her heartbeat for the heartbeat of my kingdom."

The cracks widen. Fire leaps upward, golden and blue—the colors of Drakenholt's crest. The light spreads across the chamber, racing through the runes on the walls, climbing higher until the entire cavern glows.

Outside, a deep, resonant roar shakes the mountain. I know that sound. Every dragon who ever spat flame would have known it.

The lifeblood of Drakenholt.

My chest caves. Every spark inside me collapses under the weight of it. She gave her life to save mine. To restore my kingdom.

"No," I whisper. My voice scrapes like gravel. "You don't get to stop here." I shake her gently. "Wake up! I command it!"

She doesn't stir.

The bond between us is a void now—no warmth, no hum, no light. Just absence.

Something inside me breaks. The sound that leaves me isn't human. Cradling her body, I stagger up the stairs, through the scriptorium. My vision blurs. I stumble.

I'm alive, and she's dead. My entire system quakes, anger roaring through me. It's not right. Not fair. Outside in the ruins, I trip and stagger, but I never lose my grip on her. I scream, my voice carrying into the blue sky.

My dragon embraces that anger. Flame tears from my throat as I shift. Bone becomes scale, grief becomes fire. The very air trembles from the force of my roar.

I secure her on my back, fragile and pale against my scales, and launch myself into the sky.

The mountain opens before me, sunlight searing the horizon. I climb higher, wings beating against the newborn wind, carrying her toward the heavens.

What I see below is everything I fought for.

Drakenholt lives.

The ruins blaze with golden light. The palace rebuilds itself brick by brick, spires reaching once more toward the sun. The forges along the river ignite, ribbons of smoke rising like prayer. The ink river runs clear again, reflecting the dawn.

People appear—ghosts no longer. Streets fill with laughter, shouts, and the clamor of hammers and bells. On the high balcony of the palace, two figures stand watching the sky. My mother's red hair glints in the sun. My father's hand rests over his heart.

My kingdom is alive again.

But my heart is ashes.

The grief claws its way out of me in a roar that splits the clouds. Fire pours upward, wild and endless, until the very air burns.

I would give it all back—every stone, every flame—for one more heartbeat out of her.

A tickle—light as a pulse—flutters in my chest. I'm so consumed with grief and rage, I barely notice. It comes again. Heat flares through my chest. Still, I scarcely register it.

"Ren?" The sound is a whisper against the wind, soft but unmistakable.

I freeze midair.

Her voice again, stronger this time. "Ren!"

I swivel my head. Her body glows—runic light flickering beneath her skin like fire beneath glass. Her pendant glimmers, whole once more.

The bond snaps back to life, rushing through me like lightning. "*Dessa*," I say in my mind.

I spiral downward, landing in a glen where the river curves through tall grass. Flowers push up through the ash. I lower her carefully to the ground, shifting back before my knees even hit the earth.

She blinks up at me, dazed, alive. "Did it work?" she breathes.

I laugh, rough and unbelieving. "You brought back the whole damned kingdom."

She reaches for me. I pull her into my arms, holding her against my chest as if she's the only real thing left in the world.

"I thought I'd lost you," I whisper.

"You did," she murmurs, her voice trembling. "But I found my way back."

I pull away just enough to meet her eyes. "Because of the bond."

She smiles. "Because of the bond."

"Probably a good thing I didn't ask for permission to use it. You might have said no."

And then I kiss her—because words will never be enough for what she's done, for what she is. The bond flares warm between us again, steady this time, unbreakable. Above us, the sky burns blue.

Drakenholt breathes.

And so do we.

# CHAPTER FORTY
## DESSALYN | THE SIGHT OF STORIES

*What is taken may be forgotten, but what is seen can never be unwritten.*

THE AIR SMELLS THE way I remember from my previous visit to Klamere when I was a girl. Smoke and spice and the faint, sweet tang of forges burning along the river.

Drakenholt lives again.

From the palace balcony, I see the city bustling under the first true sunset in a year. The towers gleam with new stone, the banners ripple crimson and gold, and laughter rises from the streets below. Every sound, every sight, feels like a miracle.

But inside me, there's only silence. When I reach inward for the Language, for the shimmer of stories waiting to be written, there's nothing.

The Lore is gone.

The knowledge remains—the lessons, the instincts—but the magic, the voice of it, has vanished from my heart. My chest tightens at the loss. A Lorekeeper without Lore is…nothing.

And yet…

When I close my eyes, I see light. Threads. Thousands of them, stretching through the air—some bright as dawn, others flickering like candle flame, some unraveling into darkness. They weave across the city, over mountains and rivers, vanishing into the horizon.

Not stories as they were.

Stories as *they will be.*

Ren finds me standing there, staring at the sky. His boots whisper across the marble. "You're quiet," he says gently.

I glance at him over my shoulder. "You're one to talk."

He smiles, coming to stand beside me. His fingers thread through mine, warm and steady. "I was thinking about the first time I stood here. The night my father banished your family."

I study his face in the fading light—strong, solemn, softened by something I don't remember seeing before. Peace, maybe. Or hope. "And now he's preparing a feast in our honor. The king and queen of contradictions."

He laughs softly. "My mother says it's fate's way of humbling us."

"Or rewarding us," I say, though the word feels strange on my tongue.

He studies me, his gaze lingering on my hands. "You feel it, don't you? The change."

I nod, unable to meet his eyes. "The Lore's connection to me is gone."

He squeezes my hand. "You gave it back to the world. Maybe that was always the true quest."

I want to believe him. I want to think that I'm not broken, just...rewritten.

Below us, bells begin to ring. The great hall fills with golden light, laughter, and the music of pipes and flutes. It's the same sound I remember from that long-ago night when everything fell apart—but this time, it feels like forgiveness.

In the Great Hall, the feast is dazzling.

Tables groan with food—roasted game, sugared fruits, honeyed bread still warm from the ovens. Firelight flickers over glass and gold, turning everything warm and inviting.

Ren's father rises first. His voice carries the weight of a king, but also the tremor of a man who knows he's been given a second chance.

"Once, I let fear and pride blind me," he says, eyes sweeping the hall. "I doubted the word of a Lorekeeper and lost my kingdom for it. Tonight, Klamere and Drakenholt stand because one of her blood restored it." He turns to me and dips his head. "Dessalyn Lorewyn, the realm is in your debt."

The hall erupts into applause. I manage a small smile, though my heart feels heavy. I've lost Mom again. A brother I never got to know.

Ren squeezes my knee beneath the table. "He means it," he whispers.

"I know," I murmur back. "That might be the strangest miracle of all."

Later, when the music slows and the guests drift away, I step outside. The night air is cool and rich with the scent of rain. Lanterns hang from the courtyard trees, their light soft as candle flame.

Ren follows, his cloak draped loosely around his shoulders. "You slipped away without saying goodnight to half the court," he teases.

"I needed air," I say. "Too many stories in one room."

He comes to stand beside me, eyes glinting in the lamplight. "The Lore?"

I hesitate, then lift my gaze to the stars. "Not...exactly. I see threads, now," I tell him. It doesn't seem like the right word, but it's the best I've got. Some storyteller I am. "Every person, every place. I can see where their stories touch, where they end, where they begin again."

He watches me, quiet. "And mine?"

I smile faintly. "Yours burns too bright for me to see the edges."

He brushes a hand over my cheek, thumb catching a tear. It's not one of sorrow, I realize. For the first time in weeks, it's one of joy. "Then maybe that's how it's meant to be."

I nod, leaning into his touch. At least, I still feel the bond. It comforts me. The silence inside me doesn't ache as much when he's near. It hums. Soft. Patient. Always steady.

That night, sleep doesn't come easily.

When it finally does, it's not peace that greets me but light. A thousand shimmering threads twist through the darkness, their glow sharpening until I can see where they go. Through mountains. Across oceans. Into libraries.

I follow them.

Each thread touches a story—some being told, others half-remembered—and in the dark between, shadows move. Hands reach out. Pages tear.

Someone is...stealing them.

I see ships on black water, sails stitched from parchment. I see libraries burning, ink rivers turning to smoke.

In the heart of it, a figure moves among the wreckage—cloak crimson, eyes cold as moonlight.

Not Cimarron.

Someone else.

He turns his hand, and a crown made of coral glows in his hand. In the other, a book. Its cover is marked with a Fae glyph I recognize.

*My family's.*

The realization knocks the air from my lungs. "Calliope," I whisper.

The vision shatters. I jolt awake, her name still on my lips.

Ren stirs beside me, half asleep. "What is it?"

I sit up, trembling. "He's still alive."

He blinks, confusion fading into understanding. "Cimarron?"

I nod my head slowly, thinking about one of the threads I followed. "I think so. He's wounded but not gone. Someone is helping him. Someone's stealing stories for him."

The room suddenly feels colder, the light through the window dimming to silver.

Ren sits up, the bond flaring steady and fierce. "Who?"

"I don't know, but I think Calliope's in danger."

"Then we'll stop him," he says.

I reach for his hand, my heart thudding with both fear and certainty. "Together."

He squeezes my fingers, his eyes lit with flames. "Always."

# CHAPTER FORTY-ONE
## DESSALYN | THE UNWRITTEN ROAD

*Every ending is just a pause between pages.*

MORNING SPILLS OVER THE mountains in soft gold. The wind tastes of sunlight, of things reborn.

Ren and I stand together on the ridge above Klamere, the world spread out below us like an open book. The city gleams in the dawn—towers whole again, banners rippling in the wind, the beat of forges drifting through the valley. Smoke curls from chimneys, not dark and bitter, but bright with morning rituals.

Firebrand stamps at Ren's side, mane blazing copper in the dawn. White Ash nuzzles my shoulder, patient as ever.

In the distance, the River of Ink winds its way through the hills, no longer black and sluggish but clear and silver-blue. Along its banks, the forges of Drakenholt's cities spark one by one, their flames reflecting the sunrise—a trail of light leading all the way to the sea.

It feels like a promise.

Ren's arm slips around my waist, warm and certain. I rest my head against his shoulder, letting the steady rhythm of his heartbeat drown out the wind.

"Ready?" he asks.

I look down at the Heart Quill, once more in its box. I'd planned to leave it here in the scriptorium, but another vision—I've been having them every few hours—nudged me to bring it with us.

This morning, over breakfast, Ren handed me a new journal. Not for a quest; this one is for our future together.

*Every story leaves something behind.*

The line came to me the moment I opened it. It wasn't from the Lore Language, but something else. The twin flame of his dragon and my Fae heritages braided together inside me.

My throat tightens. I hug the journal to me once last time, then slip it into my satchel. "Ready."

He smiles—that quiet, knowing smile that always steadies me—and helps me into the saddle. Firebrand snorts beside us, impatient to move.

We turn toward the east, where the light climbs higher, where the road twists beyond the horizon toward Fablehollow.

A hawk circles above, cutting through the clouds—free, fierce, and watchful. I follow its flight until it vanishes into the morning.

My quest is over.

But the story isn't finished.

Ren nudges Firebrand forward, and I follow, the sound of hooves echoing across the ridge like the turning of a page.

Ahead lies home, and somewhere beyond that, the next tale waiting to be told.

# NEXT IN THE SERIES
## TIDE OF STOLEN THRONES

*I know what he's done—and I don't know what it will cost to walk beside him anyway.*

Once, he helped steal the story that kept the kingdom alive. Now, the truth may destroy us both.

In the realm of the Five Crowns, stories are power. When Seabright's magic begins to unravel and its royal bloodline vanishes from memory, everything starts to fall apart.

I am Calliope Lorewyn, guardian of Fablehollow and keeper of truths others would rather forget. When prophecy collapses and the sea itself begins to turn, I'm sent to uncover what was taken... and who took it.

My search leads me to Henry Hawkins, a pirate with a charming smile and a past written in forbidden ink. Once an unwitting pawn of the Story Thief, he helped fracture the old fairytales and has been living with the cost ever since.

Henry doesn't deny what he's done. I don't know what it will cost to walk beside him anyway.

To restore a stolen throne, we must cross storm-tossed seas and the shattered heart of Seabright itself. But fixing a broken story may demand more than truth. It may require sacrifice—and a choice between the ending the world needs and the one my heart is beginning to write.

*Slow-burn romance meets sweeping fantasy in a tale of cursed ink, broken prophecy, and a love forged between tide and fire—where the ending is anything but guaranteed.*

# MEET MISTY

**USA TODAY Bestselling Author Misty Evans** is celebrating her 100th published novel in 2025. She loves writing urban fantasy, paranormal romance, and mystery/suspense. Under her pen name, Nyx Halliwell, she also writes supernatural cozy mysteries.

When not reading or writing (which is most of the time), she enjoys music, movies, and hanging out with her husband, twin sons, and three spoiled rescue dogs. She's a crafter at heart and has far too many projects to finish.

**Visit to check out her online store and sign up for her newsletter.**

*Read more at [MistyEvansBooks.com](MistyEvansBooks.com)*

# MEET MICHELLE

**Michelle Miles** believes every story should have a little magic, a dash of danger, and a whole lot of heart. She writes fantasy, paranormal, and young adult adventures filled with fierce heroines, unforgettable heroes, and the kind of romance that makes you believe in happily-ever-after. From angels and demons to dragons, elves, and time travelers, her books invite readers into worlds brimming with epic quests, high stakes, and enchanting possibilities.

When she's not crafting new adventures, Michelle lends her voice to other authors' worlds as a narrator and hosts *Miles Beyond the Page*, a podcast where writers share the triumphs and challenges of their creative journeys. A proud Texan, she loves getting lost in a good book, exploring hiking trails, watching her favorite movies, and savoring a glass of wine while dreaming up her next tale.

*Read more at MichelleMiles.net*

# ALSO BY MISTY EVANS

**PNR & UF by Misty Evans**
**www.mistyevansbooks.com**

**The Accidental Reaper Urban Fantasy Romance Series, available in ebook, print, and audio (through the Eleven-ReaderPublishing app)!**

Grim & Bare It, Book 1

Reaper's Keepers, Book 2

In Too Reap, Book 3

Killin' It (short story for newsletter subscribers only)

The Vampire's Kiss (an exclusive short story available in Misty's Store. Intended for matureaudiences 17+)

Grave Girl

Grave Magic

Grim Vows

Undead Ever After

**The Kali Sweet Urban Fantasy Series, available in ebook, print, and audio (through the Eleven-ReaderPublishing app)!**

Revenge Is Sweet, Kali Sweet Series, Book 1
Sweet Chaos, Kali Sweet Series, Book 2
Sweet Soldier, Kali Sweet Series, Book 3
Sweet Curse, Kali Sweet Series, Book 4
Sweet Malice, Kali Sweet Series, Book 5
Sweet Betrayal, Kali Sweet Series, Book 6

**Witches Anonymous Paranormal Romance Series**

Witches Anonymous, Step 1
Jingle Hells, WA Step 2
Wicked Souls, WA Step 3
Dark Moon Lilith, Witches Anonymous Step 4
Dancing With the Devil, Witches Anonymous Step 5
Devil's Due, Witches Anonymous Step 6
Dirty Deeds, Witches Anonymous Step 7
Wicked Wedding, Witches Anonymous Step 8

**Moonwater Paranormal Romance Series**

Soul Survivor, Moon Water Series, Book 1
Soul Protector, Moon Water Series, Book 2

# ALSO BY MICHELLE MILES

**Age of Wizards (Epic Fantasy)**
In the Tower of the Wizard King
On the Hunt for the Wizard King

**Dragon Protectors (Paranormal Shifter Romance)**
Desiring the Dragon Lord
Seducing the Dragon Knight
Tempting Her Dragon Bodyguard

**Dream Walker (Paranormal Romance)**
Call of the Dark
Blood and Bone
Flame and Fury
Smoke and Ashes
Light of the World

**Enchanted Realms (YA Fantasy Romance)**
Once Upon a Midnight Clear (Cinderella)
Once Upon True Love's Kiss (Snow White)
Once Upon an Enchanted Kiss (Sleeping Beauty)

Once Upon an Enchanted Castle (Beauty and the Beast)
Once Upon a Midnight Dreary (Poe's The Raven)

**Enchanted Realms Related Novellas**
Once Upon an Ancient Curse (Red Riding Hood)
Once Upon a Silver Strand (Rapunzel)
Once Upon a Woven Wish (Rumpelstiltskin)
**Enchanted Realms: Crossroads (Cozy Fantasy)**
Petals and Portals (Coming 2026)

**Five Towers (YA Fantasy Romance)**
The Sorcerer's Daughter

**Highland Destiny (Paranormal Romance)**
Desiring the Highland Laird
Loving the Highland Warrior
Captivating the Highland Rogue (March 5, 2026)

**Legends of the Five Crowns**
*with Misty Evans*
The Lost Kingdom
The Flame and the Dragon
Tide of Stolen Thrones (Coming Feb 2026)

**Ransom & Fortune Adventures**
**(Time Travel Action/Adventure)**
Highland Fling, Vol 1
Dead of Winter, Vol 2
The Citadel, Vol 3
Lord of the Underworld, Vol 4

**Realm of Honor (Fantasy Romance)**
One Knight Only
Only for a Knight
A Knight to Remember
A Knight Like No Other
Shadows of the Knight

**Shorts and Anthologies (Fantasy/Paranormal)**
*Newsletter Subscribers Only*
A Dance Among the Faeries, A Short Story
Eorwulf, A Short Story
Dragons of Emhain Short Story Collection

*Watch for more at MichelleMiles.net*

www.ingramcontent.com/pod-product-compliance
Lightning Source LLC
Chambersburg PA
CBHW020831030726
47496CB00001B/178